A Regency Christmas IV

~ Five new stories by ~

Mary Balogh * **Marjorie Farrell**
Sandra Heath * **Emma Lange**
* **Mary Jo Putney**

A SIGNET BOOK

SIGNET
Published by the Penguin Group
Penguin Books USA Inc., 375 Hudson Street,
New York, New York 10014, U.S.A.
Penguin Books Ltd, 27 Wrights Lane,
London W8 5TZ, England
Penguin Books Australia Ltd, Ringwood,
Victoria, Australia
Penguin Books Canada Ltd, 10 Alcorn Avenue,
Toronto, Ontario, Canada M4V 3B2
Penguin Books (N.Z.) Ltd, 182-190 Wairau Road,
Auckland 10, New Zealand

Penguin Books Ltd, Registered Offices:
Harmondsworth, Middlesex, England

First published by Signet, an imprint of New American Library,
a division of Penguin Books USA Inc.

First Printing, November, 1992
10 9 8 7 6 5 4 3 2 1

Contents

THE CHRISTMAS TART

by Mary Jo Putney

IT BEGAN with a ring. One day late in November 1809, the irritable Lady Guthrie was careless when she searched through her lacquered jewelry case for the best ornaments to adorn her scrawny person. The heirloom diamond ring that had come from her husband's family was valuable but ugly, and she brushed it aside impatiently as she searched for more attractive treasures.

Amidst the clinking of baubles, she didn't notice when the ring tumbled from the case, rolled unevenly across the lace-covered surface of the dressing table, then dropped into the narrow gap between table and wall. Halfway to the floor, the heavy ring hooked over a wooden peg that had worked loose until it projected from the back of the table.

And there the ring stayed, suspended, not to be found until the next year's spring cleaning. But by then Christmas had come and gone, and so had the young French seamstress.

A cold, heavy sky made the afternoon seem more like dusk, and it was difficult for Nicole Chambord to see the riding jacket that she was trimming. Closing her eyes for a moment, she laid the jacket down and straightened up, stretching her arms in an effort to relieve the strain on her back and neck. *Sacre bleu!* but she would be glad when Christmas was over.

During the month that Nicole had been sewing for Lady Guthrie, she had not had a single afternoon off, and every night she had worked late by candle-light to complete everything her ladyship deemed necessary for the holidays. While Lady Guthrie's important clothing was done by an expensive modiste, there were many lesser items, such as chemises and undergowns, that could be made by a household seamstress. And of course there was always mending, refurbishing older garments, and making shirts and cravats for Sir Wilfrid, the master of the house. Nicole had sewed so much that she wore white cotton gloves to prevent her sore, pricked fingers from bleeding onto valuable fabric.

Still, food in the Guthrie establishment was abundant, if bland, and most of the other servants were pleasant. Best of all, Nicole was now living in London, closer to her goal than she had been in Bristol, where she had lived for fourteen years. Come spring, she would look for a situation with a fashionable dressmaker who would be willing to take advantage of an assistant's design skills. Then someday, after much hard work and saving of money, Nicole would open a shop of her own, called Nicole's, or perhaps Madame Chambord's.

She luxuriated in the thought for a moment, then sighed and returned to her work. The happy day when she would be self-employed was many years away. Just now, her task was to use her nearly invisible stitches to attach military-style braid to the jacket in her lap.

She was just finishing the job when the butler, Furbes, swept into the small workroom without knocking. "Her ladyship wishes to speak with you, Chambord," he snapped. "Immediately."

"Of course," Nicole murmured, unalarmed by his manner, for Furbes was always rude to his inferiors and Lady Guthrie was always in a hurry. Likely her ladyship had decided that a project she had wanted completed tomorrow must instead be done today. It would not be the first time.

But instead of normal impatience, Nicole found disaster. As the French girl entered Lady Guthrie's bedroom, her mistress spun around to glare at her. "You stole the Guthrie diamond ring," she said furiously. "What have you done with it?"

Nicole was so shocked that for a moment her usually nimble tongue was paralyzed. "But no, my lady, I have never seen your ring, nor have I taken even a candle stub from your room," she said when she could speak. "Could the ring have been misplaced?"

"No, it's gone." Lady Guthrie gestured at her abigail, who stood in a corner, wearing a distressed expression. "Merkle has searched everywhere, including all the drawers and the floor under the dressing table. And tonight we dine with my husband's family, and his mother will want to know why I don't wear it!"

Still not quite believing the accusation, Nicole said in bewilderment, "I am sorry if your mother-in-law will be upset, but why are you accusing me? There are a dozen servants in this house, or a thief could have broken in and robbed you. I swear on my mother's grave that I have stolen nothing from you."

"Any thief who broke in would have taken the whole case, not just the ring, and all my other servants have been with me for years. You've been here less than a month, and you're clever—I saw that right away. You probably thought I wouldn't notice if only a single piece of jewelry was missing, especially one I almost never wear, and you've had ample opportunity, because you often worked alone in this room,'' Lady Guthrie retorted. ''As soon as I thought of you, I had your room searched, and Furbes found the proof hidden under your mattress.'' She lifted a leather pouch from her dressing table, then dropped it again, the coins inside clinking as the pouch hit the tabletop. ''Over fifty pounds! Where could you get such a sum except by theft?''

Nicole stared in horror at the bag that contained her life savings. Voice choked, she said, ''For years I have spent almost nothing on myself so I could save every shilling possible.'' All of it dedicated to the dream of a future. Desperation in her voice, Nicole continued, ''Surely if I had stolen your precious diamond ring, I would have gotten more money than that.''

''Stolen goods go for only a fraction of their true value.'' Lady Guthrie's faded blue eyes narrowed triumphantly. ''And just how did you know that the ring was a diamond?''

''Because you said so yourself!'' Nicole exclaimed, feeling as if she had wandered into Bedlam. *''Mon Dieu,* your ladyship, if you have been robbed, call a magistrate. I am not afraid to be questioned, for I am innocent.''

Before Lady Guthrie could respond, her maid Merkle said hesitantly, ''Perhaps the chit is telling the truth, my lady. Her references were splendid, and she has always done her work well, with not a shred of complaint from anyone. And there is no proof that she took the ring.''

Nicole could have kissed the other servant for her bravery in speaking up, but it did no good. Her employer's mouth tightened to a harsh line. "Bah, she belongs in Newgate, but if she blinks those big brown eyes at the magistrate, I don't suppose she'll get what she deserves, so there's no point in turning her over to the law." Lady Guthrie scowled at the seamstress as she decided what to do. "You're dismissed right now, girl, without a reference." She lifted the pouch again, her bony fingers digging into the thin leather. "This I will keep as compensation for your theft."

Appalled, Nicole gasped, "How dare you! That is my money and if you take it, it is you who are the thief!"

"Don't speak to her ladyship like that, you little slut," Furbes ordered. The butler had been a silent witness to the exchange, but now he grasped Nicole's shoulder with cruel pressure. "Shall I allow her to gather her belongings, my lady, or put her out on the street as she is?"

"Let her gather her things, but watch to see that she doesn't try to take anything else," Lady Guthrie decided. Turning back to Nicole, she said viciously, "You can thank the fact that it's almost Christmas for my mercy, girl."

And that was that. Ten minutes later, still dazed by the swiftness of events, Nicole was standing in the alley behind the house, having been escorted out the kitchen door by Furbes. Everything she owned in the world was in a canvas bag slung over her shoulder. She shivered, and not just because a cold, misty rain was saturating her threadbare cloak. She had never been so frightened in her life, even when her family had fled France to escape the Reign of Terror. Only six years old, she had seen that as a grand adventure, serene in her trust that no harm could befall her when she was with her parents.

But now both parents were dead and she was utterly alone, without a situation, money, or references to help her find another job. If she had been in Bristol, she could have found shelter with friends, but not in London, where Nicole knew no one but the servants in the Guthrie household. To make matters worse, it was Saturday afternoon and within a couple of hours all of the modistes' shops would be closed until Monday morning.

She set her chin and began marching down the street. There was nothing she could do to prove her innocence or recover her savings from Lady Guthrie, so there was no point in wasting time on regrets or curses at life's unfairness. All of her energy must go toward survival.

She had just reached the street when the kitchen door opened and a low voice called her name. She glanced back and saw Merkle standing in the door and beckoning. Nicole obeyed the summons, but as she approached the maid, she said bitterly, "Has Lady Guthrie decided I cannot take my own clothing? I should think my things would be too poor for her taste."

"She hasn't changed her mind about anything," Merkle said sadly. "I'm sorry, Nicole, I don't believe that you stole the ring, but there's nothing to be done with the old besom when she's in a mood like this. She knows her husband and his family will be furious with her for losing the ring, and she had to take it out on someone. A pity it was you. And to discharge you so close to Christmas!" The maid had a mass of scarlet fabric draped over her arm, and now she raised it for Nicole's inspection. "Take this cloak. It was one of her ladyship's mistakes in judgment so she gave it to me after one season. Too gaudy for my taste, so I've never worn it, but it's warmer than that old thing you're wearing. Here, put it on.''

Nicole's first reaction was to refuse to take anything that had been Lady Guthrie's, but practicality overcame her principles. Accepting the scarlet cloak, she draped it over her own thin garments. Immediately she felt warmer, though considering the color and the vulgar feather trimming, she understood why neither Lady Guthrie nor Merkle wanted it.

Next Merkle offered a greasy packet wrapped in newspaper. ''Here's a meat pie. It's all I could take without Cook noticing. And here's five shillings. For that, you should be able to rent a room for a few nights if you know where to look.''

''Where might I find such a place?'' Nicole asked. ''In the month I've been in London, I have learned nothing of the city.''

The maid thought for a moment. ''Around Covent Garden might be best. There are plenty of lodgings, and when the market is open you should be able to get damaged produce at a good price. But be careful, child. London streets aren't safe at night, and sometimes not even in the day, leastwise not for a girl as pretty as you.'' She sighed. ''I only wish I could've convinced her ladyship not to blame you for the ring's disappearance. God only knows what happened to the blasted thing.''

Trying to sound confident, Nicole said, ''Don't worry about me. I'm on my way right now to seek employment. The money and food you have provided will keep me until I can start work.'' On impulse, she rose on her toes and kissed the other servant on the cheek. ''Thank you, Miss Merkle. You are a good woman.''

Then Nicole turned and set off without looking back.

* * *

For a gentleman about town, there was no more desirable residence than the Rochester. The rooms were elegant and the discreet staff always ready to provide any service required. That was convenient for Sir Philip Selbourne, since his valet had a cold and had been left home in Northamptonshire. At the moment, however, Philip was not reflecting on his good fortune. In fact, as he climbed the front steps of the Rochester, head bent and mind absorbed in calculations, he was so abstracted that he quite literally ran into his best friends.

The baronet was murmuring an absent apology when a familiar voice said, "Philip! You've just arrived in town?"

Brought back to the present, Philip raised his head to discover the Honorable James Kirby and Francis, Lord Masterson, another close friend. After greeting both men and shaking their hands, Philip said, "Actually, I've been here for two days. This is just a quick trip to take care of some business."

"And you didn't let either of us know?" Kirby said reproachfully. At twenty-five he was the same age as Philip, but his round face and flaming red hair made him seem younger. "With all three of us living in the same building, you can't say that it was too much effort to call! It's been months since we've seen you in town—surely not since March." Abruptly he stopped speaking as he remembered why his friend had left London then.

Philip grimaced. "I've been deucedly busy since my father died. Having grown up at Winstead Hall, I always believed I knew something about farming, but it turns out that I knew a good deal less than I thought. And his death has caused a number of unexpected complications."

Lord Masterson's cool voice said, "Problems? That surprises me. I would have thought Sir Charles the last man on earth to mismanage his affairs."

"He didn't," Philip said, quick to defend his father. "One of the difficulties is the unexpected number of investments he left, none of which I knew anything about." He gave a wry smile. "In the last six months, I've worked harder at educating myself than all the years at Winchester and Cambridge put together."

"Come along and tell us all about it while we have lunch," Kirby urged. "It's too cold to converse here on the steps."

"Sorry, I can't accept," Philip said regretfully. "In a few minutes my solicitor is coming, and we're going to spend the afternoon finishing the business that brought me to London. I want to return to Winstead tomorrow morning."

"Stay an extra day," Masterson suggested. "So many people have left to spend the holiday in the country that town is rather thin of company." He gave a faint, charming smile. "Under the circumstances, even you offer welcome diversion."

Philip returned the smile, but shook his head. "I really must get back. This Christmas will be hard for my mother."

"Then join us for dinner in my rooms," Kirby said, undeterred. "With the three of us together, it will be like old times at Winchester."

Philip hesitated, tempted, then shook his head again. "I really can't. The solicitor will leave mountains of documents, and it will take me all evening to go over them."

"Surely your fusty documents can wait another day," Kirby said, his wide blue eyes showing hurt.

Before Philip could answer, Masterson raised his

dark, elegant brows. "You must remember to take time for your friends, Philip," he drawled, "or someday when you need them, you may find that you have none."

Philip felt color rising in his cheeks. "You still know the best place to strike, Masterson. No wonder you were so good at fencing." Then he sighed ruefully. "You are both absolutely correct. In the last six months I've spent so much time running in circles and feeling incompetent that I've half forgotten just why life is worth living. I'd be delighted to join you for dinner. Seven o'clock in your rooms, Jamie?" After the time was confirmed, he touched his hat in farewell and swiftly climbed the last steps into the Rochester.

Frowning, Kirby watched until his friend disappeared into the building. Then he turned and fell into step with Masterson as the two young men walked toward St. James, where they would be able to find a hack. "Philip's not looking at all well. He's been working too hard."

"Very likely,' Masterson agreed. "It was quite a shock for him when his father died so unexpectedly—they always got on amazingly well. And being the responsible sort, Philip's obviously feeling the weight of being head of the family."

"He really needs to relax a bit before he goes dashing back to the country," Kirby mused. "Now, what's most relaxing?"

Recognizing the tone, Masterson eyed his companion with misgiving, for Kirby's innocent face masked the devil's own capacity for mischief. "Dinner with friends is relaxing, and just to make sure, I'll send down half a dozen bottles of my best claret. That will relax all of us."

Ignoring the comment, Kirby said with an air of

great enlightenment, "*Females* are relaxing. That's it—what Philip needs is a girl." Turning his wide blue eyes to his companion, he said, "Let's find one and put her in his bed tonight."

Masterson stopped dead in the street. "You've finally lost your mind," he said flatly. "The first day you showed up to fag for me at Winchester and I saw that shade of red hair, I knew your sanity was precarious. Granted, females are sometimes relaxing, but just as often they play the very devil with one's sanity. Besides, Philip is quite capable of finding a girl of his own if he wants one, but at the moment, he has other things on his mind besides dalliance."

"Which is why he needs a girl to cheer him up," Kirby said. "A nice jolly one will make a perfect Christmas present. While Philip's dining with us, your valet can spirit her into his rooms. Now, where can we find one?" He pondered. "You can ask Michelle if she has a friend who's free tonight."

"Neither Michelle nor her friends come free," Masterson said dryly. "And as it happens, she and I came to a parting of the ways last week. If I went to her house and asked her to find another female, she'd likely drop a chamber pot on my head."

Undeterred, Kirby said, "Then we'll have to find a girl somewhere else."

The two men were still arguing as they hailed a hack and set off to lunch, but already Masterson was resigning himself to the inevitable. Kirby was bound and determined on his plan, so Masterson had better cooperate just to make sure that the thing was done right.

After more than twenty-four hours without eating, Nicole was so cold, hungry, and tired that she was

unsteady on her feet. It was time to eat the meat pie
Merkle had given her, so she turned into a small,
cluttered alley and sank wearily onto a stone step.
Then she pulled out the cold pie and held it, wanting
to postpone the moment when it would be gone.

Her spirits were as low as they had ever been in
her life, for her determined efforts to find a situation
the day before had come to nothing. Two modistes
had refused to talk to her since she had no London
references. Three more had said that they weren't
hiring and wouldn't be for months, for the Christmas
rush was over and business would be slack until
spring, when the ton returned to London to prepare
for the Season. Nicole had not expected that, and
had been frightened to realize that it might be
months before she might find a position as a seamstress.

Not wanting to spend her five shillings before she
had to, Nicole had slept rough the night before, shivering in a deserted corner of a stable yard behind an
unoccupied house in Kensington. The night was dry
and she was protected from the wind, but even so
she had been numb with cold by morning. Because
it was Sunday, she had gone to church, partly to be
under a roof, and partly because prayer seemed in
order. The vicar had read the Christmas story, and
Nicole had found herself with new empathy for Mary
and Joseph, who had found no room at the inn. Closing her eyes, she had uttered a silent prayer that she,
too, would find the shelter she so desperately needed.

She had considered asking the vicar for help, but
when she timidly approached him after the service,
he gave her a glance so contemptuous that she left
without speaking. That had been hours ago, and ever
since she had been drifting through the London
streets while she planned how best to eke out her

money and what kinds of employment she should seek.

The onset of more bone-chilling rain had brought her to a reluctant decision; since she might not survive another night sleeping rough in this weather, she must spend some of her limited funds to rent a room. Remembering that Miss Merkle had said there were cheap lodgings near Covent Garden, she had asked directions, then set off to find it.

A plaintive meow brought her back to the present. She glanced down to find a scraggly, half-grown cat sitting on the step beside her, its gaze fixed on the cold meat pie in her hands. The little creature's splotchy calico fur was matted with rain, and its huge green eyes were a mixture of hope and wariness. "Sorry, *ma petite*," Nicole said apologetically. "This is all I have to eat, and the good Lord only knows where my next meal will come from."

She bit into the pie, so ravenous she wanted to stuff the whole thing in her mouth at once. Instead, she forced herself to take a small mouthful, then chew slowly, so it would last as long as possible. Even cold, it tasted wonderful. After she swallowed the first bite, she took another. It wasn't easy to ignore the pleading green feline eyes.

Suddenly, with a small, *mrrp*ing sound, the cat jumped onto her lap and began rubbing its head against her chest. "Your manners leave much to be desired, my patchy friend," Nicole scolded as she held the pie out of reach. "But you are not as wild as most street cats. Did you also have a home until someone cruelly evicted you?"

The dangerous thought made it impossible to ignore the cat's desperate expression. "Very well, *ma petite*," Nicole said. "Perhaps it will bring me luck if I am generous to one less fortunate than I." She took a morsel of meat and offered it to the calico. Her companion did not wait for a second invitation. The fragment disappeared instantly; then, with dainty gluttony, a warm, raspy pink tongue licked Nicole's fingers. For the first time since the day before, she found herself smiling. From then on, each bite she took herself was followed by a shred for the cat.

When Nicole was done, she stood and brushed the crumbs from her hands. "*Au revoir*, my little friend, and good hunting."

Refusing to be dismissed, the cat stropped her ankles. Unable to resist such friendliness, Nicole lifted the calico and cradled the skinny little body in her arms. Immediately it began to purr so strongly that Nicole felt the vibration through her layers of cloaks. Severely she said, "Don't try to turn me up sweet, *ma petite*. The last thing I need at the moment is someone to take care of."

The cat tilted its head up and offered what looked very much like a coaxing feline smile. "Oh, very well, you silly beast," Nicole said with resignation. "If you are willing to travel in my pocket, we will give it a try. But mind you behave."

To her surprise, the cat settled happily into the right pocket of Nicole's cloak, its small body creating a spot of warmth against her side. Feeling unreasonably cheered, Nicole continued on her way to Covent Garden.

"Who would have thought that whores would be so thin on the ground?" James Kirby grumbled as he surveyed the wet, dismal intersection at Covent Garden.

"This weather would drive anyone indoors," Masterson said dryly. "Besides, even ladies of pleasure are entitled to take a few days off at Christmas.'' They had seen several raddled, gin-soaked streetwalkers, but Masterson had flatly refused to let Kirby approach them, on the grounds that the object was to give Philip a night's pleasure, not the French pox and God knew what else. ''Time to give the idea up, James. Let's go back to my rooms and make a bowl of hot punch.''

''Wait!'' Kirby pointed across the street. ''She's perfect.''

Masterson examined the object of Kirby's interest, a slim girl who stood in front of the new opera house. She was dressed in a voluminous and much-bedraggled scarlet cloak, and it was easy to see why she had caught Kirby's eye. What was visible of her face under the hood was very lovely—and also very innocent. ''She's attractive,'' Masterson agreed, ''but I'm not sure she's available. Doesn't quite have the look of a doxy.''

''Who but a whore would wear a cloak like that? And she has exactly the right look for Philip—he's never liked the brazen sort. Come on, let's ask her. If she's respectable, she'll give us a flea in the ear quick enough, and we'll be no worse off than we are now.'' Kirby started across the street.

Masterson had to admit that the garment in question was unlikely to be worn by anyone but a prostitute or a dashing society lady. Decent females didn't wear such violent, expensive shades of red, nor did they have masses of ostrich feather trim drooping about them, and they certainly did not wander alone in Covent Garden. Resignedly he followed his friend.

As soon as Nicole realized that the two young men were heading straight for her, she started to hasten away, for a day on London's meaner streets had al-

ready taught her caution. Then one of the men called
out, "Wait, miss, we want to talk to you."

The voice was polite and seemed sober, so warily
she stopped and turned to face them.

The redheaded young man who had called gave
her an ingenuous smile. "We're looking for someone to keep a friend company tonight. Would . . ."
he considered, "five pounds be sufficient?"

As soon as she realized his meaning, she gasped
in shock. How dare he! What kind of girl did he
think she was?

Misinterpreting her gasp, he said, "Very well,
ten."

Nicole realized that it was quite obvious what kind
of girl he thought she was. She opened her mouth to
give him an icy set-down, then slowly closed it when
a shocking but practical thought occurred to her. Ten
pounds was a substantial amount of money, enough
to support her for weeks if she was careful. Enough
to make the difference between surviving or starving.

Though part of her was appalled that she would
even consider such a proposition, she found herself
coolly evaluating the risks. She would lose her virtue, of course, but virtue would be of precious little
use if she starved to death. There was also the dis-
astrous chance of pregnancy, but from what she had
heard, that was unlikely to happen after a single
night.

Her hasty calculations suggested that the benefits
of being ruined would outweigh the risks. Nonetheless, the idea of allowing a total stranger such intimacy was abhorrent; the man might be revolting or
even vicious. Stalling for time to make up her mind,
she said, "Is your friend such a monster that he can-

not find a woman for himself, so he sends you to pimp for him?''

''He's a perfectly pleasant fellow,'' the redhead assured her. ''We are doing this as a surprise Christmas present, since he's been working too hard.''

Taking a deep breath, Nicole decided to put herself into the hands of fate. ''Twenty pounds,'' she said firmly. If they would pay such a great amount of money, she would take it as a sign that letting herself be ruined was the right thing to do.

''Twenty pounds?'' the redhead said dubiously. ''That seems a trifle steep.''

With a mixture of regret and relief, Nicole said, ''It is my price, monsieur. If it is more than you wish to pay, so be it.''

''Wait.'' For the first time the dark-haired man spoke. He pushed Nicole's hood back onto her shoulders. Then, while the cold rain spattered her cheeks, he took her chin in one hand and studied her with a detached gaze. ''She's very pretty,'' he said at length. ''A sweet face. I think Philip would like her.''

Nicole's companion chose this moment to stick its head out of her pocket and give a piercing yowl. Both men gave the furry, triangular head a startled glance.

''My cat,'' Nicole said, rather unnecessarily. ''Where I go, she goes.''

The corners of the dark-haired man's mouth twitched with amusement. ''James, does Philip like cats?''

''Of course. Don't you remember that great ugly ginger tom he smuggled into our rooms at Winchester?''

The dark man gave a faint shudder. ''Good God, how could I possibly have forgotten Thomas Aquinas and his unnatural attachment to my boots?'' He smiled at Nicole. ''Clearly you are singularly well-qualified to please this particular gentleman. Come, let us adjourn to more comfortable quarters.''

For a moment Nicole teetered on the verge of flight, but the streets offered nothing but cold and damp and danger. At least tonight she would be warm, and probably well-fed. In return for a few hours of endurance, she would have the money she needed to survive. Face set, she pulled her hood up over her dark hair and followed the two young men to their carriage.

Philip had not spent such an enjoyable evening since his father died. It was good to laugh with friends, to remember that he was still young and that worrying himself into a decline would do no one any good. When Kirby's clock begin to chime midnight, he got to his feet with reluctance. ''A pity to leave so soon, but I must if I want to be off at dawn tomorrow morning.''

He expected Kirby to insist that he stay, but his host said only, ''You're right. I need some rest myself if I'm to make it to the ancestral home tomorrow.'' He gave Philip a bright-eyed smile. ''When will you be in town again?''

''I'm thinking of hiring a house and bringing my mother up for the Season. She'll be out of mourning soon, and I think some gaiety will be good for her.'' Philip made a face. ''Unfortunately, she's been hinting that it's time I looked for a wife. If I bring her here, she'll throw every suitable miss in the Marriage Mart at me. She's already introduced me to every eligible female in Northamptonshire.''

Horrified, Kirby exclaimed, ''That's a dashed dangerous business, Philip. It's all very well to be a dutiful son, but if you aren't careful, you could end up leg-shackled.''

''Believe me, I'm aware of the perils. I trust that forewarned will be forearmed.'' The baronet collected his hat, shook hands, and wished his friends a happy Christmas, then went into the hall to climb the two flights of stairs to his own rooms. So convenient to live in the same building.

But that wouldn't be true much longer. Regretfully Philip realized that he really must let go of his rooms. He'd had them since leaving Cambridge, but he was unlikely to be spending lengthy periods of time in London again, so it was far more reasonable to stay in a hotel for his brief visits.

He sighed. One after another, the realities of adulthood were catching up with him. He had obligations to his family and his name that could not honorably be neglected. Which brought him back to the depressing topic of marriage.

In an attempt to preserve his good spirits, Philip counted his blessings as he ascended the shadowy steps. Though he had initially been intimidated by his new responsibilities, he now had them well in hand. He very much enjoyed being master of Winstead, for there was something elementally satisfying about working the land and seeing to his tenants' welfare. Though he did miss London friends like Kirby and Masterson, he had other friends in Northamptonshire, and family as well, so he certainly wasn't lonely. Nor did he mind bearing his mother company, for she was the most delightful of women.

As he pulled out his key and opened the door to his rooms, he realized why marriage was such a depressing prospect: he'd never met an eligible girl who was half so amusing as his mother, or his sister Marguerite. It wasn't just bias on his part; they both

really were exceptionally charming, intelligent females. It must be the French blood. A pity that the
Continent was closed to Britons; perhaps in Paris it
would be possible to find a bride who wouldn't bore
him, but with Britain and France at war he was unable to put that theory to the test.

His sitting room was warm, and he saw a glow of
lamplight coming from the corridor that led to the
bedroom. A member of the staff must have come in
to build a fire and leave a light for him. It was like
being in his own home and explained why there was
always a waiting list for rooms in the Rochester.
Whistling softly, Philip hung up his hat and walked
down the short passage to his bedroom. He was
starting to untie his cravat when his gaze came to
rest on his bed.

He stopped dead in his tracks. Kneeling in the
middle of the blue counterpane was a dark-haired
young female, a delicious-looking creature who wore
nothing but a provocative white negligee and an
enormous red silk bow tied around her slender neck.

"What the devil?" Thinking that he must have
drunk more than he'd realized, Philip gave his head
a sharp shake, but the nymph was still there. "Who
are you, and how did you get in here?"

"My name is Nicole, Sir Philip," she said in a
soft voice that contained a charming hint of accent.
"I am a present from your friends downstairs. They
said you have been working too hard, so they hired
me to . . . to entertain you for the night."

For a moment Philip felt pure exasperation at such
high-handedness. Tonight he had wanted to get a
good night's sleep to prepare him for the long drive
home; if he had been in the mood, he would have
found a girl himself.

But as he examined his visitor, he realized that he

could easily get into the mood. She was very lovely, with delicate features and huge brown eyes, and her sheer white gown revealed as much as it concealed. His fascinated gaze came to rest on the spot where the trailing ends of the red bow curved over her left breast. His pleasant languor vanished under a surge of vivid anticipation, and he began to smile. Apparently his friends knew what he needed better than he did.

Tossing his cravat over the chair, he said, ''Nicole is certainly an appropriate name for the season.'' He peeled off his coat and waistcoat and sent them in the same general direction, not bothering to watch whether they hit chair or floor. ''But I've never seen a St. Nicholas who was half so appealing.''

After tugging off his boots, Philip sat down on the edge of the bed facing the girl. She was even prettier close up, her wide eyes like dark velvet pansies. Seeing that she had green leaves twined in her hair, he leaned forward for a closer look, then chuckled. ''You really are a perfectly wrapped Christmas present.'' Touching one of the waxy berries, he added, ''Mistletoe is my favorite holiday tradition.''

Enjoying the moment, he let his fingers drift down through her silky tresses and along her graceful neck. Then he moved his hand to the back of her head and pulled her close for a kiss. He closed his eyes, the better to revel in the soft warmth of her lips and the tantalizing invitation of her spicy scent. But even as his breath and blood quickened, he realized that something was wrong. Under his hands, her shoulders were rigid, and he felt a touch of moisture against his upper lip.

He opened his eyes and found that huge tears were silently flowing down her pale cheeks. It was an unnerving sight; while he was no gazetted rake, he'd never had a girl cry when he kissed her. Uneasily he said, "What's wrong?"

Her own eyes flew open, and he saw alarm in the dark depths. "Nothing, monsieur," she whispered. Raising one hand, she wiped at the tears with the back of her wrist. "Please, just go ahead and do—whatever it is you are going to do."

As Philip mentally reexamined the last few minutes, a horrible suspicion occurred to him. "Surely this isn't your first time!"

She nodded, her expression a heartrending mixture of misery and valor.

For Philip the effect was similar to having a bucket of cold water poured over his head. While there were men who delighted in deflowering virgins, he and his friends had always preferred the practiced embraces of skilled demireps. But now that he examined the girl more closely, he saw that she was definitely not of that company; in fact, her demeanor more nearly resembled that of an early Christian trying to appear brave while lions entered the Coliseum. Exasperated, he said, "Why on earth did those idiots choose you?"

"I was in Covent Garden and wearing a truly vulgar cloak, so they assumed I was the kind of female they were looking for," Nicole replied. "Does it matter that I am inexperienced?"

"Yes, it matters," he said shortly.

After a moment's thought she understood. "I see—my ignorance will reduce your pleasure. I'm sorry—I did not mean to cheat them. Or you." Distressed tears trembled in her eyes again; while she had steeled herself to accept passively whatever was done to her, she was unprepared for talk or explanations.

With some violence, the baronet slid off the bed

and stalked across the room. Tall and powerfully built with the breadth of his shoulders emphasized by his white shirt, he was a daunting sight. Still, there was no denying that he was a fine figure of a man; in spite of what the redhead had said, Nicole had expected someone repulsive.

After muttering something under his breath, Sir Philip turned and leaned back against the fireplace mantel with his arms folded across his chest. His voice overcontrolled, he said, ''Why did you agree to do this?''

Perhaps there was a protocol for such a situation, but if so, it was not one Nicole's mother had ever explained. Well, when in doubt, use the truth. ''For the money, of course,'' she said in a small voice. ''I am a seamstress, but I lost my situation, and since I've been in London for only a month, I had no one to turn to. Even so, it did not occur to me to . . . to sell myself, but when your friends made the offer . . .'' She shrugged expressively. ''It seemed like providence.''

His brows drew together. ''So it was a choice between me or starvation?''

''Well, yes,'' she said uneasily, hoping he would not take offense.

''How wonderfully flattering,'' Sir Philip said caustically. ''Are you planning to take this up as a career?''

''Most assuredly *not*,'' she retorted. ''I will find another situation before the money runs out.''

He studied her face for a long moment, then sighed and ran one hand through his thick, light brown hair. ''Taking advantage of desperate virgins is really not a habit of mine. Perhaps it's best if you go now.''

He didn't find her attractive. It was an oddly dis-

concerting thought, even though at the same time
Nicole was so relieved that her knees were shaky
when she slipped off the bed and went to the neat
pile of possessions she had tucked in a corner. She
was sorely tempted to change into her own clothing
and leave without saying more, but unfortunately
honor insisted that she could not do that. She knelt
and fumbled with her cloak until she found the bank
notes in the pocket, then rose and walked over to Sir
Philip. "Here," she said, her voice bleak. "Please
return this to Lord Masterson, for I did not earn it."

After a still moment, his hand closed around hers,
locking the notes in her hand. "Keep the money,"
he said gently. "Neither he nor Kirby would expect
to be repaid, and your need is greater than theirs."

Nicole bit her lip, wanting to cry again because
of his kindness. Before she could become maudlin,
the baronet said testily, "Now for God's sake, put
on something more opaque before I forget to be noble."

Glancing up, she saw frank desire in his gray eyes.
Warm color flooded her face, but there was satisfaction in knowing that he did admire her.

After collecting her clothes, she went to the dressing room so that she could change away from his
intense gaze. However, she had forgotten who was
closed inside. As soon as she opened the door, small
furry feet roared across her bare toes and headed
straight for the man by the fireplace.

After a squeak of surprise, Nicole raced after the
cat and managed to scoop it up before it could as-
sault Sir Philip.

"I'm sorry, sir," she stammered as she clutched
the cat to her chest. "I forgot my cat was in the
dressing room."

Luckily he was amused rather than offended. "So it was to be a ménage à trois. What's her name?"

Nicole hadn't chosen one yet, so she made an instant decision. "Merkle."

"Merkle? An unusual choice for a cat." He reached out to scratch the cat's chin. As the little calico began to purr under his ministrations, Nicole was very aware that the baronet's fingers were within an inch of her breasts, and that she wore only the low-cut sheer negligee that Masterson had provided. How would it feel if those knowing fingers caressed her with the same gentle strength that was enrapturing the cat?

Scandalized by the direction of her thoughts, Nicole stiffened and moved away. "Miss Merkle was very kind to me when I lost my position, and I wanted to honor her. Though I suspect she mightn't be flattered to be remembered this way."

"How did you lose your situation?"

Nicole stared down at the cat, not wanting to say, but unable to lie. In a low voice she said, "I was accused of stealing."

"Were you guilty?" he asked dispassionately.

She raised her head and looked the baronet right in the eye. "No, I was not. My mistress suspected me because I was new in the household. She had my belongings searched, and when my savings were discovered, she became convinced that I was a thief. So she stole my money and threw me out onto the street with no references."

She wanted him to believe her, and was unreasonably disappointed when he frowned. Reminding herself that his opinion didn't matter, she said, "You do not believe me, but then, why should you? I am just a failed doxy." She gave him a slightly mocking curtsy. "I shall be gone in a few minutes, monsieur.

You may search my belongings before I leave to assure yourself that I have taken nothing.''

Philip raised his brows. "I didn't say that I didn't believe you. I doubt that a girl who so conscientiously tried to return money that she hadn't earned would be a thief. What bothers me is the unfairness of what happened to you, but I suppose nothing can be done.''

He was rewarded by a faint, sweet smile. With dark curls tumbling around her shoulders and her oversized negligee half off one shoulder, Nicole was a tantalizing sight. What a pity she was an innocent, for if she was what his friends had thought, the two of them could have spent a delightful night.

Instead, she looked as fragile as she was gallant, and he realized that he could not possibly send her into the December night. "You'd best stay here until morning," he said gruffly. "I don't want to be responsible for you catching lung fever.''

Her expressive eyes widened. "You are very kind, Sir Philip." She glanced at the window, where icy raindrops were softly drumming, and shivered. "It is not a night fit for man, nor beast, nor pelican. Do you have a blanket? I will sleep on the sofa in the drawing room.''

Pelican? Philip smiled at her turn of phrase as he took blankets from the top shelf of his wardrobe. She had an interesting mind. Among other things. But what would happen to her tomorrow, after he went home and she was left to her own devices? "How much did Masterson pay you?''

"We agreed on twenty pounds, but only half was paid in advance. I was to receive the other half in the morning, in return for the night's work." Unexpectedly her eyes twinkled. "Alas, I have not earned that, but the ten pounds you said I could keep is still a considerable sum.''

Philip bit his lip as he calculated how far ten pounds would go. It wasn't much of a cushion against disaster. "You're French, aren't you?"

"By birth, but I have lived in England since I was six."

Philip switched to speaking French. "My mother was born and raised in France, near Toulouse. Her family name was Deauville."

Nicole smiled with pleasure. "Then we are countrymen of a sort," she replied, answering in the same language. "Unfortunately I have never seen Toulouse, but my mother often said it was a lovely city."

Yes, the girl was definitely French, and she spoke with as refined an accent as Philip's mother. Returning to English, he said, "Are you from one of the aristocratic families who escaped the French Revolution with little more than their lives?"

She shook her head. "My family name is Chambord, and while of decent rank, we were not noble. More like one of your English gentry, for my father had a single estate of moderate size." After more thought, she added conscientiously, "My mother had a cousin who was a count, but the connection was not a close one."

Philip suppressed a smile. The girl was nothing if not honest; it was not uncommon for emigres to exaggerate the status they had had in the Old Country. Still, Nicole was clearly well-born, and her coloring and gestures reminded him a little of his own sister. A brilliant idea struck him. "Are you willing to work outside of London?"

She looked hopeful. "Of course. Without references, I cannot afford to be too particular in my tastes. Do you know of a position for a seamstress?"

"Not for a seamstress, but a companion," he replied. "My only sister married last winter, and my father died just a month later, so my mother has had a lonely year. Several times I've suggested that she hire a companion, but she always said that was unnecessary. However, if I present her with a fait accompli, I think she would be delighted to have you."

Nicole looked shocked. "Monsieur, I am an accused thief and obviously no better than I should be, or I wouldn't be here. You cannot possibly take me into your home, much less introduce me to your mother!"

He raised his eyebrows. "Of course I can. In fact, I have every intention of doing so. For over twenty years I've been bringing home stray dogs, cats, birds with broken wings, even the odd injured hedgehog now and then. If my mother can tolerate them, she can certainly deal with you."

"I am considerably odder than a hedgehog," she said severely. "Surely you can see the difference."

Philip was forced to admit that Nicole was right; it was no small thing to introduce a complete stranger into one's home, and even the most broad-minded mother was apt to look askance at a fledgling lightskirt. However, his judgment of people was usually good, and he was willing to swear that the French girl was as honest and well-bred as she appeared. "There is no need to mention how you and I became acquainted. I will just say that you are a distant connection of Masterson's who needs a situation. My mother won't question that."

Nicole frowned, and the cat batted at the red bow, causing the white negligee to dip even more precariously. "I do not want you to perjure yourself on my behalf."

Philip realized that he was getting new insight into

the expression "honest to a fault," as well as a highly distracting view of his guest's pleasing person. After swallowing hard, he said, "Allow me to worry about that. My conscience will be a good deal more troubled if I leave you here to starve." Seeing that Nicole looked unconvinced, he decided that it would be good strategy to imply that she would be doing him a favor. "If you and my mother get on well, you'll save me from a terrible fate. She's been plotting to marry me off—if she has you to fuss over, she might leave me alone, at least for a while."

Nicole smiled a little. "Clearly it is my duty to save you from disaster." Her eyes began filling with tears again. "This morning I prayed for a miracle and *le bon Dieu* has sent me one, for your generosity is truly miraculous. Thank you, monsieur."

With effort, Philip wrenched his gaze away. There was no denying that Miss Chambord was something of a watering pot—nor that she looked dangerously fetching with tears in her great dark eyes. "You stay here, and I'll sleep on the sofa tonight. Time we both get some rest, for I want to be off at dawn tomorrow." Then he beat a hasty retreat, before he found himself trying to kiss her tears away.

Philip was awakened by the faint sounds of someone building up the drawing room fire a dozen feet away. It was still dark, and it took him a moment to remember just why he was sleeping fully dressed and in such an uncomfortable position. Then he remembered and sat up, sore muscles protesting at having been laid to rest on a sofa that was hard and far too short.

He vaguely expected to find Stephens, the Rochester servant who had been looking after him for the last few days, but instead he saw a slight feminine figure kneeling by the hearth and using tongs to set lumps of coal on the embers of last night's banked fire. So the gift-wrapped girl on the bed hadn't been a dream. This morning she was fully dressed in a severe but well-cut gown whose color he couldn't determine in the predawn darkness. Merkle was curled up in front of the hearth, a pointy-eared silhouette against the increasing glow of the fire. Both girl and cat looked very much at home.

Hearing his movement, Nicole glanced up with a shy smile. "Good morning, Sir Philip. I trust you slept well?"

"Well enough." He raised one hand to cover a yawn, then pushed aside the blanket and got to his feet. As the clock began striking six, he said, "Any moment now, two of the Rochester's staff will arrive with hot water and breakfast. You'd better retreat to the bedroom; quite apart from the fact that female visitors are frowned on, the less people who know about last night, the better for your reputation."

"Why should it matter?" she asked, puzzled. "I am of no account to anyone."

"As my mother's companion, you might be coming to London for the Season. Your reputation will matter then, to her and to yourself." He stretched to loosen his knotted muscles. "In fact, after breakfast, I'll pay a brief call on Masterson, thank him for the unexpected gift, then tell him to muzzle James so this little episode doesn't become common knowledge."

"Isn't it too early to call on a gentleman like him?" she said doubtfully as she stood and hung up the fire tongs.

"If I wake him, so be it," Philip said callously. "However, in spite of Masterson's air of languor, he's an early riser. Kirby, on the other hand, hasn't had firsthand experience of dawn since he came down from Cambridge.''

After a swift, appreciative smile, the French girl said, ''When you visit Lord Masterson, will you return the negligee he lent me?''

''So that's why the thing was so large on you,'' Philip said, amused. ''His last mistress was a strapping wench.'' Then he frowned. ''Sorry. I really shouldn't speak of such things in front of you.''

Her eyes danced. ''Last night I was a fallen woman and this morning I am respectable, but in truth I feel little different.''

They were sharing a companionable smile when the servants' door at the back of the apartment swung open with a gloomy creak. Nicole immediately darted into the bedroom and pulled the door shut before the footmen could see her.

While the senior footman, Stephens, set a large tray with covered dishes on a side table, the younger servant headed for the bedroom door with the copper of hot water. Philip hastily interposed himself between the footman and the door. ''Set the water down on the hearth.''

The young man gave him a curious look, but obeyed. As he set down the copper, Merkle decided to dash across the room in a flash of calico lightning. Stephens blinked at the cat. ''Sir Philip, there is a Feline Creature here.''

''Indeed there is.'' Philip watched uneasily as the cat took position by the bedroom door and began to cry for her mistress. ''I saw a mouse here yesterday, so I enlisted expert help.''

Stephens looked scandalized. ''Mice are not permitted in the Rochester. In fact, it is against the rules to have any sort of Lower Creature here.''

The younger footmen said helpfully, ''The way

that puss is carrying on, maybe there's a mouse in the bedroom now.'' He started across the drawing room to open the door.

Once more Philip took several hasty steps to block the way to the bedroom. ''I think the cat is just interested in finding its food dish.'' Anxious to get rid of the servants, he continued smoothly, ''I know you must both be about your duties now, but before you leave, allow me to offer my best wishes for the season, and to express my appreciation for your fine service over the last several days.''

Substantial vails, augmented by a generous Christmas bonus, served to distract the two footmen from the question of what might be in the bedroom. As Philip ushered them from his rooms, he said piously, ''I will take the Feline Creature back to the country this morning, so it shan't cause any trouble.'' Then he closed the door before anything more untoward could occur.

After the footmen were safely gone, he returned to the drawing room to find that Merkle had leapt onto the side table and was now sniffing enthusiastically around the aromatic covered dishes. Before Philip could intervene, Nicole cautiously opened the bedroom door, then scurried across the drawing room and removed the cat from the table. ''I'm sorry,'' she said apologetically as the little calico protested with a heartrending wail. ''The Feline Creature's manners aren't very good.''

''Hunger will raise havoc with manners.'' Philip lifted dish covers until he found a platter of ham. ''Give her a few slivers of this so we can eat in peace.''

After Merkle had been fed and both humans had washed up, they sat down to break their fast. Nicole's interest in the food was as great as the cat's, though her manners were considerably better. In fact, with her pleasant expression and disinclination to chatter, she made an ideal breakfast companion. Philip had a brief, unpleasant mental image of her starving on the streets and gave thanks that fate had put her in his path.

After he finished eating, Philip went into his bedroom and packed the few possessions he had brought with him, plus the Christmas presents he had purchased on Bond Street. Most of the gifts were easily stowed in a leather portmanteau, but the music box he'd bought for his mother began to play when he lifted it. The box was a pretty trifle, its circular base surmounted by a delicate porcelain angel that rotated to the melody of "The First Noel."

As the sweet notes filled the room, Nicole came to investigate, then gave a soft admiring exclamation. "How lovely! A present for your mother or sister?"

He nodded and handed the music box to her. "My mother collects music boxes. I think she'll like this one because of the Christmas theme."

When the movement slowed, Nicole turned the key on the bottom again. Her small face glowed as the angel pirouetted, its gilded wings and trumpet shining in the lamplight as the carol played. "I think your mother is blessed to have a son who is not only considerate, but who has such good taste."

"I'm fortunate to have her and my sister. Losing my father so suddenly has made me aware of how fatally easy it is to take those we care about for granted." Then, more to himself than his companion, Philip added, "I never told my father that I loved him. Now it's too late."

Raising her gaze to his, Nicole said gravely, "I'm

sure that he knew. Love needn't be spoken to be understood.''

Philip found a surprising amount of comfort in her words. He had known that his father loved him, though it had never been said aloud; it made sense that his father had been equally aware of his son's regard. ''I hope you're right.'' Uncomfortable with the extent to which he'd revealed his emotions, he took the music box from Nicole, carefully wrapped it in a heavy towel, and wedged it securely into the leather portmanteau. ''My curricle will be brought around in a few minutes, so I'll go down and speak to Masterson now. Can you be ready to go in ten minutes?''

''Oh, yes.'' She smiled. ''I've little to pack.''

Philip collected the neatly folded white negligee, then took a lamp to light his way down the Rochester's dark stairs to his friend's rooms. Hair tousled and suppressing a yawn, Masterson himself answered Philip's knock.

After identifying his visitor, Masterson smiled lazily and gestured for Philip to come into the narrow vestibule. ''I'm surprised you aren't still enjoying your warm bed.''

''That warm bed is why I'm here,'' Philip said dryly as he handed over the negligee. ''While I must thank you and Kirby for your generous gift, a mistake was made. Miss Chambord is a lady, not a lightskirt.'' Then he succinctly described Nicole's background and his decision to take her to Winstead Hall.

Leaning against the wall with his arms folded across his chest, Masterson listened with amused interest. ''So the chit batted those long lashes and said she's a distressed gentlewoman. You actually believe her?''

Not liking the tone, Philip said shortly, "Yes, I do."

The other man shook his head cynically. "Be careful the little tart doesn't rob you the moment you turn your back."

"She's not a tart." When Masterson gave him a skeptical glance, Philip's eyes narrowed. "You may have catastrophic judgment about women, but not all men are such fools."

The other man's brows shot up. "A low blow, Philip," he said without rancor. "But no doubt you're right. If the girl is an innocent, it would explain why yesterday she gave me a set-down worthy of an Almack's patroness when I told her I was in need of a mistress and asked if she was interested in the position."

So Masterson had offered the girl a carte blanche. Philip teetered between satisfaction that Nicole had turned him down and a strong desire to plant a fist on his friend's jaw. He settled for saying, "Time will tell which of us is right, but until Miss Chambord's honesty, or lack thereof, is established, I'd thank you not to say anything that might ruin her reputation."

"I shall be a model of discretion," Masterson assured him. "And I guarantee that Jamie will be the same. If she is a decent girl fallen on hard times, she deserves a chance."

Satisfied, Philip offered his hand, then took his leave.

Masterson grinned as he returned to the comfort of his bed. Philip was obviously taken by the girl. If pretty little Nicole was what she claimed to be, she might turn out to be a more lasting Christmas gift than they had intended. Time would indeed tell.

In spite of his defense of Nicole's integrity, Philip found himself troubled by doubts as he made his way up the dim stairwell. He had believed without question everything the girl had said, but perhaps he'd been naive to do so. The fact that she had an air of refinement and spoke excellent French didn't mean she was honest; perhaps she was a deceitful little vixen who had been stealing his purse while he was talking to Masterson.

Frowning, he entered his rooms and glanced around, but saw no sign of his guest. He crossed the drawing room in half a dozen steps and entered his bedroom, but there was no sign of her there, or of his luggage, either. Cursing himself for a gullible fool, he spun on his heel and barked, "Nicole, where are you?"

He was so sure that she had fled that it was a shock to hear her voice floating from the narrow hall that led to the servants' entrance. "I am here, monsieur." She trotted into sight carrying a battered wicker basket in one hand. "I found this in a closet. May I use it to carry Merkle in?" Her expression became anxious. "You don't mind if I take her with me? I couldn't bear to abandon her to starve."

Her gaze was so transparently honest that Philip felt like six kinds of idiot for doubting her. After clearing his throat, he said, "Of course she can come. Put a towel in the basket to keep her warm— it's going to be a long, cold drive."

Back in the drawing room he saw that Nicole had neatly stacked all of the luggage beside the front entrance. He'd been in such a hurry when he came in that he'd rushed right by it.

He was just congratulating himself that Nicole knew nothing of his doubts when her gentle voice asked, "Did you think I had robbed you and run, Sir Philip?"

He could feel hot color rising in his face when he turned to her. "The thought had occurred to me."

She nodded with apparent approval, then laid a folded towel in the bottom of the basket. "That is only natural. What do you know of me, after all?"

Deciding to cast his lot with instinct over logic, Philip said, "I know that you are entirely too perceptive, and you have honest eyes. That's quite enough for me. How do you know that I am not a murderer, or going to sell you to a slaver who will ship you to a harem in Arabia?"

She looked up at him and laughed. "Because you are *not*. I knew you were honorable as soon as I saw you." After which placid statement, she scooped up Merkle and put the cat in the basket, making soothing noises to allay feline protests.

After staring at her dark head for a moment, Philip decided that the girl was either a genius or a lunatic, possibly both, but amiable in either case. Hearing the sound of hooves and wheels outside, he went to the window and saw that the livery groom had brought his curricle right on schedule and now waited in the street below. "The carriage is here. Don't you have a cloak? If not, you'd better wear something of mine, though you'll be lost in it."

In answer, Nicole lifted a garishly scarlet garment that had been draped over the back of the sofa. Philip blinked in disbelief as she wrapped the voluminous folds around her. Eyeing the fluffy ostrich trim, he said, "I can see why Masterson and Kirby thought you were no better than you should be."

She wrinkled her nose. "It's a most vulgar garment, *n'est-ce pas*? But warm." Then, less confident than she pretended, she set out to meet her fate, cat basket in one hand, canvas bag in the other, and ostrich feathers trailing behind.

* * *

Reluctantly Nicole left the warmth of the Saracen's Head Inn for the damp, bitter chill of the stable yard, where the curricle waited with a fresh pair of horses. As he held the door for her, Philip said, "It's getting colder. Do you think you'll be all right? I know this is not the season for a long trip in an open carriage, but this is the last stage—Towcester is less than fifteen miles from Winstead."

Nicole ached with weariness, but knew that Philip must be far more tired than she, for it took strength, skill, and continuous concentration to drive safely over the winter-rutted roads. "I'm fine," she assured him. "You have made the trip such a comfortable one. Fresh hot bricks every time the horses are changed—*quelle* luxury! And this is the third time we've stopped to eat."

"You need fattening up." Philip gave Nicole a teasing smile as he helped her into the curricle, then tucked a heavy blanket across her and the cat basket she had placed on her lap. As he climbed into his own seat, Nicole reflected that when he decided to marry, the girl he chose would be very fortunate, for his consideration made one feel cherished. She slanted a glance out of the corner of her eye. He was also kind, amusing, intelligent, good-natured, and handsome. Yes, when he was ready to marry, his chosen bride would be a very lucky woman.

A mile beyond Towcester, Philip swung the carriage from the main road onto a narrower track that led east. "This is a shortcut to Winstead. We should be home just before dark."

Nicole hoped he was right, for it was already mid-afternoon and the lowering clouds threatened to drop something unpleasant on the hapless travelers. *Eh bien;* there was no point in worrying about it, she decided philosophically as the curricle lurched into an unusually large rut. She wrapped her right arm around the cat basket and gripped the carriage rail with her left hand. "Will there be hot mulled wine when we reach Winstead?"

"If not that, something equally warming." The road was getting progressively rougher so Philip slowed the team's pace. "How did you come to England, or is that something you would rather not discuss?"

"It's not a dramatic tale," Nicole replied with a faint sigh. "We had been in Paris and were returning to Brittany. A few miles from home, one of my father's peasants, who had been watching for our return, stopped our carriage to warn us that Guards were waiting at the manor to arrest the whole family. We abandoned the carriage, and the peasant drove us to the coast in his cart. Then a fisherman took us across the Channel to England with no more than the luggage we had brought from Paris. I was only six, and everything happened so quickly that I didn't understand that I would never again see my playmates on the estate, or the nurse who raised me, or my pony. But we were fortunate—we had our lives. Others were not so lucky."

"Did you come to London?"

"Only for a few days. My mother had a cousin in Bristol, so we went there. Because there was hardly any money, my father found work driving a coach between Bristol and Birmingham, which paid enough to keep us in modest comfort for the next few years." Her voice wavered. "Then Papa's back was broken in a coach accident, and he never walked again. Since he could not work, my mother took in sewing. I was almost eleven then, so I helped her."

Philip hauled back on the reins to let a small group

of homeward-bound cows amble across the road. "What a pity. It almost seems like your family was cursed."

"It sounds dreadful, and in many ways it was," Nicole said slowly. "Yet oddly enough, the next five years were the happiest of my life. The three of us were very close. Papa became my teacher, for he said that an informed mind was the true mark of gentility. A gentleman who lived nearby let us borrow any book in his library, so I learned Latin and some Greek, read the classics, debated the ideas of the great philosophers. Then Papa died of lung fever, and my mother's heart died with him."

Nicole used the icy rain as an excuse to brush at her eyes, which were disgracefully moist. "Maman survived another three years, mostly from a sense of duty to me, I think. Then when I was eighteen and she knew I was capable of taking care of myself, she just . . . drifted away."

"And ever since, you've faced the world alone."

"It hasn't been so bad," she assured him, staunch once more. "I have friends in Bristol, and I had a good position there. But I was ambitious and wanted to work in London and someday have a shop of my own. That is how I came to Lady Guthrie's household." She made a face. "Going to work for her was the worst mistake of my life, but it seemed like a good opportunity at the time."

He gave her a quick, warm smile. "You are a remarkable young lady, Mademoiselle Chambord."

She laughed. "There is nothing remarkable about making the best of one's lot, Sir Philip. Not when one considers the alternative."

After that, conversation flagged, for the weather was steadily worsening. The mizzling rain froze wherever it touched, and the muddy ruts began to solidify to iron-hard ridges that rattled the curricle and its occupants to the bone. Earlier there had been a steady trickle of traffic in both directions, but now they were alone on the road.

The Northamptonshire terrain consisted of wide rolling hills that took a long time to climb. It was at the top of one such ridge that the curricle's wheels got trapped in a deep, icy set of ruts that ran at a tangent to the main direction of the road. Caught between the pull of the horses and the ruts, the curricle pitched heavily, almost spilling both passengers out.

"Damnation!" Using all of the strength of his powerful arms, Sir Philip managed to bring the carriage to a safe halt. Glancing at his passenger, he said, "I'm sorry, Nicole. In a heavier carriage we could manage, but the curricle is just too light for these conditions. We've scarcely eight miles to go, and I'd hoped to make it home, but it's dangerous to continue. There's a small inn about a mile ahead. We can stop there for the night."

Struggling to keep her teeth from chattering, Nicole nodded with relief. "Whatever you think best, monsieur."

He urged the nervous horses forward again. "What a polite answer when you would probably rather curse me for risking your neck."

"I'm in no position to complain," she said. "Two days ago I was this cold, but then I had no prospect of finding a warm fire at the end of the day."

The road down the hill was steep and dangerous, so icy that the horses sometimes slipped. The light was failing, and visibility was only a few yards, but with Philip's firm hands on the reins, they made it almost to the bottom without incident. Then they reached a bare spot where the wind had turned a wide puddle into a treacherous glaze of ice. As soon as the curricle's wheels struck the slick surface, the vehicle slewed wildly across the road.

The horses screamed, and one reared in its harness. Philip fought for control, and Nicole clung to railing and cat basket for dear life, but to no avail. The curricle tipped over, pitching both occupants onto the verge. Nicole struck the ground hard and rolled over several times, coming to rest in an ice-filmed puddle, too stunned to speak.

While she struggled for breath, a piercing cry split the air. Immediately Philip shouted, "Nicole, where are you? Are you hurt?"

Another shriek came from the vicinity of Nicole's chest and she wondered dizzily if that was her own voice and she was too numb to know what she was doing. Then she realized she was still clutching the cat basket in her arms. Poor Merkle had been tossed and rolled as much as her mistress and was now protesting in fierce feline fashion. As she pushed herself to a sitting position, Nicole gasped, "I'm all right. At least, I think I am. Merkle is the one carrying on."

"Thank heaven!" Sir Philip emerged from the gloom and dropped to his knees beside Nicole, then pulled her into his arms, basket and all. She burrowed against him, grateful for his solid warmth.

"You're sure you're not hurt?" he asked anxiously, one hand skimming over her head and back, searching for injuries.

Nicole took careful stock. "Just bruised. A moment while I check on Merkle." She would have been happy to stay in Philip's embrace, but conscience made her sit up and lift the lid of the basket. Merkle darted out and swarmed up her mistress's arm, crying piteously until she found a secure position on Nicole's shoulder, claws digging like tiny needles.

"Merkle can't have taken any injury either or she'd not be able to move so quickly," Sir Philip observed as he got to his feet. He helped Nicole up. "Just a moment while I see if the curricle is damaged."

Nicole tried to brush away mud and crushed weeds with one hand while soothing the cat with the other. The puddle had finished the job of saturating her cloak, and the bitter wind threatened to freeze her into a solid block of ice.

Sir Philip muttered an oath under his breath. "The horses seem to be all right, but the curricle's left wheel is broken."

"Surely it can't be much farther to the inn you mentioned," Nicole said through numb lips. "We can walk."

"Up one long hill and down another," he said grimly. "That's too far on a night like this. Luckily there's an old cottage just a few hundred yards from here. I don't know who lives there, but it's always well-kept so I'm sure it's occupied. Just a moment while I get the curricle off the road and unharness the team."

To reduce her exposure to the wind, Nicole hunkered down beside the road and returned an indignant Merkle to the basket. The baronet undid the leather harness straps, tending the job horses as carefully as if they were his own. Nicole's father would have approved; he always said that how a man treated his beasts was a good guide to his character.

When Philip had freed the team from its harness, Nicole stood and joined him, the basket handle slung over one arm. "Which way, monsieur?" she said with a hint of chattering teeth.

"Just along here." Taking the reins in his right

hand, Philip put his left arm around his companion, wanting to warm her. He felt her slim body shaking under her damp cloak, but she did not complain. She really was the gamest little creature.

The lane had a surprisingly smooth surface, which meant that it was now treacherous with sheet ice. Even with Philip's arm to support her, Nicole was skidding with every step. After she had barely survived several near-falls, he turned and scooped her up in his arms, cat basket and all.

When Nicole gave a little squeak of surprise, he explained, "Like the curricle, you are too light for these conditions."

She gave a gurgle of laughter, then relaxed trustingly against him. Between carrying her and leading the placid horses, progress was slow, but ten minutes of trudging through the dark brought them to the cottage, which was a small thatched building of undoubted antiquity.

Fortunately a light was visible inside. Philip set Nicole on her feet and looped the reins around the gatepost, then guided his companion to the cottage's front door. A knock produced no results, so after a moment's hesitation he tried the knob.

The door swung open with a creak, and Philip ushered Nicole into the cottage's large main room. A fire burned in the hearth, and the air was warm and rich with the scent of simmering soup, but there was no one in sight. As he looked around uneasily, a soft female voice with only a trace of country accent came from the chamber behind the main room. "Emmy, what kept you? I've been expecting you all day."

A moment later the owner of the voice appeared. A small, elderly woman with straying white hair, she was dressed plainly, but with neat propriety. Seeing the unexpected visitors, she stopped still, her eyes widening with alarm.

Nicole said reassuringly, "Your pardon, madame, but we are travelers who had a carriage accident on the road outside. The wheel is broken, and to walk to the next village in this weather would be dangerous. I know this is a great imposition, but may we spend the night here?"

The woman went to a window and pulled the curtain aside with one gnarled hand, knitting her brows at the sight of the icy rain beating against the thick old glass. "I was napping and hadn't noticed how beastly the storm is. That must be why Emmy didn't come." She pursed her lips, then dropped the curtain and turned to her visitors. "Of course you and your husband can stay."

Philip said, "May I put my horses in your shed?"

"By all means. It's no night to be traveling." After Philip went outside, the woman turned to Nicole and smiled apologetically. "You must think me a poor hostess. I'm Mrs. Turner. Let me take your cloak, my dear."

"I am Nicole Chambord," Nicole said as she handed over the mantle. Even soggy, it caused Mrs. Turner to raise an eyebrow, but the older woman made no comment as she hung the garment on a peg by the door.

Nicole continued, "My companion is Sir Philip Selbourne. He is not my husband, but—" she hesitated fractionally, "my cousin. We were on our way to his home, Winstead Hall."

Mrs. Turner's eyes brightened with interest. "So he's the squire of Winstead. I know of the family, of course, they're important folk hereabouts. His father died last winter, didn't he?" She gave an appreciative smile. "I didn't know Sir Philip was so young. He's a handsome lad, isn't he?"

Nicole nodded agreement. Sir Philip *was* handsome, not with the flamboyant, Byronic dash of Lord Masterson, but he had a pleasing aspect that was more appealing every time she looked at him. Knowing it was not her place to say any such thing, she asked, "May I let my cat out? Poor Merkle has had a difficult day." She lifted the lid of the basket. Pushed beyond the limits of patience, Merkle instantly scrambled out and jumped to the floor, then swung her head back and forth as she suspiciously examined her new surroundings.

Before the little calico could take a step, a menacing feline growl sounded from a shadowy corner by the wood box. The growl was followed by a large, bristling tabby who slunk into the center of the room with flattened ears and a dangerous gleam in its green eyes.

Judging discretion to be the better part of valor, Merkle raced across the flagged floor and darted under a low chest of drawers, the tabby flying in hot pursuit. "Oh, dear!" Nicole said unhappily. She took a step toward the cats, but Mrs. Turner put her hand up.

"Don't worry," the older woman said. "Moggy won't hurt your puss. She just wants to make it clear whose house this is."

Sure enough, Moggy didn't follow the smaller cat under the chest. Instead, the tabby crouched down, tail flicking, in a waiting position that effectively trapped the calico under the furniture, but offered no real threat.

With crisis turned to stalemate, Mrs. Turner said, "I'll make you and Sir Philip a nice cup of tea. You must be freezing."

As the older woman hung a kettle on the hob so that the water could be brought to the boil, Nicole drew her chilled self closer to the hearth. "Forgive me, madame, for this is none of my business, but who is the Emmy you were expecting? A member of your family who has been caught away from home by the storm?"

"No, she's a girl from Blisworth, the nearest village. She helps out sometimes," Mrs. Turner explained. "My son is coming for Christmas tomorrow and bringing his new wife, Georgette. Robert is a solicitor in London and doing very well for himself." She gave a rueful smile. "Vanity doesn't diminish with age, child. I wasn't well enough to go to the wedding so I've never met my daughter-in-law, but I do know that she's the daughter of a judge, and my cottage will appear poor to her. Still, I wanted everything to be as nice as possible. Emmy was going to help me with the baking and decorating, but she must have decided to stay home because of the weather." Mrs. Turner sighed and spread her hands, which were twisted with arthritis. "So much for vanity. I can't manage everything myself, so Georgette will just have to accept me the way I am."

"It is not vanity to wish to put one's best foot forward," Nicole said. After a moment's hesitation, she offered shyly, "Will you allow me to help you? With a whole evening in front of us, together we can accomplish most of what you wish."

After pouring boiling water over the tea leaves in the pot, Mrs. Turner gave her guest a shocked glance. "It wouldn't be fitting for you to do such humble work. You're gentry."

Thank heaven her kind hostess didn't know what Nicole had been just the night before! Coaxingly Nicole said, "Preparing a home for Christmas is not work, but great pleasure."

While the older woman debated, Philip returned, accompanied by a gust of damp, icy air. He was carrying the baggage. As he hastily closed the door, Nicole said gaily, "We are in luck, Philip. Mrs. Turner is planning her Christmas preparations, and if we are very, very good, perhaps she will let us help her."

Mrs. Turner chuckled. "You're a clever minx. Very well, I'd be delighted to have your help, but first, you both need some tea and bread and soup. Take your coat and hat off, Sir Philip, and come warm yourself by the fire."

"You're very kind, Mrs. Turner," he said as he complied. Holding his chilled hands toward the flames, he continued, "My sister and I are very grateful."

The older woman gave him a sharp look. "I thought you and Miss Chambord are cousins."

Without missing a beat, Philip said, "We are, but Nicole is so much a member of the family that I think of her as another little sister."

Nicole watched with admiration; if this was a sample of his skill at dissembling, he should have no trouble convincing his mother that the scandalous female he'd brought home was actually a respectable poor relation of Lord Masterson's.

Her levity faded as she perched on the oak settle and accepted a teacup from Mrs. Turner. Even if Sir Philip could lie like Lucifer, it simply wouldn't do. Nicole had done considerable thinking on the long drive from London and had reached the miserable conclusion that she must tell Lady Selbourne the truth, for it would be impossible to work for the woman under false pretenses. If Lady Selbourne was as tolerant as her son, perhaps she would not mind Nicole's appalling lapse from grace . . . but more likely she would be outraged and refuse to have such a doxy under her roof.

Nicole knew she should tell the baronet of her determination to confess all, but he would try to change her mind and it would be difficult to resist his arguments. With a sigh, she stirred sugar and milk into her tea. At least when Lady Selbourne ordered her out of the house, Sir Philip probably wouldn't allow Nicole to be tossed into a snowbank; likely he would consider it his duty to buy her a coach ticket back to London. She would be no worse off than she had been yesterday.

She gave Sir Philip a surreptitious glance from the corner of her eye. He was standing, his head almost touching the smoke-darkened beams of the ceiling as he smiled and chatted with their hostess. He seemed too large and energetic for such a small cottage. And as Mrs. Turner said, he was a handsome lad.

No, not a lad, a man, one who was kind and considerate and wonderfully solid. Returning her gaze to her tea, Nicole felt a small, dangerous twist deep inside her. As an émigrée separated from her own class by poverty, she had resolved to build a life as an independent, respected businesswoman. There was no husband in that picture, for Nicole had never met a man for whom she could feel more than liking. But it would be easy—so, so easy—to fall in love with Sir Philip Selbourne. He was very close to the dream husband she had imagined for herself when she was a child, before she realized that the Revolution had made it impossible for her to meet such a man as an equal.

Appalled at the thought, she swallowed a huge

mouthful of tea, scorching her tongue in the process.
Mon Dieu! What a fool she was; her situation was
quite difficult enough without developing a hopeless
tendre for a man she could never have. The baronet
thought of her as a waif, a hapless female who reminded him of his sister. From kindness he was
helping her, but that was all there would ever be
between them. When he was ready to marry, he
would choose a wife of his own class who could
bring him a dowry and an impeccable reputation; the
sort of honorable female who would starve rather
than sell her virtue.

As Nicole sipped more cautiously at her tea, she
realized with a bitter pang that she might have been
better off braving the hazards of the London streets.
Instead, by impulsively accepting Sir Philip's offer,
she was risking her heart.

Working gingerly to keep from being stabbed by
the needlepointed leaves, Philip used a length of dark
thread to attach the last silver-paper ornament to the
last branch of holly. Then he got to his feet and
arranged the brightly decorated sprays of holly, pine,
and ivy along the narrow ledge of an oak beam that
ran across the wall about a foot above the fireplace
mantel.

After all of the greens had been tacked to the
beam, he took a length of shining scarlet ribbon and
twined it through the boughs, working from the left
end to the right, then back again. When he was done,
he stepped back and surveyed his efforts with great
satisfaction. Mrs. Turner's new daughter-in-law
would have to be very hard to please not to enjoy
the results, for the mass of fragrant, brightly decorated greenery turned the whole cottage into a fes-

tive bower. Turning to his hostess, he said, "What do you think—should I use more ribbon?"

Mrs. Turner sniffed the pine-scented air with delight and touched a silver paper star that hung from a spray of holly. "No, it's perfect just the way it is. I only hope your mother won't mind that you gave away the ribbon and silver paper she ordered."

"There's still ample left for Winstead Hall." With an elaborate show of casualness, Philip sidled over to the table where Nicole was assembling the last batch of mince pies. "Can I have one?" he asked hopefully.

Nicole looked up just in time to swat his hand before he could snatch one of the three-inch-wide tarts cooling on the end of the table. Laughing, she said, "You are exactly like an impatient six-year-old, Sir Philip."

"In my family it's traditional to try to wheedle sweets from the cook." He made another attempt to steal one of the tarts, this time successfully eluding Nicole's not-very-determined effort to stop him. The warm, crumbly shortcrust pastry disappeared in two bites. "Mmm, delicious." The same could be said of Nicole, he noticed as she slid the last tray of mince pies into the oven built into the wall by the fireplace. With a towel tied around her waist and a dab of flour on her nose, she was adorable. More than that, her bright good nature created happiness all around her.

Mrs. Turner chuckled as she watched her young guests. "Now that you're finished, Nicole, it's time for us to relax and enjoy the results of all our hard work. Besides, I want you to sample a Turner family tradition." Their hostess lifted a poker that had heated to red-hot in the fire, then plunged it into a wide-mouthed jug of spiced cider. The cider hissed and bubbled around the glowing metal, releasing the rich scent of apples and nutmeg.

After Mrs. Turner had poured them each a mug of mulled cider, Nicole brought over a platter of baked tarts and they all took seats by the fire. Moggy, who had long since given up watching Merkle in favor of the more fascinating study of food preparation, promptly leaped onto Mrs. Turner's knees and raised her nose for a sniff of pastry. Not to be outdone, Merkle slunk out from under the chest of drawers, darted across the rag rug, and hopped onto Nicole's lap, where she turned in a circle three times before settling down.

Outside, the freezing rain still fell, but in the old cottage, all was warmth and good fellowship. As they chatted back and forth, Philip had trouble remembering that he had known Nicole less than a day, Mrs. Turner for only four hours. The chance that had brought them together and the time spent cooking, cleaning, and laughing had made them almost a family.

Halfway through her second mug of mulled cider, Mrs. Turner said, "All we need now is Christmas music. Do you both sing?"

"Willingly, but not well," Philip replied. Then he remembered the music box in his baggage. "But I have something that will get us started properly."

It took only a moment to retrieve the music box from his luggage and wind the key. As he carried the box across the room, the bright notes chimed through the cottage, easily rising above the sounds of crackling fire and spattering rain.

After the mechanism had slowed to a halt, Mrs. Turner reached out and touched the delicate porcelain angel, her lined face glowing with pleasure.

"Such a lovely thing." She glanced at her guests. "Shall we sing along with it?"

Philip wound the music box again, and together they sang "The First Noel." From there they moved into other carols. While none of them had an outstanding voice, all could carry a tune, and together they made a very decent set of carolers.

Eventually Mrs. Turner yawned, covering her mouth with one thin hand. Then she removed Moggy from her lap and got to her feet. "Gracious, but I'm tired. You'll find that when you reach my age, sleepiness comes on you very quickly. You young people can stay up late if you like, but I'm going to bed."

"Not quite yet." Philip stood and picked up the sprig of mistletoe that he had earlier tied with a loop of ribbon. It took only a moment to hang it from a hook on a beam in the center of the ceiling. With a smile, he said, "I'll not let you go without a Christmas kiss."

Mrs. Turner laughed and joined him under the sprig. "You'll turn my head, Sir Philip. I can't remember the last time a handsome young man tried to lure me under the mistletoe."

When Philip started to give her a light kiss on the cheek, she firmly grasped his shoulders and pulled his face down for a solid buss. "I'm not going to waste this opportunity," she declared. Then she scooped up Moggy and retired to the tiny bedroom behind the main chamber.

Nicole followed Mrs. Turner with a hot brick for the older woman's bed, then returned to the main room. "I'm tired, too," she murmured. "It's been a long day."

"Stay until we've finished the mulled cider." Philip divided what was left into their two mugs. Then they took seats on opposite sides of the hearth.

After a few minutes of companionable silence, Philip mused, "I never would have guessed that I'd spend such a fine evening with two females I'd not even met twenty-four hours ago."

Nicole smiled. Curled up in Mrs. Turner's cushioned Windsor chair, she and Merkle were a picture of domestic bliss. "Moments like these are gifts, as lovely as they are fleeting."

"A pity that we can't stop time when we're happy, but life changes so suddenly and unexpectedly," Philip said, regret in his voice. "A year ago at Christmas my father was alive and seemed in the best of health. Then he died, and nothing will ever be the same again." Perhaps it was the result of the alcoholic kick of the cider, but he found himself adding, "And change begets more changes. A year from now, my mother will probably have remarried."

Nicole's gaze shifted from the fire to his face, and her brows drew together. "She is planning to take another husband?"

"Not yet, but I think she will. The estate next to ours is owned by the Sloanes, who have been family friends forever. John Sloane was my father's best friend, just as Emily was my mother's. The children of both families grew up together. Emily died three years ago, and now my father is gone too." Philip swallowed the last of his drink. "Just before I went to London, John Sloane spoke to me in my capacity as head of the family. He wanted to let me know his intentions for when Mother is out of mourning. He and she have always been very fond of each other. Now he hopes that in time she'll marry him." Philip smiled humorlessly. "It's an odd experience when a man who has been like an uncle asks one's blessing to marry one's mother."

"I can see where it would be," Nicole said gently. "How did you feel about it?"

Philip grimaced. "I felt a brief desire to hit him. Then I shook his hand and said that if Mother accepted his proposal, I would wish them both happy."

"Well done." She gave him a warm smile. "But I think you still feel some guilt and resentment?"

"I'm afraid so," he said ruefully. "Not very admirable on my part. Yet I honestly want my mother to be happy and I'm sure she will be with John Sloane." He smiled with self-deprecating humor. "When I told my sister what John Sloane had said, Marguerite raised her brows and said that of course they would marry—that if John and my mother had died, my father would probably have married Emily after a decent interval had passed. Apparently my understanding is not very powerful."

"No, it's just that women take a deeper interest in things like love and marriage." Nicole cocked her head to one side thoughtfully. "Will it help if I say that being possessive of your mother was a perfectly natural first impulse? I would have felt the same way if my mother surprised me with the announcement that she intended to take another husband. It's common for families to oppose the remarriage of a widowed parent. But your second impulse was generous, and that's the one you obeyed."

Philip let out a slow breath. "It does help to hear you say that. Though I don't quite understand why I've confessed such unworthy thoughts to someone I hardly know."

"It is precisely because we are almost strangers," Nicole said with a trace of sadness. "I am a safe repository of unworthy thoughts because I am transitory in your life."

"But if you become my mother's companion, you

will be part of the household.'' At least, until his
mother remarried. Then she would no longer need a
companion, and Nicole would need a new position,
Philip realized. Still, she would be safe at Winstead
for at least a few months.

Nicole muffled a yawn. ''Time I went to bed. If
you wish to stay up longer, I'll take the bed in the
loft and you can sleep down here.''

Philip got to his feet. ''No, I'll take the loft. It's
drafty up there, and I wouldn't want you to take a
chill.'' He smiled. ''If I haven't given you lung fever
yet today, I don't want to do it now.''

Nicole picked up the empty mugs and placed them
on the kitchen table. As she crossed the room toward
the quilts that Mrs. Turner had provided, she passed
under the mistletoe, an opportunity that Philip was
not about to pass up.

Intercepting her under the sprig, he took her
shoulders and said, laughing, ''Happy Christmas,
Nicole.''

She looked up at him, lips parted and brown eyes
wide, her delicate features framed in dusky curls.
''Happy Christmas, Sir Philip,'' she replied in a
husky whisper.

He bent his head and kissed her. Nicole melted
against him, her arms sliding around his neck, her
soft mouth spicy with apple and cloves. She felt as
delicious as she had the night before in his bed, but
this time she did not simply yield. Instead, she welcomed him, and what began as a Christmas kiss rapidly developed into an embrace for all seasons. It
was a moment of fire and sweetness that Philip
wanted to last forever.

Then, with a shock, he realized that once again
tears were running down Nicole's cheeks. Abruptly
he ended the embrace, using his hands to support

her when she swayed. "Why are you crying?" he asked in bafflement. She had not been unwilling, he was absolutely certain of that. "This is not like last night."

"No," she whispered as she brushed the back of her hand across her eyes. "That's why I'm crying."

He looked at her a little helplessly. "I don't understand."

Nicole gave him a faint, sad smile. "It's better that you don't." She closed her eyes for a moment, then opened them again, her manner matter-of-fact. "If I am going to be your mother's companion, we really mustn't kiss like that. It's . . . it's distracting. It lacks propriety."

Perhaps, but it didn't lack anything else. In fact, Philip very much wanted to kiss her again, so that he could savor the nuances more fully, but clearly the moment had passed.

More than a little confused, he lifted one of the lamps. "Good night, Nicole. I'll see you in the morning." The ladder to the loft was in a corner of the room, and he lost no time climbing up, taking off his outer clothing, and crawling into the narrow bed that had once been used by Mrs. Turner's son.

However, in spite of a tiring day, it took Philip a long time to fall asleep. He kept wondering just what it was that he was better off not understanding.

Christmas Eve morning dawned clear and bright. Outside, ice sparkled on every surface and coated leaves and twigs with crystal brilliance, but the magical conditions were short-lived. By the time the inhabitants of the cottage had finished a breakfast of bacon, eggs, and apple muffins, most of the ice was gone and traveling conditions were safe again.

Nicole was grateful when Sir Philip left to go into

Blisworth to make arrangements for repairing the curricle. She had made an absolute fool of herself last night, and this morning she could not look him in the eye. Thank heaven the dear, foolish man didn't understand how the female mind worked, or he'd realize how silly she was. He had been quite right that last night's kiss was different from the one the night before. When she'd been hired to warm his bed, she had been frightened and stoic, but under the mistletoe she had been eager. She loved his touch, loved his taste, and wanted with all her heart to follow the kisses to their natural conclusion.

But, sadly, *her* heart was the only one engaged. Perhaps Sir Philip did not think of her quite as a sister, but he had made it clear that he was not the least bit interested in acquiring a wife. And nothing less would do; Nicole had been willing to sell her virtue rather than starve, but she wasn't going to give it away to a man who didn't love her.

Years from now, when Philip was ready to marry, he would choose a bride whose family and fortune were similar to his own. It was ironic, really. Nicole was too well-born to be Philip's mistress, but too poor, too déclassé, to be his wife.

It was a depressing train of thought, so Nicole determinedly started decorating an old vine wreath that Philip had found in the shed. The addition of sprigs of holly, fragrant crab apples, and a flamboyant red bow made the wreath perfect for the outside of the front door. After it had been hung and admired, Mrs. Turner said, "You have a gift for making things pretty."

"Thank you." Nicole closed the door again. "I'm sure that Georgette will have a fine time here."

"I hope so." Mrs. Turner rubbed absently at one of her gnarled knuckles. "Robert keeps asking me to come live with him in London, but it will never do if his wife and I don't get on.''

"Ah-h-h, I see," Nicole said softly. "That's why you are so particularly concerned about this visit.''

Mrs. Turner nodded. "I'm just a country woman of yeoman stock. I'm afraid Georgette will be ashamed to have someone like me in her house. To make it worse, her own mother died when she was a child, so likely she's used to having things her own way. She won't want me around.''

Nicole wished there was some comfort she could offer, but any words would sound hollow, for there was a very real chance that the judge's daughter would not wish for too much intimacy with her husband's rustic mother. "If Miss Georgette doesn't appreciate you, it will be her loss.''

Mrs. Turner sighed and changed the subject. "Your feelings for Sir Philip aren't sisterly, or even cousinly, are they?''

At the unexpected comment, Nicole's face flooded with hot color. "Am I that obvious?''

"Only to someone who notices such things," the older woman said. "I doubt that he does. Most men don't notice love until it hits them over the head. You'll just have to be persistent. In a discreet sort of way, of course.''

Attaching Philip's interest would take more than persistence, and it was far too late for discretion. Not wanting to explain, Nicole said, "Is there anything else you'd like me to do? It will surely be hours before the carriage is repaired.''

As Nicole's mother had often said, work was the best antidote for the dismals.

It was early afternoon when Sir Philip drove up in the repaired curricle. Nicole came out to greet him.

"I was in luck," he said cheerfully. "The wheel-
wright wasn't too busy. Are you ready to go? We
can be home in an hour."

"Splendid," Nicole said, her voice a little hollow.
If they were at Winstead in an hour, in two hours
she would be on her own again. Briefly she considered postponing her confession for two days, until
Boxing Day was over, but that would be too dishon-
est. She gave Philip a false, blinding smile. "I'll put
Merkle in her basket and get my cloak."

After Philip had loaded cat and baggage into the
carriage, Mrs. Turner came out to say farewell.
Philip took her hand. "You saved our lives, Mrs. T.,
and gave us a splendid evening as well. Will you
allow me to compensate you for your trouble?"

She shook her head. "Taking you in was the
Christian thing to do, and I'll not accept money.
Besides, I had a fine time, too. Perhaps sometime
when you and Nicole are driving by, you'll stop for
a cup of tea."

Philip wished he could do more, but accepted her
comment at face value. Then he straightened up and
saw Nicole's gaze go very deliberately from him, to
Mrs. Turner, to the leather portmanteau that held the
presents, then back to him.

For a moment he didn't understand. Then he
smiled. Of course; why hadn't he thought of that?
He unpacked the music box and offered it to his
hostess. "I understand why you don't want money,
but will you accept this, as a reminder of a special
evening?"

Mrs. Turner took the music box with reverent
hands. "You've found my weakness, young man.
Thank you—this is the prettiest thing I've ever owned
in my life."

She opened the box, and they all listened with

pleasure as the carol chimed through the crisp winter air. Nicole knew that never again would she hear "The First Noel" without thinking of Sir Philip and Mrs. Turner, and these brief, happy hours when their paths had crossed.

The music was just ending when the rattle of a carriage could be heard coming up the lane. Mrs. Turner's expression became tense. "That must be Robert and Georgette."

Philip went to hold his horses' heads while Nicole took the music box from the older woman. "I'll put this inside for you." Under her breath she added, "Courage! I'm sure Georgette will love you."

Nicole set the music box on the kitchen table and was stepping through the front door when the approaching chaise entered the yard, passing by Philip's curricle, which was drawn over to the side. As soon as the chaise stopped, a stocky, dark-haired young man tumbled out and swept Mrs. Turner into his arms. "Happy Christmas, Mother," he said exuberantly. Clearly the young solicitor was not ashamed of his countrified parent.

Then Robert turned to the chaise to help his wife down. As Nicole watched, Mrs. Turner touched her hair nervously.

Then came the Christmas miracle. The girl who climbed from the carriage was not the haughty judge's daughter whom Mrs. Turner had feared. Instead, she was a golden-haired elf whose huge blue eyes mirrored Mrs. Turner's own nervousness. As the two women came face-to-face, Robert said proudly, "Mother, this is Georgette. Isn't she everything I said?"

Mrs. Turner smiled. "Welcome to my home, Georgette. You're even lovelier than Robert said."

The elf blushed. "I've been looking forward so

much to meeting you. Robert speaks often about you
and growing up in the country—the way you and he
and Mr. Turner worked and read and laughed together. It sounds like the most wonderful childhood
imaginable.'' Wistfulness showed in the depths of
her wide blue eyes. ''May . . . may I call you
'Mother'? I've never had a mother of my own, and
I've always wanted one.''

Her face transformed by joy, Mrs. Turner said,
''Nothing would make me happier, my dear.'' Then
she stepped forward and hugged her new daughter.

Nicole was edging her way toward Philip when the
newcomers belatedly realized that there were
strangers present. After introductions and hand-
shakes all around, Nicole and Philip drove off down
the lane. Nicole's last glance over her shoulder
showed the Turners going into the cottage, Robert
in the middle with one arm around his mother and
the other around his wife.

Nicole felt a prickle of bittersweet tears. She did
so love a happy ending. There wouldn't be one for
her, but she didn't doubt that the three Turners would
be happy.

Philip was silent during the seven-mile drive to
Winstead Hall, but not because the familiar road required all of his attention. Instead he found himself
thinking of the young woman sitting quietly by his
side. In the day and a half he'd known her, he had
seen her many different ways: as a pretty little tart,
as a gallant waif, as an uncomplaining traveler, as a
young woman with warmth and kindness for everyone. She was lovely, desirable, intelligent, and
agreeable; everything, in fact, that a man would want
in a wife. No dowry, of course, but he could afford
to marry for love.

But he didn't want a wife! Moreover, he couldn't possibly be in love with a girl he'd just met. Could he?

The more Philip thought, the more confused he became. He'd never been in love, apart from one or two infatuations when he was younger, and even at his most infatuated he'd known that what he felt was passing madness, not true love. But his feelings for Nicole were different from anything he'd experienced before. He liked the idea of having her around all the time, day and night. Definitely at night, but equally definitely during the day. He liked talking with her, and listening to her, and he couldn't imagine ever growing tired of having her around. Was that love?

He had not reached any conclusions when they arrived at Winstead. As they drove up the sweeping entrance road, Nicole drew her breath in sharply, and her reaction made Philip see his home as if for the first time. Winstead Hall was only a few decades old, built for comfort rather than defense. It was also quite beautiful, a triumph of the Palladian style. As Philip drew the curricle to a halt in front of the portico, he tried to visualize Nicole coming down the stairs as mistress of Winstead. It was surprisingly easy to conjure the image up.

A manservant came to take the reins of the curricle, and Philip helped Nicole from the curricle. She was very silent as she accepted the cat basket and accompanied him up the stairs and into the hall. She had the same nervous expression that Mrs. Turner and Georgette had worn when they met, and for the same reason. Philip gave his guest a reassuring smile, knowing that his mother would quickly put her at her ease.

Even as the thought crossed his mind, Lady Selbourne came floating down the stairs. She was a remarkably youthful-looking woman, with dark hair and a face marked by a lifetime of laughter. She did raise her brows at the sight of the appalling scarlet cloak, but made no comment. She'd always been hard to perturb, even the time Philip had led his pony into the vestibule with the intention of having it to tea.

Giving her unexpected visitor a friendly smile, Lady Selbourne said, "Philip, I'm so glad to see you. I was beginning to fear that you might not be back in time for Christmas. Did the weather cause you trouble?"

"A bit. We had a minor accident near Blisworth and had to spend the night, but it was nothing serious." After kissing his mother's smooth cheek, Philip ushered the two women into the drawing room. "Mother, this is Miss Nicole Chambord."

Her dark eyes bright with curiosity, her ladyship said, "I'm pleased to meet you, Miss Chambord. Let me ring for some tea. You must both be chilled from the drive."

Philip's gaze went to Nicole. Her hands were clenched around the handle of the cat basket, and she looked as if she were riding in the tumbril to the guillotine. Yet her head was high, and she had a grave dignity that touched him in ways he couldn't explain. Wanting to relieve her anxiety, he said, "Miss Chambord is a distant relation of Masterson's and in need of a situation. I thought we had a position here that would suit her."

Lady Selbourne nodded with understanding. "I see. You were thinking she could be a companion for me?"

"Perhaps." Philip looked into Nicole's enchanting, expressive brown eyes, and pure madness struck him. "Or if she's interested, there's another position available. As my wife."

A bomb thrown into the drawing room couldn't have struck with greater impact. Both women stared at him with identical expressions of shock, and Nicole almost dropped Merkle's basket. Philip hastily took it and released the cat.

As he did, the silence was broken by his mother going into gales of laughter as she looked first at her son, then at the young woman she had just met. "Oh, Philip, my only and adored son," her ladyship gasped when she could speak again. "Have you learned nothing of French savoir faire from me? This is *not* the way to offer a young lady a proposal of marriage!"

Face scarlet, Nicole blurted out, "The situation is much worse than that, Lady Selbourne, for I am not a young lady. My only relationship to Lord Masterson was that he hired me to spend the night with your son as a . . . a Christmas present." She blinked hard. "If Sir Philip really meant what he said, it is only because he wants to save me from ruination."

Lady Selbourne's laughter ceased, and she plumped down on a velvet-covered chair rather quickly. After a long, alarming silence broken only by the ticking of the mantel clock, she said, "It sounds as if you are already ruined." Aiming a gimlet gaze at her son, she said in a dangerously reasonable tone, "I have trouble believing that you would bring a doxy to Winstead. Am I wrong, Philip?"

Philip winced, realizing that he couldn't have handled the matter more badly if he had tried. "I did meet Nicole in an irregular manner," he admitted, "but she's not a doxy. As an orphaned émigrée, she had been forced to earn her living as a seamstress.

Several days ago she was unjustly discharged, so she accepted Masterson's offer because she was penniless and totally without prospects. When I realized that she was gently bred, of course I couldn't take advantage of her situation. So I brought her here." After a moment, he added stiffly, "I assure you, nothing improper occurred."

"God forbid that I should consider her turning up in your bed as improper," Lady Selbourne said dryly. Her shrewd gaze went back to Nicole. "Is what Philip says true, Miss Chambord?"

Nicole nodded miserably.

Her fingers drumming on the right arm of her chair, Lady Selbourne studied her potential daughter-in-law. At length she said, "Well, you've a practical mind, and that's no bad thing." Switching to French, she said, "Tell me about your family."

Seeing that Nicole was speechless, Philip said helpfully, "Her mother is related to a count."

"Which one?"

Finding her tongue, Nicole said in French, "The Count du Vaille, but the connection is remote."

Lady Selbourne bit her lip absently. "The Count du Vaille? He's also a distant relative of mine, so you and I are in some way related. Where in France did you live?"

Still in French, Nicole sketched in her background and the story of how her family had been forced to flee to England. After listening intently, Lady Selbourne thought for a moment, then began tapping one dainty foot. "*Très bien.* With the du Vaille connection, the world can be told that you are a cousin to whom we offered a home. After a few months of proximity, no one will be surprised if there is an interesting announcement."

Nicole gaped at Lady Selbourne. "You mean that you would approve of such a match?"

Philip's mother gave her son an affectionate glance. "I have been doing my best to find my son a suitable bride, and you are the only girl who has caught his fancy. Philip is very like his father—an easygoing Englishman, but once he makes his mind up, nothing will shake him from his path. While I would certainly not approve of him marrying a courtesan, I have heard nothing about your past that disqualifies you from becoming his wife."

Voice choked, Nicole exclaimed, "But he can't possibly marry an unknown female with no reputation! He knows nothing of me."

"I know that you're honest and lovely and brave and kind, and enchantingly unexpected," Philip said. "What more do I need to know?"

"But . . . but I could be lying about everything," she said helplessly.

"You are the most ruthlessly honest female I've ever met," he retorted. "I may not have much savoir faire, or a deep understanding of the female mind, but I do know that."

Lady Shelbourne gave a low chuckle. "Resign yourself, Miss Chambord. If Philip has decided that he wants to marry you, you had best accept it. Granted, his proposal was cabbage-headed in the extreme, but I've always found his judgment to be sound."

She got to her feet. "I think it's time to leave you young people to sort this out." Leaning over, she scooped up Merkle, who was sniffing inquiringly about her slippers. "You're a pretty little puss. Would you like a Christmas ribbon around your neck? Not red, that would clash with the orange in your fur. Green would be better." She floated out of the room, the calico cat draped across her shoulder.

Nicole stared after her until the door closed. "I've never met anyone quite like your mother," she said weakly.

"She is rather remarkable. You remind me of her a bit." Philip caught Nicole's hand and drew her over to sit beside him on the sofa. "Now, *ma petite,* shall we discuss our future?"

"How can we have a future?" she protested as she settled next to him. "We hardly know each other." She swallowed hard, determined to keep her head. "Why do you want to marry me?"

He smiled. "I rather think I'm in love with you. Isn't that the best of reasons?"

She gave him a level look. " 'Rather think' isn't enough. I don't want to be one of your broken-winged birds or injured hedgehogs that you take in from pity."

Philip's laughing face sobered. "I might try to help a waif because of pity, but I'm not foolish enough to marry for such a reason. I enjoy your company, I admire you, and I desire you. If you turn me down, it's myself I'll pity, not you, for I've never met another woman with whom I could imagine spending my life." His hand tightened on hers. "But just as you don't want me to propose from pity, I don't want you to accept from gratitude or desperation."

"I wouldn't," Nicole assured him. "I've seen what love should be like between man and wife, and I won't settle for a marriage that is merely convenient."

He caught her gaze with his. "Do you think that someday you might be able to love me?"

Philip's nearness and the warmth of his eyes were

rapidly disabling her logic. Looking away from his face, she whispered, "Last night I realized that I was falling in love with you, but it never occurred to me that you might reciprocate. You made it very clear that you didn't want a wife."

"I didn't. I still don't want 'a wife.' What I want is you, *ma petite,* for now and always. I've never thought of marrying before. Now that I've met you, I can think of nothing else." He gently brushed a curl from her temple. "I know this is very sudden. There's no need to rush to a decision—since this is a house of mourning, it will be several months before a betrothal could be announced. That will give us time to become sure of our feelings. As my mother said, you can be a distant cousin come to keep her company. No one will question that."

"I don't really need more time," Nicole said shyly, looking at him from under her dark lashes. "You make my heart sing with happiness. I think it must be love, for I can't imagine anything better or more right."

"Neither can I." With a burst of exuberance, Philip scooped her up in his arms and whirled her around, not caring if she thought him a Bedlamite. Setting his laughing lady back on her feet, he said, "Shall we seal our agreement with a kiss?"

Not waiting for a reply, he drew her into an embrace. Nicole received him eagerly, her pliant body molding to him with the sweet enthusiasm of a playful kitten. And she was a quick learner; she had gotten better at kissing just since the night before.

That being the case, it was a distinct shock for Philip to realize that Nicole was weeping. Lifting his head, he said wryly, "My dearest Christmas tart, why are you crying this time?"

She smiled and ducked her head against his chest.

"Because I'm so happy. I'm sorry, Philip, I'm just a watering pot." She looked up with sudden anxiety. "Perhaps you should reconsider."

"I suppose I'll become accustomed to tears, as long as they are mostly of the happy variety," he said philosophically as he pulled her back into his arms. "Besides, if I cried off, I'd never again see you sitting on the bed with a red ribbon tied around your neck." He grinned. "The best Christmas present I ever had."

"With you, *mon coeur*, every day will be Christmas." Then Nicole laughed mischievously. "I shall have to think up something very special for Guy Fawkes Day."

This time when they kissed, she didn't shed a single tear.

A SEASONAL STRATAGEM

by Sandra Heath

THE TWO fashionable gentlemen were most definitely bored as they rode slowly across the frosty heath toward the tavern known as the World's End. As the crow flew, they were near Chelsea and only three miles away from St. Paul's Cathedral in the heart of London, but here it was open countryside, with only the spire of a church to mark the presence of an adjacent hamlet.

It was three weeks before Christmas, the weather was bitterly cold, and the gentlemen were suffering from a surfeit of the hospitality at Holland House, where they were among a large party of guests for the festive season. Too many late nights and lavish entertainments had jaded their appetites, and they were in the mood for diversion of a different kind. That is to say, Leon, Earl of Holmwood, was thus disposed, whereas his more easily pleased friend, Lord Peter Bristow, was simply suffering the after-effects of too much maraschino the night before.

Lord Peter was a plump, freckled, red-haired follower of the fancy, and sport of every kind was to his liking, even though his rather rotund figure frequently made such pastimes somewhat difficult. There was one sport, however, which always defeated him, and that was the successful pursuit of the fair sex, for it was his misfortune that very few ladies were content to converse endlessly about the merits of such-and-such a prize fighter, or upon whether or not a Yorkshire-bred racehorse could outstrip a Newmarket nag.

Leon, Earl of Holmwood, on the other hand, was notorious for his success in the love stakes. A string of broken hearts lay in his wake, for he was one of London's most handsome and eligible lords, as well as one of its most charming and well-liked. He had as yet to submit to the need to take a wife, but had had mistresses too numerous to mention, and there was not one among these ladies who had relinquished him willingly to her successor. In short, Leon had yet to meet his match, and had yet to even suffer the ignominy of being given his congé.

He was tall, dark-haired, and very dashing, with a roguish smile and vivid blue eyes. It was whispered that his great-grandmother had succumbed to the charm of an engaging Gypsy, and it could not be denied that there was something of the Romany in Leon's restless spirit and flashing smile, but he was also an aristocrat to his fingertips, with the sort of blue-blooded good looks that told of centuries of breeding. It was the roguish side of his nature which was to the fore now, for he was finding the hothouse atmosphere of Holland House very tedious, and he longed for something new and refreshingly different.

The two friends didn't have much to say to each other as they rode toward the ancient wooden tavern which stood just where open heathland and pasturage gave way to the first of the market gardens for which Chelsea was so famous. It was this isolated situation which gave the hostelry its dramatic name, the World's End, but in spite of its lonely position it was a very busy establishment, much frequented by the many workers from the surrounding farms and the market gardens. But busy as it was, its clientele seldom included noblemen, so that the arrival of two fine gentlemen on glossy thoroughbred horses caused something of a stir. Leon and Peter ignored the stares, and remained in the taproom only long enough to purchase two tankards of much-needed mulled ale before adjoining to the fresh air again to enjoy their drinks where they had tethered their mounts. Behind them, the tap room resumed its former noise.

Both men sipped their drinks appreciatively, for the mulled ale served at the World's End was without equal. The laughter and general clatter of the taproom was so great that at first it drowned the sound of two more approaching horses, but Leon became suddenly aware, and turned to see a young lady on a cream mare, accompanied at a discreet distance by a mounted footman.

He lowered his tankard, for the young lady was bewitchingly attractive. She was dressed in an aquamarine velvet riding habit and a plumed black beaver hat, and her bright golden hair tumbled in bouncy ringlets over her left shoulder. Who was she?

By now Peter had also observed her, and he gave a brief grin as he noticed his friend's keen interest. "It seems I have the advantage of you, for I am acquainted with her," he said tantalizingly.

Leon's quick blue eyes swung toward him. "Who is she?" he demanded.

"Her name is Miss Rosalind Faraday, and she is Lady Jenford's niece. Thus she is also a distant relative of mine. Very distant."

Leon was taken aback. "I didn't know Lady Jenford had a niece."

"She has two, actually, for Miss Faraday has a younger sister who is still at the family home in the depths of the Cotswolds, somewhere near Cirencester.''

Leon's attention returned to the approaching riders. "How long has she been here? I'd remember if I'd seen her before.''

"She arrived about two weeks ago, and is returning home on the day before Christmas Eve. I only met her myself about a week after she came to Jenford House. As you know, Lady Jenford is disposed to regard me as family, even though the link is very involved, and so when there was a large dinner party, I was invited to make up the numbers.''

Leon continued to gaze at the dainty figure on the cream horse. "Is she as delightful as she looks?'' he asked softly.

"Well, if your taste runs to pale beauties with soulful green eyes and the word 'chaste' written across their delicate hearts, then yes, she is as delightful as she looks.'' Peter took a long breath. "Look, Leon, she isn't the type for an idle dalliance, she's far too properly brought up for that, so that if you're contemplating another seduction, please put the notion from your head. Besides, I have no desire to run the gauntlet of Lady Jenford's wrath. The woman's a dragon of the highest order, and I've been singed by her anger before now when I've overstepped any mark.''

"And what mark would you be overstepping now, pray?'' Leon asked idly.

"The mark of simply introducing you to Miss Faraday. Lady Jenford would regard you as most definitely unsuitable, my friend, lofty title or no.''

"An introduction is hardly an invitation to ruin,'' Leon murmured, his gaze still upon Rosalind as she and the footman rode along the ice-hard track past the tavern. "I must know her, Peter, so please attract her attention before she rides by."

"Leon—"

"Speak to her, damn it!"

Without further ado, Peter raised his arm to wave. "Good morning, Miss Faraday," he called.

Rosalind reined in, startled to hear someone say her name, for she hadn't seen the two gentlemen by their horses. She smiled as she recognized Peter. "Why, Lord Peter, I didn't notice you there," she said, turning her mount and riding slowly toward them.

Both men put down their tankards and removed their tall hats, and then Peter reluctantly made the desired introduction. "Miss Faraday, may I present my friend, the Earl of Holmwood. Leon, this is Miss Faraday, Lady Jenford's niece and a very distant cousin of mine."

Leon reached up to take her gloved hand and drew it fleetingly to his lips. "I'm honored to make your acquaintance, Miss Faraday," he murmured, gazing into her wide green eyes. Close up, she was even more lovely than he'd realized, with the sort of beguiling innocence he hadn't encountered in far too long.

She smiled at him. "And I yours, my lord," she replied.

Peter cleared his throat. "Are you enjoying your ride?" he inquired politely.

"Oh, yes, even if it is a little cold this morning. I love riding, and come out whenever I have the opportunity, which I fear isn't as often as I would like."

Leon was curious. "Why is that?" he asked.

"I'm afraid my aunt does not approve of ladies riding, for she regards it as most unbecoming."

He smiled. "I doubt if you could ever look unbecoming, Miss Faraday," he said gallantly.

Rosalind flushed a little at the compliment, for the smile accompanying it had been lazily warm, almost caressing, and it forced her to look at him again. She realized with a jolt that she found him devastatingly attractive, almost heartstoppingly so, and it was a realization that brought a flood of warm color to her cheeks.

At that moment the distant sound of a church bell echoed across the winter countryside from the direction of Chelsea, and she gave a gasp of dismay as she realized the time. "Oh no! Is it that late already? My aunt instructed me to be home by now to discuss our engagements, and she'll be furious with me for not being prompt. Please forgive me, gentlemen, but I simply have to hurry back." With a rather flustered nod of her head, she urged her horse away toward the market gardens and Chelsea. The attendant footman rode after her.

Leon exhaled slowly as the sound of their hoofbeats died away into the crisp December air. "Enchanting, quite enchanting," he breathed after a moment.

Peter eyed him with dismay, for he recognized the signs. "Leon, I didn't want to introduce you, for I know you too well. I also know Lady Jenford, and my hide will be nailed to the nearest wall if you set about seducing Rosalind Faraday."

"I merely said . . ."

"I know what you 'merely said,' " Peter interrupted. "You have that look in your eye which usually denotes a certain intention, and I would be much obliged if you would leave this particular beauty well and truly alone. Not that I think you'd succeed with her anyway," he added as an afterthought.

Leon raised a quizzical eyebrow. "Are you casting doubt upon my prowess?"

"No, I'm merely crediting the lady with too much sense to risk her reputation for the sake of your charms. I'm also hoping against hope that I can dissuade you from all thought of meddling with a member of my family, no matter how distant and tenuous the blood connection may be. Lady Jenford wields a great deal of influence with my old man, and I have no desire to be not only skinned alive, but also denied my allowance! Oh, and there is one thing more."

"Do tell."

"Miss Faraday is set to be betrothed in the New Year. I gather that the son of a neighboring landowner has been away on some sort of grand tour for the past year, but that he is about to return, and a match has been arranged. I believe his surname is Lincoln. Yes, that's it. Mr. Granville Lincoln. His family owns half of Gloucestershire, and so it's an excellent match."

"And this intended marriage of convenience makes the lady impervious to my lovemaking?" Leon inquired smoothly.

"I didn't say it was a marriage of convenience, indeed I have no idea at all how Miss Faraday feels about it. She may be wildly in love with the fellow for all I know. And as to her being impervious to your advances, well, yes, I rather think she would be."

"Such a challenge cannot be ignored, my friend, and so the matter must be put to the test. A thousand guineas says I can win a kiss."

Peter stared at him. "Eh? Oh, now look, Leon, I know I'm a gambling man, but this—"

"Ha! So you don't have all that much faith in the lady's virtue after all!" Leon cried tauntingly.

Peter hesitated. "That isn't what I said."

"No? Either you think she will resist me, or she will surrender. Which is it?"

"She will resist."

"A thousand guineas?" Leon grinned at him.

Peter sighed and nodded. "Oh, very well. But only a kiss, mind you, and even that is going too far if Lady Jenford gets a whiff of it."

Leon gave him a rather wry smile. "My dear Peter, why is it that you and the rest of society insist upon branding me a shameless libertine?"

"Perhaps because you are," Peter replied crushingly.

"No, my friend, I'm not. If you go back through my admittedly long list of conquests, you will not find one name there belonging to a real innocent. I have only ever seduced those who have made it clear they are willing and available. A rogue I may be, but I'm not a villain. I will be content to pocket your guineas by persuading the lady to part with a single kiss, but it cannot be simply a peck on the cheek. No, it has to be a passionate kiss." Leon gazed in the direction Rosalind had ridden. She had vanished from view now, but he could see her as clearly as if she were still before him. It would be a sweet moment indeed when she surrendered her lips. Rousing himself from such delicious reverie, he looked at Peter again. "How long do I have to effect this momentous triumph?"

"Well, she leaves for Gloucestershire the day before Christmas Eve."

"That gives me two weeks. Shall we say until midnight on the twenty-second?"

Peter nodded. The wager intrigued him in spite of

his alarm over Lady Jenford. Perhaps he was beyond redemption, a gambling man who simply could not resist temptation. But, oh Lord, if the dragon should ever find out what he'd been up to . . . He finished his ale and tugged on his tall hat. ''Come on, it's time we returned to Holland House, otherwise we'll be too late for the shooting party.''

Leon paused for a moment, his attention returning to Chelsea, where Lady Jenford's elegant residence overlooked the Thames in Cheyne Walk. He meant to win this wager, and the chase would have to commence without delay. He had long since found out that one of the best ways to discover all he needed to know about a lady was to cross her maid's palm with silver, and thus Rosalind Faraday's maid would be approached this very day. He would be crying off Lord Holland's shooting party, for he would be embarking upon the first moves in his seductive design.

As he and Peter rode away from the World's End, Leon grinned to himself. Suddenly his ennui had vanished, and he knew he was going to enjoy the next two weeks. The pursuit of such a delightful quarry was going to be very pleasurable indeed, as was the whole of this seasonal stratagem. He had wanted a new and refreshing diversion, and now he had it.

By the time Leon and Peter had set off back to Holland House, Rosalind and her footman escort had almost reached Cheyne Walk. Jenford House was a beautiful seventeenth century mansion facing the river from behind a leafy garden and a high red brick wall. A screen of evergreen trees shielded it from any prying gaze which might be directed through the magnificent gilded wrought-iron gates, and the dormer windows in the roof enjoyed a matchless view over the Thames.

Cheyne Walk was one of Chelsea's most fashionable streets, part elegant houses, part superior shops, and it was a place to see and be seen in. Even in the depths of winter there were numerous ladies and gentlemen strolling beneath the elm trees at the water's edge, and a constant stream of fine carriages passed to and fro along the cobbles. The Thames itself was very busy, with sailing barges making full use of the incoming tide, and as Rosalind rode toward Jenford House, there were seagulls swooping low over the water, their haunting cries echoing all around.

Leon would have been aggrieved to know that he didn't figure at all in his quarry's thoughts as she dismounted at the door of her aunt's house, for she was far too preoccupied with how she was going to satisfactorily explain her tardiness. Her formidable aunt was looking for an excuse to ban her from riding, and now such an excuse was going to fall into her hands. Being late for an appointment was an unpardonable social sin, and she, Rosalind Faraday, was over fifteen minutes late on this occasion.

Pushing the reins into the hands of her footman escort, she fled into the house, entering a wide paneled hall where firelight danced upon the walls and a grand staircase rose at the far end, but as she reached the lowermost steps she was halted by the pattering sound of little paws. She looked up to see her aunt's three white spitzes running excitedly down to greet her.

They were named Hera, Hestia, and Demeter, and they adored her because she frequently took them for walks along the river. She had become very fond of them as well, and in spite of being late now she paused to give them the fussing they sought. Their curling feathery tails wagged with pleasure, and they tried to jump up to lick her face.

The moment was brought to an abrupt end by an imperious voice from the top of the staircase. "And what time do you call this, pray?"

Rosalind straightened reluctantly, and looked up at her aunt's black-clad, ramrod straight figure. "I . . . I must beg your forgiveness, Aunt Jenford. I have no excuse except that I simply did not realize how late I was."

"I permitted you to go out on the strict understanding that you would return by eleven. It is now almost twenty past."

"Yes, Aunt Jenford." Rosalind lowered her eyes guiltily.

The town carriage was being brought to the front of the house, and it was only then that she realized that in her haste she had dashed past her aunt's maid, who was waiting in the hall with her mistress's carriage cloak.

Lady Jenford began to descend the staircase. She was fifty years old, and even though she had been widowed for fifteen long years she insisted upon wearing unrelieved black. She powdered her hair, and there was a judicious application of rouge on her cheeks. Her face was fine-boned and even, with a questing nose and rather penetrating gray eyes, and everything about her exuded displeasure as she came down toward her niece in a rustle of black bombazine.

She halted at the bottom, teasing her slender hands into her tight-fitting black kid gloves. "Well, I fear that since you were not prompt, it is not now possible to discuss our social engagements with the care which is necessary, and so I have taken it upon myself to make the decisions without you. I trust you will pay heed to what I am about to say.''

''Yes, Aunt Jenford.''

''On the eleventh, that's in three days' time, we are to attend a breakfast party at Syon House. On the thirteenth we are going to the masque at Devonshire House, followed on the sixteenth by a concert recital at Lansdowne House. After that we have been invited to join Lady Kinnear's party at Covent Garden. Mrs. Siddons and Mr. Kemble are playing in *Coriolanus*, which is my favorite play.''

''Yes, Aunt Jenford,'' Rosalind responded meekly, but her heart sank. She loathed *Coriolanus,* indeed she loathed all Shakespeare except *Twelfth Night* and *A Midsummer Night's Dream.*

''That brings us to what will be your final engagement before leaving for Faraday Park on the twenty-third. I refer to the Christmas ball at Holland House on the twentieth.''

Holland House? Rosalind's thoughts suddenly winged back to the World's End tavern, and the Earl of Holmwood's handsome face and warm smiles.

Lady Jenford flexed her fingers in her gloves. ''I hope that you took full note of everything I said, Rosalind?''

''Yes, Aunt Jenford.''

''Good. You may count yourself fortunate, missy, for if I did not have to break my word to you about the shopping expedition the day after tomorrow, I would be obliged to deal firmly with you over your tardiness today. I fear that we will no longer be able to go as planned because the ladies of Chelsea are meeting here to discuss how best to distribute food to the needy at Christmas, and such a worthy cause must naturally take precedence over your Yuletide gifts.''

Rosalind was filled with dismay. "But cannot I go anyway, Aunt Jenford?" she pleaded. "I could go directly to the jeweler's in Piccadilly where they have the very thing I wish to purchase for Verity."

Lady Jenford hesitated. "You only require to purchase something for your sister?"

"Yes, Aunt Jenford, and that particular jeweler has a wonderful selection of silver pincushions. You know how very much Verity enjoys needlework," she added persuasively, being fully aware that her aunt approved greatly of her sister's industry.

"Oh, very well, I will put my town carriage at your disposal, but you must be sure to take your maid as a chaperone. Piccadilly is not suitable for a young lady alone."

"Yes, Aunt Jenford." Rosalind smiled gladly, not only because she would now be able to complete her purchases as planned, but also because she would escape her aunt's worthy cause. She had already sampled the laudable deliberations of the Chelsea ladies in question, and their prim manners and tinkling teacups were altogether too awful for words.

Lady Jenford nodded. "That is all I have to say to you for the moment, my dear, except that I would be pleased if you could take the spitzes for a walk this afternoon."

"I will, Aunt Jenford."

"Oh, and a letter has arrived for you from Verity. I have left it on the mantelshelf in the drawing room."

Rosalind couldn't hide her delight. A letter from Verity?

"Good-bye for the moment, my dear." Lady Jenford presented a cheek for a dutiful kiss.

Rosalind duly obliged and then waited impatiently as her aunt donned her carriage cloak before rustling out of the house accompanied by her maid. As the butler closed the door and the carriage drove off, Rosalind gathered her skirts and ran up to the drawing room, the excited spitzes scurrying at her heels.

The drawing room stretched across half of the front of the house, its windows facing the evergreen trees in the garden, with now and then a glimpse of the Thames beyond the high wall. It was a sumptuous room, with paneled walls and crimson velvet furniture, and it was upon an elegant sofa that Rosalind settled to read her sister's letter. The spitzes jumped up beside her, resting their chins on her lap and gazing adoringly up at her as she began to read.

Faraday Park, Friday, December 5th, 1811.
My dearest, much-missed elder sister,

Before I write another word, I will break the news I suspect you've been longing to hear. Mr. Granville Lincoln has returned to England, and comes over from Lincoln Place every day in the hope that you've come home early. Rosalind, I do believe that the match pleases him greatly, for he expresses himself deeply disappointed that you are absent, and is always recalling things you once said, and where and when you said them. I fear that he is having to make do with my company, and that he is far too much of a gentleman to show how dismally I compare.

I vow you would hardly recognize him now, for the foreign sun has changed him. You will recall that his complexion was once pale, and his hair light brown, but now he is tanned and glowing, and his hair is the color of honey. He is altogether a handsome fellow, and I have become the envy of the neighborhood, for he takes me out driving in his new curricle. He is very skilled with the ribbons, and we skim along the Gloucestershire lanes like the wind itself, so fast that I once lost my bonnet and he had to retrieve it from a branch!

He accompanied Father and me to church last Sunday, and I observed many a jealous cat turning her gaze upon him. I refer in particular to the Robertson twins, who were even bold enough after the service to invite him to their paltry ball. To their fury, and my unutterable delight, he politely declined.

I fear I cannot write more now, for Father and Granville are waiting to leave for Cirencester. Father's magisterial duties require his presence, and Granville and I are to amuse ourselves as best we can.

Oh, dear, I was going to write such a long letter, but now there isn't time. Please hurry home before the twenty-third if you can, for Christmas cannot possibly begin until you are here. I'm longing for our usual holly-gathering expedition in the woods by the lake, and I'm brimming with new ideas for decorating the house and the church.

All my love.

Verity.

Smiling, Rosalind folded the letter and then leaned her head back against the sofa. Granville was home at last. Oh, how she was looking forward to seeing him again, especially now that a match was to be arranged between them. They had known each other since they were children, and they'd always been the best of companions. Now they would be husband and wife.

With a glad cry she scooped the startled spitzes into her arms and buried her face in their white fur. This was going to be the most wonderful Christmas ever, and the next two weeks simply wouldn't pass quickly enough.

* * *

It was the afternoon of the same day, and Rosalind was almost ready to take the spitzes for their walk. She was dressed in her emerald-green pelisse and matching gown, and her golden hair was swept up beneath a wide-brimmed hat which had a white gauze scarf tied around its crown. She turned for her maid to hand her her gloves, but the maid's thoughts were elsewhere, indeed she was gazing out the window.

Rosalind paused. "What is it, Daisy? You've been acting most strangely ever since you came up to my room. Is something wrong?"

The maid jumped guiltily. She was a bright-eyed country girl with dark hair which she wore plaited and coiled on top of her head. Her figure was slender and a little flat-chested, and she liked to starch her clothes so much that they crackled when she moved. "Wrong? Oh no, Miss Rosalind."

"Are you sure? I wondered if you'd had an argument with Thomas, the underfootman." Rosalind smiled, for Thomas had quite set the maid at sixes and sevens since she'd arrived.

Dull color rushed into Daisy's cheeks. "No, Miss Rosalind, I haven't quarreled with him."

"So, what is it? Your mind is quite obviously elsewhere."

Daisy didn't reply, but lowered her eyes. The truth was that she had allowed herself to be bribed by the Earl of Holmwood, whom she had told all sorts of things about her mistress's plans, and now she was conscience-stricken. "There's nothing wrong, Miss Rosalind," she said, wishing that Rosalind would stop probing.

"Oh, very well. That will be all."

"Miss Rosalind." With a thankful curtsy, Daisy made good her escape.

A footman was waiting for Rosalind in the entrance hall, with Hera, Hestia, and Demeter straining impatiently at their red leather leads. They wagged their feathery tails and whined excitedly as Rosalind descended the staircase, and then their paws slithered on the floor as they strove to drag her out of the house into the pale winter sunshine of the December afternoon.

A light breeze whispered through the bare branches of the elm trees at the edge of the river as she made her way downstream along Cheyne Walk, with the footman bringing up the rear a few paces behind her. Carriages bowled along the cobbles, and the pavement opposite was crowded with people, but there weren't many beneath the trees. She passed the wall of All Saints' churchyard, and then walked on toward the stone bench opposite the apothecary's shop, where it was her custom to halt for a while so that Hestia, the least robust of the spitzes, could rest before making the return journey.

Christmas was most definitely in the air. A man was selling hot chestnuts by the churchyard steps, and nearby there was a young girl with a tray of pretty gilded paper stars to adorn Christmas garlands. For the first time the sound of Christmas carols could be heard, not from the church, but from a trio of wounded ex-sailors on the corner by the circulating library as they sang "I saw three ships come sailing in."

It wasn't far to the bench now, but poor Hestia's strength was flagging so much that Rosalind bent to scoop her up into her arms and carry her the rest of the way. Verity's letter was on her mind. Was Granville with her sister now? Were they perhaps driving in his curricle? Oh, how frustrating it was to be here in Chelsea, and not at home where she so longed to be.

She didn't see Leon waiting by the bench, his cane swinging idly in his gloved hands as he pretended to gaze across the river at the sailing barges. But his attention wasn't upon the river, instead it was upon Rosalind herself. He knew she would be here at this time, for her maid had informed him. The sunlight flashed on the diamond pin in his starched neckcloth, and he cut a very stylish figure indeed in his dark blue coat and cream kerseymere breeches. His tall hat was pulled well forward on his dark curls, and his blue eyes were speculative as they rested upon her. Well, one thing was certain, he still found her as delightful now as he had this morning. There was something about her, something quite exquisite and alluring.

Rosalind remained unaware of his presence, for out on the river two barges came close to collision, and their respective crews hurled abuse at each other. On the shore, where some stone steps led down to the water and a jetty where rowing boats were moored, a large marmalade cat had found itself a sheltered corner in the sun, where it groomed itself with leisurely satisfaction. It paused in its licking as it detected the spitzes, but although it was now perfectly still, the dogs perceived its presence. With a sudden furious burst of barking, they flung themselves toward it, almost jerking Rosalind from her feet. Even Hestia became excited, jumping down from her arms and yapping excitedly. Hera and Demeter were so beside themselves that they lunged at the cat again, and this time they did indeed unbalance Rosalind. With a frightened cry she teetered at the top of the steps, and would have fallen had not

Leon dashed forward in time to pull her back from the brink. The leads were snatched from her fingers as the cat leapt up the steps and the spitzes gave chase, followed in turn by the dismayed footman. Only Hestia remained, but that was because she was still too weary after the long walk from Jenford House.

Rosalind was shaken by the suddenness with which it had all happened, so that Leon had to keep his arm around her waist to steady her.

"Are you all right, Miss Faraday?" he inquired anxiously, for she had come within a heartbeat of falling into the river.

She managed to nod. "I . . . I think so . . ."

"Come and sit down," he said firmly, ushering her to the bench and then sitting next to her. "Is that better?" he asked, still looking anxiously into her eyes.

Her gaze went to the steps and the water beyond, and she shivered. "If you hadn't been here . . ." she began.

"You're quite safe now," he said, briefly taking her hand and squeezing it reassuringly.

"I don't know how to thank you," she said.

"There is no need." He smiled, perhaps a little too warmly.

Something in his gaze disconcerted her, and she felt a flush suffusing her cheeks. "I . . . I wonder if he will catch Hera and Demeter?" she asked, sitting forward and looking along the cobbles in the direction the unfortunate footman had run.

"I'm sure he will," Leon replied, realizing that he'd allowed his interest in her to come a little close to the surface. If she wished to change the subject, then by all means let them change it. "Hera and Demeter? How very classical and superior," he said with a slight laugh. "And what is this one called?" He stroked Hestia's head.

"Hestia," she replied.

"Are they yours?"

"No, they belong to my aunt. She named them after the Queen's dogs. I believe she saw a painting by Mr. Stubbs of the royal spitzes, and she liked it so much that when she acquired these three, she decided to give them the same names."

His brows drew together thoughtfully. "A painting by Stubbs?"

"Yes, I understood it is at Windsor Castle."

He shook his head. "No, for I've seen it recently, and it's some time since I graced Windsor with my presence. In fact, I'm sure I've seen it at Holland House."

"Really?"

"Yes. You will be able to see for yourself when you attend the Christmas ball."

She looked at him in surprise. "How do you know I will be at the ball?"

"I, er, happened to notice the guest list just before I came out this afternoon. Having made your acquaintance only today, your name did rather catch my eye." The untruth slid easily from his lips, for he hadn't seen any guest list, he'd found out from her maid, just as he'd also found out about her walk to this particular bench, and that she and her aunt worshipped at All Saints', just down the street from where they sat. He also knew about the Syon House breakfast party, the Devonshire House masque, the Lansdowne House concert recital, and the visit to see *Coriolanus*. He even knew that the day after tomorrow she would be sallying forth to a certain jeweler's in Piccadilly to purchase her last Christmas gift.

At that moment the breathless footman returned with the two disobedient spitzes, and Rosalind rose quickly to her feet, giving Leon an apologetic smile. "I should go back now, my lord," she said.

Leon got up as well. "Allow me to walk with you, Miss Faraday."

"There is no need . . ." she began.

"I would like to," he insisted, smiling.

His smiles affected her, and she accepted his offer a little self-consciously. "Then if that is your wish, sir," she murmured.

Leaving the footman to bring the spitzes, they began to walk back along the water's edge. Rosalind was very aware of her handsome escort, for there was no denying that he was one of the most winning gentlemen she'd met since arriving from Gloucestershire. Verity had teased her that she would be spoiled by legions of such gallants, but the truth was that the Earl of Holmwood was the first she, Rosalind, would have described as truly dashing and good-looking. He was certainly the first one she'd found so very attractive.

They reached Jenford House just as Rosalind's aunt returned, and Lady Jenford did not seem at all pleased as she alighted from her carriage and saw her niece on the arm of the notorious Earl of Holmwood. She accorded him the courtesy of a nod, but it wasn't a warm greeting, and she finished it by instructing Rosalind to come inside without delay.

Astonished at her aunt's manner, Rosalind took her leave of Leon. "I . . . I had better do as I'm instructed, sir," she said.

He caught her hand and drew it to his lips. "I fear you are about to be sternly warned of the perils of my company, Miss Faraday."

"Am I?" Her eyes widened. "And would such a warning be justified?"

He smiled a little. "Probably," he murmured, "but I promise you that I am not as black as I am painted."

She searched his eyes for a moment and then drew her hand away to hurry after her aunt into the house.

Lady Jenford waited in the hall, her lips pursed with disapproval. "I was not aware that you were acquainted with the Earl of Holmwood, Rosalind," she said the moment her niece entered.

"I . . . I only met him today, Aunt Jenford."

"Where?"

"While I was out riding."

"I trust he did not simply present himself to you?"

"Oh no, Aunt Jenford, we were formally introduced by Lord Peter Bristow."

Lady Jenford's eyebrow rose. "Lord Peter? I will have to have words with that gentleman. Rosalind, the Earl of Holmwood is an infamous womanizer and rakehell, and as such is not at all suitable as an acquaintance for a young lady like you. Do I make myself clear?"

"Yes, Aunt Jenford." Rosalind lowered her eyes to the floor.

"You are to avoid situations that will bring you alone into his society. Is that also clear?"

"Yes, Aunt Jenford."

The older woman softened a little then. "My dear, I have to say these things in order to protect you from folly. A very advantageous contract has been arranged for you with Mr. Lincoln, and your name being linked with someone like the earl might endanger that match. You do understand, don't you?"

"I do, Aunt Jenford."

Lady Jenford smiled. "We will not speak more of it. Now then, I have requested tea to be served in the drawing room, so you go and take off your outdoor clothes, and we will meet there in a few minutes."

Rosalind hurried up the staircase, but as she did so her thoughts were not of any vague danger to her forthcoming match with Granville, but rather of the novel and somewhat exciting experience of meeting a gentleman as notorious as the Earl of Holmwood.

She next encountered Leon at the jeweler's in Piccadilly, when she went to select the silver pincushion for Verity.

Piccadilly was such a bustling and crowded thoroughfare that it quite put Cheyne Walk in the shade. It was a place of shops, inns, lodging houses, stagecoach ticket offices, private residences, and all manner of other establishments, and it was only in the small hours of the night that it was ever quiet. The world and his wife appeared to be on the pavements now that Christmas was approaching, and the carriageway itself was a constant crush of every vehicle imaginable. As a consequence, Lady Jenford's coachman was hard put to maneuver the town carriage through the jam to the curb outside the jeweler's bow-windowed shop opposite the Egyptian Hall.

The noise of the street seemed to leap at Rosalind as she and Daisy alighted to the pavement. Footsteps, hooves, wheels, and voices echoed all around, and there was music from a fiddler and a man with a penny whistle who were playing "God Rest Ye Merry, Gentlemen." There was a poster on a wall announcing that this year's pantomime at the Sadler's Wells theater would be *Bang up, or, Harlequin Prime*.

It was dark in the shop, and after the cold brightness of the street it was a moment or so before Rosalind's eyes became accustomed to the gloom. She didn't see the only other customer, a gentleman standing at the far end of the dark oak counter, but Daisy saw him straightaway and hung guiltily back near the door, for he was only there because she had told him her mistress's plans today.

Leon smiled a little as he observed Rosalind enter and approach the other end of the counter. She wore gray today, a full-length pelisse that was fitted tightly at the waist, and a matching bonnet that was lavishly trimmed with white fur. Her hands were plunged deep into a white fur muff, and the sound of her footsteps was light upon the shop's polished wooden floor.

A young man assistant went to serve her. "May I be of assistance, madam?" he inquired.

"Yes, I wish to see the tray of silver pincushions you have on display in the window."

"Madam."

As he went to bring the tray, Leon decided it was time to acquaint her with his presence. "Why, if it isn't Miss Faraday, again," he said, walking toward her.

Rosalind gave a start and whirled about. Her aunt's strictures sounded warningly in her ears, and for several seconds she was so flustered that she couldn't respond to the greeting.

Leon smiled and sketched her an elegant bow. He wore a pine-green greatcoat with an astrakhan collar, and the mother-of-pearl handle of his cane gleamed softly in the shadowy light as he placed it on the counter next to her, together with his tall hat and gloves.

Rosalind's confusion was too marked for him not

to comment upon it. "It would seem that I've suddenly sprouted horns and a tail," he murmured.

"I . . . You startled me, that's all, sir," she offered by way of lame explanation.

"No doubt I did, Miss Faraday, but I also fancy I detect the hand of Lady Jenford."

She lowered her eyes. "I do not deny it, sir."

"I sincerely hope that you are not forbidden to even exchange the usual courtesies with me?"

She met his eyes reluctantly. "I'm told you are all that is unsuitable, my lord."

"My fame may travel before me, Miss Faraday, but I assure you that I do not deserve quite such a reputation."

His gaze was amused and rather teasing, and the faint smile playing upon his lips made her feel a little foolish.

The assistant returned with the tray of pincushions, which he placed before her. To conceal her continuing embarrassment, she made much of giving her full attention to the gleaming selection of silver.

Leon studied her profile, thinking how very engaging she was when self-conscious. There was a bloom on her cheeks, and a shyness in her green eyes which made him want to reach out and touch her. But that wouldn't do just yet. Not just yet. For the moment his stratagem would be best served by treading with infinite care, and by joining her in the study of the pincushions.

"Are you purchasing for yourself, Miss Faraday?" he inquired.

"For my sister. It is to be her Christmas gift," she replied.

"You certainly have a vast choice," he murmured, picking up a cushion in the shape of a gondola, with a crimson velvet pad in the middle for the pins.

"I simply don't know which one she would like," she said.

"Well, if *I* were choosing . . ." He put the gondola back and picked up a little shoe instead. It was a lady's high-heeled shoe from the middle years of the previous century, and it was filled with a bright blue satin pad. He held it out to her. "This is the one I like most, Miss Faraday."

"Yes, it is very pretty," she said, taking it and studying it more closely.

"But then this is also very stylish and novel," he went on, picking up a little silver carriage, the roof of which was hinged to reveal another crimson velvet pad.

"And this," she replied, putting the shoe down and taking a little chair, the green silk seat of which was the pad for the pins. For a long moment she studied them all, but then her attention returned to the shoe he had selected. It *was* very pretty, and somehow she felt that it would appeal to Verity. She decided on the spur of the moment that no other pincushion would do, and she gave it to the assistant. "This one, if you please," she said.

"Madam." Bowing, he spirited it away to the back of the shop to wrap it very carefully in tissue paper before placing it in one of the shop's little boxes.

Leon was determined not to allow Rosalind to escape from him just yet. "Miss Faraday, may I beg a very great favor of you?" he asked suddenly.

"A favor?" She looked warily at him, her aunt's warnings returning.

"It is nothing shocking, I promise you. You see, I also have Christmas gifts to purchase and am finding it impossibly difficult when it comes to my great-aunt in Berwick. I know that the perfect choice for her would be a Cashmere shawl, and the haberdashery next door to us now boasts a selection second to none, but even though I have studied every shawl they possess, I simply cannot decide which one would be best for my aunt." It happened to be the truth.

"My lord, I cannot see how I can be of any . . ."

"It's just that my aunt and Lady Jenford are very alike indeed, and I was hoping that your knowledge of *your* aunt might be put to good use for *my* aunt as well." This also happened to be the truth. He smiled disarmingly. "Will you lend your invaluable advice, Miss Faraday?"

She hesitated, for it seemed churlish to decline.

He noted her indecision and pressed home his advantage. "I'm sure that propriety will not be flouted, Miss Faraday, for your maid is with you, and we need only step from this shop to the one next door. Your carriage need not move, and I swear upon my honor to be all that is gallant and gentlemanly. I also swear that I will be eternally in your debt."

She was forced to smile at that. "There is no need to feel quite so beholden, sir, for assistance with the choice of a shawl is hardly a grand gesture on my part."

"Then you will help me?"

How could she refuse? "Yes, of course."

He took her hand and drew it gratefully to his lips. "You are an angel, Miss Faraday."

Color flushed to her cheeks, and she pulled her hand slowly away. "I would not go that far, sir," she murmured, turning gladly as the assistant returned with her little parcel.

A few moments later, with the pincushion safely

purchased and reposing in her reticule, she emerged from the jeweler's shop on Leon's arm. Daisy waited awkwardly by the door and then followed them into the haberdashery. The maid's conscience was weighing heavily, and she wished that she hadn't accepted the earl's bribes. What if something should befall her mistress because of all this? What if the Earl of Holmwood wasn't the gentleman he appeared to be? But it was too late now, the information had been imparted, and all Daisy could do was hope that all would be well in the end. To confess to her mistress would be to risk instant dismissal, and that was a prospect which terrified the maid. No, she must keep her fingers crossed and pray that the earl's interest was honorable.

A very agreeable half hour was spent examining the shawls, and Rosalind had little difficulty in at last deciding upon a silver-gray square with a lavish border of embroidered pink roses. It was just the thing her aunt would have chosen, and she felt sure that the equally formidable lady in far-off Berwick would like it as well.

Leon expressed his undying gratitude and then escorted her back to the waiting carriage. He kissed her hand once more and smiled into her eyes for a last time before closing the carriage door and instructing the coachman to drive on. As the vehicle vanished amid the throng of traffic choking Piccadilly, Leon's blue eyes were alight with satisfaction. Things were proceeding well, and Peter's guineas were as good as in his pocket. The winning of this wager was proving even more agreeably diverting than he had expected, and the moment of victory was something to anticipate with immense pleasure.

He still had to proceed with care, however, for one false move would put his quarry to flight. For the next few days he would let the matter rest, and then he would seek her out at All Saints' Church, when he would brave Lady Jenford's wrath by acknowledging both her and her niece. Then there would be the Devonshire House masque, which would surely present a number of suitable opportunities. He had been forced to abandon all thought of the Syon House breakfast party, for he would be out of town at that time, staying overnight with friends in Windsor, nor would he be able to make use of the Lansdowne House concert, because he had a prior engagement from which he couldn't properly extricate himself, but there was the visit to the theater still to come, as well as the Christmas ball at Holland House itself, at which occasion he trusted he would achieve his goal.

There was a large congregation for Sunday morning service at All Saints' Church. It was Advent, and the new young clergyman had taken the unusual step of permitting the singing of a carol normally reserved for Christmas Eve. The well-loved notes of "While Shepherds Watched their Flocks by Night" resounded around the ancient stone walls where once Sir Thomas More and his family had worshipped, and the excitement of the approaching season was almost tangible, especially among the children.

Lady Jenford's private pew was near the front of the aisle, and she and Rosalind were its only occupants. Lady Jenford wore her customary black, but Rosalind wore a very becoming sage-green spencer over a cream fustian gown, and there were flowers around the crown of her green silk hat. She wasn't gleaning as much enjoyment from the carol as she usually would, for she was still very tired indeed after the Devonshire House masque the night before.

The masque had gone on until dawn, and her aunt had chosen to remain there until almost that hour.

Her thoughts slid away from Chelsea to her parish church at home in Gloucestershire. It wouldn't be long now before she and Verity went gathering evergreens for the house and the church. Perhaps Granville would come with them this year. She hoped he would.

Leon stood a few rows behind her, on the opposite side of the aisle. The collar of his greatcoat was turned up, and the brim of his tall hat put his face in shadow. His attention was upon Rosalind, so near to him, and yet so far. She didn't know he was there, for he had entered the church after she and her aunt had taken their places, but if she turned her head just a little, she would look straight at him.

His stratagem hadn't gone as planned the night before at Devonshire House, for fate had decreed that Rosalind should elude him completely. She was so distinctive with her bright golden hair and dainty little figure that it hadn't occurred to him that he might not be able to find her among the many masked ladies present. That was what had happened, however, and even though he had searched throughout the night, he hadn't seen her once, let alone managed to speak to her. It had proved a very frustrating experience.

The service came to an end at last, and the congregation began to leave. Rosalind opened the door of the pew, and as she did so her gaze was drawn inexorably toward Leon, almost as if she suddenly felt his eyes upon her. For a long moment she stared at him, and then he saw the telltale color warm her cheeks as she quickly lowered her eyes and stepped out of the pew.

She and her aunt walked past him. Lady Jenford

didn't even notice he was there, but Rosalind met his eyes again for a moment and gave him a shy little smile before hastening on at her aunt's side.

He followed them from the church and watched from the churchyard as they entered their waiting carriage, which then conveyed them along Cheyne Walk toward Jenford House. The silent encounter had proved satisfactory, for that small smile had told him one very important thing. The lady liked him. And so his next chance would be at Covent Garden, on which occasion he would be armed with the knowledge that Rosalind Faraday was prepared to form her own judgments and not be entirely influenced by others.

Lady Kinnear's box at the theater was very crowded, as were all the other boxes, for *Coriolanus* was playing to a very large audience indeed. Mrs. Siddons and her equally famous brother, Mr. Kemble, were always assured of a full house, and society had turned out in strength to watch them tonight.

The Covent Garden theater was the third to have occupied the site, its predecessor having burned to the ground in 1808. It was a very handsome building, with a vast red-and-gold auditorium and three tiers of private boxes. So many people and the large number of lamps required to light such an area, ensured that the auditorium was always very warm, but tonight the heat was almost unendurable. Fans proliferated everywhere, and several ladies had already fainted.

Rosalind also had frequent recourse to her fan, but it was failing to keep the oppressive heat at bay, and she was beginning to feel too uncomfortable to concentrate properly on the stage. She wore a delicate white silk gown with a daringly low scooped neckline and tiny sleeves, and there was a tall diamond-studded comb in her hair, which was thankfully pinned up off her neck, without even so much as a ringlet to brush against her hot skin.

Her fan wafted to and fro as she gazed down at the players on the brilliantly lit stage. Suddenly it seemed her vision was unsteady for a moment, and she realized that she was in danger of passing out. Anxious not to cause a scene of any kind, she slipped quickly from her seat, which was toward the back of the box. No one noticed as she went out and closed the mahogany door softly behind her.

The air was cooler in the passage behind, but she knew it would be cooler still in the nearby anteroom she had noticed on arriving. There had been a casement window there, and if she could open it and breathe a little of the cold night air outside, she was sure she would soon feel a great deal better.

To her relief the anteroom was unoccupied, and she gathered her white silk skirts to hurry across to the window. A welcome draft of icy air breathed over her as she opened it. It was just beginning to snow, with at first just a few flakes fluttering past, but then more and more until it was quite heavy. The chill night air swirled into the room, shivering through the delicate crystal droplets of the chandelier behind her.

Leon had been wondering how to manage another meeting with her, and so the moment she left her box he left his own, intending to "encounter" her yet again. But as he walked in the direction he was sure she must come, he was puzzled to find no sign of her. Then he remembered the anteroom, and as he reached the open doorway he immediately saw her by the window. The soft silk of her gown clung revealingly to her figure, more revealingly perhaps than she realized, and there was a sheen to her hair which reminded him of spun gold. The slight motion of the chandelier made the diamonds in her comb flash now and then, and there was something very sweet and appealing about the tilt of her head as she gazed up at the dark snow-laden skies.

At last he spoke. "Two minds with but a single thought, Miss Faraday," he said, going toward her.

She turned, strangely unstartled this time by his sudden appearance. "Good evening, my lord," she said.

"It is suffocatingly hot here tonight, is it not?" he went on, joining her at the window.

"Yes. I'm afraid I wasn't able to give the players the attention they deserved," she replied, wishing that she didn't find him quite such unsettling but interesting company. She should hurry back to Lady Kinnear's box instead of remaining here with him, but somehow that was the last thing she wished to do. She was conscious of a frisson of forbidden pleasure as his sleeve brushed momentarily against her arm. This man was all that she should turn away from, but, oh, he was exciting to be with.

He gazed out at the snow. "What were you thinking about a moment ago?" he asked.

"Oh, nothing in particular."

"You seemed very preoccupied. I wondered perhaps if Mr. Lincoln was on your mind."

She looked at him in surprise. "Mr. Lincoln? But how on earth . . . ?"

"Peter told me," he explained.

"Oh. Well, no, I wasn't thinking of him."

"I understand you intend to marry him?"

She met his eyes again. "A match has been arranged."

"Is it something you wish for?"

She drew back a little. "Sir, I cannot see that that is any concern of yours."

"I am concerned with everything about you, Miss Faraday. Arranged matches can be good or bad, depending upon whether both partners wish to be so joined in matrimony. It seems to me that you are the sort of young lady who would wish to marry for love."

Her green eyes were a little challenging. "Indeed? And are you an expert on marriage, my lord earl?"

He smiled ruefully. "Hardly, but I *am* an expert on love."

"So I understand."

He smiled again and returned his attention to the snowflakes falling past the window. "A loveless marriage must be a wretched thing, Miss Faraday. Don't you agree?"

"Sir, it isn't as if Mr. Lincoln were entirely unknown to me. On the contrary, we've known each other since childhood, and I promise you that there is a great deal of warmth and affection attached to this proposed match."

He searched her lovely eyes. So, it wasn't an out-and-out love match. It pleased him to know it. "Forgive me, Miss Faraday, for my interest obviously offends you," he murmured.

"It doesn't offend me, sir, but it certainly puzzles me. Why are you concerned as to whether my marriage plans are based on love, or upon more mundane practical considerations?"

"I didn't suggest that mundaneness figured in it, Miss Faraday," he protested lightly.

"No, but you did use the word 'loveless,' " she pointed out.

"True, and I had no business so doing. Forgive me."

She glanced at him. "What of your marriage plans, my lord? Is there a lady in your life?"

"No."

"Why not?" She faced him properly.

He smiled a little wryly. "It's my turn to answer probing questions now, is it?"

"It seems fair."

"You have the capacity to surprise me, Miss Faraday. Very well, let us discuss my marital future. I said that I believed you to be the sort of young lady who would wish to marry for love, and I felt able to make that judgment because I am the sort of gentleman who wishes to marry for love. A marriage of convenience or an arranged match wouldn't do for me, and since I have yet to meet the love of my life, I remain single. Does that answer your question?"

"Yes, for it is what I had judged for myself," she replied truthfully. She had given him some thought and had concluded that he needed only to fall properly in love to change his ways completely. Perhaps she was being naive to view him in that light, for he was a sophisticated scion of London's highest society, and she was little more than a country rustic, with only a few weeks of London experience behind her, but nevertheless that was indeed how she thought of him.

"So, I've been assessed, have I?" he asked.

"As much as I have," she countered.

A wry smile played upon his lips. "Touché," he murmured.

There was a burst of applause from the auditorium, and she turned toward the sound. "I really should return to my seat," she said.

"Stay a little while."

Their eyes met, and she shook her head. "My aunt may miss me, indeed she may have done so already."

"And it wouldn't do for you to be discovered in my company?"

"It wouldn't do at all."

He smiled again. "Very well, I shall not impose upon you to stay, but will content myself with but one more question."

"What question?"

"Shall I see you at the Holland House Christmas ball?"

"I will be there, yes."

"That isn't quite what I asked. I wish to see you again, Miss Faraday. I wish that very much."

She stared at him. "I'm very flattered, my lord, and I have no doubt that our paths will cross at Holland House." With that she turned and hurried from the room.

She was quite flustered when she returned to her seat, and she was thankful that she was able to slip back without anyone having realized she'd gone. Her aunt was still intent upon the stage, and no one else had observed the coming and going from the rear of the box. But as she tried to concentrate on the players, all she could see was Leon's face, and all she could hear was his voice. *I wish to see you again, Miss Faraday. I wish that very much.*

It was as if he were all around her still, and at any moment she would feel the touch of his hand upon her shoulder. She was playing with fire by allowing him to come as close to her as he had so far. Her aunt had cautioned her, but she hadn't really paid any heed to what had been said. She was drawn to the devastatingly attractive Earl of Holmwood like a moth to a flame, and if she didn't take care, she would soon be burned. Common sense bade her to keep him at arm's length, but common sense had precious little to do with the feelings that had begun to stir deep within her. He was everything she should resist, and perhaps that was what was making him so irresistible. It was as well that she would soon be out of harm's way at home in Gloucestershire, but between now and then there was the ball at Holland House. What would happen then?

There was a thin carpet of snow on the ground as society prepared for the famous ball, but the night was still and clear, with stars shimmering in the black velvet sky.

Rosalind was nervous as Daisy helped her to dress. Her hair was piled up into a loose knot at the back of her head, and the knot was sprinkled with tiny artificial pink rosebuds. Her gown was made of gossamer light pink gauze over a sleeveless slip of white satin, and there were spangles on the hem and neckline which caught the light at the slightest movement. She wore long white gloves, and there were deep pink rubies at her throat and trembling from her ears. Her fur-lined evening cloak was keeping warm over a chair by the fire, and her only remaining accessories were the dainty white silk reticule and the folded ivory fan lying upon the dressing table as Daisy put the finishing touches to her hair.

The maid wasn't herself tonight, indeed, she had fumbled with the pins and had dropped the comb several times. She was also pale and looked as if she hadn't slept well the night before. Rosalind was greatly concerned and at last felt she had to say something.

"Daisy, there *is* something wrong, isn't there? I know you denied it when last I asked, but it's quite plain to me that you have something weighing upon your mind."

The maid met her eyes in the dressing table mirror. "No, Miss Rosalind," she said again.

"Are you quite certain?"

Daisy looked wretchedly at her, wanting to admit the truth, but too afraid of the consequences to do so. "Quite certain, miss."

There was nothing more to be said, for if the girl was going to insist all was well, then no advice or assistance could be offered.

There was a tap at the door. It was a footman to tell her that the carriage was at the door and her aunt awaited her in the entrance hall.

Daisy brought the warm cloak from the fireside and then gave her the reticule and fan. A minute or so later she left the room and went down to the entrance hall.

Daisy watched from an upstairs window as the carriage drove away into the night. She should have said something. She should have had the courage and belated loyalty to tell her mistress that the Earl of Holmwood's encounters with her had not happened by accident. Tears filled the maid's eyes, and she turned away from the window.

Holland House was a splendid Jacobean mansion on the outskirts of London at Kensington, and in daytime it was only visible from the main highway as a cluster of tall, rather ugly chimneys rising above a screen of trees. At night, however, especially on nights such as this, it was ablaze with lights which twinkled through the darkness.

Lanterns had been strung in all the trees in the park, and every window of the house itself was brilliantly lit, even those in the attics. The main entrance was decked with Christmas greenery, and with the first of the many kissing boughs which had been strategically placed through the house.

The strains of a polonaise carried out into the ice-cold night as carriage after carriage drew up at the house, and from the chill of winter the guests stepped into the hothouse temperature of summer, for every fireplace boasted a roaring log fire.

Rosalind was trembling inside as she and her aunt alighted from their carriage and entered the dazzling house. Would she see the earl again tonight? Yes, of course she would, but what would he say to her? More and more she felt like a moth to his flame.

The house echoed with laughter and music as they approached the top of the ballroom steps, where their hosts, Lord and Lady Holland, were waiting to greet each new arrival. There were so many guests that a queue had formed, and Rosalind had some time in which to survey the magnificent ballroom below. An ocean of richly clad ladies and gentlemen moved to the music, and jewels and decorations flashed beneath the light from the huge chandeliers. The delicate silks and satins of the ladies' gowns were complimented by the dark shades of the gentlemen's formal evening wear, and by the bright scarlet of the army uniforms which were scattered so liberally among the gathering. She toyed with her fan as she searched every face, but of Leon, Earl of Holmwood, there was as yet no sign.

At last she was being presented to their hosts. Lord Holland was genial and kindly and was at great pains to put her at her ease as she sank into a curtsy before him. His eyes were agreeably direct as he quickly raised her, and he patted her gloved hand before turning his attention to the next guest. Lady Holland, once very beautiful indeed, was now a little on the plump side, but she still looked handsome in a rose taffeta gown.

She smiled as Lady Jenford introduced her. "Miss Faraday? Now where have I heard your name mentioned recently? Someone spoke of you to me." Her brows drew thoughtfully together, and then she shook her head. "I'm afraid it eludes me for the moment, but I'm sure I will remember sooner or later. Now then, my dear, I do hope that you will enjoy our little entertainment this evening."

"I'm sure I will, Lady Holland," Rosalind replied. Little entertainment? This was a very lavish occasion indeed, in fact it was a ball to end all balls!

She accompanied her aunt down the ballroom steps and stayed with her as Lady Jenford made her way around the ballroom toward the tiers of chairs and sofas ranged down one side. There she took her seat, and did so in such a way as to indicate that she had no intention whatsoever of taking part in the dancing, for she was soon surrounded by a coterie of her closest friends, and Rosalind was left to sit at the end of the sofa, passing the time as best she could. Not that she was left to twiddle her thumbs or toy endlessly with her fan, for it wasn't long before the first gentleman approached her to dance, and soon she was enjoying measure after measure with a succession of partners, although there was still no sign yet of Leon.

It was to be over an hour before she saw him at last, and even then it was only to exchange a brief glance. She was partnering an elderly colonel in a *ländler,* and as they circled the crowded floor, she suddenly found herself looking into the quick blue eyes she'd been seeking.

He was leaning against a holly-garlanded column, and although he was talking to Lord Peter, his attention was upon her. He wore a close-fitting coat made of very dark purple velvet, and there was an amethyst pin in the lacy folds of his unstarched neckcloth. His dark hair was a little disheveled, as if he had but a moment before run his fingers through it, and there was a faint smile curving his lips as his gaze followed her around the floor.

Her heart tightened as their eyes met, but then the dance took her away, and he was soon lost to view beyond the crush of other dancers. When the measure had ended and the colonel had returned her to her aunt's sofa, she looked toward the column where he had been, but Lord Peter was standing there alone.

Disappointment washed keenly through her, but she had no time to dwell upon it for at that moment Lady Holland approached her. "My dear Miss Faraday, I have been quite racking my brains to remember where I heard your name, and at last it has come to me." Arranging herself carefully on the arm of the sofa, Lady Holland bent close to be heard above the general hubbub of the ball. "It was the Earl of Holmwood who spoke of you, and it was concerning a painting we have here. A painting by the late Mr. Stubbs of three of the Queen's spitzes?"

"Oh, yes, the earl and I did speak briefly about it," Rosalind replied, glancing uneasily toward her aunt, but Lady Jenford and her friends were sitting with their heads together in some scandalous whisper or other, and no one had even noticed Lady Holland's presence at the other end of the sofa.

Lady Holland went on. "I gather that there was some confusion about the painting's whereabouts, and I can confirm that it was indeed at Windsor Castle, but that my dear husband managed to purchase it from Her Majesty two summers ago. Would you care to see it?"

"Why, yes, I would," Rosalind answered.

"Then I will take you to it. Oh dear, I see I am required over there." Lady Holland glanced across the ballroom to where her husband was urgently beckoning her. "Still, no matter, you shall still see the painting, Miss Faraday. I will instruct a footman to conduct you to it." Getting up from the arm of the sofa, Lady Holland attracted the attention of a footman and briefly told him what was required. Then she turned to Rosalind again. "Go with him, my dear, and he will conduct you to the painting in question."

"You're very kind, Lady Holland."

"Not at all, my dear."

As Lady Holland hurried away to see what her husband wanted, Rosalind politely interrupted her aunt's conversation. "Begging your pardon, Aunt Jenford, but is it in order if I go to see one of Lady Holland's paintings? She has instructed a footman to show me the way, and . . ."

"Yes, yes, my dear," Lady Jenford replied, waving her away and then bending close to continue with what appeared to be a particularly shocking item of chitter-chatter, one which was certainly of much more concern to her than whether or not her niece went to look at a painting.

Without further ado, Rosalind nodded to the footman, who conducted her up the steps and out of the ballroom. He led her through the great house, and then up to the next floor to a small chamber in the northeast corner, where the painting hung in an alcove next to the fire. The room was as brilliantly lit as all the others in the house, but the alcove was deep, and so the painting was in shadow. Taking a candelabrum from the mantelshelf, the footman lit it with a spill which he held to the fire.

Rosalind put her fan down upon a table. "There is no need for you to stay with me, for I wish to look at the picture at my leisure."

"Will you be able to find your way back to the ballroom, madam?" he inquired.

"Yes."

"Very well, madam." He gave her the lighted candelabrum and then withdrew.

When he had gone, she held the light up and looked at the painting. It was like looking at her aunt's spitzes, except that those belonging to the Queen had black patches around their eyes. The brilliant Mr. Stubbs had captured the exuberance of the excitable little dogs and had painted their coats so realistically that she felt she could reach out to stroke them.

As she stood there, Leon was accosting the footman at the top of the ballroom steps. He had seen Rosalind being conducted from the ball, but hadn't been able to find where she had gone. Seeing the footman return alone, he decided to make a few discreet inquiries and was rewarded with Rosalind's precise whereabouts. A smile touched Leon's lips. How very obliging of Lady Holland to mention the matter of the portrait. Had he planned it, he could not have done better in order to get Rosalind alone. Turning, he caught Peter's eye and gave a single nod. It was the signal that he was about to bring his carefully laid stratagem to the necessary conclusion, and he hummed softly to himself as he made his way up through the house toward his delightful quarry.

Rosalind heard his steps approaching and knew instinctively to whom those steps belonged. Her heart leapt, and she was conscious of an immediate thrill of excitement at the thought of speaking to him again. Her hand trembled, and her pulse quickened as she turned her head slightly to look at the window, where the doorway was clearly reflected in the glass. His tall figure appeared there, and in that brief, heart-stopping moment, she knew that she loved him.

She struggled to keep her composure and returned her attention to the painting as she spoke to him. "It seems you were right after all, my lord, for the painting is indeed here at Holland House." Could he hear the telltale quiver in her voice? Perhaps he could even hear the wild beating of her treacherous heart?

He came toward her. "It is not often that I am privileged to be in the right, and Lady Jenford in the wrong."

"Not entirely in the wrong, for the painting was at Windsor until two summers ago." She knew that she was failing to appear calm and poised and that her distraction was only too clear in her manner and voice, but there was nothing she could do to help herself. She was shaken to know that she loved this man, for such a love could only be the height of folly and could only cause her pain.

He felt the atmosphere which had sprung into being. Unspoken thoughts and feelings swirled invisibly but tangibly, and he knew that he was no longer entirely the master of the situation. She affected him, dear God how she affected him.

Suddenly she turned to face him, and there was an unexpected directness in her wide green eyes. "Why are you taking such an interest in me, my lord? Do you see me as another name to add to your list?"

The question caught him momentarily off guard, for it confronted him with the realization that he felt guilty where she was concerned. He wished the wager had never taken place; he wished so many things. . . .

"Have you no answer, my lord?" she inquired, searching his handsome face.

"Yes, Miss Faraday, I have an answer. I promise you that I do not have your seduction in mind, and that I am not intent upon appending your name to any list." It wasn't a lie, but then neither was it entirely the truth. Plague take that thousand guineas, and the ennui which had led him to this, for now he was on the wrong side of honor, and the knowledge filled him with wretchedness.

"My lord, I may be unused to London ways, but I am not a fool, and I have to admit that it cannot be coincidence which has brought you and me together so frequently of late."

Her gaze was unsettling, and he ran his fingers through his hair. He didn't know how to respond, and it was an entirely new experience for him. Never before had the notorious Earl of Holmwood been reduced to this.

His silence confirmed her suspicions, and she turned away to hide her hurt. "So, your purpose does not err on the side of propriety, does it, my lord?" she said quietly.

"Nor does it lean toward inpropriety, Miss Faraday," he replied.

"Whatever it is, my lord, you cannot lay claim to entirely creditable motives, can you?"

Was it time to be truthful? Should he admit what really lay behind his actions? No, he couldn't do that, for he could not bear to see reproach in her eyes, nor could he bear to sink so low in her opinion. Oh, Lord above, what was happening to him? At last he met her gaze. "And what of your motives, Rosalind?" he asked softly.

''My motives?'' The sound of her first name on his lips was like a caress.

''Yes. If you are so suspicious of me, why didn't you flee from this room the moment I came in? Can you answer me, Rosalind?'' He had to touch her, to feel her warmth against his fingertips. Gently he put his hand to her cheek, his thumb moving slowly against her skin.

She was at the point of no return. She knew she should leave, but desire coiled around her, denying her the will to escape. His closeness electrified her, and her entire body tingled with a wild confusion of emotion.

The need to hold and kiss her overwhelmed him, and he drew her close. She did not resist, and her body yielded as she raised her lips to meet his. She was soft and pliable in his arms, and he could feel her heart beating close to his.

She threw all caution to the winds as she gave herself to his embrace, and there was no thought in her head of how a proper young lady should behave. She was aflame with a passion of which she had never dreamed herself capable, and her whole body ached with the desire to surrender completely.

The kiss seared through him as no other kiss ever had, and suddenly he was exposed to a new truth. The hunter had become the prey, and he knew he had paid a very high price indeed for the winning of a wager. His seasonal stratagem had rebounded upon him, for if he had won her kiss, he had lost his heart in the process. This sweet golden-haired innocent had stolen his soul, and for all his experience he had not realized it until it was too late. He was her slave now, hers to do with as she pleased.

Her eyes were dark and her face flushed as she

drew back. "This is wrong," she whispered. "I should not stay here with you like this. . . ."

He cupped her face in his hands, and kissed her again, his lips moving softly and luxuriously over hers. Then he gazed into her eyes. "I love you, Rosalind," he murmured. "I love you with all my heart."

She hardly dared believe she heard the words on his lips. Please don't let this be a dream from which she would suddenly and cruelly awaken. . . . His thumbs caressed her cheeks. "Tell me you love me too," he whispered.

"Of course I love you," she breathed, closing her eyes with ecstasy as he kissed her again.

He didn't want to let her go, but knew that he must. "There is much to say, Rosalind. When can I see you again?"

"I will walk the dogs tomorrow and will be at the bench at about two in the afternoon." She was aglow with incredible happiness.

"I will be there." He caught her hand and drew it palm-uppermost to his lips. "I love you," he said again, "and you must never believe that my intentions are anything other than honorable."

Her fingers curled briefly around his, and then she hurried from the room. She so walked on air that she didn't see Peter's stout figure draw back out of sight behind a curtain, nor did she remember her fan, which still lay upon the table where she had placed it earlier. It wasn't until she had reached the ballroom that she thought of the fan, and she hurried back to retrieve it. As she neared the room, she heard voices. One belonged to Leon, the other to Lord Peter Bristow.

Uncertain of whether to return later for the fan,

she hesitated for a moment and thus overheard some very damning words indeed.

Peter's tone was perplexed. "Leon, did we have a wager, or didn't we?"

"Yes."

"And from what you've told me, you've won it fair and square."

"Yes, but . . ."

"Either the lady delivered the required kiss, or she didn't. Which is it to be?"

"The kiss is fact, Peter, and so I have indeed won the wager, but . . ."

"What is there to 'but' about? You've won, and I must part with one thousand guineas. Oh, plague take you, Leon, for I was so sure of Miss Faraday's inviolability."

At the door Rosalind's heart had frozen within her. With a stifled sob of shame and mortification, she turned and fled. What a fool she'd been! He'd gulled her, and all for the sake of a shabby wager. She wanted to hide away and never show her face to the world again, and when she reached the top of the ballroom steps, she felt as if everyone present could see how guilty she was of the utmost folly. It was as if they had all witnessed her fall from grace and knew how much she had welcomed the most improper advances from London's most infamous rake.

To her immeasurable relief, she returned to the sofa to discover that the onset of a headache required her aunt to return home immediately, and within a quarter of an hour they were ensconced in the carriage and on their way back to Chelsea. As the lights and gaiety of the Holland House Christmas ball faded away into the snowy darkness behind her, Rosalind knew she had courted ruin. She had been the subject of a wager, and she had been lured into shocking conduct. No doubt the story would soon be all over town and the name of Rosalind Faraday would be on every amused lip.

Tears filled her eyes, and she was glad of the darkness in which she could hide. She would have to tell her aunt what she had done, and it was a confession she dreaded to make.

Lady Jenford rose very late the next morning, and Rosalind was forced to wait in the breakfast room until her aunt chose to come down. There had been a little more snow just before dawn, and the garden outside sparkled very white in the sunshine. A fire crackled in the hearth in the morning room, and to the smell of coffee, toast, and bacon there was added the refreshing scent of pine from the garlands which had been arranged around the window and mantelshelf the day before, when Lady Jenford had decided on the spur of the moment that it was time to put up the Christmas greenery. A bowl of holly stood upon the white-clothed table, and the sunlight streaming in through the window made the berries look very bright indeed against the shining pointed foliage. Christmas was only four days away now, but Rosalind took no pleasure at all in the happiness of the season, for she had never felt more miserable and dispirited in her life.

Her face was pale and strained as she waited for her aunt, and her eyes were still red from weeping. She wore a simple cream muslin gown with a blue velvet sash, and her hair was tied back with a blue satin ribbon. The Rosalind Faraday of this morning was a very far cry indeed from the joyous, glowing creature who had left the Earl of Holmwood's arms the night before.

The rustle of taffeta told of her aunt's approach,

and she steeled herself for what was bound to be a very difficult interview.

Lady Jenford came in and halted immediately as she saw her niece standing there so nervously. "Whatever is it, child?" she asked without preamble.

"I . . . I have something to tell you, Aunt Jenford."

"Something very disagreeable, from the look of you," Lady Jenford replied, going to take her seat at the table. "Well? What is it?"

Rosalind couldn't meet her gaze. "I've let you down, Aunt Jenford. I ignored your advice, and I've fallen into a scrape."

Her aunt's eyes were shrewd. "My advice? Well, since your manner is one of shame, I can only deduce that it was my advice concerning a certain gentleman. Has this anything to do with the Earl of Holmwood?"

Rosalind bit her lip and nodded.

Lady Jenford's breath escaped on a slow sigh. "You had better tell me what you've done."

With a supreme effort Rosalind explained all that had happened, and with each word she saw her aunt's face become more and more cold. When she'd finished, Lady Jenford rose slowly from the table.

"You foolish, foolish chit! How *could* you have been so empty-headed as to dally with him like that?"

Fresh tears wended their way down Rosalind's pale cheeks.

Her aunt paced up and down for a moment. "This is bound to get out, and soon there won't be a drawing room where your name isn't being sniggered over. You realize that, don't you?"

Rosalind closed her eyes.

"Well, I will have to see what I can do to limit the damage. I may not have any influence with the earl, but I certainly have with Lord Peter, who is most definitely going to feel the full force of my anger. How *dare* he involve you in such a mean and low trick! He had better prevail upon the earl to say nothing of all this, otherwise I will see to it that his father withholds his allowance. And, believe me, I am well able to cause that to happen. As for you, well, I think the best thing would be for you to leave for Gloucestershire without further delay. It's best that you are placed out of harm's way."

"Yes, Aunt Jenford."

"I'm deeply disappointed in you, Rosalind, for I thought you had more sense than to fall by the wayside like this. You've put your match with Mr. Lincoln at risk, you realize that, don't you?"

Rosalind looked miserably at her.

Lady Jenford drew a heavy breath. "I have no option but to inform your father what has happened. I would be failing in my duty if I did not, and I take my duty very seriously."

"Yes, Aunt Jenford."

"You will leave for home after breakfast. I will instruct my traveling carriage to be made ready, and your maid can commence packing immediately. The weather may not be all that could be desired for such a journey, but I am sure you will reach your destination by nightfall."

"Yes, Aunt Jenford."

Two hours later the carriage was loaded and waiting as Rosalind and Daisy came down to the entrance hall, where Lady Jenford stood waiting, the three spitzes at her side. Rosalind wore a fur-lined brown velvet cloak over her emerald pelisse and gown, and there was a small beaver hat on her head.

She carried a warm beaver muff, and there were tightly laced ankle boots on her feet. The marks of her tears were still on her face, and her voice shook a little as she took her leave of her aunt.

"I'm sorry to have failed you, Aunt Jenford," she said, striving to sound level.

"You have let yourself down, my dear, but I trust that your prompt removal to Gloucestershire will help to quieten the matter. I have written a letter which I wish you to give to your father."

Rosalind reluctantly accepted the letter her aunt held out to her.

Lady Jenford smiled a little. "I have not been unkind to you, my dear, for although you and I know how much you were at fault, I have placed the blame squarely upon the Earl of Holmwood."

"Thank you, Aunt Jenford."

"Good-bye, Rosalind."

"Good-bye, Aunt Jenford." Rosalind kissed the cheek her aunt presented to her and then remained where she was as the older woman walked to the staircase and ascended without a backward glance.

Rosalind bent to give the spitzes a final fuss. Their tails had wagged hopefully when she came down in her outdoor clothes, for they had anticipated a walk, but now their tails were still. Hestia whined a little as Rosalind choked back a sob, and Hera and Demeter tried to reach up to lick her face.

Daisy stood unhappily by the door. She wore a simple blue cloak with a hood, and she was very quiet and withdrawn. She had confessed her part in it all to her mistress and knew she was very fortunate indeed not to have been dismissed on the spot.

Rosalind straightened, and then gathered her skirts to hurry outside to the waiting carriage. When Daisy had climbed in as well, the coachman's whip cracked, and the team strained forward on the first stage of the journey to Faraday Park.

The moment the carriage had departed, Lady Jenford sent a running footman to Holland House to summon Lord Peter to face the music.

It was snowing again as Leon waited by the bench in Cheyne Walk. The falling flakes were large and fell so thickly that the far bank of the Thames was obscured from view. There were few people abroad in such weather, and as the minutes passed, he became more and more doubtful that Rosalind would venture out with the spitzes.

He leaned on the railing, his silver-topped cane swinging to and fro. Rosalind's fan was in his pocket, for he had noticed it on the table the night before. The night before. He gazed at the river without seeing it, for all he could see was Rosalind, and all he could feel was the exquisite softness of her lips and body as she returned his kiss.

There was a step behind him, and he whirled eagerly about, but the smile died on his lips as he saw not Rosalind, but Peter. "What on earth are you doing here?"

"I've just come from Jenford House, Leon, and I've come to tell you that Rosalind will not be keeping the tryst with you."

Leon misunderstood. "Well, I suppose this isn't exactly the best weather for walking small dogs."

"It has nothing to do with the weather, my friend. I fear that the wager is known to her."

Leon became very still. "What are you saying?" he demanded sharply.

"I'm saying that you and I were overheard last night. It seems that Rosalind came back for her fan, and our incriminating conversation conveyed the unpalatable truth to her. At least, it conveyed the original truth to her. Unfortunately, she did not wait to hear you confess to me that you loved her and wished to forget all about the wager.''

"I must go to her and explain. . . ." Leon began.

"She isn't there, she left for Gloucestershire this morning. Lady Jenford sent for me, and I've just come from having my ears twisted in no uncertain terms. The pressure is being put upon me not to spread any unwelcome tittle-tattle over town, and if I don't prevail upon you to be equally reticent, I will have my allowance withdrawn indefinitely.'' Peter sighed heavily and leaned his hands on the railing. "I think you can forget all thought of your sweet Rosalind, my friend, for she won't have a whisker of you now.''

"But, damn it, didn't you explain?'' Leon cried, seizing his arm.

"Of course I did, what do you take me for?'' Peter protested. "But no matter how much explanation there is, one thing cannot be denied, and that is that the whole damned business began with a wager upon whether or not Rosalind could be seduced into a kiss. The fact that the biter has been bitten is rather beside the point when it comes to the honor of the situation. We behaved shabbily, Leon, and I fear that Rosalind regards your sins as unforgivable.''

"But they must be forgiven,'' Leon breathed. "They must, Peter, for I cannot be without her.''

Peter fell silent, for what could he say? Having just faced a justifiably and dauntingly furious Lady Jenford, he knew only too well that it was very unlikely indeed that Rosalind Faraday would ever have anything more to do with Leon, Earl of Holmwood.

Leon took the fan from the pocket of his greatcoat and slowly opened it, running his gloved fingers over the delicate carved ivory spines. "I cannot submit without a fight, Peter," he said quietly. "I must go after her and try to win her back. She loves me as much as I love her, I know she does, and if I have to grovel before her to beg for forgiveness, then that is what I will do. She means more to me than I ever dreamed would be possible." He smiled wryly. "The biter has indeed been bitten," he murmured, closing the fan and replacing it in his pocket.

Peter pursed his lips. "I wish you well, my friend, but I think it will prove a fruitless errand."

It had been dark for some time when Rosalind's carriage at last turned in through the stone gateposts of Faraday Park. Snowflakes fluttered past the beams of light from the carriage lamps, and the coachman was hunched wearily on his box as he tooled the tiring horses along the winding tree-lined drive. The wooded park stretched over the Cotswold hills on either side, but only the nearest trees were visible in the darkness. The harness jingled and the wheels crunched through the snow as the horses traveled the final mile.

At last the curve of the drive brought the lights of the house into view ahead, and Rosalind gazed at them with trepidation as she wondered what her father would say when he read her aunt's letter, for however carefully it had been worded, it would be clear to him that unwelcome goings-on had touched upon his daughter's hitherto immaculate reputation. For the thousandth time she reproached herself for her foolishness. She would never have believed herself capable of such incredible indiscretion. Lowering her eyes, she pushed her hands further into the depths of the beaver muff. How was she going to be able to look anyone in the eye after this? How was

she going to be able to face Granville, who had returned to England to marry her? She blinked back
the tears which had been so close to the surface every
minute since the heartbreak of the ball.

The carriage drove over the stone bridge that
spanned a narrow neck of the ornamental lake before the house, and then swept up the final yards to
the two-storied stone porch jutting out from the cen-
tral bay of the rambling Tudor mansion. In daylight
the house was very beautiful indeed, with mullioned
windows, gables, and a lichen-covered stone-tiled
roof, but now it was merely a silhouette with a
lighted window here and there as the carriage drew
to a halt and Rosalind and Daisy alighted.

Rosalind did not knock at the door, but went
straight into the great hall, where once her ancestors
had entertained Henry VIII and his retinue of court-
iers. It was a magnificent baronial chamber, with
fine tapestries on the oak-paneled walls, and wheel-
rimmed candle-holders suspended from the beamed
ceiling far above. A huge log fire crackled in the
hearth of the vast stone fireplace, and a grand oak
staircase rose directly opposite the main entrance.
The staircase divided at a half-landing, where a full-
length portrait of Bluff King Hal had pride of place.

Rosalind advanced across the stone-flagged floor
and put her muff down upon the polished oak table
which ranged down the center of the hall. Then she
paused for a moment, trying to compose herself for
the coming minutes.

Daisy lingered by the door, afraid that her activities might yet lead to summary dismissal. If she
could have turned the clock back and declined the
Earl of Holmwood's bribe, she would, but it was far
to late for that.

Taking a deep breath, Rosalind glanced around,

wondering where her father and sister would be. They would have dined by now, and so her father would probably have adjourned to the library, where he liked to enjoy his pipe and spend a few agreeable hours reading, or at least nodding sleepily over a volume. As for Verity, well, no doubt she was in the drawing room with her needlework.

With a heavy heart, Rosalind walked across the hall toward the two doors at the far end. One was the door of the library, the other of the billiard room. The library door stood slightly ajar, and as she suspected she saw her father asleep in his favorite green leather chair. He wore a blue paisley dressing gown over his shirt and breeches, and there was a tasseled cap on his gray hair. He wasn't a large man, indeed he was frail and thin, for he had never had a robust constitution. She hesitated about disturbing him, for he looked so comfortable and contented, and she knew that Aunt Jenford's letter was going to distress him a great deal.

It was then that she heard Verity's low voice coming from the billiard room. Curious, she left the library and went toward the next door. Pushing it open a little, she peeped inside.

The low lamps above the green baize billiard table cast pools of light which did not extend far into the room on either side, but she could still make out the two figures standing by the green velvet curtains at the window. It was Verity and Granville, and they were locked in each other's arms, their lips joined in a lingering kiss.

Rosalind stared at them and then drew stealthily back. Verity and Granville?

Daisy came anxiously toward her. "What is it, Miss Rosalind?" she asked.

Her voice seemed to echo loudly around the silent

hall, and Rosalind put a swift finger to her lips and shook her head. The maid fell silent as her mistress drew her back toward the table.

"Miss Rosalind?" she whispered. "Is something wrong?"

"We have just entered the house this very moment, Daisy. I did not go to the billiard room door, is that clear?"

The maid stared at her. "Yes, Miss Rosalind," she replied, although it was plain that nothing was clear at all.

Yet again Rosalind had to pause for a moment to compose herself, and then she called out. "Hello? Is anyone at home? It's me, Rosalind."

For a moment the silence continued, but then the billiard room door opened and Verity hurried out in some flusterment. She was two years Rosalind's junior, and very like her to look at, with the same golden hair and green eyes, but she wore her hair short, and her figure was much more rounded than her elder sister's.

Granville followed her into the hall, and he too looked a little disconcerted. As Verity had said in her letter, his hair was no longer the light brown it had once been, but had been bleached by the foreign sun, and his face was tanned by that same sun. He wasn't as tall as Rosalind remembered, but was still as good-looking, with warm brown eyes, a finely chiseled mouth, and a firm, square chin. He had discarded his coat, and wore a frilled white shirt and beige breeches. There was guilt in his eyes as he looked at Rosalind.

Verity recovered first and hurried toward her sister, her blue dimity gown pretty in the light from the candle-holders hanging from the beams high above.

"Rosalind! Oh, Rosalind, how good it is to see

you again!'' she cried, flinging her arms around her sister's neck.

Mr. Faraday's fragile figure appeared at the library door. ''Rosalind?'' he inquired in astonishment. ''My dear, we did not expect you for several days yet.'' He smiled and opened his arms for her to come to him.

Leaving Verity, Rosalind took a hesitant step forward, but the kindness in his eyes and smile proved too much, and suddenly she burst into tears and hid her face in her hands.

It was midnight, and Rosalind sat on the floor by the fire in her bedroom. She wore her nightgown, and her golden hair was brushed loose about her shoulders as she sat with her chin resting upon her knees. The firelight was reflected in her sad eyes, and her thoughts were of Leon, whom she had trusted, but who had betrayed her so sadly.

She had given her aunt's letter to her father and had been grateful to him for not questioning her at any great length about what had happened. It would all have to be said sooner or later, however, just as she would have to speak to Verity about Granville. It had become clear during the evening that her father was unaware of the love which had sprung up between his younger daughter and the man who was supposed to be marrying his elder daughter. It had also become clear that Granville believed himself obligated to continue with the original match, even though his affections had been transferred from one sister to the other. As for Rosalind's own feelings, well, she could hardly blame anyone else for something of which she had been guilty herself. If Granville had deceived her with Verity, then she, Rosalind, had deceived him with the heartless Earl of Holmwood. She knew her sister and Granville well enough to be certain that neither of them would have entered lightly into their love, a love of which they both felt a terrible guilt, and she knew that she had to release them both from that guilt. She did not seek to marry Granville, for her feelings for him were pale and insignificant beside the rich emotion Leon had stirred in her heart, and so she meant to reveal to them both that she knew how they felt about each other. Let them at least be free to be happy. No doubt she would one day find happiness too, when the pain of loving unwisely had faded away at last.

Someone knocked softly at the door behind her. "Rosalind? Can I come in?"

It was Verity. "Yes, of course."

Her sister came in. She wore a lilac wrap over her nightgown, and her short golden hair was tousled. She hurried across to where Rosalind was, and sat down beside her, drawing her knees up in the same way. They had sat together like that as children.

For a long moment neither of them spoke, but then Verity glanced at Rosalind. "What happened in London?" she asked gently.

"I don't want to talk about it just yet, Verity."

"I want to help you, to comfort you. . . ." Verity's voice died away, and she bowed her head.

Rosalind knew that her conscience was stinging her again over Granville. "Don't feel guilty, Verity, for there is no need. I know about you and Granville."

Verity stared at her. "You know?"

"I saw you together in the billiard room."

"Oh, Rosalind, if only you knew how dreadful we've both been feeling. We didn't mean it to happen, it just did."

"I know. I don't mind, truly I don't."

"You don't mind?" Verity looked intently at her in the firelight. "Rosalind, you and Granville were to be betrothed, you were happy about the match and longing to see him again. Now you simply say you don't mind if he loves me instead?"

"There's nothing simple about it," Rosalind replied, gazing into the fire again.

Verity's eyes suddenly cleared. "There was someone in London, wasn't there?"

Rosalind nodded.

"What happened?"

"I was made a fool of. No, I made a fool of myself," Rosalind corrected.

"Please let me help. I'm very good at listening."

Rosalind smiled fondly at her. "I know you are, and when I'm ready, I'll tell you everything. But not just yet."

"You love him very much, don't you, whoever he is?"

"Yes. Gull that I am, I still love him."

Verity hugged her tightly. "I won't press you anymore for the time being. Now then, I think it's time I tried to get some sleep." She scrambled to her feet and then paused. "Shall we gather the holly tomorrow?"

"In the woods by the lake?"

"Yes, unless the snow is too deep. If it is, Father has agreed that we may pick what we need from the trees in the walled garden. I hope we can go to the woods, though, for it's become a little tradition, has it not?"

"Yes, it has."

Verity bent to drop a kiss on her hair and then hurried from the room again.

Rosalind did not move from her place by the fire.

She was more tired than she had ever felt before, but she knew she would not sleep. There were too many thoughts milling around in her head, and too great an ache in her heart.

"Oh, Leon, Leon," she whispered, her eyes shimmering with tears.

The snow did not lie too deep the next morning, and once again the skies were clear. The lake sparkled in the sunshine, and the park stretched crisp and white toward the horizon as the two sisters emerged from the porch to climb into the pony and trap to go holly-gathering. They both wore warm cloaks, Rosalind's the brown velvet in which she had traveled from London, and Verity's a bright shade of orange wool. They were to drive themselves to the woods, and Verity climbed into the trap to take the reins.

Granville had ridden over early, and his heart had been gladdened when he learned that Rosalind willingly relinquished him to her sister. He stepped out of the porch behind them, carrying his top hat and riding crop, for he was about to ride home again, and he detained Rosalind for a moment before she joined Verity in the trap.

"You'll never know how grateful I am that you're not angry with us," he said, looking earnestly into her eyes.

"It's plain that you and she were meant for each other," she replied, smiling.

"Whereas you and this unknown gentleman in London were not?"

"Verity has been tittle-tattling," she murmured.

"I'm so very sorry that you are unhappy, Rosalind." He took her hand and pressed it to his lips.

She smiled again and then climbed into the trap

beside Verity, who immediately stirred the plump gray pony into action.

They drove smartly down the drive to the bridge and then took the track which led by the lakeside toward the woods. A party of men had been sent out earlier to collect the huge yule log for the fire in the hall, and the track had been cleared a little, so that the pony could trot along at a spanking pace. They passed the men, who raised their hats and waved as the trap sped by.

The air was sharp and clean in the woods, and as the sun shone through the naked branches overhead, it cast a lacework of shadows on the snow. Wild ducks flew noisily by on their way to the lake, and a magpie's jarring call echoed through the trees as Verity at last drew the pony to a standstill by a grove of holly trees.

They had gathered several armfuls when at last Verity could no longer refrain from bringing up the subject of what had happened in London. Dropping her load of holly into the trap, she turned to face her sister.

"Are you able to confide in me yet?" she asked.

Slowly Rosalind put her own holly into the trap as well and then nodded. "Yes, I suppose so."

"Who is he, this mysterious gentleman?"

"His name is Leon, and he is the Earl of Holmwood."

Verity blinked. "An *earl*?" she gasped, for it had not occurred to her that Rosalind might have become involved with someone of such high rank.

Rosalind smiled a little. "An earl who also happens to be one of the most handsome, charming, and untrustworthy gentlemen in England, an earl who thinks it amusing to lay siege to me in order to win a base wager."

Verity's eyes widened. "A wager?"

"My kiss is apparently worth one thousand guineas, would you believe? I suppose I should be flattered, for how would I have felt to know I'd been tricked for a paltry few pennies?"

"Tell me about it," Verity urged gently, putting a hand on her arm.

Determined not to give in to tears again, Rosalind took a long breath and began to tell her all that had taken place, ending with the painful truth she had overheard at Holland House.

Verity listened with increasing anger. "How monstrous!" she cried when Rosalind had finished. "What a despicable insect he is!"

"I was at fault as well, for I should have taken heed of what Aunt Jenford said. Well, I've learned a very salutary lesson, of that you may be sure, and now I can only pray that at the very least he and Lord Peter will have the grace not to spread my name over London."

"You didn't commit all that heinous a crime, Rosalind," Verity said kindly. "A kiss is hardly complete capitulation; if it is, then I am guilty of the same."

"Do you honestly imagine that society will believe it was only a kiss? By the time the story has spread from drawing room to drawing room, I will be credited with having surrendered my virtue several times over."

Verity fell silent, for the excesses of scandalous gossip did not need to be dwelt upon.

Rosalind gave a brisk smile. "Shall we continue with our gathering? There's some ivy over there, and Father tells me that a Scots pine had been felled on that spit of land at the southern corner of the lake, so we'll be able to pick some of that as well."

Verity nodded, and they made their way through the snow to the ivy. After that they found some mistletoe growing on an ancient crab-apple tree, and managed to pick most of it before setting off for the Scots pine. It was while they were collecting this last that Rosalind glanced across the lake toward the house and saw a gleaming maroon traveling carriage drawn up at the porch. It was a very expensive vehicle, driven by a liveried coachman and drawn by a team of four perfectly matched dapple-grays.

She straightened in surprise. "Who has called?" she asked, thinking that her father must have made an influential new acquaintance while she had been away.

Verity was equally as puzzled, however. "I don't know. I've never seen the carriage before."

Rosalind continued to look across the lake for a moment, but then put the strange vehicle from her mind as she turned back to the pine. Carrying as much as they could, they made their way back to the trap.

"That's enough, I fancy," Verity said, looking at the mountain of greenery they had gathered. "Oh, when I think of decorating the house with all this, I feel very seasonal all of a sudden. I think we should toast our industry on our return. What would you say to a cup of warmed claret flavored with roasted orange and cinnamon?"

"It sounds the very thing," Rosalind replied, smiling at her.

They drove quite sedately back to the house, fearing that any speed would mean the greenery bouncing off the trap and having to be gathered again. As they emerged from the woods they saw the carriage was still at the house.

"Who on earth could it be?" Verity wondered

aloud. ''Whoever is it must be a person of consequence, for I am sure there is a coat-of-arms on the
carriage door. Yes, there is, I can see the gold against
the maroon.''

They halted the trap near the carriage, and Rosalind had taken an armful of holly to carry inside
when the owner of the carriage emerged from the
porch. Her breath caught with shock, and the holly
fell into the snow, for it was Leon.

He wore his greatcoat and was about to put on his
tall hat when he saw her. His steps faltered. ''Rosalind!''

''I have nothing to say to you, sir,'' she breathed.

''But I must explain . . .'' he began.

''How dare you come here after what you've done!
What has happened, sirrah? Is there some doubt as
to whether or not the wager has been properly won?
Or is there perhaps another thousand guineas resting
upon your chances of duping me into another indiscretion?''

''It isn't like that at all,'' he said, taking a hesitant
step toward her. Her hurt and anger cut through him
like a knife, and he wanted to take her in his arms
and tell her how much he truly loved her.

''I don't wish to have anything more to do with
you, my lord. You behaved very cruelly toward me,
and I think you a toad of the lowest order. I cannot
believe that you have actually had the face to come
here, and I wish you would leave again.'' Choking
back a sob, she hurried past him into the house.

''Rosalind! Please!''

She ignored his calls.

He turned and found Verity's frosty gaze upon
him. Her voice was as cool as her eyes. ''My lord
of Holmwood?'' she inquired.

"Miss Faraday, I presume?" She was so like Rosalind that he knew she had to be her sister.

"I trust you mean to comply with my sister's wishes?"

"I have already been instructed to leave the property, Miss Faraday. Your father made his opinion of me more than plain."

"It is no less than you deserve."

"I know."

"Well, that at least is something," she replied.

"You are obviously fully acquainted with the extent of my misconduct, Miss Faraday."

"Yes."

"I know that my original purpose did me no credit at all, but I vow that it has all rebounded upon me, for I have fallen in love with your sister."

Verity's lips parted in surprise. "Can I believe you, sir?"

"Do you really imagine I would make such a statement if it were not true?"

"I know of no reason why I should take your word for anything, my lord."

The faintest of smiles passed over his face. "I suppose I cannot blame you for that. Miss Faraday, I have come here to try with all my heart to make amends for having hurt Rosalind. Hurting her was the very last thing I ever wished to do, for I love her and wish to win her hand."

Verity's eyes widened. "You wish to marry her?"

"Nothing less will do. Will you tell her what I have said, Miss Faraday?"

"If that is what you wish."

He glanced back toward the house. "If she will but give me a chance to speak to her myself . . ."

Verity hesitated and then nodded across the park to where the spire of the parish church in a nearby village rose in a fold in the hills. "Do you see that church spire, my lord?"

"Yes."

"Be there at noon tomorrow. I cannot promise that my sister will meet you, but I will endeavor to persuade her that she should."

He looked gratefully at her. "Thank you, Miss Faraday."

"Do not thank me yet, sir, for it could be that I will fail."

"I can ask no more of you than that you try, Miss Faraday."

Inclining her head, Verity walked past him into the house. Rosalind's earl was indeed possessed of a disarming smile, and it was plain that there would be very few women with whom he would not be able to have his way, but she still believed him when he said he loved her sister. Maybe there would be complete happiness yet this Christmas.

Outside, Leon bent to pick a small spray of the holly Rosalind had dropped. He twirled it between his gloved fingers for a moment. How ironic it was that he should fall victim to one of his own stratagems. He deserved to suffer a downfall, there was no denying it, but would Rosalind's be the sweet hand that would consign him to eternal misery? Tucking the holly into his buttonhole, he climbed into the carriage, and a moment later was being conveyed away from Faraday Park.

Rosalind watched from her bedroom window. Why had he come here? Wasn't it enough that he had made a fool of her in London? Was it necessary to repeat the exercise here, in her own home?

She heard Verity come in, and turned to look at

her. "You and he appeared to have much to say to each other, Verity," she said.

"He loves you, Rosalind."

"I find that hard to believe."

"Nevertheless, it is true. Rosalind, *I* believe him, and I have to tell you that even Father is inclined to give him the benefit of the doubt."

"Father?"

Verity nodded.

Rosalind looked out of the window again. "The Earl of Holmwood can be a very accomplished actor when he wishes to be."

"Possibly, but he wasn't acting when I spoke to him just now."

"An accomplished actor, and a plausible one."

"The truth frequently is plausible, Rosalind. Anyway, I told him that I would tell you what he said, and so I am. He not only loves you, he wishes to marry you."

Rosalind stared out of the window, not moving at all.

Verity paused and then went on. "If you wish to speak to him, he will be at St. Nicholas's Church tomorrow at noon. I will go there with you if you want me to, you have only to say."

With that, Verity left the room again, closing the door softly behind her.

Rosalind gazed down from the window at the track his carriage had left in the snow. What should she do? In London she had allowed her heart to rule her head, and she had been cruelly deceived. Was it time now to let her head rule her heart? If so, that head was bidding her to spurn him and protect herself from further pain.

It was snowing very lightly the next morning as Leon waited in the churchyard by a spreading yew

tree which overhung the stone wall and the lane below. Rooks wheeled above the copse of elm trees in
an adjacent field, and in the church itself there was
singing as the choir rehearsed for the Christmas services. He listened for a moment. They were singing
"The Holly and the Ivy."

Turning, he glanced along the lane. Would Rosalind come? It was nearly noon now, and the minutes seemed to be dragging by on leaden feet. He
reached up with his cane to dash some snow from a
low-hanging branch of the yew tree. He had spent a
dismal night in a Cirencester inn, tossing and turning without sleeping because he was so anxious as
to whether or not Rosalind could be prevailed upon
to at least hear him out. No doubt society would find
it all highly amusing, to observe the armor-hearted
Earl of Holmwood brought to such a pitch by an
inexperienced girl who hadn't even had the benefit
of a London Season to equip her.

The snow began to fall more heavily, and he
turned up the collar of his greatcoat and tugged his
tall hat further forward. From now on snow would
always remind him of these hours of agony and sus-
pense, and so would "The Holly and the Ivy"! His
carriage was drawn up a little further along the lane,
and the coachman was busily attending to the comfort of the horses. He'd placed blankets over their
backs and had gone to each one to rub its nose and
pat its neck. Leon looked back at the church clock,
and as he did so it began to strike midday.

At almost the same moment the sound of an approaching carriage carried along the lane. Leon's
breath caught hopefully, and he leaned over the wall
to gaze toward the sound. The lead horses appeared
around a corner, and then the pair behind, and at
last he saw the carriage itself. It was an elegant ve-

hicle with gleaming brass and indigo panels, and somehow he knew that it was from Faraday Park. But was Rosalind inside?

The second carriage drew up at the ivy-covered lych-gate, and the coachman climbed down to open the door. For what seemed to Leon to be an age, no one inside alighted, but then he saw a lady's ankle-booted foot and the swansdown hem of a rose-pink pelisse. His heart leapt with hope, but then plunged into despair again as the lady who stepped down proved to be Verity, not Rosalind. But even as he thought all was lost, a second lady alighted, and at last he found himself gazing at the woman he loved to distraction.

Rosalind was pale and tense, her little face framed by the rich white fur around the hood of her leaf-green velvet cloak. At first she didn't see him by the yew tree, but then Verity touched her arm and pointed. She turned then, her large eyes unsure.

Verity spoke to her, evidently urging her to go to him, for after a moment she stepped beneath the lych-gate and walked slowly through the snow toward him. She halted a short distance from him, somehow unable to go any further. She was filled with doubts, but in spite of what he had done, she knew she still loved him. If only he hadn't proved false, if only those brief wonderful moments at the Christmas ball hadn't been shattered by the truth behind his actions.

He had removed his hat the moment she approached, and now the snowflakes began to cling to his dark hair. "Thank you for coming, Rosalind," he said quietly.

"I do not know if I should have, sir, for I can only view you with mistrust."

"I have much for which to crave your forgiveness."

"You are a very skilled lover, my lord, far too skilled for me to know even now if you are being sincere. You used your cleverness upon me, and in a most unworthy cause."

"If you wish to hear me say I am ashamed, then I say it without hesitation. I wagered one thousand guineas upon your kiss, Rosalind, but in truth it has cost me much, much more than that. I lost my heart to you, and now my fate is in your hands."

She met his gaze, wanting to believe him, but too afraid to do so. In her dilemma she took refuge in further reproach. "Is this another wager, sir? Is Lord Peter hiding somewhere nearby to see whether or not I can be gulled yet again?"

"You wrong me now."

"Do I?" Her voice trembled, and tears stung her eyes. She had to look away.

Her tears affected him. "Please don't cry," he said softly, going to her and taking her by the arms. "Look at me, Rosalind. Do you really believe that I would go to lengths such as this simply in order to amuse myself with another wager?" He removed his gloves and put a warm hand to her cheek, making her look into his eyes. "In my heart of hearts I haven't deceived you at all, for the wager was immaterial to my actions, and I believe that I began to fall in love with you the first time we met. You've seldom been out of my thoughts since then, and when I at last took you in my arms and kissed you, I knew I was lost forever. You've conquered me, Rosalind, you have to believe that. I love and need you, I want to make you my countess and to spend the rest of my life with you."

She closed her eyes. As always, his touch wrought havoc with her heart.

He cupped her face in both his hands. "At Holland House you told me you loved me. Please tell me that you love me still."

She stared up into his eyes. "Oh, Leon . . ." she whispered.

It was the first time she had used his first name, and a surge of gladness swelled through his heart. Tenderly he bent his head to kiss her on the lips.

Her hood fell back, and her hair tumbled loose from its pins. She could feel the iciness of snowflakes upon her face, but it was the fire of his lips that she felt the most. His fingers twined richly in her warm hair, and his kiss became more urgent as he pulled her into his arms.

A low moan escaped her as she abandoned all lingering doubt and allowed her own passion to meet his. There was no innocence in her now, just an open acknowledgement of the love and fierce desire she felt for him.

He broke off from the kiss, his eyes dark and intense. "Say you will be my wife, Rosalind. Say it, I beg of you."

"I will be your wife, Leon," she whispered, her words barely audible because she trembled so much.

"Do you require witnesses to my request? I will repeat it again in front of your sister, in front of the whole choir in the church, even in front of our coachmen!"

She smiled through the foolish tears which shone in her eyes. "I do not need witnesses, my love," she said softly.

He kissed her again, and they were oblivious to everything except each other. The snow continued to fall, and the carol-singing still drifted out over the quiet churchyard.

As Leon held her close, he thought again of how his stratagem had proved his undoing. But oh, how sweetly. How sweetly.

By the lych-gate Verity watched them as they stood wrapped in each other's arms. She smiled, deeply happy for them both. All would be well after all this Christmas. She and Granville could be together openly, and now Rosalind was to be a countess. Oh, what a feather in the Faraday family's cap! It would be one in the eye for all the jealous tabbies in the neighborhood.

THE PORCELAIN MADONNA

by Mary Balogh

THE GENTLEMAN strolling along Bond Street was doing so purely because he had spent all morning at White's reading the papers and arguing politics, and he needed the air and exercise. And perhaps he walked along that particular street when he might have chosen a quieter one because he derived a cynical sort of pleasure from watching the world indulging in its annual observance of the great myth.

Christmas! He touched his hat to two ladies of his acquaintance and stepped off the pavement into the gutter to let them pass. And he grimaced as he stepped back up again. Yesterday's light snowfall, which had been hailed by the populace of London as a sure herald of that rare phenomenon, a white Christmas, had turned to muddy water on the streets and pavements and to brown slush in the gutters.

Christmas! He looked down at his top boots and frowned at the spatters of mud that overlaid the high gloss his valet had produced that morning. And he hunched his shoulders inside the twelve capes of his greatcoat and would have been quite prepared to swear on a stack of Bibles without fear of perjuring himself that the damp cold had penetrated to his very bones. He almost wished that his beaver hat had flaps to cover his ears. The thought amused him, though his pale blue eyes did not lose any of their cold cynicism.

A carriage drew to a halt alongside him, and he grimaced anew at the spray of murky water thrown up by the wheels and the horses' hooves. He drew to a halt too as two ladies hurried from the shop to his right and a liveried servant jumped down from the box of the carriage to relieve them of the numerous boxes, bandboxes, and other parcels they carried. They must have been shopping for hours, he thought, dithering over exactly what gift would suit this aunt or that nephew or the other brother. And doubtless the carefully wrapped gifts would be torn open on Christmas Day, exclaimed over, and dropped into an upstairs drawer never to be looked at again.

And yet both ladies, neither of whom he knew, turned to him when their arms were empty to thank him for giving them the right-of-way and with the most perfectly cheerful smiles wished him a happy Christmas.

Nonsense and fiddlesticks, he thought as he touched his hat and wished them a good day. And everywhere it was the same. People rushing hither and yon and spending and smiling and calling out cheerful greetings for all the world as if they believed that peace and goodwill really would float down to earth and to mankind in three days' time and remain there forever after. They would eat their goose and Christmas pudding and drink their wassail and their punch, and then they would settle before the warmth of the Yule log and have a comfortable gossip before nap time, massacring the reputations of all acquaintances not then present.

Not for him. Not this year. This year he would stay in London and behave on Christmas Day as if it were any other day of the year. Though that would prove not quite possible, of course. The servants would expect their gifts and their time off, and they would expect him to have a goose and mince pies and all the rest of the traditional Christmas fare so that they might enjoy their portion.

He sighed inwardly. And Lady Lawrence, having heard that he was to remain in town for the holiday, was after him to attend her Christmas party and dance on the evening of the twenty-fifth. Who had told her? he wondered. He had certainly not been going about blabbing the good news.

And then his footsteps slowed and his lip curled. Now was not that the perfect picture of Christmas sentimentality, he thought, looking ahead and across the street to a jeweler's shop. It was enough to make anyone of any sensibility grab for a large handkerchief and dab at moist eyes. He wondered what she was gazing at so intently in the window.

Whatever it was, it was without a doubt many fortunes beyond her means. She was shabby and as out of place on Bond Street as he would have been at Newgate. Her cloak had once been blue, he guessed, though now it was faded to a nondescript gray. Her bonnet had never been anything else but gray and very plain. She must be cold, he thought. But if she was, then it was partly her own fault. Gazing at some bauble, she was, her back to him, dreaming the impossible dream. Dreaming Christmas.

He withdrew his eyes from her. And yet something drew them back again, and he found himself hesitating, shrugging, and stepping out into the street to cross over. He wanted to see what it was she gazed at. He wanted to see the extent of her foolishness.

She was not the only person out of place on Bond Street, of course. There were always varying numbers of young men and urchins lounging against the corners of buildings, darting in and out between the legs of horses and the wheels of carriages, yelling out their willingness to carry parcels for a small pittance. Christmas time was especially lucrative for them, with its extra parcels and its extra goodwill.

He noticed the one particular urchin because he was behaving atypically. The boy was strolling down the street, minding his own business, just as if he had a definite destination in mind. And he was eyeing with darting glances—there was no head movement—the reticule that the shabby lady dangled carelessly from one hand. And then not only the boy's eyes darted—his left hand followed suit, snatching the reticule deftly, and then his feet.

Except that his feet ran out of a place to run as the collar of his patched jacket somehow hooked itself over the gold-headed cane of a tall, well-caped, and cynical-looking gentleman—the very one who had been crossing the street to look into the jeweler's window. The boy moved both hands defensively to loosen his collar at the front and prevent strangulation, dropping the reticule in the process.

"Not clever enough, my lad," the gentleman said, the boredom in his voice suiting the expression on his face. "Boys of your stamp do not stroll along Bond Street unless they are up to no good. It is an observation you might wish to remember as this will be a thrashing you might wish to forget."

Turning the boy beneath his arm was the matter of a mere moment despite the flailing of thin arms and ill-shod feet and despite the fact that the urchin cursed the air blue with vocabulary that even the gentleman found original. He raised his cane.

"Don't." The word was not shrieked or even spoken loudly, but the gentleman's hand and cane paused in midair. Several interested spectators sidled past, too well-bred to stop, but curious to witness the thrashing.

"Don't," she said again, her voice a little firmer. "I thank you for recovering my reticule, sir, but please do not strike the boy."

Good Lord. She was Christmas itself—shabby and dignified and softly spoken and beautiful. Her face was oval and delicately featured. It glowed with color from the cold. Her hair beneath the drab bonnet shone golden. But of course she was beautiful, and of course she was educated, and of course she was impoverished, he thought scornfully. What else could he have expected? And she had been admiring, not a golden bracelet or a diamond necklet, but a porcelain Madonna with a curled and naked baby in her arms, enough to melt any tender female heart.

And this female obviously had a tender heart. He lowered his cane and let the boy up, keeping an iron hold on his collar.

"Ah," he said. "I will wish him a happy Christmas, then, ma'am, and send him on his way. The thrashing might have done more to warm him up, though."

She did not argue with him or look at all annoyed by his sarcasm. But of course she would not. She was all sweetness and sensibility as well as tender heart. The brim of her bonnet was on a level with his chin. And her eyes were green, an interesting and unusual shade of green. He pursed his lips.

She looked steadily at the boy, who was trying to wriggle his face right down inside his collar. He had succeeded in hiding only his chin. "Why did you need it?" she asked.

The gentleman closed his eyes briefly. She would be far better advised to swing the reticule back and belt the boy across the head with it. But, of course, she was the spirit of Christmas.

The boy wisely did not answer.

"Are you hungry?" she asked.

The boy sniffed wetly, and the gentleman actually caught himself in the act of reaching toward a pocket for a handkerchief. He raised his eyebrows and left his handkerchief where it was.

"Are you all alone?" she asked. "Or do you have a family?"

The boy seemed finally to have realized that the iron hand on the back of his collar had made it impossible for him to duck his face down quite out of sight. He gazed up at her instead with eyes that became instantly soulful, so much so that the gentleman felt an inward wave of amusement. He tightened his grip and pursed his lips afresh. He waited for the inevitable description of the family.

"There's me muvver," the boy said, his voice high and piping, "an' there's Vi'let an' Roddy an' me pa." His eyes would have done justice to an offspring of Garrick or Kean. "An' there's the new one wot me ma is 'xpecting."

Oh Lord. The gentleman turned up his eyes to the gray skies above. And she would fall for it too. There was no doubt in his mind. But the boy had missed his most golden chance. He had not explained how he was the sole breadwinner for the family.

"Me pa works on the wharves, missus," the child said. "But 'e 'ad 'is 'and crushed last month an' I'm the man of the family now, missus, an' 'as to feed 'em all."

He had done the boy an injustice. Apart from the nonchalant and inappropriate sauntering down the street, he was showing himself to be a remarkably intelligent young man.

"You poor boy," the shabby, beautiful lady said gently. "But if you steal, you know, you will be thrown in prison or even hanged, and then your family will certainly starve. And grieve for you too."

The gentleman looked down at the boy and almost smiled outright when he saw what looked suspiciously like a tear beading on the child's lower lashes.

"I wish you had asked me for help instead of trying to take it," she said. "But there, you did not know that I would not have frowned and spurned you, did you? I shall give you something."

"Ma'am." The gentleman could hold back no longer, much as he had been enjoying the thoroughly predictable drama unfolding before him. "The rascal probably lives with a den of thieves. He has probably never even known a mother or father."

She looked up at him with those remarkable green eyes, just as if she had forgotten his existence until that moment. "Then his lot would be all the sadder, sir," she said. "However it is, he would not be stealing if there were not the need."

And she bent her head to her cracked and ancient leather reticule and unclasped it. And doubtless, he thought, she would withdraw an equally ancient purse from it and open that to reveal two lone pennies, one of which she would give to the boy, who would cheerfully have helped himself to both and laughed about it too.

"Wait!" the gentleman said, and there was irritation now for the first time in both his voice and his heart. For he was about to step up onto the stage and take a part in this most despicable of melodramas. "Put your purse away, ma'am." After transferring his cane to the hand that clutched the boy, he reached into an inner pocket with his free one and came out with his own bulging purse of new and soft and expensive leather. "Here, lad." He finally released the boy, judging—correctly—that he would not run away at this interesting juncture. And he handed the boy half a crown, cursing himself for passing over both the sixpence and the shilling, cursing himself for falling into the trap in the first place. "But next time it will be my cane across your backside no matter who is pleading for me to stop."

The half crown disappeared as neatly as in any magician's trick. The tears had disappeared too, the gentleman noticed without the least surprise.

"You are very kind," the lady said. "Thank you, sir." But she was turning her attention back to the boy even as the gentleman was wondering idly how creamy her complexion must look when not rouged by the cold. She smiled. "You can buy some food for your family now, child. What is your name?"

"Charlie Cobban, missus," the boy said.

The gentleman was somewhat surprised that the boy had not taken to his heels the instant the half crown had disappeared among the rather ragged folds of his clothes. But perhaps he had realized the imminence of the ultimate sentimentality, as the gentleman had not.

"Are you hungry, Charlie?" she asked. "And cold? Shall we find a pastry shop, and I shall buy you a meat pie?"

Good Lord. The woman must have escaped from Bedlam. The gentleman looked at her in fascination. The boy sniffed and tried the disappearing act with his head again. With considerably more success this time.

"Ma'am." The gentleman felt the terrible compulsion to interfere again. "I would not so encourage vice if I were you."

"Vice?" She looked up at him once more. "Not poverty and desperation and despair?" She looked as if she must have firsthand knowledge of at least one of those three.

"Well," he said, and he blamed the words that he knew were about to issue from his mouth entirely on the green of her eyes, "I know of an excellent pastry cook's a mere few steps farther along. Their specialty is meat pasties." In reality he had no idea what their specialty was. "Allow me to treat you both."

Two sharp eyes were peering upward from the boy's frayed collar. The lady was possibly blushing, but it was impossible to tell for sure since her cheeks had been scarlet to start with.

"It would not be proper, sir," she said. "I do not know you."

Lord. Oh Lord. Perhaps he should go running for one of the dragon hostesses of Almack's to effect an introduction.

"Allow me to present myself," he said, removing his hat and making the woman a bow, to the interested view of the crowds moving along the street. "Darcy Austin, Earl of Kevern, at your service, ma'am."

"Oh," she said while the urchin's eyes swiveled back and forth between the two of them.

"Now do you know me well enough to come with me and this urchin into the warmth of the pastry cook's?" he asked.

The boy shifted from one foot to the other.

"Thank you, my lord," she said.

"But I do not know you, ma'am," he said.

"Julie Bevan, my lord," she said.

Julie. A thoroughly sweet name. He might have expected it, the Earl of Kevern thought. And he offered his arm to her and watched her hesitate before accepting it. He sallied forth along the street with her, the thieving urchin bobbing along at his other side, one foot in the gutter and the other on the curb.

Christmas, he thought. It was like an octopus with a thousand tentacles or a fishing net of infinite size. Or like a giant hand covered with jam, to which anyone it touched would stick fast. There was no escaping it. It was happening all around him, and there he was in the midst of it all, a shabby lady on his arm, a ragged child bouncing along beside him, the three of them on their way to a pastry cook's to partake of meat pasties and some hot beverage.

The child had already told his heartrending story. Doubtless there were many more details to be wrung from his fertile imagination. He would hear some of them as soon as they were in the warmth of the shop, the earl decided. And he had yet to hear the touching details of Miss Julie Bevan's impoverished existence. It was something to anticipate with some pleasure.

It was a good thing he had not given his handkerchief to the boy, he decided. Before he left the pastry cook's, a free and a sane man again, he would doubtless need it to mop up the moisture from his own eyes.

If he had accomplished nothing else that day, Lord Kevern thought a few minutes later—and without a doubt he had not, beyond encouraging a budding criminal by rewarding him with half a crown instead of thrashing him and turning him over to a magistrate as he deserved—if he had accomplished nothing else, he had provided food for conversation in fashionable drawing rooms that evening.

Fashionable heads turned as he entered the pastry cook's with a shabby lady on his arm and a more-than-shabby urchin tripping along at their heels. And fashionable eyebrows rose when he seated the lady at one of the tables before seating himself. He also raised no objection to the urchin's taking a vacant chair at the same table and drumming his heels against its metal legs.

Fashionable heads, he thought, could go hang. And he winced as the boy sniffed wetly and solved the problem of the lack of a handkerchief by cuffing his nose dry.

Miss Julie Bevan would not have a meat pasty, though she looked as if she needed one, the earl thought, his eyes passing over her slightly too slender figure. She would have only a cup of tea and a cake when one was pressed on her. Charlie Cobban had a meat pasty and two cakes without having to be pressed at all—and a cup of steaming chocolate, which he eyed with something resembling awe. Certainly his legs drummed a louder tattoo against the legs of his chair when it was set before him.

"Charlie," Miss Bevan said quietly and with a gentle smile, "keep your legs still, dear. You will be disturbing the other customers."

The tattoo ceased. The sounds of a meat pasty being thoroughly enjoyed and a cup of too-hot chocolate being sipped took its place.

"Christmas!" the earl said, fixing his pale blue eyes on the lady and trying to guess the story she must have to tell and determining that he would draw it from her and thereby amuse himself. "The time for peace on earth and goodwill amongst men. The most wonderful, heart-warming season of the year. The time for family and gift-giving and feasting."

"Yes." She smiled at him.

He had known, of course, that she would agree with all the foolish clichés he had mouthed.

"And how will you spend the holiday, Miss Bevan?" he asked her.

"At home," she said, "where Christmas should be spent, my lord."

"And where is home?" he asked.

"London." She smiled again. "It does not really matter where home is, does it, provided there is one. Especially at Christmas. Home is where one's loved ones are. Where one belongs."

Ah, he thought, toying with the handle of his teacup and ignoring the plate of cakes, but what if there was a home—more than one, and all of them large and lavishly furnished—and no loved ones in it? What if one belonged to no one but oneself? If one discounted a brother and two sisters and their spouses and numerous offspring, that was, and their undying custom of coming together at Christmas? One could be even more alone in such company than in only one's own.

"Are there loved ones?" he asked. "In your own home, I mean."

"Yes." Her eyes softened, and he wondered for the first time if that home contained a husband and perhaps some children. She had not said that she was Miss rather than Mrs. Bevan. But she wore no rings. Perhaps Mr. Bevan could not afford rings.

He turned his attention to the boy and wondered how the pastry cook would react when the crumbs that liberally dotted the tattered jacket were decorating the floor after the boy stood up.

"I suppose," he said, "you would like to stuff the rest of those cakes inside yourself, Charlie, but find to your chagrin that there is just no more room in there."

"I would like for Vi'let an' 'Arry to taste them," the boy said.

"Never fear." The earl pursed his lips. "We shall have them wrapped up, and you shall be allowed generously to share your treat with Violet and Harry—or is it Roddy? You must be careful of such details, lad."

Sharp eyes darted to his. " 'Arry is my friend wot lives next door to us," Charlie said. "Roddy is too little to eat cakes. Well, maybe 'alf a one."

"Ah," Lord Kevern said. "If you cannot always have a perfect memory, lad, then a quick and fertile imagination is the next best quality." He raised his hand to summon a waiter and directed that the cakes remaining on the plate be wrapped up to take and that another meat pasty be wrapped separately. And if the next three days did not hurry on by, he thought, he would be joining the world in its collective insanity. The boy should have been soundly thrashed and long forgotten by now.

When he returned his attention to Miss Julie Bevan, it was to find her eyes fixed on him thoughtfully. "You are kind," she said, "though you pretend not to be, I think. And what will your own Christmas be like, my lord?"

He grimaced. "Soon over, it is to be hoped," he said. "I shall shut myself inside my town house and try to ignore the merriment of my servants and try to forget what day it is. I choose not to be a part of the universal hypocrisy that seizes everyone during the second half of December."

"Oh," she said, and she looked so infinitely sad that he felt the urge to look over his shoulder to see who could have aroused such a tender emotion in her. "Do you have no family, my lord?"

"A brother and sisters and nephews and nieces galore," he said. "For the first time I shall keep myself away from their Christmas gathering. Why should I be a witness to all the affecting maternal and paternal tenderness that afflicts my brother and sisters and my in-laws on Christmas Day and to all the unbounded affection for their parents that the receipt of gifts inspires in the bosoms of my nephews and nieces?''

"And to have no part in it yourself," she said quietly, the sorrow still in her eyes.

They were almost an emerald green, he thought. But he was feeling too irritated to enjoy the admiration of her eyes. He had come there to amuse himself with the stories of his guests, not to tell his own. He rose to help the lady to her feet, and Charlie gulped down the last two mouthfuls of his chocolate.

"Thank you, my lord," she said, offering him her hand when they stood outside the shop. "May Christmas bring you a blessing as you have brought one to this boy today."

Lord, he thought, she must have been rehearsing the speech all the time she was sipping at her tea. But he took her slender little hand and applied a polite degree of pressure to it.

"Will you allow me to call you a hackney coach?" he asked her. "The wind is cuttingly chill." He was in grave danger, he thought wryly, of falling headlong into Christmas as into a vat of treacle and finding himself quite unable to pull himself out again. What an unspeakably awful fate!

"Thank you, my lord." She smiled. "But I do not have too far to walk."

And she turned from him and proceeded on her way while he watched. She looked briefly into the jeweler's window as she passed.

The Earl of Kevern glanced down at Charlie Cobban, who was still standing beside him, looking from him to the disappearing figure of Julie Bevan, and clutching his bundle tightly in one hand.

"That was a mistyke, guv," he said in his piping voice. "Lydies like 'er don't take carriage rides from gentlemen."

"Don't they, indeed?" the earl said. "But ladies like her rescue worthless thieving rascals from the thrashings they deserve, lad, and fill their bellies instead. And don't you forget it. And next time you decided to thieve—I do not doubt that there will be a next time—steal from someone who looks as if he or she can spare what you take. Now be off with you. And don't eat that food all at once, or it will make you sick."

The boy darted away in the same direction Julie Bevan had taken and was soon lost among the crowds and conveyances. The Earl of Kevern stood where he was for a few moments longer and felt a little emptier than he had felt before. The great myth had beckoned him for a moment and then laughed in his face again.

He turned about with a cynical curl of the lip and continued on his way.

The Earl of Kevern was in a bad mood. At least that was the word being spread belowstairs in his town house on Hanover Square. He had barked at his valet for producing the wrong coat when he got up from bed, though no particular coat had been asked for. And he had commented with caustic tones to his butler at breakfast that there was enough food on the sideboard to feed the five thousand, and Cook would do well to remember that despite his exalted rank, he was but one man in possession of but one ordinary-sized stomach.

Christmas was approaching again, his servants reminded one another, as if any of them needed reminding, and they nodded sagely to one another as if that fact alone accounted for their master's irritability. And he was not going down to Buckland Abbey this year even though it was his own country home and the rest of the family would be there as usual.

It would have taken his mind off things if he had gone, the housekeeper gave as her opinion. All those children would cheer anyone's heart at Christmas.

But it was the very children who made it so hard for him, Cook said, shaking her head and muttering "Poor dear gentleman" into the large pot of soup she was stirring. It was Cook's philosophy that the very best way to help a man forget bad things was to fill his stomach with tasty dishes. And so it was unlikely that future breakfasts would diminish in size or in the variety of foods prepared.

Whatever the cause of the bad mood, it was there. It was to be contended with. The butler, therefore, tapped on the library door at some time after breakfast with the firm conviction that he might be committing suicide by so doing—or at the very least ensuring that he would be out on the streets, jobless, for Christmas.

"Set it down," the earl said, glancing up briefly from his book at the salver full of the day's post that his butler clutched. And then his look became irritable. "What is it, Horrocks?"

Horrocks had coughed, a genteel clearing of the throat, the sure signal that he had something to say.

"There is a person, my lord," he said in the haughty tones that usually turned mere persons into quivering jelly. "A bundle of rags. An impertinent boy."

His lordship looked at him coolly from pale blue eyes.

"In the kitchen, my lord," Horrocks said. "Sidling up to the fire, trying to warm himself despite discouragement." Horrocks warmed to his story as perhaps the boy had to the fire. He coughed again.

"Throw him out," the earl said and prepared to turn his attention back to his book, though truth to tell he might as well have been holding it upside down for all the attention he had been giving it before the interruption. "Give him some bread and a coin first."

"He demands to speak with you, my lord." Horrocks spoke as if the noose were being lowered over his head. "Says it is a matter of life and death."

Lord Kevern lowered his book and Horrocks stiffened his upper lip. "His name is not by any manner of chance Charlie Cobban, is it?" the earl asked.

"Yes, my lord." The brief answer seemed the best defense against such an unexpected question. But the boy had told the housekeeper that it would mean certain death and dismissal—though he had not said they would come necessarily in that order—to deny him admittance to His Highness.

"Show him in by all means," the earl said, laying aside his book altogether and getting to his feet.

Horrocks disappeared rather like a shot from a gun, only with far greater dignity.

The Earl of Kevern stood before the fire and warmed his back and his hands, which he clasped behind him. He had spent the night dreaming alternately of emerald green eyes and urchins swinging in the breeze from a gibbet at Tyburn and had woken in the blackest of moods because Christmas was still two days off instead of being comfortably behind him already. He might as well amuse himself with the sight of an intelligent and inventive urchin who still had his feet firmly on the ground.

Why was it, he wondered, that he was in no way surprised by the arrival of Charlie Cobban on his doorstep?

"Good morning, Charlie," he said when his butler ushered the boy into the library and disappeared again at a nod from his master.

"Cor blimey, guv," the boy said, "is there as much stuff as this in Carlton 'ouse?"

"I daresay there is a great deal more," the earl said. "Did you come for a guided tour?"

"Naw!" Charlie said scornfully. "You don't know where she lives, do you, guv? And you wants to know. I seen that yesterday when you watched 'er walkin' down the street. I'll tell you where she lives. I followed 'er."

"Did you?" his lordship said, beginning to feel the first stirrings of good humor that he had experienced that morning. "And will you? For a small fee, I assume?"

"One guinea, guv," Charlie said firmly. "I figures you wouldn't miss a guinea."

"Ah," the earl said, "I see you have taken to heart my final words of wisdom to you yesterday afternoon, my lad. But one guinea is a prodigious amount to pay for information I have never considered necessary to my existence or well-being."

"Or 'alf a guinea to tell you where she went this mornin', guv," Charlie said.

The earl's eyebrows rose. "Gracious," he said. "You *have* been doing your homework. Perhaps I should search your person, Charlie, to see if you have any of the lady's property about it. If you have, you know, it will be over my knee with you and a spanking with my bare hand that you will never forget.''

"Naw," Charlie said scornfully. "I decided to give up thievin', guv. She came to an 'ouse quite close to 'ere. She must work there."

Yes, she must, to be up and out at an hour when most ladies were still abed. Close to Hanover Square. Bond Street was perhaps, then, on her route to and from work.

"So you have decided to make a more honest living by, ah, selling information," the earl said dryly. "Were you sick on the cakes and pasty, by the way?"

"Me muvver an' Annie ate the pasty," Charlie said, "an' . . ."

"Annie being Violet's middle name, I suppose," the earl said.

"Naw," Charlie said, "Annie's me older sister, the one wot 'ad a job wiv 'er needle 'til she lost it day before yesterday."

"Ah," the earl said. "So the burden on your shoulders becomes more and more onerous."

"We always 'ad meat for Chris'mus," Charlie said, his eyes soulful as they had been the afternoon before for Julie Bevan's benefit. "But this year there won't be none."

"My heart is rent in two," the earl said. "Now, then, Charlie, I shall send you back to the kitchen with instructions that you are to be fed dinner. Here is a crown with no information asked for in exchange. I suppose you gave yesterday's half crown to your mother, like a good boy?"

"Yes, guv," Charlie said.

"I thought you would have," his lordship said dryly. "Make sure you do the like with this. Your mother doubtless has the wisdom to spend it carefully."

"Yes, guv," Charlie said. "But for anuvver one like this I'll tell you where she lives. Special price, guv, for Chris'mus."

"Spying on a lady," the Earl of Kevern said, "will earn you only a session with the heavy side of my hand, Charlie. Mr. Horrocks, my butler, will be waiting outside the door for you. Go belowstairs with him, eat your dinner, and then take yourself off. I feel compelled to add that I will not grieve dreadfully if I never set eyes on you again."

"Cor, guv," Charlie said, his hand on the knob of the library door, his free arm gesturing through the door with a jerking thumb, "I thought 'e must be a duke or somethin'."

The earl waited for the door to close behind the boy before grinning. Yes, Horrocks would make the perfect duke—on stage.

But his grin faded quickly enough. If she worked for a living, the chances were that she worked regular hours. She probably walked to work at exactly the same time every morning and home again at exactly the same time in the afternoon. And along the same route.

The earl frowned down at the carpet before his feet and tried to reconstruct his movements of the day before. At exactly what time had he left White's? Had he stopped off anywhere along the way before arriving opposite that jeweler's shop?

And was he seriously making these calculations? he asked himself suddenly, his frown deepening. Why would he want to know the answers if he was not planning to be in the same place at the same time today?

Was he mad?

Very probably, he decided. Because that was exactly what he was planning to do unless he could talk himself out of it within the next two hours.

He had threatened to beat Charlie for spying on a lady. And what was to be his punishment for attempting to do the exact same thing? Except that he did not mean to follow her home. Did he?

Good Lord, he thought, he should go down to Buckland Abbey now, this very minute, before it was too late. He could still be part of the wassailing and the caroling and the gift-giving. No, anything but that. Not again. Better to slink about in the shadows of Bond Street shops spying on shabby ladies with emerald eyes. Better to amuse himself again with the image of the perfect spirit of Christmas—a shabby, impoverished lady with a heart of gold.

If she passed along Bond Street again that day. The odds, he supposed, were very much against her doing so. But he would go along anyway and see. There was not much else to do with his time until Christmas was over.

She did come, but surely a little later than the day before. The Earl of Kevern had sauntered up and down that particular stretch of the street three times, examining the contents of every shop window on both sides, keeping an eye out for her so that he could duck out of sight if and when she appeared, nd generally trying not to look conspicuous.

He touched his hat twice to Lady Goodborough, once on one side of the street as he walked in one direction, and again on the other side of the street going the other way. Well, he thought, she would merely assume that he was having particular trouble selecting a gift for an aunt or a sister. Which was perhaps exactly what was happening to her.

There was Christmas all around him again, but it

made him uneasy and irritable today. He could not view it with the satirical detachment he had felt the afternoon before. For it was Christmas that had brought him back out again. What else? Christmas always brought the delusion that the impossible might happen and that one might be happy and remain happy. Though what that idea had to do with a shabby stranger he did not know.

He saw her finally and stepped into the doorway of a bootmaker's. She was walking in the same direction as the day before and dressed the same—a small, slender, drearily clad young lady, who should not even have caught his eye. She certainly ought not to have held it. There was nothing there to attract.

Except that ridiculous and affecting spectacle she had made of herself, staring in through a jeweler's shop window on Bond Street. Though that had not been attractive, but merely pathetic. And those eyes, of course, which he had not even seen until he had committed himself to crossing the street and rescuing her from a little street thief. So he could not say that they were what had attracted him.

He held his breath without realizing that he did so until she stopped almost opposite where he was standing and looked in the jeweler's shop window. She would not be disappointed. The Madonna and child were still there, an elegant group in painted porcelain. Though there was something more than mere elegance, he had conceded earlier when he himself had stared in at it. It had been shaped by a feeling hand, by someone who knew something about mother love or father love. Or perhaps merely by someone who had an eye to the purse of a sentimental lady who would view it in a shop window.

Only that this lady viewer's purse was doubtless far too light to oblige.

The Earl of Kevern lounged in the doorway trying to look as if he was not lurking. What was he to do? Merely stand there and watch until she moved away homeward, as she must do soon? Follow her when she did so? The thought was highly distasteful. Or cross the road to speak to her? But what to say? Merely to touch his hat and wish her a good day? Make some comment on the Madonna? Inquire after her health? Ask her to kindly not haunt his dreams tonight?

But as he stood there undecided, someone else was far more bold. Denbridge's son Colley, the young jackanapes. He had been sent down from Oxford the year before for some unknown crime and had proceeded to sow his wild oats in London. And wild his oats were too by all accounts. Having a wealthy and indulgent father and possessing the looks of a blond god ensured that he had not yet reaped the harvest of those oats. But he probably would in time.

He had stopped and was talking to Julie Bevan. The earl could see his practiced smile in profile. She took one step sideways away from him and continued to stare in at the window. Colley took one step after her. And then she turned to face him, as if to step past, but he touched her arm and she stopped.

By God, the earl thought, grasping his cane and taking one step out of the doorway in which he stood, there was going to be one crushed beaver hat and one cracked skull when he got himself across the street. And one set of bruised knuckles for himself and a shower of teeth from the mouth of Denbridge's brat.

She was looking up at Colley and speaking, and he was smiling back at her. To give her her due, she did not look panic-stricken. She was not falling into a fit of maidenly vapors.

And then the earl stopped, one foot on the pavement and one on the road. Good Lord. Oh, good Lord. Was he in his dotage already and soft in the brain? She was a working lady. Of course. A working lady. Shabby and genteel and working probably for only half the price she might have commanded if she could have dressed herself in more expensive clothes.

He clamped his teeth together and returned his forward foot to the pavement.

And then she turned so that he could see her face, and there was distress in it. She was clearly trying to draw free of the hand that held her arm without drawing undue attention to herself.

Before the earl could get halfway across the street to her, a little ragged missile launched itself headfirst at the gentleman's middle, and two thin fists pounded against the expensive capes of a greatcoat, and two ill-shod feet kicked at well-booted thighs. There was a high-pitched roar of rage.

By the time Lord Kevern arrived on the scene, the Honorable Mr. Cuthbert Colley was shaking a foully cursing little urchin like a rat by the scruff of the neck and Julie Bevan was watching, her hands to her bosom, making no attempt to effect her escape while it was possible. Even some of the polite shoppers on Bond Street had stopped to witness the outburst.

"Let him go, Colley," the earl said in the bored tones that characterized him. "It does not look good, my dear fellow, to be brawling with a mere infant."

"Not until I have given the little varmint a lesson in good manners," Mr. Colley said, his voice tight with fury.

"After you, then," Lord Kevern said. "I shall await my turn."

"He has offended you too, Kevern?" Mr. Colley asked, shaking Charlie Cobban once more and listening with distaste to the stream of unrepeatable language that issued from the child's mouth.

"No, no," the earl said. "Not this afternoon, anyway. It is a big varmint I am waiting to chastise. Though given the very public setting, you may prefer to apologize to the lady and be on your way, Colley. In which case we will forget about the incident, provided it is never repeated."

"Lady?" Mr. Colley looked at Julie Bevan incredulously, appeared somewhat embarrassed by what he saw, and released his hold on Charlie, who kicked him once more on the shin. "My apologies, ma'am. I mistook you for, er, someone I know." He touched his hat, turned on his heel, and was gone without a backward glance.

"What took you so long, guv?" Charlie asked, wriggling his threadbare clothes back into their proper position. "I might of got the stuffing shook out of me."

"Oh, Charlie," Julie said, "how incredibly brave of you to come to my rescue. I do thank you." She turned to the earl. "And you, my lord. I am very much afraid that Charlie would have been hurt if you had not been here."

"*Charlie* would have been hurt," he said. "Are you all right, ma'am? May I offer you my arm? Would you like to sit down at the pastry cook's again and have some tea?"

"No." She smiled. "Though it is very kind of you to offer, my lord. But thank you." She took his offered arm and her voice wavered a little. "Perhaps I will lean on you for a few steps if you are walking my way."

She was small and fragile and trembling—all the things he most despised in women because they knew so well how to exploit their weaknesses. And yet

Julie Bevan did not press her advantage as he fully expected her to do and willed her not to do. She turned her head aside instead and beckoned Charlie to walk on her other side.

"Did he hurt you, Charlie?" she asked. "Oh, you poor brave boy." And her hand continued to tremble on the earl's arm, and her voice continued to shake. "Will you walk home with me? There are some cakes being baked for Christmas today, and you shall take some home for yourself and your family."

All the boy needed, Lord Kevern thought, was another evening of cakes to stuff into himself and he would be ill in good earnest.

"Do give him instructions not to eat them all at once," he said, "or he will spend Christmas with a sore stomach."

She smiled up at him. "Not if he shares," she said. She stopped walking and withdrew her arm from his. "Thank you for your support, my lord. I am better now. I shall bid you a good day."

He should do the same for her, he thought. He should hurry home and shut himself away from Christmas before he was further infected by it. Before he was caught up more fully in the hypocrisy and the artificiality and the sheer unreality of it.

"I shall see you to your door, ma'am," he said, "with Charlie as your chaperon. I shall see to it that you are not accosted again."

Her smile was a little sad, he thought. "It was my fault for stopping," she said. "I should know from experience that that only invites unwelcome advances. But I always avoid them when I keep my head down and walk briskly. I shall be quite safe, my lord. And there is quite a distance yet to walk. I would not take you out of your way."

"If you will not take my arm and let me accompany you," he said, "then I shall follow along behind like a watchdog. Which would you have?"

Her smile showed some amusement. "Your arm, then," she said. "I must confess it will be a rare treat to feel thoroughly safe. But what a strange coincidence that you should be there again today, my lord, at the same place."

"Yes," he said. "A strange coincidence."

"And Charlie too," she said with a laugh.

Charlie, the earl noticed when he looked, was engaged in his usual bobbing motion along the curb, one foot on and one foot off, and was glaring back at him accusingly. His lordship raised his eyebrows.

She lived on a street of shabby, down-at-heel gentility. It was not exactly a slum, but it would be before too many years had passed. She stopped before a terraced house and withdrew her hand from the earl's arm.

"This is home," she said, "and you have brought me safely, my lord. Will you come in so that I may present my grandfather to you? He sees so little company. And offer you some tea?"

Oh Lord, no. He had no desire to be drawn into the lives of people who had fallen on hard times. He had no wish to view genteel despair at close quarters. His heart strings did not need to be tugged upon. He was quite satisfied with the state of his heart as it was. It had taken him almost two years to deaden it, and that was the state he liked it to be in.

"I understand," she said, bobbing him a sudden curtsy, her eyes fallen away from his. "Good day, my lord, and thank you again for your great kindness. Charlie? Come along, dear."

She understood what? That he was too high in the

instep to pass beyond the door of the house behind her and to drink tea with her grandfather?

"I would like to meet your grandfather, Miss Bevan," he said, "and to drink some hot tea." Though her eyes, which turned back to him and smiled, could warm his blood quite as effectively as a hot or even intoxicating beverage, he thought. And frowned at the thought.

An ancient servant with a back bent into the shape of a bow shuffled into the narrow hallway as Julie opened the front door with a latchkey. He must be ninety if he were a day, the earl thought.

"Oh, Mr. Stebbins," she said, "you should be in the kitchen where it is warm. I can let myself in and see to my cloak and bonnet, as you know. Mm, wonderful." She breathed in deeply. "Mrs. Stebbins has been baking. Her legs are better today, then?"

"No, missy," the servant said. "But you know my Martha."

"I do indeed," she said. "This is Charlie Cobban, Mr. Stebbins." The earl watched, fascinated, as she set an arm about the boy's thin shoulders and hugged him to her side. "He rescued me today from someone who was being discourteous. Take him back to the kitchen, if you please, and let him eat his fill of lemon tarts and mince pies. Let Mrs. Stebbins know that he is my champion." And to his lordship's amazement, she bent her head and kissed the boy on the cheek before releasing him to the ancient servant's care.

"Charlie," the servant said in the quavering voice that suited his appearance to perfection, "come along, my good boy. Mrs. Stebbins will feed you to the brim." He laughed at his own little joke.

"And tell Mrs. Stebbins that she is not to climb the stairs with the tea tray," Julie said firmly. "I shall come for it myself in a few minutes."

She turned back to the earl and smiled. "Will you come this way, my lord?" she asked, turning to the closed door at her left and opening it.

It was not the dark and gloomy room Lord Kevern had expected, though it might have been. A cheerful fire burned in the grate and candles had been lit already. The rather shabby chairs were strewn with gaily embroidered cushions, and the old gentleman dozing in a chair beside the fire was covered by a brightly colored rug from the waist down.

And there was Christmas again, even in this shabby house of old age and poverty. Boughs of red-berried holly liberally decorated the room, and a sprig of mistletoe hung from the ceiling a little forward of the fireplace.

"Grandpapa," Julie was saying, bent over the old gentleman and smoothing back a lock of thin white hair that had fallen over his forehead. "I am home. And I have brought someone with me."

"Eh?" The old gentleman woke with a start and gazed upward with fierce eyes from beneath bushy white eyebrows. And then his eyes softened with warmth and with love. "It is you, Julie, is it? Home again? And home to stay until after Christmas?"

"No, Grandpapa." She spoke loudly and distinctly. "I have to go in tomorrow again, but only to play the pianoforte so that the young people can practice their dance steps, not to give a lesson. I have brought someone with me."

"Eh?" the old gentleman said, and she straightened up and stood to one side of the chair.

"My lord," she said, "may I present my grandfather, Sir Richard Bevan?" She raised her voice again. "This is the Earl of Kevern, Grandpapa. He was kind enough to escort me home after someone was rude to me."

"Eh?" he said. "Someone being disrespectful, Julie? The Earl of Kevern?" The old gentleman set his hands on the arms of the chair and made as if to get to his feet.

"No, no," the earl said, stepping forward, one hand outstretched. "No need to get up, sir. I would say you are in the best place today. It is chilly outside."

Julie offered him the chair opposite her grandfather's and next to the fire, and she left the room in order to fetch the tea tray. The earl watched her go and resisted the unfamiliar urge to jump to his feet to offer his assistance.

Sir Richard was inclined to talk, the earl found, and spoke of former days and better days when he had lived on his own property in the country and had had friends that extended over the whole county. And of his son, the Reverend Peter Bevan, who might have been a bishop if only he had had some ambition and accepted patronage when it was offered. Instead of which he had died of a fever with his wife and not a penny to his name.

"But Papa was a happy man, Grandpapa," Julie said. She had returned to the room long since and had poured the tea and handed around a plate of cakes and tarts and mince pies. "And well loved."

"And left you without a penny for a dowry," the old gentleman said. "And me to burden you after everything was lost."

"You are not a burden, Grandpapa," she said, setting aside her own plate and crossing the room in order to adjust the rug, which had slipped down to his knees. "You are my family. My only family."

He touched her smooth golden hair with a gnarled hand before she straightened up and sat down again. "You should have your own family by now, Julie," he said. "You should have married young what's-his-name when you had a chance and be hanged to me. I had had my life. You should have children of your own.''

''Well, I do not,'' she said briskly, and she looked acutely embarrassed, the earl saw. ''We moved to London, my lord, so that I might take employment. I could not take a governess's post because that would have meant leaving Grandfather and Mr. and Mrs. Stebbins, who were too old to get other positions. I teach music and sometimes French.''

''And she has to go out alone every day,'' Sir Richard said, ''without a maid or chaperon. And no carriage. It is not right, Kevern, for the granddaughter of a baronet. Now, is it?''

''Oh, grandfather,'' she said.

The earl declined a second cup of tea and got to his feet. She was clearly uncomfortable, and he was uncomfortable. Good Lord. She had made a home and a life out of such an appalling situation. And there was love in her eyes for the old codger who had held her back from either taking regular employment or marrying. And yet she was prepared to enter into the spirit of Christmas, he thought, looking about again at the holly, just as if it could really bring some joy into her life.

He shook hands with the old gentleman and followed Julie into the hall.

''You said that you have learned from experience,'' he said to her, staring down at her broodingly when she had closed the door of the sitting room behind her. ''Does that mean you have been accosted before this afternoon?''

''When a lady who looks as I do,'' she said, looking down at her plain gray dress, ''is standing still on a street, gentlemen draw their own conclusions. Even a clergyman's daughter from the country learns that lesson fast, my lord. And when one works in the homes of the wealthy, there are always gentle-men who assume that one wishes to augment one's income. I have learned to look after myself."

"And yet," he said, "you were shaking like a leaf after your ordeal this afternoon."

"Because you were there," she said, "and Charlie. It is easy to give in to feminine vapors when one knows that one does not have to cope with a situation alone."

"Tell me where you work," he said, "and I shall go and give the male inhabitants of the house a sermon on gentlemanly conduct."

She laughed, a low sweet sound. "How very kind you are," she said, "and how different from what your eyes and your facial expressions proclaim you to be." She flushed and lowered her eyes as if realizing too late what she had said.

"And what do they proclaim?" he asked.

She looked up at him again and hesitated. "That you are a man who cares for no one and nothing," she said. "Would you really have beaten Charlie with your cane?"

"And he would have deserved every stroke," he said. "Thieving little urchin."

"You are wealthy, I suppose," she said. "Have you ever tried to put yourself mentally in the place of someone who does not know where his next meal is coming from? Or someone who has on his thin young shoulders all the burden of having to provide for a family that cannot provide for itself?"

"Muvver and Pa and Vi'let and Roddy?" he said. "And the metamorphosis of the sister and brother into Annie and 'arry, who then had to become a friend from next door and an older sister, who of course—did it need to be said?—had just lost her employment? And I suppose the mother—if we were to ask the question—would be nine months less one week with child. Come, Miss Bevan, you are not still naive enough to believe that cock-and-bull story, are you? How long have you lived in London?''

''I have *lived*,'' she said, ''for almost twenty-five years, my lord, and I learned from my mother and father to love people and to accept their stories without question. It is true that Charlie tried to steal from me yesterday, but today he risked his own safety to save me from harm. And he is a little child. Do you think he is more than ten years old? And poorly fed and poorly clothed.''

''Is this the point at which I withdraw my handkerchief from my pocket to dry my eyes and blow my nose?'' he asked.

''Your eyes are cold again,'' she said, ''and such wonderful blue eyes. But you cannot deceive me, my lord. I remember the cakes and the extra pasty yesterday and the half crown. And I remember your walking home with me this afternoon when you must be accustomed to riding such distances.''

''Perhaps I walked home with you because of your golden hair and emerald eyes,'' he said.

She flushed again. ''I think not, my lord,'' she said.

''Well.'' He looked about him for his coat and drew it on. ''I shall have that child hailed up from the kitchen before I leave. Otherwise he may forget to leave altogether and become a permanent recipient of your charity.''

''I think Charlie is of a more independent spirit,'' she said with a smile, but she walked to the doorway at the back of the hall and called down the stairs.

''Now,'' he said before Charlie appeared, ''tell me where you work so that I may be waiting close to there tomorrow to escort you home. It will be

Christmas Eve, and there are likely to be some inebriated revelers about, looking for a little sport.''

She flushed once more. "I cannot ask it of you," she said.

"You did not," he said. "Where do you work?"

She hesitated and then named an address on Brook Street, quite close to Hanover Square.

"I shall see you tomorrow, then," he said as Charlie appeared from the kitchen. "Ah, I see you are carrying away the spoils of war with you, my lad."

Charlie looked down at the bundle clutched in his hand. "The old woman give me some to take to Vi'let an' Annie," he said.

"My congratulations," the earl said. "Your memory is improving, Charlie. Come along. It is time to go home."

"Good-bye, dear," Julie said, and she bent down to hug the child tightly to her and kiss his cheek again. And she slipped something into a tattered pocket before releasing him, Lord Kevern noticed.

"Cor blimey," the boy said when the two of them were out on the street and Julie Bevan had waved to them and closed the door. "I bet you would of give a bag of guineas to be in my place then, guv." He walked along the curb, balancing on it with arms outstretched.

"Two bags," the earl said. "And I owe you a guinea and a half, Charlie. Here they are."

"Cor blimey," Charlie said again, gazing down at the coins in his hand and forgetting to secrete them about his person with his usual magician's swiftness. "Chris'mus must be comin'."

"No," the earl said. "It is not that. It is just my conscience smiting me, for without your hint I could not have found out the information that you offered to sell to me, Charlie. Now be off with you to whatever hovel you call home."

Charlie stood still on the curb and muttered an address absently as he continued to stare down at his newfound fortune. And then he looked up and grinned cheekily. "I'm goin' to buy 'em presents," he said, and he darted off down the street and disappeared less than a minute later into the dusk.

The Earl of Kevern was left with that feeling of emptiness again. Dusk and cold and an empty street. And Christmas gone, no sign of it at all about him. Just the way he wanted it. But that empty feeling.

But not quite, either. "Number Five, Brook Street," he muttered to himself as he began the long walk home.

He really should have gone to Buckland Abbey, the earl told himself the following afternoon. Did it matter that last year he had felt like an outsider there, even though the property belonged to him and even though every single guest there had been a member of the family of which he was the head—and close family members at that? Did it matter that he had not been happy there, but had seen to the very heart of the cruelty of Christmas with the illusory joy it pretended to offer?

At least he would have retained his sanity there.

He was not at all sure that he was remaining sane in London. For one thing, he had delayed all morning, as late as he possibly could, before going out, not because the nature of his errand—purchasing gifts for his servants—was distasteful, although it was, but because he was expecting a visitor. And he found himself not only disappointed when Charlie Cobban did not come, but also worried. Why on earth was he disappointed, and why in heaven's name had he been expecting him anyway?

Worried about a street urchin whose neck would

probably be stretched by a rope collar long before he reached manhood? Worried about a ragamuffin who could steal from someone almost as poor as himself and extort money for useless information and lie without blinking an eye and curse like a navvy?

Why in hell was he worried? The child had walked off with a minor fortune in the past two days. And yet his lordship could not shake from his mind images of the boy spending Christmas in a den of thieves, stripped of the coins that had been given him and sent out to beg or steal more. Or of the boy all alone, seeking warmth and comfort in an alley somewhere, waiting for people to come outdoors again once Christmas was over. Or of the boy dreaming of a family—of two sisters and a brother, and a mother about to give birth again.

Of a boy lonely as he was lonely, except that the boy was only a child and should have had a right to love and security and a family.

An address kept repeating itself in the earl's mind, the street one he had never heard of, certainly one he had never traversed. He did not even know where the address had come from except that he could hear the boy's piping voice reciting it.

The Earl of Kevern did his shopping eventually and then waited restlessly until it was time to wander out close to Number Five Brook Street. But he was not in a good mood and snapped at his valet for handing him his gold-topped cane when he wanted the silver, and scowled at a footman who jumped to open the front door one second later than he ought.

He was in a savage bad mood. He might have known that Christmas would open wounds that he had thought quite healed. He might have known that it would not be possible merely to laugh at the great myth. But it would have been possible too, he thought, if he had only ignored her standing before that damned jeweler's window and walked on by. Had he done so, he would not even have seen the boy steal her reticule. And Charlie would have succeeded, and she would have been destitute.

She was walking briskly along Brook Street, her head down, though twice she lifted it to look anxiously about her. The second time she saw him, and she paused and bit her lip.

"Miss Bevan?" he said and raised his hat to her.

She smiled, and her smile was like a soothing balm to his pain. He found himself smiling back.

"Oh," she said, taking the arm he offered, "you look quite different when you smile, my lord. You look human."

"I will not ask what I look like when I do not smile, then," he said. "You smile all the time. Are you never bitter that your life has turned out as it has? You are the granddaughter of a baronet, and yet you must work for a living and put up with the insults of men who think themselves your superiors—and the even worse insults of women, I would not doubt, because you have the misfortune to be beautiful. You refused a marriage proposal because you have an aged and infirm grandfather and his retainers to care for. How can you smile?"

"Because I am alive," she said, "and enjoy good health and have people to love and be loved by. And I did not care for him a great deal, though he was a perfectly eligible gentleman."

"You are happy, then?" he asked.

"My father used to say that happiness can never be achieved in this life," she said, "except in brief moments. Brief glimpses of heaven he used to call them. There is always something else we want. Always something we yearn for even if we are not selfishly greedy persons. I believe he was right. I have yearnings just as you must. As everyone must.''

"No," he said. "Not me. Not for the future. I wish there were no future."

"Ah." She did not smile when she looked up at him. "Something has hurt you. I have felt it from the beginning—was that only two days ago?"

But he was saved from having to answer her. There was a group of carolers a little farther along Bond Street, and the merry sounds of singing caught their attention. They walked closer and stopped, as several other pedestrians and shoppers had done.

If one were to paint a picture of perfect Christmas bliss, the earl thought, one surely could not do better than to draw a group of carolers, bundled up against the cold, their cheeks and noses rosy from the cold, their faces glowing with the happiness of the season and the birth of the child they proclaimed, their mittened hands holding the sheets of music for all of them to see.

The only touch missing from this particular live picture was snow. The pavements were still quite wet and dirty. But even so the scene oozed sentimentality. Just two days before it would have delighted his satiric heart. But no longer? Had anything changed in two days?

"Oh," Julie Bevan said, and her head tipped sideways and almost touched his shoulder for a moment, "the nostalgia. It was what we used to do in the country every year on Christmas Eve when Papa was alive."

Her eyes, he saw when he looked down at her, were glistening with unshed tears, and yet she smiled. And then she fumbled with the clasp of her reticule. The carolers were collecting donations for a foundling hospital.

"Put it away," he said, touching her hand with his own before reaching into an inner pocket for his purse. He dropped a few gold coins into the hat upturned on the pavement, and they moved on.

He might have brought his curricle. Not his carriage. She was a lady, however impoverished, and would not feel easy riding in a closed carriage, alone with a gentleman, but the curricle would have made the journey shorter and easier for her. But he had been too selfish to do so. He had wanted her company for as long as possible.

And so their steps took them along Bond Street and past the jeweler's shop window. Her steps lagged, and she turned her head, but she did not stop.

"Ah," was all she said, but it was more an expelling of breath than a word.

"It is gone," he said, "and has been replaced by a silver clock. Why did you like it so?"

She looked up at him in some surprise. "The porcelain Madonna?" she said. "Have you been admiring it too, my lord? My father always placed one of carved wood at the front of the church at Christmas, though some people used to think it popish. When I first saw it in the window a week ago, it was Christmas to me and memories and home. And hope. I think it must have been wonderful for Mary to give birth to Jesus on Christmas Day. Don't you?" She laughed suddenly. "Though of course it is Christmas Day only because she did so."

But he had swallowed and closed his eyes. And swallowed again.

"What is it?" Her words were whispered.

"Nothing." The word sounded harsh even to his own ears. He had her hand clamped to his side with a rigid arm. "It is just all this talk of Christmas. It is merely a day in the year like any other. And yet one is asked to spend a fortune on gifts and to stuff oneself full of rich foods and liquor and pretend that human nature had been transformed and will remain so. We are asked to believe that nothing bad can ever happen at Christmas, only peace on earth and good-will among men.''

''Did something bad once happen to you?'' she asked.

But he would not answer her. He walked on, drawing her with him, reducing his pace when he realized that he was striding, but not talking. And he was sorry again that he had not gone to Buckland Abbey, and sorry that he had turned his head for a second look at her outside the jeweler's shop two days before. And sorry for every incident that had led him to this moment.

''I was sorry,'' she said at last, when they were quite near her house, ''not to see Charlie on Bond Street today. Somehow I expected to. Is that not absurd? I wonder what sort of a Christmas he will have. The family should at least be able to buy some food with the half crown you gave him.''

''And with the money you slipped into his pocket yesterday,'' he said. ''Don't believe too much in that family. Charlie is a street urchin.''

''I have to believe in the family,'' she said, ''or my heart will break. He is just a child. I wish I knew where I might find him. I wish I had asked him.''

''I believe I do know,'' he said. ''At least, an alien address keeps running through my head, and it repeats itself in Charlie's voice.''

Her face lit up. ''Oh, do please tell me,'' she said. ''I shall go there. Tomorrow. I shall take more of Mrs. Stebbins's cooking, and I shall see if I can find something to take as gifts for Charlie and the little children.''

''Violet and Roddy?'' he said. ''Have you always been so gullible, Miss Bevan? But you must not go. It is doubtless a rough neighborhood.''

''I shall go anyway.'' She smiled up at him. ''Oh, I shall look forward to seeing Charlie again and to wishing him a happy Christmas.''

Leave well enough alone, an inner voice told him. *Say good-bye to her now and leave well enough alone.*

''If you insist on going,'' he said, ''then I shall come too. I shall escort you there and watch your disappointment and disillusion when you find that the address is that of a den of thieves.''

''Is that what you wish to find?'' she asked.

No. And damn the boy for pulling at his heart strings and twining himself about them. ''I'll take him home with me,'' he said. ''Doubtless my house-keeper can find him some tasks to do suitable to his age and strength and talents. Perhaps I shall train him to be my tiger. Would that satisfy you?''

''Would you do that?'' she asked. ''For Charlie? Even if you are right and he is no more than a waif and a thief and a liar?''

''He is a child,'' he said irritably.

''Yes.'' Her smile was warm, though her cheeks shone scarlet with the cold. ''Once he was like that little porcelain baby in Mary's arms.''

''I shall come for you tomorrow morning, then,'' he said. They had come to a stop outside her house.

''Won't you come in for tea?'' she asked. ''Grandpapa would be happy to see you again. And you have a long walk home.''

''No,'' he said. ''Not today.'' But he did not im-

mediately bid her a good day and turn on his heel as
he ought to have done.

There is always something we yearn for, she had
said earlier.

Not me, he had said.

And yet he yearned now for he knew not what.
He took her gloved hand in his, felt with his own
glove the hole in the palm that she had concealed,
and turned her hand over to look at the worn patch
in the leather. And he lifted her hand to set his mouth
against her skin.

Well, he told himself with all the old inner cynicism, *say it.* He might as well become a part of it
all just like everyone else so that he could jeer at
himself as well as at the whole world. Why should
he be the only sane one in an insane universe? The
only one immune to the myth?

And so he said it. He touched her cheek with his
other hand, resting his gloved thumb briefly against
her lips. ''Happy Christmas, Julie,'' he said.

Her eyes grew bright with tears again before he
turned abruptly away. ''Happy Christmas, my lord,''
he heard her say as he strode away.

Christmas Day. It was the first thought to lodge
itself in his mind when sleep abandoned him, even
before he opened his eyes. The Earl of Kevern rolled
over onto his stomach and burrowed his head beneath two pillows as if in so doing he could block
out the knowledge and will twenty-four hours to pass
in a moment.

Two years ago. It had all started to happen already
by this time, although it had continued on through
the whole day and into the night. It had not put a
dampener on anyone's spirits. Quite the contrary.
How very wonderful at Christmas, his family had

said. How very appropriate. And even he, restless and anxious as he had been, quite unable to think of gifts or the Christmas dinner, had been excited and happy too. Christmas. The most glorious day of the year. The most glorious day of his life.

The earl lay for a long time beneath his pillows before finally throwing them off. Even beneath the pillows he could smell Christmas—the mince pies and the plum pudding and the goose. And the greenery with which the house had been decorated the day before while he was out. There were things to be done, most notably the distribution of gifts and Christmas bonuses among his servants. There were smiles to be worn and jokes to be made and hands to be shaken.

And then there was something else to be done. There was Julie to be called upon—when had he begun to think of her as Julie rather than Miss Bevan? he wondered—and that mad visit to be made to the house that might or might not be Charlie's hideout. And to the mythical family.

Lord Kevern looked with a wry smile at the packages lying on top of a chest of drawers across the room—scarves and mittens he had bought after leaving Julie the afternoon before for Charlie and Violet and Roddy, a shawl for Annie. And another longer parcel, which he had bought earlier, during the morning.

He should walk straight to Bethlehem Asylum, he thought, and save someone the trouble of having to take him there to commit him in a few days' time. For undoubtedly he had taken leave of his senses. And yet the very sight of the packages and the knowledge of the strange journey he was going to make later somehow made the day seem less impossible to face.

He sat on the edge of the bed and ran his hands through his hair before ringing for his valet. His yearning of the day before had been for a nameless something. And yet at least one longing he had been able to identify even at the time. He had wanted to place his mouth against the lips he had touched with his thumb.

He was glad after all that he had not gone to Buckland Abbey. Ah, he was glad.

"Grandpapa." Julie leaned over the old gentleman's chair and tucked the rug more snugly about his waist. He had drawn it up over his feet so that he could look at the slippers she had given him for Christmas. "Lord Kevern and I are going out for a short while to visit Charlie, the little boy I told you about who rescued me the other day. It is time for your sleep anyway. When I return I shall play another hand of cards with you and read to you."

"Yes, go," Sir Richard said. "Go, Julie, and give the boy my best regards." He looked with some keenness at the earl, who had risen to his feet after sitting and conversing for almost half an hour. "Go, and have a merry Christmas of your own, girl. There is no hurry for you to get back. I am tired."

She kissed his cheek.

"I have a basket to take," she said, when she and the earl had left the room. "I shall run and fetch it."

It was the first time he had seen her in out of the cold. Her complexion was as delicate and creamy as he had expected it to be, though there was a flush of color in her cheeks. And her eyes shone with Christmas, even though there seemed to be precious little in her life to cause the sparkle—only three elderly dependents and a boy who would have stolen all her money if he could have got away with it.

And himself. Was he a part of her Christmas? he wondered. Had she woken up that morning and remembered that she was to see him and thought that perhaps after all the day would be bearable?

She returned wearing the gray-blue cloak and the plain bonnet and the worn leather gloves and carrying a covered basket only a little smaller than the one that stood on a seat of his carriage outside her door. She had declined his suggestion that she might want to take Mrs. Stebbins with her as a chaperon.

"This is a sort of holiday for her too," she had said. "Besides, my lord, I am past the age of needing chaperons."

Perhaps she would have changed her mind, he thought, if she could have known how his eyes had drunk in the sight of her on his arrival and whenever she had looked away to address a remark to her grandfather. Or how his raw, repressed emotions were soothed by the sound of her voice. He handed her into the carriage and climbed in after her.

"At least," she said, laughing when she saw his basket, "they will not starve, will they? I have brought handkerchiefs for the children, plain for Charlie and Roddy and embroidered for Violet and Annie. They are not very grand presents, are they? But I know how you noticed poor Charlie's absence of a handkerchief at the pastry cook's."

Her face was alight with warmth and happiness.

"Julie," he said, "don't count on finding him. The address I have may not be his. It may not even exist. And it is very probable that the family does not exist."

"It is Christmas," she said. "Only wonderful things happen at Christmas."

He turned his head to look out of the window. Already the streets were getting narrower and less familiar.

"I am sorry," she said softly. "Your face is shuttered again. It was a thoughtless thing to say. Something less than wonderful happened to you, did it not?"

"It is only," he said stiffly, "that I do not wish to see you disappointed."

"I will be sorry," she said, "if we do not find him at all, because I wish to hug him and wish him well. I will be sad if we find him and there is no family, because he will have been deprived of what all children should have a right to. But the whole day will not have been a disappointment. For you have come out, though something has happened to make you hate Christmas, merely to find and to feed a young boy who should be quite beneath the notice of an aristocrat. A boy you would have beaten with your cane just three days ago although his only crime was being unwilling to starve."

"Julie," he said, his eyes still directed to the drab streets passing by the carriage windows, "you are too sentimental for your own good, you know. He would have understood the thrashing far more than the hugs."

"Understood, yes," she said. "He would have understood what he must expect of life. But you do not believe that the beating would have been better for him. I know you do not."

"Oh, well," he said, turning his head again to look at her, "if you know what is in the depth of my heart, then there is no point in further discussion, is there?"

But she refused to be cowed by the set-down. She set her head to one side and smiled at him. "Those cold cynical eyes," she said. "But they do not fool me any longer. If your eyes denoted truly what was in your mind and your heart, my lord, you would not be seated in this carriage at this moment on this particular errand."

He pursed his lips. "I am on this errand," he said, "in order to save you from certain attack by ruffians. Have you glanced out of the window yet? And to show you how foolish it is to be sentimental and to believe everything a thieving brat cares to tell you. I came so that I may say 'I told you so' as we ride back home again."

"And you came with a full basket." She laughed. But she did not try to continue the conversation. She turned her head to look out through the window. And there was much to see that was shocking and even mesmerizing to someone unaccustomed to the slums of London. But apparently the carriage of the Earl of Kevern was as shocking and as mesmerizing a sight to the inhabitants of those streets.

The address was certainly not a fictitious one, the earl discovered when his carriage slowed and eventually stopped outside a tall and gloomy rooming house in a narrow street of equally gloomy run-down buildings. Ill-clad men and women lounged in doorways and sat on steps despite the coldness of the weather, and ragged children, many of them barefoot, darted about the street. Most of them were darting in the direction of his carriage and then stopping, saucer-eyed, watching as if he had just dropped in from another planet.

"The King of England lives two 'ouses down on your left, guv," one wag yelled as the coachman opened the carriage door and, after one pained look of inquiry directed at his master, let down the steps.

"An' the Queen of England an' all 'er maids lives on yer right," someone else called out.

The loungers made merry with the two remarks and embellished them with witty directions to the Regent's house and those of all the royal dukes and princesses.

"Could he possibly live here?" Julie asked, looking almost fearfully out through the door.

But her question did not need answering.

"Cor blimey," a piping voice cried, "it's the guv. *Now* I'll prove it to you, Pa."

Charlie had been walking along the street with a small, wiry man, whose right arm was wrapped in ragged yet clean bandages.

The Earl of Kevern stepped down from his carriage. A Daniel into the lions' den, he thought. But *Pa*? Was he to be proved wrong after all? And then he closed his eyes briefly as the man sank to one knee. He did not even notice the loud jeers of the lookers-on.

"Sir," the man said, "I've already belted 'im one good, sir, though I 'ave only my left arm to do it wiv, sir. An' tomorrow mornin' sharp, sir, 'e was to bring it back and take the consequences, sir. But beggin' your pardon, sir, 'e's a good boy, sir, an' 'as felt the burden of our troubles 'eavy on 'is young shoulders. Don't tyke 'im to jail, sir. Don't 'ang 'im. 'Is ma would grieve."

Good Lord, the earl thought. At any moment he expected the man to try to kiss the hem of his greatcoat.

"Charlie!" he could hear Julie saying. "Happy Christmas, sweetheart. Oh, how good it is to see you."

"I think there is some misunderstanding," his lordship said. "Good heavens, man, get up on your feet. I have not come to take Charlie away to jail. I have come because Miss Bevan wished to see him and, er, hug him, and because I, ah, wanted to wish him a happy Christmas.''

''*See*, Pa?'' Charlie said, triumph in his voice. Then he turned an accusing glare on the earl. ''Got me into trouble proper, you did, guv,'' he said. ''When I showed Pa the guinea an' an 'alf, not to mention the lydy's 'alf a crown, Pa wouldn't believe that I come by them honest. Only glad I was that 'is right arm is bandaged up.''

''Whatever 'e did for a guinea an' an 'alf, guv,'' one woman onlooker shrieked to the delight of the growing audience, ''I'll do double for a single guinea.''

''For such an 'andsome gent, she'd do it for free, guv,'' someone else said.

Good Lord. The earl started to regret Buckland Abbey again. Did Buckland Abbey belong in the same world as this?

''Charlie earned his guinea and a half,'' he said to Mr. Cobban. ''Miss Bevan and I have brought some Christmas cooking and some gifts for the children. Is there somewhere more private we can go for a few moments?'' He glanced dubiously at the rooming house.

Mr. Cobban smote himself on the brow suddenly at the same moment as a young girl of sixteen or seventeen, neatly though shabbily clad, appeared at the door and looked out anxiously.

''Oh, Pa,'' she said, ''ain't she with you?'' And then she saw the carriage and the coachman and the earl and her eyes widened.

''She couldn't come, Annie,'' Mr. Cobban said. ''She 'ad gone somewhere else.''

"Oh," the girl said, still eyeing the carriage. "But there is no one else, Pa. What are we goin' to do?"

Mr. Cobban looked back to the earl. "Beggin' your pardon, sir," he said, "I can't invite you into my 'umble abode, sir. The missus is 'avin' another young 'un, sir, an' 'er time 'as come. An' there ain't no midwife."

Lord Kevern felt suddenly as if someone were draining him of blood, starting at the top of his head and working downward.

"I don't know what to do, Pa," the girl wailed. "An' Vi'let and Roddy are cryin' because they're frightened."

"Lord bless us," Mr. Cobban said, scratching his head. "Beggin' your pardon, sir, but I'll 'ave to go. An' if Charlie didn't steal that money, sir, I thank you kindly."

The earl would have handed his basket to the man and left without another word. He felt closed in by the narrow street and the tall buildings. He felt as if there were no air in the street. He had to have air. But Julie was speaking.

"I have some little experience, Mr. Cobban," she was saying. "I have worked with a midwife, though never alone. May I see what I can do to help?"

No! He wanted to grasp hold of her, to pick her up bodily and bundle her back inside the carriage. He wanted to instruct his coachman to spring the horses. He needed air.

"Lord love you, miss," Mr. Cobban was saying. "Oh, Lord love you. Sent from 'eaven, you was, the two of you, to bless us for Chris'mus."

"Julie." The earl caught at her arm as she turned toward the house. "This is not your responsibility. Come back home and I shall send a physician."

She smiled. "A physician come here?" she said.

"No, no, I shall help. Annie looks like a sensible girl and will be an able assistant once there is someone to tell her what to do, I am sure. There is going to be a new child for Christmas. Is that not wonderful and appropriate, my lord?"

His hand slipped from her arm.

She looked searchingly at him. "Go home, my lord," she said. "Thank you for bringing me here. I shall stay for as long as I am needed, and then I shall get Charlie to show me the way home. He will be an adequate bodyguard."

She turned and hurried inside the house.

"If you go," Charlie's piping voice said from his elbow, "you'll be a fool, guv. After 'elpin' Ma, she'll be glad of them soft seats an' your shoulder to rest 'er 'ead on."

"Charlie," the earl said, taking a deep breath and finding that, after all, there was air left in the street, "you have the head of an eighty-year-old on your shoulders. But your advice is unnecessary. Why should I leave Miss Bevan to your escort later on when she might have mine?"

" 'Xactly what I was sayin', guv," Charlie said. "What's in them baskets?"

It had to be the strangest Christmas of them all, the Earl of Kevern decided over the next two hours. Indeed, it had to be the strangest day of his life. He would perhaps have been amused by it all—*very* amused—if he had not been feeling sick at the thought of what was proceeding inside the rooming house.

For two hours he held court in his carriage. He retired there after Julie had gone about her self-imposed duty as midwife, and Charlie climbed in behind him without invitation, curious to discover the contents of the two baskets. Mr. Cobban came inside by invitation, and soon afterward a tiny boy, ragged but immaculately clean, climbed the steps, using hands as well as feet, and raised two arms to be lifted into his father's lap, where he snuggled up and proceeded to suck his thumb. And then a girl, two or three years older, appeared and sat down close beside Charlie and stared at the earl from solemn, soulful eyes.

"What's in the baskets, guv?" Charlie asked, though his father had warned him to watch his mouth when he had asked the same question on the pavement.

"That basket," the earl replied, indicating the smaller of the two, "belongs to Miss Bevan. This one contains a ham and some pastries and bread for your family."

"Lord love you, sir," Mr. Cobban said.

"And a Christmas gift for each of you children," Lord Kevern added.

Violet sat even more still and solemn. Roddy forgot for the moment to suck his thumb. His eyes swiveled sideways to regard the earl fixedly.

"Let's 'ave 'em, then, guv," Charlie said, bouncing up and down on the seat and earning for himself another paternal warning.

"Lord love you, sir," Mr. Cobban said again five minutes later, when the parcels had been opened and scarves wound about chill necks and mittens drawn onto cold hands.

"Cor blimey, guv," Charlie said, his high-pitched voice sounding excited and more childlike than usual, "I'll never be cold again." He wormed his chin down inside the coils of the green scarf until only his eyes were visible.

Violet touched her brother's arm with a red mitten

and smoothed it along his sleeve. "Charlie," she said, her eyes shining up into his, "I got two presents for Chris'mus." She looked shyly across at the earl and half hid behind her brother's arm. "Charlie give me soap."

Roddy sat looking at his blue mittens, which were several sizes too large, and holding up his hands for his father's inspection. Then he discovered that he had to remove one mitten in order to suck his thumb and nod off to sleep against his father's chest.

The earl found himself involved in a lengthy discussion of the strange tendency life displayed of having its ups and downs. At least, he supposed *discussion* was an inaccurate description of the proceedings since his own part in them consisted of strategically placed yeses and nos and other monosyllabic acknowledgements of the wisdom of Mr. Cobban's observations of life.

But one thing was very obvious. The Cobbans were currently living through—*barely* living through—one of the deepest of life's downs. Mr. Cobban's arm was not healing as it ought. The wound kept festering. And without a healthy right arm there was no working. Mrs. Cobban had chosen the worst of all possible times to decide to present Mr. Cobban with another young hopeful, though he generously acknowledged his own part in that inconvenient state of affairs.

"The thing was, you see, sir," he said with significant looks at the children, "that the deed was done, if you get my meaning, before I 'urt my arm."

The earl did indeed get Mr. Cobban's meaning. He knew a thing or two about procreation.

And then Annie Cobban had lost her job as a dressmaker's assistant when the dressmaker's niece arrived from the country in search of employment.

And Charlie was a good boy, but just a lad of eleven, and his father worried about where his zeal to provide for his family might lead him.

"I was sure when 'e come 'ome with a guinea an' an 'alf yesterday that 'e 'ad stole it," Mr. Cobban said. "An' then when 'e ups and gives the little uns presents this mornin', I was certain. I belted 'im a good un, I did, sir. Stealin' was never the way of the Cobbans, sir."

The earl assured Mr. Cobban that such firm parental moral training was bound to have its effect in making Charlie and the other young ones honest citizens. Charlie stared at him the while, his eyes narrowed speculatively.

"I 'ope so, sir," Mr. Cobban said. "We might be poor, sir, and fallen on 'ard times, but we still 'as our pride, sir."

Mrs. Cobban's labor had already reached an advanced stage before the earl's carriage had arrived. Less than two hours later, Annie Cobban came rushing from the rooming house to announce the birth of another son.

The Earl of Kevern sat in the corner of the carriage watching as the father, who half an hour before had been lamenting the imminent arrival of yet another mouth to feed, hugged his sleeping child to himself and wept with joy over the compounding of his problems. And he watched Charlie bounce on the seat again and explain to Violet that they had another brother. Violet looked up at him in silent wonder. Annie meanwhile was explaining in a fast, excited voice how she had helped the lady and watched the baby being born.

Neither Mr. Cobban nor the children were permitted to enter the house immediately. Apparently the lady was still busy, and Annie had to return to

help her. But soon enough they were summoned inside and wasted no time in scrambling out of the
carriage to view the new Christmas arrival.

"A son born on Chris'mus Day, sir," Mr. Cobban
said before he left. "Imagine that. My son an' Jesus
both." He chuckled. "A man couldn't arsk for a
better gift, now could 'e?"

No. A man could not ask for a better gift.

He waited quietly until she came out a few minutes later, without her bonnet, her face flushed, one
lock of hair come loose from her smooth chignon.

"My lord," she said, "I did not know until Charlie came inside that you had waited. It must have
seemed a dreadfully long time. But I am glad my
basket is still here. I forgot it earlier. Will you give
me a moment to take it inside?"

"Take mine too," he said. "They forgot about
the food in their excitement."

She hesitated and looked up into his eyes. "Come
inside too," she said. "Just for a moment. Come
and see the baby and wish Mrs. Cobban a happy
Christmas."

But he retreated farther into his corner.

"Please," she said softly. "I think you need to
see that a child has been safely born."

Strange words. He would have liked to ponder
them, but she had reached inside for her basket, and
she was smiling at him—a smile full of the wonder
of Christmas and the event in which she had just
played an active role. And a smile that was directed
right into his eyes, right into his heart.

"I shall carry the basket inside," he said. Good
Lord and good Lord. He could be playing billiards
now at Buckland Abbey.

They had two rooms, poorly but neatly furnished.

Clean. How could a family of six—now seven—live in two rooms? And with no steady income?

He nodded to a tired Mrs. Cobban from the doorway between the two rooms and gazed down at the red and wrinkled new bundle of humanity that Mr. Cobban brought proudly for his inspection. Ugly. Life. Human life safely launched on its journey into the unknown. Beautiful.

Annie was exclaiming over her shawl and thanking him profusely. And they were all unwrapping handkerchiefs, and Violet was running a finger over the embroidery on hers and telling Charlie, awe in her voice, that she had had three gifts for Christmas.

Charlie was loudly demanding to know when they could eat. He already had the ham out of the earl's basket.

"Mr. Cobban," Lord Kevern said as the man laid the sleeping baby beside his wife and came back out into the other room, "would you miss the wharves if you worked in a large house instead? Perhaps in the stables? Or even in the country, perhaps, in Dorsetshire? As a gardener? Would you care to work for me?"

Mr. Cobban merely stared.

"My lodgekeeper at Buckland Abbey is due for retirement in the spring," the earl said. "Perhaps you would care for that job. There is a comfortable lodge in which to live. I am sure work could be found for Annie in the house there, or here if she would prefer to stay in London. And small jobs could be found for Charlie when he is not at school."

"School?" Charlie said. "Cor. I always wanted to learn to read, guv."

"Working in an 'ouse?" Annie's hands were clasped to her bosom. "Oh, sir, I always dreamed of workin' in an 'ouse an' wearin' one of them uniforms.''

"Then you shall do so," the earl said. "Mr. Cobban?"

"Lord love you, sir," the man said. "But me arm." He held it up.

"I shall have it tended to by a physician," the earl said. "In the meantime my head groom and my housekeeper must find you duties that can be done with one arm. If you want the employment, that is."

"If I want the employment!" Mr. Cobban's tone implied that there was no doubt about his wanting it.

Lord Kevern was feeling embarrassed, and he was very aware of Julie, standing silently in the background.

"Report to my housekeeper on Hanover Square tomorrow morning, then," he said. "The three of you. She will be instructed to offer you immediate employment until such time as we can work out some permanent place for you." He nodded dismissively and picked up his empty basket from the table. "Charlie knows the way. A happy Christmas to you all."

A chorus of Christmas greetings and blessings followed him from the rooming house. He handed Julie into his carriage and followed her inside. He sank into the seat beside her and closed his eyes with relief as his coachman put up the steps and shut the door. A few moments later the carriage lurched into motion.

"Well," he said after a few minutes of silence, "you are missing your chance. 'I told you so' would be a quite appropriate remark."

"I only feared," she said, turning her head to

look at him, "that perhaps the parents were uncaring and were deliberately driving Charlie into crime. But there is much love and much pride in that family despite their poverty."

"I suppose," he said, "there is even a friend next door named 'Arry."

"You did a wonderful thing," she said. "May you never turn those cynical eyes on me again, my lord, for I will not believe in them for one moment."

"Oh," he said, "I rather fancy having a cockney lodgekeeper. Mr. Cobban should be a source of endless amusement."

They lapsed into silence again, and he stared unseeing from the window. Several minutes passed while he felt the weight of a great sorrow descending on him with the early dusk.

"Tell me about it," she said at last, her voice little more than a whisper.

He did not ask her what she meant by *it*. He rested his head against the cushions and continued to stare out the window.

"My son died on Christmas Day," he said. "Two years ago." He swallowed. "He died making the perilous journey from his mother's womb to a world he never saw."

Silence stretched like a tangible thing.

"My wife survived him by two hours," he said. He closed his eyes and breathed in slowly and deeply. "It was Christmas. Even though she was upstairs all day moaning and occasionally screaming, everyone was in the best of spirits, even me for all my anxiety. Nothing bad could ever happen at Christmas. Only all that was good. The birth of my first child. What more appropriately joyous event could there be for Christmas than the birth of one's firstborn son?"

Still the silence.

"My wife and my son died on Christmas Day," he said.

The pain was intense. It had all the rawness it had had when it was new. The rawness had never worn off, in fact. It had not been given the opportunity. He had very deliberately suppressed it. He had stopped thinking of them. He had refused to have them mentioned the previous Christmas and had put off his mourning for the day in order not to dampen the spirits of the rest of his family. His own mood had been determinedly festive. He had suppressed his pain and not suffered through it.

Now the pain made it difficult to breathe.

He turned his head sharply away when she took his hand in hers, carefully removing his glove before she did so. He could feel the hot tears on his cheeks and felt suddenly ashamed. Why had he felt compelled to burden her with his personal hell on this of all days?

And then he closed his eyes again as she lifted his hand, and he felt first her lips against the back of it and then the softness of her cheek.

"I am sorry," she said. "I am so very, very sorry."

"And yet," he said, turning his head to look at her a few moments later, "life goes on. It is the most atrocious of clichés, but I have been learning the truth of it in the past few days. There are other Christmases without pain. There are children born live into the world every day. Even on Christmas Day. That is what Christmas is all about, I suppose. Birth. Life. Hope."

"Yes," she said. She was holding his hand against her cheek with both of hers.

"Even happiness," he said. "I have been happy today."

"Have you?" She smiled at him. "Did you notice the little one's mittens, my lord? Each one of them was as big as his head."

He chuckled. "I did not realize he would be that young," he said.

"You did not even know he existed," she said. "But I think you hoped he did."

He gazed into her eyes, their emerald darkened by the dusk. "I did not know it would be possible to live again and not just exist," he said. "I did not know I could ever laugh again."

"You will do both," she said. "Your period of mourning is over, my lord."

"I did not know it would be possible to love again," he said.

She took his hand away from her cheek and returned it to his side, though she did not release her hold of it. "You loved Charlie when he came into your life," she said, "just as I did. And now you love his whole family."

"I did not know it would be possible to love a *woman* again," he said.

She was looking down at their clasped hands.

"Will you take your Christmas dinner with us, my lord?" she asked, raising her eyes finally to his. "I am sure it is a foolish question when you must have a sumptuous feast planned at your own home or elsewhere. And I can offer no entertainment beyond my grandfather's company and my own. I am sure there must be a grand *ton* party somewhere."

"At Lady Lawrence's," he said. "I am invited."

"Ah." She smiled.

"Since it is Christmas," he said, "I fully intend to avoid an evening of dullness at all costs. And it seems I have a choice. Boredom or certain entertainment—which shall it be?''

She was smiling and nodding. "I understand," she said.

"Certain entertainment, I think," he said. "If you are sure I will not be intruding."

She looked up into his eyes, and her lips parted.

"I accept your invitation," he said and watched light leap into her eyes and felt hope and joy leap into his heart.

"Bring on Christmas, Julie," he said, and he felt the unfamiliar sensation of smiling. "I am ready for it."

"He has fallen asleep," she said very quietly when the old gentleman's chin finally came to rest against his chest and the sounds of low snoring became unmistakable. "It has been a very exciting evening for him, my lord. But he tires easily, I am afraid. This is already past his usual bedtime."

"You do not have to sound apologetic," he said as she rose to her feet. "I understand. Where are you going?"

"To ring for Mr. Stebbins," she said. "He will help me to get Grandpapa to bed."

"I shall help you when the time comes," he said. "But does it have to be immediately, Julie? If your grandfather goes to bed, I shall have to take my leave since you have no chaperon."

She sat down again in the chair close to his own that she had just vacated. "It must have been a dreadfully dull evening for you after all," she said. "I am afraid Grandpapa likes to reminisce about the old days. I do not mind because the stories are about my own ancestors and some people I remember. But you were wonderfully patient to listen so attentively.''

"My grandmother died less than three years ago," he said. "She could have outtalked your grandfather with no effort at all. I still miss her."

"You are kind," she said. "And he was so very pleased to discover that you could play chess. I have never learned. But it was such a very long game. I thought a few times that he had fallen asleep."

"A good chess player likes to spend time thinking out his moves and picturing his opponent's next move and his own next and so on," he said. "Your grandfather was a worthy opponent. I barely defeated him."

"But I am glad you did," she said. "He gets ferociously angry with me sometimes when he suspects me of deliberately allowing him to win at cards."

He smiled at her and watched the color mount her cheeks and her hands twist in her lap.

"But it was kind of you to spend the evening with us when you might have been at Lady Lawrence's," she said. "Grandpapa was happy."

"And you?" he said.

"And I was happy too," she said and looked down to the absorbing task of smoothing her dress over her knees.

"I have a Christmas gift for you," he said. "All day I have hesitated to give it to you. It is not quite proper for single ladies to accept gifts from single gentlemen, is it?"

Her eyes shot up to his, and she reminded him for a moment of Violet Cobban as she had appeared in his carriage earlier at the mention of Christmas presents.

"Oh," she said, "what is it?"

He smiled at her. "If I had had advance notice of the invitation to dinner," he said, "I might have brought wine with me with the greatest propriety, might I not? Will you accept a gift instead?"

"Where is it?" she asked.

"I remembered to put it in my greatcoat pocket," he said, "before sending my carriage home. My greatcoat is in the hall?"

She nodded.

He brought back the long package a few moments later and handed it to her. Her eyes sparkled.

"Oh," she said, "it is heavy."

He watched her unwrap it carefully so as not to tear the paper and perhaps to prolong the anticipation as he and his brother and sisters had always done at Christmas many years before—long ages before. And then he watched the stillness of incredulity on her face before she caught her lower lip between her teeth. And he watched her raise her emerald eyes to his.

"*You* bought it," she said. "That was why it was missing. I could have cried when it was not in the window yesterday." Tears sprang to her eyes as if to prove her point.

"You gazed at it," he said, "as if nothing in this dreary world mattered because there was Christmas and a mother and child."

She looked down at the porcelain Madonna and touched a finger to the chubby baby in its arms. Her finger was trembling.

"Oh," she said, "it is the most wonderful, wonderful thing I have ever owned. Thank you." And he watched a tear fall onto the back of her hand.

"Perhaps," he said, "when you look at it, you will remember this strange Christmas and the hap-

piness it brought to someone who had lost his faith
in happiness.''

She looked up at him, tears swimming in her eyes.
''But I have no gift for you,'' she said.

''Ah,'' he said softly. ''Then you will have to pay
a forfeit.''

''A forfeit?'' she said.

''Why did you hang the mistletoe there?'' he
asked, indicating the sprig hanging before the fireplace.

''Oh.'' She laughed breathlessly. ''It does not
seem quite Christmas without mistletoe and holly.
Grandpapa said to hang it there.''

''Go and stand beneath it, then,'' he said, ''and
pay your forfeit like the honorable gentlewoman you
are.''

She bit her lip again, and her cheeks grew pink.
But after a moment's hesitation, she stood the Madonna carefully on a table, got to her feet, and went
to stand beneath the mistletoe. She turned to face
the room.

He framed her face with his hands, feeling her
soft skin and her smooth hair. He watched her swal-
low, though her eyes did not flinch from his, and he
lowered his head and kissed her.

Softness and sweetness and subtle fragrance. And
warmth. And happiness. And home.

He lifted his head and smiled at her. ''Happy
Christmas, Julie,'' he said.

''Happy Christmas, my lord.''

''Darcy,'' he said. ''It is my name. Nothing so
ordinary as Richard or Robert or John when my
mother gave birth to my father's heir.''

''Darcy,'' she said.

''I love you,'' he said.

She shook her head. ''It is Christmas,'' she said.

"And it is the first one you have known for three years. It happens at Christmastime—warmth and happiness and love. It is wonderful, but it is not real life. Tomorrow you will feel differently."

"Now who is the cynic?" he asked.

She stared mutely back at him.

"I will not feel differently tomorrow," he said. "You may ask me when tomorrow comes. I love you."

She shook her head again.

"I want to marry you," he said.

She smiled and swallowed again and raised her hands to grasp his wrists. "You are an earl," she said.

"And so I am," he said.

"I am a clergyman's daughter," she said. "I work for a living."

"But no longer," he said. "Your only task as my wife will be to make yourself and me happy, as mine will be to make you happy. Marry me, Julie."

She shook her head. "There is Grandpapa," she said. "And Mr. and Mrs. Stebbins. I cannot abandon them."

"Oh," he said, and he drew back the length of his arms, though he still held her face in his hands, and frowned down at her. "I thought we could just marry and forget about them, Julie. They are just elderly folk after all."

"You would take them on too?" she asked.

"Of course I would take them on," he said. "Who else am I to play chess with except your grandfather? You have confessed to me that you do not play."

She bit her lip once more.

"Well?" he said, closing the gap between them again. "Julie, I cannot tell you all you mean to me. There are not words meaningful enough. I saw you gazing at the Madonna and had to cross the street to you. And then Charlie, bless his heart, chose that moment to attempt his quite inexpert theft and gave me the chance of a lifetime to speak to you. I have thought of you every waking moment since and dreamed of you every sleeping moment. I think you are the spirit of Christmas sent to release me from bondage. But I am greedy and want Christmas every moment of every day for the rest of my life. Don't cry.''

''I c-can't help it,'' she said, tipping her head forward to rest her forehead against his neckcloth. ''I turned from that window and saw you holding Charlie and raising your cane to hit him, and I was horrified. And then I looked into your eyes—those lovely blue eyes—and I knew you were not cruel. And I think my heart turned over inside me at that moment. I thought I would never see you again after we came out of the pastry cook's, but I knew I would dream of you for the rest of my life. And then the next day you were there again and coming to my rescue and insisting on walking all the way home with me.''

''I think it is settled, then,'' he said. ''I would accept no for an answer, you see, Julie, only if you did not care for me. But you do.''

''Yes, I do,'' she said, lifting her head again and staring up at him in wonder.

''The mistletoe must have been difficult to hang,'' he said.

''It was.'' She looked up at it. ''I had to balance a chair on a table. And grandfather and Mr. Stebbins kept giving me advice and declaring that they were the ones who should have gone up there. And Mrs. Stebbins had her apron up over her head and was calling on the blessed Lord to keep me safe. Which he did.'' She laughed merrily.

''Well, then,'' he said, ''it would be a shame for all that work to result in only one kiss, would it not?''

She looked into his eyes and blushed rosily again. ''Yes, Darcy,'' she said, ''it would.''

He took his hands away from her face finally and set one arm about her shoulders and the other about her waist in order to draw her against him.

''We had better put it to good and thorough use,'' he said. ''Do you think ten minutes, or even fifteen, would be sufficient to count for thorough use?''

''Yes,'' she said and laughed breathlessly. ''I think ten. Or perhaps even fifteen.''

He smiled at her, and the outer rim of his vision took in the mistletoe above her head and the log fire burning cheerfully at her back and the sprigs of holly decorating the pictures beside the fireplace and her grandfather nodding in his chair.

Christmas! There was no time quite like it to make a person believe in eternal peace on earth and everlasting goodwill among men.

''I love you,'' he said, and he lowered his head and opened his mouth over hers before she could reply. But she did not need to say the words. He saw them in her eyes and felt them in her body and tasted them in her mouth. Her arms came about him and held him close.

The old gentleman in his chair snored gently on and opened only one eye—and even that only partly and only for a moment—to satisfy himself that the silence meant what he thought—and hoped—it meant.

Julie was having her happy Christmas, bless her dear loving heart.

CHRISTMAS ROSE

by Marjorie Farrell

I

ON THIS COLD December night, not quite a fort-night to Christmas, Jonathan Holford, Earl of Meare, would have been quite willing to admit he was drunk. Not disguised, mind you. Not falling-down, unable to get up drunk, which was lucky on such an icy evening, but what he called "fizzy," a condition once removed from bosky. Unfortunately, it was a state with which he had become familiar over the last six months.

Getting fizzy meant that for a few hours each night he felt buoyed up. If not full of joie de vivre, he was at least not blue-deviled. Of course, the golden bub-bliness was gone by morning and he was left feeling as flat as left-over champagne, again fully aware of the failure of his marriage and by evening, driven again to seek escape with brandy or claret or what-ever was being served by his host.

A hitherto naturally abstemious man, he some-times wondered whether this mild beginning would lead to a progression in drunkenness, and to years of being tossed in cabs and sent home by his friends. He hoped not. But despite his worrying in the morn-ings when his mouth felt like cotton batting, he was incapable of turning down the one thing in his life that gave him a few moments of happiness.

On this particular evening a light snow was beginning to fall. The streets and sidewalks were slick, and Jonathan came close to falling down several times. "But I am not drunk, mind you," he announced to the lamppost which had saved him. "Just fizzy." He bowed and continued on his way, slipping and sliding as he turned the corner into Grosvenor Square.

Almost all the houses along South Audley Street were dark, for most of Lord Meare's neighbors were long gone into the country. As he passed by one house and then another, he pictured Lord and Lady Boxborough decorating the halls of their Sussex home with their grandchildren, and Sir Hubert Barrand and his lady seated before a cozy fire in Kent, Lady Barrand with her feet up, rounded belly covered by a cashmere shawl. Even Major Downing. a self-declared bachelor, was gone to Bath to be with his sister and her family. He had left two days ago, his carriage piled high with presents for his nieces and nephews.

And there, down at the end of the street, was the residence of Jonathan and Madeline Holford, Lord and Lady Meare, who had remained in London for the past two Christmases. Who had started their married life with every reason to believe they would only become happier with each other. Who now could hardly bear to be in the same room together. Who were childless.

Theirs had been that rare thing, an arranged marriage that was also a love match. Their families' estates in Somersetshire marched together, and they had been expected to wed for years. Jonathan was older than Madeline by a few years, and she had worshipped him, tagging along every chance she got. Luckily for both of them, Jonathan's absences at school and then his short stint in the Peninsular campaign enabled both of them to question what they had for years taken for granted. Jonathan's fancy was captured by more than one dark-eyed Spanish beauty, and during Madeline's first Season she was an overwhelming success and had her heart interestingly bruised by a tall, handsome, totally ineligible viscount.

They were also lucky that both sets of parents were eager but not desperate for their match. Neither Jonathan nor Madeline felt badgered, and indeed, Madeline knew that had the aforesaid viscount been eligible or interested in marriage, her parents would have approved the match. Reluctantly, perhaps, but they wanted her happiness above all things.

But when Jonathan walked into Lady Sedgewick's ball, the first ball of Madeline's second Season, dressed in full regimentals, his golden hair bleached almost white by the sun of Portugal, Madeline took one look at him and thanked God that Viscount Richmond's father had gambled away the family estates. There he was, the friend of her childhood, looking so familiar and yet so strange, and utterly desirable.

And Jonathan, who had not seen Madeline for two years, was just about to have himself introduced to the stunning brunette when he realized that the statuesque beauty was no other than his long-legged, formerly skinny neighbor. All his plans to speak to his parents about his desire to seek his own bride went completely out of his head.

It took only two weeks for them to announce their betrothal. Society agreed that it could hardly be called a whirlwind courtship, since their engagement had been expected for years. But it was very romantic, wasn't it, when two such well-matched young people were also clearly head over heels for each other.

They were the golden couple of the Season, and for three Seasons after that. While neither sat in each other's pocket, it was obvious from the expression on their faces when one or the other walked into a room, that their love had not faded at all. They had everything: love, health, beauty, and happiness. They had everything but children.

At first it had not mattered. After all, not every couple produced children immediately. And so, for the first few years, Jonathan and Madeline stood the teasing and then the sensitive questions from their friends and family good-naturedly. And if there was a direct relation between physical pleasure and conception, as Jonathan remarked one morning after a particularly passionate night, we would be the parents of a baker's dozen.

After two years of marriage Madeline visited the family doctor in Somerset. After three years, a specialist in London. And during the fourth year of their marriage, she tormented Jonathan and herself by either swallowing or applying any and every folk remedy recommended by women from the Duchess of Devonshire to any old woman she encountered in London or the country.

At the time Jonathan had not thought he could stand it. But at least they had still been talking and making love. At the oddest times, perhaps, and in the most ridiculous positions and hardly spontaneously, it was true, but they had still shared a bed. And now he looked back on what he had thought of as a year of torture with something resembling nostalgia.

After that he had felt utterly helpless. Madeline clearly felt a failure as a woman. He had tried to reassure her again and again. And he tried to laugh her out of her sadness by pointing out that at least she would never lose her figure or her sleep, that his cousin would make a perfectly competent earl when the time came, and wasn't his love enough for her? Nothing worked and Jonathan began to doubt his own abilities as a husband. Surely she couldn't love him as much as she claimed if he wasn't enough for her. And from time to time he wondered if it were possibly some lack in him. . . . But of course not. Everyone knew that childlessness was the fault of the woman.

By the fifth year of their marriage they hardly ever made love. At first Madeline had just cried through Jonathan's lovemaking, not wanting to give up trying, but utterly hopeless about the outcome. Then she just lay there silently. It began to seem to Jonathan that he was raping his own wife, although she was willing enough, and so he stopped initiating contact. As soon as he did, the physical side of their marriage was over.

They kept up appearances as well as they could, but it soon became clear to the *ton* that the Holfords had gone the way of many another couple, into polite indifference. Jonathan was punctilious in his attentions to his wife, but spent all the time he could with his friends and the occasional willing widow. His flirtations were never more than that, though no one would have believed him, including Madeline.

Madeline, who had had only the normal interest in gossip, fashions, and flirting, became obsessed with them. Her natural companions, under any other circumstances, would have been friends of her own age. But all her friends had become mothers, and the main topics of their conversation was their children. And so she frequented the company of the faster ladies of the *ton,* those who had no interest in family or children and left them to their nannies and nurses. A few years ago Madeline had watched these women from afar, wondering how anyone lucky enough to have children could desert them. Now, she was so dead to her old self that she was happy to have found a group of friends whose concerns were utterly frivolous.

Neither husband nor wife questioned the other. They went together to most occasions, but returned separately, often in the early hours of the morning. For the past two years they had not shared a bed, had not had a real conversation, and were each privately convinced that the other had taken at least one lover.

They spent every Season in town. During the summer, of course, they were at Meare, but for the past two years, they had remained in London for the holidays. Neither had offered reasons beyond "Not wanting to miss the Cross soiree, you know," or "The traveling being so tedious at this time of year." Both knew that it would have been unbearable at Meare, with Madeline's brothers and sisters there with their children. They always received invitations from friends, but consistently refused, knowing that a Christmas with a happy family would be impossible. And so, during the holidays they increased their socializing, Madeline flirting madly and ever on the verge of finally giving way to one of her devoted followers, and Jonathan getting slightly drunk, as he was this night.

Afterward he wondered if he had had one glass more whether he would have missed it altogether. At first as he made his way down his street, walking slowly to keep his balance, the snow falling more thickly, he had his eyes only on the pavement in front

of him. His buoyant mood was fading, and a fall
would have no longer amused him. When he saw the
woman, he only thought how odd it was for a laundress to be leaving her basket on the front steps. He
had passed the house in question before it struck him
as more than odd that on a cold and snowy night—
or make that early morning—a woman would be delivering laundry. To the Barrand home, moreover.
The Barrands had been in Kent for ten days.

The woman was almost out the front gate by the
time he turned around. When he got closer, he could
see she was no laundress. She was wearing a dark
red velvet cloak trimmed in what looked like er-
mine. No working woman would be dressed like
that. But neither would a lady. The cloak was far too
flamboyant for a lady. But then what was a woman
from the demimonde, for so she must be, doing here
on South Audley Street, delivering laundry?

Jonathan put his hand on the gate, holding it closed
so she could not get out. She looked up in surprise
and alarm, and he could make out her face under the
street lamp. She was a good-looking woman, and
younger than she looked under her powder and paint.

"Let me out, sir," she demanded.

"I will let you out when you have given me a
satisfactory explanation," Jonathan answered. "Just
what are you doing here?" He could see the basket
on the steps, gathering snow. Perhaps she was a thief
and had left the basket for a co-conspirator in the
Barrand home. There was always a skeleton staff of
servants left behind, but as far as he knew, they were
all trustworthy. But suppose there was someone new,
whom he didn't know, who had decided to take advantage of their employer's absence?

The woman glanced back at the basket and the
worry on her face when she turned to Jonathan was

very real. But she should be worried, he thought, if she was intending to rob the house.

"I cannot tell you, sir. Please let me out."

"I am going to call the watch, but first we are going to see just what you have in that basket." Jonathan pushed his way in, grabbed her arm, and marched her to the steps.

At first when he looked in the basket he thought it *was* laundry. For there was a mound of blankets. The snow had accumulated on the inside as well, and the woman leaned down and carefully brushed the mound clean.

Jonathan was still thinking theft and wondering if the woman had already been inside the home and the basket was piled high with silver wrapped in the family linens? Maybe she was leaving it for an outside accomplice?

He leaned down and started to jerk at the linens, when the woman grabbed his arm.

"Please, sir. She'll freeze to death if you do that. I swear I will tell you everything."

"She?" Jonathan knelt down and tugged more gently at the coverings, and there she was, not a silver tea setting or a priceless bit of porcelain, but a baby, sound asleep.

Jonathan stood up and almost bellowed, "What on earth is going on here? Whose child is this?"

"Hush, sir, hush, you'll wake the household."

"Not to mention the baby," he added sarcastically.

"No, she will sleep for a few more hours," the woman replied. "I gave her a small dose of laudanum."

"I *will* have the watch and see you arrested, you heartless whore." Jonathan was horrified at the thought of a drugged baby abandoned to freeze on a *ton* doorstep.

Tears fell from the woman's eyes and froze on her cheeks. "*Please* listen to me."

"You have a minute to explain. If I am not satisfied, you will find yourself in prison within the hour."

"I am a whore, sir," she began in a dignified tone. "Or I was," she continued. "I started out in a brothel five years ago, but I was one of the lucky ones. I was pretty, and I could speak well, and a gentleman, a regular customer, took me out of there and set me up as his mistress."

"A common story, I suppose," muttered Jonathan.

"Oh, no, sir," the woman answered bitterly. "Not common enough. If it were, so many young girls wouldn't be dying of the pox. No, I was one of the lucky few."

"I suppose you got pregnant?"

"I did, once before. It was his baby, but I knew he would leave me if I had it, so I . . . got rid of it."

Jonathan shuddered with distaste.

"We were together for a year after that, but then his family bought him a commission. I found out I was increasing just before he left, but this time I couldn't bear to get rid of it. I had come to love him, you see, and I wanted something of him, should he be killed. And I hoped, perhaps, he had come to love me."

Jonathan gave a derisive snort.

"Well, it has happened, sir. But he will be home within the week, and I all of a sudden realized I have been dreaming. No gentleman marries his mistress, much less claims his child. I had to find a place for her. I had hoped that a good family might take her in and raise her as their own. I can't keep her, for we would both be out on the street, and what good would that do her?'' the woman ended in bitter, but determined tones.

''And just who did you think was going to pick her up off the steps? Lord and Lady Barrand have been in Kent for over a week. Didn't you see that the knocker is off?''

''But I saw lights in the back of the house. I never looked at the front door.''

''They have left a few servants here, but I hardly think you could trust them not to abandon the baby to the parish.''

The woman leaned down and picked up her daughter. ''What can I do then,'' she whispered, holding the baby close. ''If I keep her, I lose him and any chance of a good life for her anyway. I'd be back on the street within days. Oh God, what will become of us?''

Jonathan suddenly and completely believed her. She was a bit mad, he thought, of course. But who wouldn't be under the circumstances. Only a mad or panicked woman could have thought that leaving a baby on a Mayfair doorstep would mean adoption into the family!

''How old is she?'' he asked, for want of anything comforting to say.

''Almost seven months.''

''What will you do now?''

''I don't know, I don't know,'' the woman moaned, rocking the baby to comfort herself. ''Isn't there anyone else home on this street?''

''General Drummond's widow. But she's in her eighties and not likely to take in an infant.''

''But what about you, sir?'' the woman asked desperately. "You are still in London. Surely there must be others still in town?"

"My wife and I are still here because we have no . . ." Jonathan stopped. He was either madder than this woman or drunker than he had thought. Surely he couldn't be thinking . . . ? "It *is* a girl, you say?"

"Yes, sir. Rose, because she always reminded me, from the very first, of a pink rosebud."

"Let me see her."

The woman clutched the baby tighter.

"Please," said Jonathan gently, "I am not going to hurt her. I just want to hold her for a moment."

She passed the bundle over, and Jonathan pulled open the blankets. Long, silky black eyelashes over perfectly rounded cheeks. A little lock of brown hair protruding from under her wool cap.

"What color eyes does she have?"

"I beg your pardon, sir?"

"What color are her eyes?"

"Blue, sir. Dark blue."

"Hmm . . . well, there are enough blue eyes on both sides of the family."

"Why, no," said the woman. "I have blue eyes from my mother's side, but my father . . ."

"I meant my family and my wife's."

"Oh, sir, could you . . . would you?"

"You don't even know me, woman, and you are willing to leave your daughter with a drunken stranger?"

"Not drunk, sir, merely a little bosky."

"I can assure you not even a little that," said Jonathan wryly. "Suddenly I am perfectly sober. And quite likely a madman, not a drunk. Would you let me have her? It will mean never seeing her again, you know," he added gently.

"I knew that already."

"My wife and I have never been able to . . ." Jonathan's voice broke.

"I understand sir. Some men can't."

"I believe the problem is my wife's," he informed her.

"Yes, sir, of course sir," she reassured him, thinking of the whores she knew who had gotten pregnant as soon as they changed protectors.

"It has been a great disappointment to us. Indeed, it has affected our marriage. But if your daughter were found on *our* doorstep . . . ?"

"Oh, God bless you, sir."

"I am not doing it for you, but for my wife."

"But what if she doesn't want Rose?"

"Then I promise you I will send her into the country, where she will be cared for by a tenant's family. Of course, then she would not grow up as a lady, but she would be well-cared for."

"I want what is best for her, that she be in no danger of the street. Of course, she is a lady because of her father, which is why I came here, to give her that chance, but above all, I want her safe."

Jonathan gently placed the baby back in the basket. "All right then," he said. "I will carry the basket to our steps and pretend to have tripped over it. I will wake up my wife with a great deal of drunken amazement and then see what transpires. If she responds to the baby, we will keep her. If not, she will go into the country, as I promised."

"I hope she stays with you, sir. Perhaps you need her as much as she needs you." The woman held out her arms. "May I have her just for a minute?"

Jonathan hesitated, afraid that she meant to take her back, and was surprised at how naturally his arms tightened around the baby.

"I only want to say good-bye, sir."

"Of course," said Jonathan gently. The woman turned her back on him, and he could see her whispering and crooning to her daughter and then saying good-bye in a tear-choked voice. He had tears in his own eyes by now, for he had begun to appreciate the magnitude of the sacrifice.

"Here, sir, take her, and God bless both of you." The woman thrust the baby at him and was down the steps and out the gate before he could stop her. "And I don't even know her name," he thought. Well, he'd not want to see her again, after all.

He looked down at the small bundle in his arms. The baby was still sleeping soundly and didn't move when he placed her back in the basket.

"All right, little Rose, we are in this together, so don't betray me."

He carried the basket clumsily down the street, wondering how the woman had handled it. Presumably she had taken a hansom cab.

When he reached his own house, he stood outside the gate for a moment. He was much later than usual tonight, and so he assumed his wife was already in bed. The servants would also be sound asleep. He would have to make quite a racket to wake anyone, and he wished he were still drunk. He had, however, gained some renown at Oxford for his amateur acting, and he hoped his talent had not deserted him.

He banged himself against the door, cursing and swearing in a loud voice and calling for their butler, and then began to bang with his hand.

He could hear the household stirring. And then he heard his wife's voice, demanding to know what the dreadful racket was and why that drunken reveler hadn't been turned away from the door.

Jonathan was about to beat the knocker once more

when the door flew open and he lost his balance and almost fell in. There was their butler, Stoughton, his throat, which had been sore for a few days, wrapped in goose-grease-coated flannel, his feet thrust into floppy slippers, holding a candle before him.

"My lord!"

"Yes, it is I, Sshtoughton, but what is this, I want to know." Jonathan leaned against the doorjamb as though he needed its support and pointed to the basket.

Stoughton looked and shook his head. Unfortunately the flannel was wrapped so tightly that he only started coughing.

"Stoughton, what on earth is going on?" Jonathan heard his wife coming down the stairs, and then, there she was, in her blue silk wrapper, her hair all around her face, and God, how he wanted her at that moment. Had wanted her hopelessly for the past two years. By now, however, he was into his role of a drunken sot of a husband, and he decided to play it to the hilt.

"You may indeed ask what is going on," said Jonathan, in the tones of an affronted drunk. "I have come home and almost killed myself over this laundry basket. It is a miracle I didn't break my shoulder," he whined, rubbing his left one. "I expect my wife," he continued with drunken dignity, "*not* to leave our dirty laundry out for everyone to see."

Madeline's face flushed with anger.

"You are drunk, sir!"

"Oh, and why not, when I have a wife who cares nothing for her own husband. I wonder what secrets this dirty laundry holds? I will investigate," he added wisely.

It was fun to be acting again, he thought, as he watched his wife's color drain from her face. He was so tired of being so damned understanding, so damned cool. He had wanted to know if she had been unfaithful for months now, but had played the fashionable husband. Now, in a way, he was being more himself. Which was the better acting job, he couldn't have said.

He mock stumbled and leaned over the basket, making it look like he was ripping apart the covers, but in truth, being careful not to disturb the baby. There she was, little Rose.

"My God, what is this?" Stoughton and his wife were immediately by his side, gazing down in wonder at the contents of the basket.

"Jonathan, wherever did this baby come from?"

"Why, I imagine where all babies come from, my dear."

Madeline grimaced and turned to their butler.

"Stoughton, as you can see, Lord Holford is foxed. Could you get him inside and see that he gets some strong coffee into him immediately. I will take care of the basket."

Stoughton grabbed Jonathan by the arm and led him in, Jonathan protesting all the way that he was not really foxed. "Of course not, my lord," murmured the butler, leading him down to the kitchen.

Madeline stood bemused for a moment, looking down at the little face which peeped out of the cocoon of blankets. It took her a minute to realize that it was snowing and that the snow and cold were beginning to penetrate her light wrapper. And fall on the baby's face. She dragged the basket through the door, expecting the child to wake up at any moment.

Once the door was closed, she lifted the baby out and brought her into the drawing room. She placed the child on the sofa and sat next to her. Who on earth would leave a baby on their doorstep? And whatever would they do with it?

Reporting it to the authorities was of course the logical thing to do, she decided immediately. Perhaps it had been kidnapped. No, more likely abandoned. How could any woman abandon a child on such a cold night, she wondered. How could any woman lucky enough to have a child not want it?

The baby's cheeks were getting pink, and she realized how well wrapped it was. Clearly it had not been abandoned to die in the cold, she thought as she began to loosen the flannel covers. And the little white wool cap that she slipped off the baby's head had been hand-crocheted and threaded with pink velvet ribbon. And there were little pink roses embroidered on it. Someone had loved this child. And someone had lost this child, whether purposely or through some criminal act, she didn't know.

Madeline reached out a finger and traced the round cheek. How could a baby sleep through all this commotion, she wondered, and then worried. She leaned over and smelled the baby's breath. A faint trace of the sickly sweet smell of laudanum remained.

Madeline felt rather than heard someone come up behind her. "This poor baby has been dosed with laudanum," she announced without turning her head.

"Most likely so it wouldn't cry," said her husband.

She turned to look at him. His hair was disheveled and his eyes bleary, but he looked almost sober.

"Do you have any explanation for this, Jonathan?" she demanded.

"Explanation? I fell over the basket. I am sorry for making such a racket, but I was a little drunk."

"More than a little, sir. Whatever shall we do?

We shall have to call the authorities,'' she sighed, almost to herself.

"The authorities?" Jonathan had not thought of this as a possible response. He had hoped she would fall in love with the baby immediately.

"Jonathan," Madeline explained, slowly, as though she were talking to the child on the sofa, "someone, we don't know who, has left a baby on our doorstep. Some mother out there might be frantic."

"Or relieved. Did you think of that?"

"I have, although I cannot believe that a mother who would go to such pains to embroider tiny roses and thread expensive ribbon through her baby's cap would abandon it."

"Maybe she couldn't take care of her?"

"Her?"

"The baby."

"We don't even know if it is a boy or a girl," Madeline realized.

"Well, you did say embroidered roses. Hardly likely to be a boy," replied Jonathan. He had better be careful.

"A very drugged little girl. I think, in addition to calling the authorities, we should call a doctor."

"In the morning, my dear."

"It *is* the morning, Jonathan. You were out almost all night."

"Well, but it is too early to drag a constable or doctor here."

"Doctors and constables keep early hours, Jonathan. Please send a footman out. I will wait here until the baby wakes up."

The doctor, when he arrived, concurred with Madeline's diagnosis. "Laudanum. Probably given to keep the child quiet. But other than that she looks like a perfectly healthy baby to me,'' he continued. ''She will be a bit groggy when she wakes up, but if you have any other concerns, don't hesitate to call me.''

An hour after the doctor left, the baby began to stir and finally opened her eyes. They were a deep blue, and Madeline, who had looked down just at the moment they were opening, felt something stir in her that she thought was dead. All the longing for a child which she had buried under her frantic social activities, was suddenly back, stronger than before, and she reached down, picked the baby up, and held her on her lap. She ran her hand lightly over the baby's head, which was covered with fine, silky brown hair, and then touched her round cheek. The little one turned and reached up her arms, and Madeline lifted her up to her shoulder, where she nestled in, sucking her thumb.

And so Jonathan and the constable found her there on the sofa, sitting upright, as though not quite used to this new role. The baby's head lifted as they came into the room, and Madeline turned, real fear in her eyes as she saw who accompanied her husband.

''This is Constable Durham, my dear. I have told him the whole story.''

''Good morning, my lady. That's a fine fat baby you've had dumped on you.''

''Do you think she was abandoned then, Constable? I was afraid she might have been stolen away.''

''We have no kidnapping reports, my lady. Indeed, the kidnapping of babies is not one of your common crimes. Abandoning children unfortunately is. This little one is lucky she landed on your doorstep. Or any doorstep,'' said the constable, thinking of the numerous babies he had found dead in such places as dust heaps and abandoned buildings. "I would say that the mother hoped she would be well taken care of."

"I was just telling the constable that if the child were not claimed, we would both make sure of that, Madeline. I was thinking of sending her to the Coopers." Jonathan turned to the constable. "One of our tenants, Constable. A good family." Jonathan had decided that the fate of the little girl *must* depend upon Madeline. She must be the one to want her, while he raised objections. He was too afraid, given the state of their marriage, that if it were his idea, for that reason alone she would reject it.

Madeline's eyes opened wide at the thought of the Coopers. Her hand automatically went to the baby's head, to cradle it and hold her closer.

"They would surely make fine parents," she replied slowly. "When would we be sure, Constable, that she is ours . . . or could be theirs?"

"I'll put the word out today, my lady, and if we haven't heard anything in a day or two, I'll let you know."

"Thank you, Constable. That will give us time to discuss what the best plan would be for the baby."

"Of course. I will be taking my leave, then."

Jonathan showed him to the door and then returned to his wife. "She is finally awake, I see, Maddy," he observed.

"Yes, although she seems quieter than a baby this age should be."

"What do they do at six or seven months?" asked Jonathan without thinking.

"However did you know she was that old?"

"Well, uhm, I have observed your sister's children, as well as our friends'. And didn't the doctor tell us she was about that?"

"Did he? I suppose he did. Well, I think she can sit by herself, can't you sweetheart?" Madeline placed the child on her knee while gently supporting her back. The baby gazed placidly around her.

"Do you not think that the Coopers would make good parents?" asked Jonathan, holding his breath.

"Jonathan . . ." his wife began hesitantly.

"Yes? Do you think that the Gunns would be better? But they have four of their own already."

"How would you feel . . . what if we kept her?" His wife's voice sounded softer than it had in years.

"How could we keep her?" he asked, trying to sound surprised. "How could we tell people we have adopted a child who was dropped on our doorstep? Who knows who her mother is? Probably some whore."

"Her mother must be a loving, caring one, whatever her . . . profession. She could as easily be an upper servant or shop girl as a whore, Jonathan. And she left her on our doorstep. Perhaps she knew of us in some way. Maybe she knew we had no children of our own," continued Madeline softly.

"Are you seriously suggesting we take this child in as our daughter?"

"Couldn't we say that some little-known relative named us as her guardian? Don't you have a distant cousin in the West Indies?"

"Yes, but it is hardly likely that he would have sent us his child in the middle of winter!"

"Oh, then, we'll make someone up, for God's sake. I want to keep her, Jonathan," said Madeline firmly. She would not beg, Jonathan knew. She would not let herself be vulnerable.

"I'll ask Henshaw if he can dig up some forgotten relative from the family tree, if you are sure you want to do this."

"If she had been a boy, we couldn't, Jonathan, and I'd understand that. But there is no question of inheritance here. And it would seem to be our only chance to become parents."

"All right, Madeline, if you are sure. We'll engage a nurse immediately."

"A nurse? Oh, yes, of course. But she can sleep in my room until we find someone appropriate."

"Do you think that wise, Madeline? After all, you will be coming in late at night, and babies get up quite early in the morning?"

"Oh, for a night or two I can cancel my obligations."

"Of course, my dear. Whatever you wish."

Miracles do not occur overnight, even at Christmas time, Jonathan knew. But as he watched his wife over the next few days, he saw a slow but steady transformation. Madeline canceled her engagements for three days until they found a suitable nurse and opened up the small bedroom they had set aside as a nursery years before. She kept most of her afternoon commitments, but instead of coming home late from a shopping trip laden with ribbons and reticules which she did not need, Madeline came home early so that she could be there when the baby awoke from her nap and give her the brightly painted blocks that she had purchased.

One afternoon, almost a week after the baby had arrived, Jonathan went up for a nursery visit himself and found his wife stretched out on the floor in front of the baby, who was on her stomach batting at the block towers Madeline was building and laughing delightedly when she managed to knock one down.

Madeline looked up at her husband and gave him the first genuine smile he had had from her in years.

"She is such a bright little girl, aren't you?" she cooed. Jonathan sat cross-legged on the rug and constructed a few more towers which the baby again knocked down. He reached over and pulled her in front of him so that she was sitting up, and he gave her a block. She had a hard time getting her chubby fingers around it, but she did and brought it immediately up to her mouth.

"She has two teeth, don't you sweetheart? Show your papa."

Jonathan felt a thrill go through him as Madeline continued her cooing and baby talk. He was sure his wife wasn't aware of what she had said, but the fact that she had said it meant they were on their way to becoming a family. And if they were a family, then surely they could again be husband and wife. He stuck his finger in the baby's mouth, and she clamped down hard.

"Ouch! She certainly does have teeth!"

"Oh dear. Well, you have to get your finger in between them, Jonathan, or you will get bitten," Madeline giggled.

Jonathan turned the baby around and put her on his knee. "This is such a small nursery, little one." He began bouncing her gently. "How would you like to visit the country for Christmas?" The baby began to smile and then gurgle. "You would like that, wouldn't you? A bigger room? And a yule log?" He bounced her higher, and she crowed with delight. He turned to his wife.

"What do you think, Maddy? We could pack up and be there in time for Christmas Eve. Or do you prefer to stay here with your friends?"

"I think that our daughter has convinced me that she would be happier at Meare. My friends will not miss me."

"Then I'll send Stoughton ahead and tell him to help Mrs. Rogers start cleaning and decorating."

"And how will we explain the baby to my parents, Jonathan? I have been putting off writing. It is one thing to lie to the *ton,* but quite another to ask them to be grandparents to a foundling."

"We will tell them the truth, Maddy. And they will not be able to resist her, our little pink Christmas Rose, will they, Miss Rosie?"

"Why, that is the perfect name for her," exclaimed Madeline. She looked just like a little rosebud in her basket. And perhaps it was her name. Maybe that's why there were rosebuds embroidered on her cap."

"Well, Rose she is. Lady Rose Holford of Meare," announced Jonathan to the laughing baby.

They managed to arrive at Meare two days before Christmas. The servants there had been told the same story as those in town: the master and the mistress had adopted a second cousin's child. The only ones who knew the truth were Stoughton and the footman who had gone for the constable, and they were sworn to secrecy.

The house had been turned inside out and the nursery was spotless. And all week hired boys from the village had been out cutting greens, and the house looked and smelled like an evergreen forest.

The weather had been dry and cold, and Madeline shooed the nurse who was carrying Rose ahead of her into the house. Mrs. Rogers was there to greet them, of course, as were some of the servants. The others had placed themselves strategically so that they could catch a glimpse of the baby. They were all hoping that the little orphan would prove just the thing to bring the master and mistress the happiness they seemed to have lost.

Mrs. Rogers had taken Rose from the nurse, and when Madeline and Jonathan got inside she was lifting her up to let her bat at the mistletoe hanging in the main hall.

Madeline looked around her. The smell of fir and pine reminded her of the Christmases of her childhood. She had shut those memories away when she had realized she would never be recreating them for her own children. But one whiff had opened the door to that closed room, and all the anticipation and excitement from the past returned.

"You have done a splendid job decorating, Mrs. Rogers," said Jonathan.

"Thank you, my lord. And the nursery is ready for the baby."

"Rose, Mrs. Rogers. Lady Rose," replied Madeline, reaching her arms out for the little girl. "Let me take her up, Jonathan, and get her settled, and then we can have our supper."

"It will be served within the hour, my lady."

"Thank you, Mrs. Rogers." Madeline hurried up the main staircase, murmuring to Rose about her new room, which was "ever so big."

"She is a lovely child, my lord," said Mrs. Rogers.

"Yes, isn't she? We were lucky my cousin died, although that is not quite the way I meant to put it," replied Jonathan with a rueful smile.

"And you had no idea at all that you were named guardians?"

"None at all. She just . . . ah . . . arrived on our doorstep, in a manner of speaking."

"Well, she has come to a good family, lucky child," said Mrs. Rogers.

"I think so, Mrs. Rogers. I think so too."

Of course they had to visit Madeline's parents the next day. Both the baron and his lady were speechless with surprise as they were introduced to their new grandchild.

"But Madeline," her mother said when she had found her voice. "Wherever did she come from?" She stopped, confused and embarrassed.

"We are telling people that she is the orphaned daughter of one of Jonathan's far-flung cousins, and he was made guardian in the will."

"You are *telling* people?"

"Yes, Mother. The truth is . . ." Madeline thought she had been prepared to tell them, but all of a sudden it seemed so preposterous. And what if they couldn't love Rose the way she herself was beginning to?

"The truth is," said Jonathan, quite calmly and matter-of-factly, "that she was left on our doorstep. We thought it only right, however, to tell you the truth."

"On your doorstep?" said Madeline's father. "Why she could be anyone's child!"

"We know she was not kidnapped, Father, for we had a constable investigate. But you are right—there is no way of knowing who her mother was, except that she was a good one."

"A good one, to abandon her child!" exclaimed Lady Mansfield.

"The baby's clothes were clean and well made, and she wore a little hat that was hand-crocheted and hand-embroidered. And she left her with us, and not on some ash heap. And we are going to keep her, Mother," finished Maddy in a rush.

"Well, well, she seems a healthy enough child, Dorothy," said the baron to his wife. "And it is a little girl. No question of her inheriting the title. And we have wanted another grandchild.'' He pulled out his watch and dangled it in front of Rose, who smiled and grabbed it and put it directly in her mouth to start chewing it.

''You'd better take it back, Father, or you will have her teeth marks all over it,'' protested Maddy.

''Then they will just join her mother's,'' said the baron with a smile. ''This was one of your favorite toys when you were little Rose's age.''

They all watched the baby teething and drooling for a few minutes, as though it were quite the most intelligent thing she could be doing, and a few tears slipped down Madeline's cheeks. It felt as though some pattern had been made complete, something made whole, as Rose added her teeth marks to her mother's. At that moment Maddy realized she *was* a mother. Unconventionally, suddenly, and miraculously, a mother.

That night was Christmas Eve, and after an early supper Rose was sent up to bed so that Jonathan and Madeline could wrap her presents. She had needed a whole wardrobe, of course, but Madeline hadn't been able to resist a silver teething ring and an exquisitely dressed French doll.

''She'll break her, you know,'' said Jonathan as she unfolded the tissue paper and showed it to him.

''For now, she will only be to look at.''

''Good, because I got her this one.'' He pulled out a soft rag doll with yellow yarn hair and bright red cheeks and mouth.

''Oh, Jonathan, she looks . . .''

''Like a tart. I know, I know,'' he said with mock despair. ''But she is soft, unbreakable, and the only one they had left in the store.''

They both looked at each other and started to

laugh. It was the first time they had laughed together in a long time, and it closed the distance between them better than anything else could have done.

"Oh, Jonathan, this is so much fun," said Madeline when she was finally able to stop giggling.

"It is, isn't it?"

"Of course, she won't know what it is all about anyway, but she'll love tearing the paper." Madeline stood up, her arms full of ribbons and paper. Her cheeks were flushed and her eyes bright, and Jonathan thought she had never looked so beautiful.

"She will have a lovely Christmas. Her first."

"That is right. It is her first, and it will be with us. She won't remember, of course, but somehow, it is important to me."

Jonathan got up and moved over to his wife.

"Madeline."

"Yes, Jonathan?" Just as she looked up, Jonathan leaned down and kissed her gently on the lips. Her eyes opened in surprise.

"You are under a bunch of mistletoe, Maddy," he said, unwilling to let her know that she could have been standing under a bunch of straw for all he cared. He couldn't have stopped himself, for she looked so much like the old Maddy, the girl he had married.

"Oh." Madeline blushed. The kiss had been quick and light, but it had awakened memories of their first kisses. She had not wanted Jonathan to touch her for so long, for his touch and her response had reminded her of the uselessness of their loving one another. Other men had kissed her over the years. Some of their kisses she had enjoyed, some not. But she had never gone further than those kisses, whatever the gossips had thought. But now she both wanted and was afraid of wanting Jonathan's kiss. What if it was merely a whim?

"I had better go up," she said, her voice shaky. "Rose wakes early, and I want to see her face when she sees all the presents." Madeline turned and hurried up the stairs.

Well, thought Jonathan, that kiss, quick as it was, was the first physical contact they had had in years. Perhaps it was the beginning of something better.

Christmas morning dawned clear and cold. Rose was up with the sun, and the nurse brought her into Maddy's room just as she had been instructed. Madeline was sitting up in bed with one of Rose's presents beside her.

"Just put her here next to me, Nancy."

The nurse plopped Rose down, and Maddy handed her the package.

It went into her mouth, paper and all, of course. Madeline laughed. "No, no, Rosie. It *is* for chewing, but first we must unwrap it." She helped pull the paper off, and Rose's eyes got wide with delight at the shiny silver teething ring. "And listen," said Madeline, "there are some lovely beans inside that make it rattle." Rose grabbed for it and chewed on it contentedly. "Shall we wake your papa?" Maddy asked, almost without thinking. "He has something for you too."

Madeline knocked at the connecting door, and Jonathan groaned.

"Are you awake, Jonathan?"

"Now I am," he muttered into his pillow. "Yes, Madeline. Is something wrong?"

"No, no, Rose wanted to show you her present."

"Bring her in."

And so Rose and Madeline came in and perched

on his bed. Both looked delightfully tousled and informal. ''Now where is Papa's gift for Rosie?'' asked Madeline.

''Right here.'' Jonathan reached over the side of the bed. ''Here you are, sweetheart. Right into the mouth, paper and all!''

''Of course. It seems to be what they do at this age.''

Jonathan retrieved the package and removed the paper. He held the rag doll up in front of Rose. ''Good morning, Lady Rose,'' he said in falsetto.

Rose dropped the silver ring and put out her hands for the doll. She patted its cheeks and pulled its hair and immediately started chewing on an arm.

''Oh, poor Miss Jones,'' said Jonathan.

''Miss Jones?''

''That's the way I think of her. Miss Jones, no better nor she should be,'' said Jonathan with a twinkle in his eye.

Madeline hit him playfully. ''You are terrible, Jonathan.''

But Miss Jones she remained. Miss Jones came to breakfast with them and watched while Rose mushed her scrambled eggs with her fingers. Miss Jones came to church with them and then came out of church with Jonathan and Rose, who had started to cry at the first Christmas carol. Jonathan felt like one in a long unbroken line of papas carrying their infants out before they disrupted the service. Miss Jones came to Grandma and Grandpa's with them for dinner. And Miss Jones, that night and every night, went to bed with Rose. And indeed, after a week, Jonathan announced that Miss Jones was beginning to look much more respectable, as her paint began to wear off a little. It was just as well, for respectable or not, Rose would not go anywhere without her.

On New Year's Eve, after Rose fell asleep, Madeline joined Jonathan by the fire. They had made some visits during the day, and he had been dressed in his blue superfine. But she noticed that he had changed into buckskins and corduroy. He looked so handsome sitting there, quietly drinking brandy by the fire, that she felt a sharp pang of longing. She missed his arms around her, she missed his kisses, and most of all, she missed their lovemaking. But she didn't know whether he did. There were all those widows, after all.

"Why have you changed, Jonathan?"

"It is New Year's Eve, Maddy. The night for wassailing. I thought I'd go up to the apple orchard with everyone."

"Oh, Jonathan, I had forgotten. Can I come with you?"

"Now, Madeline, remember the trouble we got into the year you got caught!"

"Well, I was only twelve! I'm a grown married woman now. Surely I can do what I like."

"You'll have to change," warned Jonathan.

She was down in ten minutes, dressed in a worn gown and with an old woolen cloak thrown over her. She had tucked her hair into an old woolen cap, and her eyes were bright with excitement. Jonathan realized he hadn't seen her look so alive in a long time.

It was a cold night and there was frost on the ground, so Jonathan reached out and grasped her hand as they walked over the uneven grass to the orchard. Most of their neighbors were there before them, carrying pine torches and guns and bearing

buckets of cider. They gathered around the oldest of
the apple trees, one whose main branches were as
thick as a man's body, and formed a large circle,
and Maddy and Jonathan were separated by the jos-
tling, good-natured crowd. Old Jared Cooper started
them off, his bass voice booming out as they began
to circle the tree:

> "Old apple tree, we'll wassail thee
> And hoping that thou wilt bear
> The Lord does know where we shall be
> To be merry another year.
>
> To blow well and to bear well
> And so merry let us be
> Let everyone drink up his cup
> Here's health to the old apple tree!"

As they circled round, Madeline felt herself a part
of a whole larger circle. Generations and generations
of villagers had sung this song and poured their cider
into the ground around the tree to make it rich and
fertile, and so the trees would bear, even the oldest.
Any other year she would have been reminded of her
barrenness. But this year, with Rose, she felt a part
of it all, and she threw her head back and shouted
with them, feeling the last of her bitterness leave her
with the yelling and the shooting.

There was, of course, a jug of apple brandy that
did *not* get poured on the ground, but passed around.
She and Jonathan drank their share and by the time
they had joined hands to return home they were both
"fizzy" but with drink or joy they could not have
said.

Jonathan did not let go of her hand even when they
were inside the house. They stood there in the hall,

hands linked, smiling at one another, the loving feeling of their shared childhood returned to them.

"Jonathan."

"Yes, Maddy?"

"Perhaps you didn't notice, but we are standing under mistletoe."

"Oh." He just stood there. Maddy stood on tiptoe and pulled him down for a kiss.

"Maddy."

"Yes, Jonathan?"

"We could go on kissing here, but it would be much warmer upstairs?' Jonathan ended with a question in his voice.

Madeline tugged at his hand and led him upstairs. "Your room," she whispered. "In case Nancy brings Rose in early."

They dropped their clothes on the floor and crawled under Jonathan's comforter. Suddenly they were as shy as newlyweds. Jonathan leaned over and kissed Maddy long and hard. She slid underneath him and ran her hands over his body.

"Oh, Maddy," he groaned, and buried his face in her shoulder. She could feel him getting hard against her, and all of a sudden she wanted him, wanted him for his and her pleasure alone—not to make a baby, not to make her feel like she had accomplished what women were supposed to—just to feel him slip inside her and bring them as close together as it was humanly possible to be. She reached down and lightly brushed him with her fingers and he seemed to himself and to her to grow even bigger.

Their first coupling was quick and fierce. It had been so long for both of them that neither could wait. But they made love twice more that night, each time more slowly, as both realized that they had years ahead of them to enjoy each others' bodies again and again.

By the time morning came, neither could tell where one left off and the other began. Her pleasure became his pleasure, and they both smelled and tasted of one another. At one point, in fact, Maddy had licked the sweat off Jonathan's shoulders, and he had turned over and touched each breast, lifting the nipples gently with his tongue. She had pulled him close, wrapping her legs around him, and that had started off another round of lovemaking.

As the sun rose, Jonathan looked down at his wife, who was cuddled close into his body. He gave the top of her head a kiss, just to see if she was awake. She turned in his arms and smiled up at him.

"Oh, Maddy," he said without thinking, "I have missed you so much these past few years." He wished he could take the words back almost immediately, for they revealed so much to her. And she had seemingly done very well without him.

"Have you, Jonathan? Even when you were making love to your widows?"

Jonathan smiled a wry smile. He was already in, he may as well go all the way. "I never did make love to any of those widows, Maddy. Oh, I kissed a few, but that is as far as it went." The closeness between them was so precious and new that Jonathan had no desire to question his wife along the same lines. He didn't want to know the truth; nay, he didn't care, now that he had her back.

Maddy was silent a moment. "Aren't you going to ask me about Lord Wrentham or Sir Humphry?"

"Whatever happened between you has happened already. I don't need to know."

"You are the more courageous in loving, Jonathan," confessed Maddy. "I was afraid to tell you how much I had missed you. And my pride may not have let me admit that nothing happened between me and my cicisbeos. Oh, sometimes I wanted it to happen, but just when we were at a dangerous moment something made me stop. I think I still had some hope, buried down deep, that our marriage could return to what it once was."

"And what about that hope now, Maddy?" Jonathan asked gently, pushing back a lock of her hair with his finger.

"Oh, Jonathan, I couldn't have you touch me, I couldn't feel like a wife to you and feel such a failure as a woman."

"Madeline, I never felt you were a failure. And I have been thinking lately . . . That is . . . Perhaps sometimes it is the man who is at fault?"

"Let us not even think of it again. We have Rose now. I am so grateful you let me keep her."

"And I am so happy you wanted to, Maddy." He glanced out the window, where the sun was shining on the frost-covered fields and trees, making the whole world sparkle. "Look," he said, and she turned her head. "It is a beginning of another year. I wish you a happy new year, my dear wife."

"Happy new year, Jonathan."

II

If it had not snowed, if she had not taken Rose out into the garden to see her first snow and make her a little snowman, if she had only sent Nancy out to look for Miss Jones, whom Rose had set down and forgotten in the excitement, if she had not been down on her hands and knees looking behind a bush . . .

If, if, if, thought Madeline as she sat stiffly on the edge of her bed, looking down into the garden.

But she had gone out herself, for as she had told Nancy, "I'll find her quicker." And she had been on her hands and knees for a moment. Just the moment when the scullery maid came out to empty dirty water from the sink and get a quick hug from the stable lad, who just "happened" to come along. Madeline had stayed there, so as not to embarrass them. She had smiled at their little rendezvous and then decided that she had better speak to the cook since it wouldn't do to have Mary Ann in the family way. She was cold, crouched there, but not as cold as she felt when she heard their conversation.

"It be a mortal shame, what you told me, Jeffrey."

"Aye, well, but these things 'appen, luv."

"But to pass your own child off as someone else's . . ."

Madeline wondered whom they were talking about. She felt ridiculous on her hands and knees, but knew she would feel even more so if she got up.

"I never told anyone, Mary Ann, so don't you go spreading the word. Lord 'Olford is a good master, and men understand these things better."

"But you saw 'er talking to 'im on the step?"

"It were snowing, like last night. I 'ad come out front because I 'eard a noise. And there they were, next door, with the basket between them."

"Do you think it were 'is 'ore?"

"She were a 'igh class one, from what I could see of 'er cloak."

"And then she left, and 'e pretended to be drunk. A banging on the door and saying as 'e tripped over the basket."

"So Lady Rose's mother were the master's light-skirt?"

"So I would surmise, Mary Ann," Jeffrey said solemnly.

"Well, what do you think of that. And 'er lady-ship not suspecting a thing. Shameful."

"I dunno. They been 'appier this year than in a while, hit seems to me. So maybe it was all for the good."

Mary Ann gave him a quick kiss. "I 'ear the cook calling for me. Tomorrow then?"

"Tomorrow, luv," Jeffrey said with a wink. "And you remember to keep your mouth shut."

Madeline then would have found it quite easy to have crouched there forever, turning herself into an oddly shaped hedge or piece of topiary. But she forced herself to get up and stumbled back to the house, numb with cold and with what she had over-heard. She handed Miss Jones to Nancy and told her to put Rose down for her nap.

"Won't you be joining us for a cup of chocolate, my lady? You look so cold."

"No, thank you, Nancy. I think I will go up for a nap myself."

And so here she was, looking out at the frozen garden and the end of her marriage.

This past year had been happier even than the first years of their marriage. They had come through the hard times, they had been tested, and their joy in one another was much deeper than it had been at nineteen and twenty-four. And Rose? She was what had brought them together. And now it seemed she would tear them apart.

How could Jonathan have lied like that? How could he have expected her to take in his bastard? How could he have lied about their years of estrangement? Only kisses indeed! Although, thought Madeline ironically, maybe he was telling a half-truth. Maybe he *had* done no more than kiss his widows, because he had a whore to do the rest with.

And Rose! Somehow it had not bothered her, who Rose's mother was. She could make up any story she wanted: that she was a poor seamstress or a shopgirl. Or even a governess. The child of a good woman who had stumbled once. Not the child of a fallen woman, who once down, never got off her back and, moreover, one who had had Jonathan!

What was she to do? She had been feeling unaccountably tired and ill these past few weeks. At the moment she was so utterly exhausted by her discovery that she was surprised her blood was still able to move through her body.

She would just leave them both. Let him raise his bastard alone. Let him explain to the society why his wife suddenly left him. She would go home to her parents until she decided where to live for the rest of her miserable life.

She pulled out a valise and threw in the first clothes that came to hand. She summoned a footman and ordered the coach readied for the trip to Somerset. He appeared surprised, but quickly straightened out his features and obeyed her bidding, wondering all the while why the mistress, who was standing there so wide-eyed and pale, was on her way to Mansfield alone.

Madeline decided to take one last look at Rose. She made her way to the nursery, almost unwillingly, and sent Nancy off downstairs.

There she was, their Rosie, lying peacefully, the ever-faithful Miss Jones in her arms. Miss Jones's face had faded over the year, so she finally appeared respectable. A gentlewoman down on her luck, rather than a successful tart, Jonathan had commented a few months ago. Madeline choked a sob back and truly looked at Rose. How could she leave her? She loved her, whoever's child she was. And why should Jonathan have her? He was the true villain in all of this. Rose was *her* daughter, no matter who had conceived her. She scooped her up, murmuring softly to keep her sleeping for a few more minutes. At least she had a child from this marriage. Jonathan would have nothing, which was what he deserved.

When Jonathan returned home, he immediately went up to the nursery. It was his custom to have a cup of tea with Maddy while Rose was having her own supper, and then he joined in on the prebed rituals. When he got upstairs, he was surprised to find the nursery dark and deserted. No sign of Rose, Maddy, or the nurse.

He was puzzled, but not overly concerned. Something must have kept them later than usual. Probably Maddy had told him their plans while he was engrossed in his newspaper. He went down to the library, pulled out a book, and settled in to wait for them.

When they had not returned over an hour later, he began to worry, and summoned the butler.

"Stoughton, I am sure whatever her engagement, Lady Holford would not keep Rose out this late. Did she say where she was going?"

The butler looked down at the carpet, as though trying to discover an answer to the question there. "I believe Lady Holford said she was going to Mansfield, my lord," he finally answered.

"Mansfield? Whatever do you mean, Stoughton?

Of course she wouldn't have gone to Mansfield. We are not leaving for the holidays for another ten days.''

"Nevertheless, she summoned the coach, and she and Lady Rose and Nancy left three hours ago.''

Jonathan was speechless. Why in God's name would Madeline leave like that? And without telling him? He might have been absorbed in his newspaper this morning, but an announcement like that would have gotten his attention.

"I see,'' he finally replied, although he didn't, not at all. "Well, then, tell Cook I will dine within the hour.''

"Yes, my lord.''

Belowstairs, of course, was buzzing.

"I can't imagine why Lady Holford would leave like that,'' said the cook as she was sitting down later to eat her own meal. "Why this past year they have been happier, I wager, than ever before. It just doesn't make sense.''

Mary Ann could not resist the opportunity to become the center of attention. "I bet I know why she left.''

"Oh, go on, Mary Ann. You are hardly her ladyship's con-fee-dante,'' drawled James, the first footman, in his most irritating way.

"She left because the master fobbed 'is bastard off on 'er, that's why,'' she said, with a triumphant smirk.

"Wherever did you get that idea, Mary Ann? The baby was left to them by a distant cousin.''

"What if that's what his lordship wanted us to think? What if 'e and 'is 'ore set the 'ole thing up?''

"Enough of your lying gossip, girl,'' said the cook, brandishing her spoon. "You'll scrub the pots twice tonight.''

"I ain't lying. Jeffrey *saw* them. Call 'im in and ask hif 'e didn't.''

"And so I will, to end this once and for all,'' replied the cook. But when Jeffrey repeated his story reluctantly, it was so convincing that there was dead silence at the table.

"You never told the mistress this, did you, Jeffrey?''

"Go on. I never come within ten feet of 'er. And from what I know of 'er, I like 'er.''

Mary Ann piped up. "We was talking about it out in the garden this morning. I didn't see nobody, but maybe somehow she 'eard us.''

"We certainly don't know for sure, but I think she must have,'' said Stoughton after a moment's thought. He had been sitting quietly, hoping that Mary Ann would be discredited. Who would ever have guessed that Jeffrey had been a witness last winter? "I think I will have to tell his lordship.''

Mary Ann blanched. "Oh, no, Mr. Stoughton. 'E'll turn me out, and my family needs the money I give them.''

"Lord Holford is not that sort, Mary Ann. Although it would be no less than you deserve, for spreading this gossip.''

"I'll tell 'im, Mr. Stoughton,'' said Jeffrey. "Arter all, it were me as saw 'im.''

"Yes, perhaps you should come upstairs with me, Jeffrey, and we'll ask to see him. And the rest of you,'' said Stoughton threateningly. "If I hear one word gets out of this house, I'll sack you all.''

Jonathan was surprised by Stoughton's knock, but let him into the library, followed by one of the stable lads.

"Good evening, my lord,'' said the butler.

"Good evening, Stoughton. And, Jeffrey, isn't it? Is there something wrong with one of the horses?"

"Jeffrey has something to tell you that we think will cast some light on Lady Holford's precipitous departure," said Stoughton at his most formal.

"Yes?" asked Jonathan, unable to think of anything a stable lad would know.

"Er, yes, sir, I mean, yes, my lord. You see, I were talking to Mary Ann this morning."

"Mary Ann?"

"The scullery maid, my lord. We are a bit sweet on one another," admitted Jeffrey, blushing to the roots of his hair. "And I were telling 'er . . . this is 'ard, my lord. It isn't that I don't respect you, and I 'ave never, never told anyone else, but I wanted to impress 'er, you know."

"Yes, Jeffrey, get on with it," said Stoughton impatiently.

"I told Mary Ann I 'ad seen you and your . . . er . . . lady friend the night Lady Rose arrived. You were a' talking on the steps next door, the basket between you. So I told Mary Ann I thought Lady Rose was your . . . yours. And your lady friend's," he added almost inaudibly.

"But whatever does your mistaken gossip have to do with Lady Holford's departure?" asked Jonathan. "And you *are* mistaken, Jeffrey."

"We think, my lord," said Stoughton, "although we are not sure, that Lady Holford might have overheard their conversation. She *was* in the garden this morning, *that* we do know."

"Oh my God." It hit Jonathan full force. Maddy had left him, and nothing else would have made her leave. She *must* have overheard the wretched stable lad's gossip.

"Stoughton, get Jeffrey out of here before I do

something I will regret later, like sacking him.'' Or killing him, thought Jonathan, as the two left.

What had Maddy thought? That he had asked her to raise his whore's child? That he had lied to her about those painful years of abstinence? What else could she think? She might have asked me, he thought. She might have trusted me. He was both distraught for her and furious at the same time.

Well, it was an accurate account he thought bitterly. Jeffrey was not lying, only misinterpreting. There I was, talking to that woman, and Rose lying between us. What else was he to think? And I suppose I am lucky that he seems to be loyal enough not to have spread it all over town. Maddy would not have as quickly believed town gossip, Jonathan knew, but a conversation overheard by accident would hold weight.

He would leave early in the morning and let Stoughton close the house behind him. He would get there and tell Maddy the truth, and all would be well between them again, he was sure. She would be a little upset when she heard he had practiced a small deception. But surely it was not such a bad thing, to have wanted her to want Rose?

The two women had spent a miserable night in an inn. Maddy was unable to sleep at all and Rose was restless and irritable, having sensed her mother's distress. They arrived at Maddy's parents' past midday and were greeted warmly, but with surprise.

''Please don't ask me yet why we are here, Mother,'' Maddy begged. ''Let me get Rose down for a nap, and I will join you for tea and tell you everything.''

But Maddy never came down, and when her mother went up to look for her, she found her daughter curled up next to Rose. "Looking like two children, with that silly Miss Jones between them," she told her husband. "And I know she had been crying."

Lady Mansfield went back up an hour later and sat quietly, waiting for her daughter to awaken.

"Mother. . . ?" asked Maddy, surprised when she was awakened by her mother's presence in the dark room. "What time is it?"

"Time to get up, Maddy and tell me why you are here," answered Lady Mansfield quietly.

Maddy pulled herself up, careful not to disturb Rose, and straightened her dress. She found she could not look at her mother and tell her story, so she gazed at the floor as she told her of Jonathan's deception.

Lady Mansfield listened carefully. "And when you spoke to Jonathan, what was his explanation?"

"I didn't wait to speak to him. Why would I need to? This wasn't *ton* gossip, Mother. Those two did not know I was there, and what reason would a stable lad have to lie?"

"Still, there may be some other reason Jonathan was talking with the woman."

"What other reason than that they were conspiring to have their . . . child introduced into the household?"

"It does look that way, Maddy," her mother said and continued thoughtfully, "But what difference, in the long run, would it make? We all assumed Rose's mother was no better than she should be, and we all love her, knowing that."

"Mother," said Madeline, lifting her eyes to her mother's face, "you do not know what it is like to be a childless woman. To have tried, month after month, year after year. It has been hell, and it contaminated our marriage. But at least, all that time, in some way Jonathan and I were suffering together. Neither of us could produce a child, or so I thought,'' she concluded bitterly. ''But now, to think that he succeeded, that he was able to have one with another woman and then fob her off on me . . . I can never forgive him.''

''And Rose?''

Madeline looked down at her sleeping daughter and said quietly and vehemently, ''She is my daughter, no matter that he is the biological parent. I tried, but I could not leave her behind.''

Her mother rose and extended her hand. ''Come, let us go down and talk with your father. You know that Jonathan is sure to come after you?''

''Let him,'' said Maddy, her voice so cold that a shiver went through Lady Mansfield.

By the time Jonathan arrived the next day, the baron and Lady Mansfield had decided that they would not involve themselves in the quarrel beyond giving Maddy and Rose refuge. Lady Mansfield was inclined to sympathize with her daughter, and Lord Mansfield with Jonathan, but both decided not to discuss it further between themselves. They concentrated their attentions on Rose, who toddled about, delighted to be with her grandparents, and delighting them with the range of her vocabulary.

Maddy went for a long walk in the afternoon and had just taken off her cloak when Jonathan rode up the drive. She looked beautiful, her cheeks flushed with exercise and cold, and as Jonathan shrugged out of his greatcoat, he had a hard time holding on to his anger at her willingness to believe what she had heard and to run off without even giving him a chance to explain.

Madeline sent the footman off immediately to order some tea for herself and Lord Holford, but as soon as he left, Jonathan looked at her and said, "No tea, Maddy. No polite rituals until we have spoken. Is Rose here with you?"

"Of course. Where else would she be?"

"I don't know. You left me no word at all, so I have been worried."

"Worried that I would abandon your bastard the same way her real mother was supposed to have done?" Maddy's eyes were blazing with anger.

"Madeline," Jonathan said, controlling his voice with great difficulty, "we are not going to talk about this in the hall. Come into the library, please."

Madeline turned on her heel and having walked down the hall, flung open the door to the library. Jonathan followed and closed it gently after them.

The room was chilly, for it was in the east wing of the house and had had no sun since morning. There was a fire in the grate, but it was almost out, so Jonathan calmed himself by adding a few logs and stirring it up before he turned to face his wife.

"I know why you left, Maddy," he said quietly. "But you at least owe me the chance to explain."

"How do you know?" she asked, tight-lipped. Now that she was facing him the only way she could keep herself from weeping was to hold on to her anger.

"Evidently, Mary Ann, the scullery maid, offered her explanation of your departure in front of Stoughton. He got the whole story out of her. *Were* you in the garden?"

"Yes. I was looking for Miss Jones, and I overheard them."

"And believed a stable lad without question, without even asking for my side of the story?"

''What reason would he have to make it up? Had he come to me directly, I might have thought about blackmail. But he has kept your secret for a year, so he is clearly loyal and only trotted it out to impress his 'lady.' He *saw* you with her, Rose's mother and your . . . whore.''

''Yes, he did see me with Rose's mother,'' Jonathan said quietly.

''There, you don't even bother to deny it!'' Maddy sank down on the sofa. A wave of exhaustion passed over her, and she suddenly felt quite sick. She had believed the stable lad, but somehow had been hoping that Jonathan would deny everything.

''There is nothing to deny, Maddy. I came home late that night, and just as I was almost at our door, I saw a woman leave a basket on the steps next door.''

''But the Barrands were out of town.''

''Yes. Which is why I stopped and asked what she was doing. She told me her story, and all of a sudden I thought of our taking the baby. But I wanted *you* to want her. So I lied about tripping over the basket. I had no idea anyone saw me. But that was the only thing I lied about, Maddy. Surely you can forgive me, since it brought us Rose?''

''If I believed you I could forgive you, Jonathan. But I do not believe you. What was such a woman doing in our neighborhood? And how did you persuade her to give the baby to us? It is a preposterous story.''

''It may be preposterous, but it is true, nevertheless. She was desperate. Her lover was on his way home from the war. She would have lost him, her home, everything. She was afraid of the street. And so she hoped a rich family would do something to provide for her child.''

"I am sorry, Jonathan. They say appearances are deceiving, but in this case, I believe the appearances. You were her lover, you fathered her child. I am willing to grant you had kind intentions, but the fact remains that you were able to become a father with your mistress, and you wanted your barren wife to raise your child."

Jonathan was furious. "How can you think that of me? I could never act to cause you such pain. And I have had no mistress, I've told you that."

"You told me no *widows*. You didn't say anything about whores."

"I am not that sort of man, Maddy, and you know it."

"Why should I, Jonathan? Men have needs. And most men have their needs met, one way or another, especially if they are not sleeping with their wives."

"And women don't have needs?" replied Jonathan. "You did not miss sharing my bed? That is not the impression I have gotten this past year. And yet I believe you when you tell me you never went with any of your admirers."

"I am sorry, Jonathan," Maddy said as calmly as she could. "I am staying here with my parents. I am keeping Rose. You have not convinced me that your story is true."

"And what *would* convince you, Maddy, if not my word," Jonathan replied bitterly.

"The word of Rose's mother. That should not be too difficult to obtain, should it? Or is she another man's now?"

Jonathan would never know what kept him from shaking or striking his wife at that moment. He thrust his hands into his weskit, ripping both pockets with the force of his anger, and let her go out the door. He knew her anger came from the pain of betrayal, just as his did, and he didn't want to do anything to irrevocably separate them. Although how he would ever convince her, he didn't know. Find one whore amongst the thousands in London? Impossible!

Jonathan spent the night at Meare. The servants were in the process of cleaning and decorating for the holidays, and Jonathan could not help remembering the happiness of last Christmas. He rode over to Mansfield in the morning, but Madeline refused to see him, and so he left directly from there for London. All he could think of during his journey back was the night he had met Rose's mother. Had there been anything, anything at all that she had said that would help identify her? Her lover had been in the army and had been away on campaign for at least a year. He was presumably Rose's father. Rose had been about seven months old when they had gotten her, her mother could have been breeding two or three months without him guessing . . . so that could put him on the Peninsula from October or November of 1810 to last December. Of course, thought Jonathan, thousands of other men were there too, so how this could help him find her, he didn't know.

He took the problem to bed with him that night and in the morning spent hours in the library trying to remember every detail about that snowy night. Had she spoken any names at all? Had she given any clue?

She had clearly not been a street whore. As a gentleman's mistress she would have been set up in her own house. There were only a certain number of areas in the city where men set up such women, so that narrowed things down a bit. But what was he to do? Tramp the streets, knocking on the doors of love nests until he found her? Think, Jonathan, think. There must be a better way.

The house felt so empty and cold around him, despite the fires in every room and the servants going quietly about their duties. Without Rose and Maddy it felt like a mausoleum. He missed his daughter's energetic curiosity, her babbling that made more and more sense every day, her smiles, and her chubby arms lifted up to him in the morning. In a few days it would be Christmas. It was to have been their first real Christmas together as a family, for last year they were barely used to being three.

Jonathan heard a quiet knock at the library door and said, "Come in."

Stoughton entered apologetically. "I am sorry to disturb you, my lord, but it is impossible not to be aware of your . . . troubles, particularly since someone under my supervision caused them."

"Don't blame yourself, Stoughton. It could just as easily have been a servant from next door who saw us. To give credit where credit is due, Jeffrey held his tongue all this time when he could have made us the laughingstock of society. If there is loyalty in this household, we owe it to you."

"Thank you, sir. May I be so bold to ask whether you will be here for the holidays or will be going to Meare?"

"Lady Holford has returned to her family, as no doubt you have guessed. Unless I can convince her that I'd never seen Rose's mother before, she will, I fear, seek a formal separation. And I don't know how to find the confounded woman, damn it." Jonathan groaned and put his head in his hands.

"I, er, have a suggestion, if I may propose it, sir," said Stoughton after a moment or two of sympathetic silence.

"Go right ahead, Stoughton," said Jonathan, lifting his head and giving the butler an ironic grin.

"Why don't you call in a runner, sir?"

"A runner?"

"Yes, sir. The runners go anywhere they are needed. They get paid, of course, when they are on private business."

"Hmmm. And do you think a 'robin redbreast' could find Rose's mother?"

"If anyone could, my lord."

"You may be right, Stoughton. A runner would have his informants, wouldn't he? He could cover the ground much more quickly and efficiently than I could," said Jonathan, feeling a small stirring of hope.

"I could send a footman down to Bow Street for you."

"Yes, why don't you send George, Stoughton. And thank you," added Jonathan with such strong feeling that his voice shook.

"No need to thank me, my lord. We all want to bring Lady Holford and Lady Rose back where they belong."

While Jonathan was trying to remember anything he could about Rose's mother, Maddy was becoming more and more miserable. After the first flash of anger she was left with only a heavy sadness. She slept late and left Nancy to take care of Rose. She most certainly did not want Jonathan to have their daughter, but she found it difficult to be with the little girl and not look for some likeness to her father. Aside from the blue eyes, she could find none, but assumed that the resemblance would emerge as Rose grew older, and then how could she stand it?

Lady Mansfield was so delighted to have her

granddaughter for a long visit that her attentions more than made up for Maddy's neglect. And Rose was so excited to be in a new place with all the holiday hustle and bustle that, for the moment, she seemed not to notice Maddy's absence.

A few days after they had arrived, however, Lady Mansfield sent her husband up to bed early and sat down with her daughter in the drawing room.

"Madeline, you cannot go on this way. It is not fair to Rose."

"What do you mean, Mother?"

"You are ignoring her."

"I have spent time with her every day we have been here," protested Maddy.

"Yes, a short amount of time during which you hold yourself quite aloof. The child is not responsible for her birth, Madeline," her mother reminded her.

Maddy's eyes filled with tears at her mother's reproof.

"I know, Mother. But I feel so . . . I don't know, so far away from everything. I keep looking at Rose, searching for something of Jonathan. And I keep imagining what her mother must look like."

"Do you love Rose?" her mother asked quietly.

"How can you even ask that, Mother? Of course I do."

"Then whatever the circumstances of her birth, whatever you feel about Jonathan, you must continue to show her that love."

"I know," sobbed Maddy. "I hope I will be able to."

"You will, my dear. And what about Jonathan?"

"What about him?"

"Do you intend to seek a separation? There will be gossip, which will affect Rose. Would it not be better to find a way to live with this revelation and to return to him? Especially now.'' her mother continued gently. ''Maddy, I have been wondering if you could possibly be carrying his child?''

''What! Whatever do you mean, Mother. You know I am unable to conceive.''

''I also know that you have been very tired. That you have eaten little these past few mornings. And that you have thrown up what little breakfast you have tasted, according to your maid. I have borne three children, my dear. I know the signs.''

''It is impossible. Of course my stomach is upset. The last few days have been very upsetting. It is the heartache and shock that are making me tired and sick.''

''I don't think it impossible, Maddy. I have known, over the years, a few women who conceived after years of barrenness. And I have an old woman's feeling that you are sick because you are increasing. It is a shame that it may happen after all these years, and we cannot be rejoicing.''

Madeline sat very still. It *was* true that her menses had not occurred recently. But that had happened before over the years, leading to false hopes and bitter disappointment. And her tiredness? Well, it did go back to before finding out about Jonathan's deception. But surely her sickness was only because of the state of her nerves? She passed her hand lightly across her belly. It was flat, of course. If what her mother suspected was really true, she wouldn't show for months anyway. Oh, but how could it be true now, after all these years of waiting. Now, when she hated Jonathan more than she thought it possible for her to hate anyone.

George came back from Bow Street with the news that a runner would wait on Lord Holford by the next day. Jonathan was in the library when he was announced. "Send him in, Stoughton."

A moment later the door was pushed open and in walked a mild-looking man, sandy-haired, pale, and holding a leather hat in his hand. He looked to be in his late thirties, Jonathan guessed from his face and receding hairline. He was not attired in the distinctive blue coat and trousers and the scarlet waistcoat which Jonathan had expected, and had he not known his identity he would have guessed him to be a clerk.

"Gideon Naylor at your service, my lord."

Jonathan rose and motioned the runner to sit by the fire. He himself took a seat opposite.

"I understand it is possible to acquire the services of a runner like yourself for a fee?"

"Yes, my lord. A guinea a day as a retainer."

The runner spoke with a slight west country accent. "You are not originally from London, Mr. Naylor?"

"No, my lord. From Somersetshire."

Jonathan smiled. "Then we are fellow west-countrymen, Mr. Naylor. What brought you to London?"

"I was a soldier, my lord. After I resigned from the 47th foot, I landed in London. I had no family left in Somersetshire and no knack for anything but soldiering, so I joined up with the runners. I've been with them for over fifteen years."

"You don't look like what I expected, Mr. Naylor. I thought you would be in uniform and . . . bigger. More threatening."

Naylor grinned. "Only patrol members wear uniforms, sir. And some of us look more like pugilists than others, my lord. As for me, I've found meek and mild as good an appearance as any. It lulls suspicion, it does. And a few times it has saved my life,

I might add. The element of surprise, you know. But I assure you, my lord, I've grabbed my share of flash coves and murderers.'' Naylor patted his pockets. ''And I know how to use these.''

Jonathan hadn't noticed the bulges under his coat until they were brought to his attention.

''You won't need your pistols for this job, Mr. Naylor. I only need you to find a woman.''

The runner lifted his eyebrows inquiringly.

''A whore. Well, not really a common whore. A gentleman's mistress.''

''Her name, my lord?''

''That is exactly the problem. I do not have a name,'' Jonathan confessed and told Naylor the story.

''She never mentioned any names at all, my lord? Try to remember.''

''I've been racking my brains for the past week. Do you think it is hopeless?''

''Well, not hopeless, exactly.''

''We *do* know that her lover was on the Peninsula. We know she wasn't a common streetwalker or in a high-class brothel. She had been set up in her own house. Surely that would narrow the search. . . ?''

''To a few hundred,'' said the runner with a grin.

''Oh God,'' groaned Jonathan in despair.

''Now, don't let's give up hope, my lord. We can assume it was her lover's baby?''

''I think that is a safe enough assumption. From what she said, I gather she had been set up and well-taken care of in his absence.''

''So, we are looking for a young woman in Kensington. Or maybe Chelsea. Who had been set up in a house or lodgings. Who had an officer . . . we can assume an officer since she claimed he was a gentleman, as a protector . . . who lived alone from. . . ?

"Let me see. Rose was almost seven months last Christmas. That would make her birthdate around May. Say her mother was three months along when the fellow left. That makes it a year ago last November. Who will even remember that far back?"

"If we are lucky, my lord, the gentleman came back, resumed his protection, and she hasn't moved. The fact that he was away for a time and that she did give birth would make her stand out in a neighbor's mind. It may take a while, but I'll start my inquiries right away."

Jonathan's face lit up. "Do you really think there is any hope?"

"Some, my lord. Some. I've had less information to go on and still found my man. Or woman," he added with another quick grin.

"I don't suppose . . . I know this is ridiculous to ask. . . . Could you find her by Christmas?"

"Five days, my lord? Well, if it can be done, I will do it."

"Thank you, Mr. Naylor. I can't tell you how much this means to me."

"I think I can guess, my lord," said Naylor.

But as soon as he left, Jonathan's confidence in him seeped away. He summoned Stoughton. "How did George come to hire Mr. Naylor, Stoughton? Do you think he is capable? He is so ordinary-looking."

Stoughton smiled. "George told me he went into the Garrick's Head for a pint after speaking with the officer in charge. He overheard someone talking about Naylor. It seems he is one of their most courageous officers. He has been in more than mere hand-to-hand confrontation, evidently. They said he was like the famous MacManus, 'mild with the mild, terrible with the terrible.' "

"Mild I can believe. It is the terrible part . . ."

Stoughton grinned. "I think you can rest assured, my lord. He'll do his best for you."

"He has to be able to do it better than I, at least," admitted Jonathan.

While Jonathan and Maddy suffered through the week, Naylor quietly and patiently went about his investigation. He was a slow and methodical investigator, for the most part, who, from the outside could appear plodding. What outside didn't show, however, was that his patient disciplined turning of every stone was a technique he practiced to quiet his quicksilver intelligence, so that intuition would have time to surface. He had found, from years of experience, that mysteries were not solved by the rational mind alone, but also by hunches. And so he liked to keep the rational mind at bay by keeping it busy through a go-by-the-book search, while giving his intuition complete freedom.

He patiently blocked out a number of neighborhoods where gentlemen tended to keep their ladies, and he visited each in turn, making inquiries of the neighbors and tradesmen. He also had a number of informants whom he contacted to help in his search. It took him three days to cover the neighborhoods he was interested in, where first inquiries had brought nothing. On the fourth day, he was in the Garrick's Head himself, enjoying the company of a few out-of-work actors. He considered himself an actor at times, considering the disguises he had utilized occasionally, and he enjoyed listening to all of them talk about makeup and costume and method. Several of them who had gotten him drunk once or twice and made him show them one of his characters had been amazed at how so neutral a countenance could be transformed. He had the required plasticity, they agreed, and could have become anyone: a toff, the lowest of flash coves, and even an old woman. Gideon Naylor disappeared and reappeared. That same intuition which enabled him to enter the mind of his prey also enabled him to enter a disguise wholeheartedly. On this night he only listened and drank, letting the ale and tiredness slow his brain. He glanced out of the window occasionally, watching the traffic go by. And at last, by the time the fourth hansom cab passed, he knew. Oh, not who she was. Or exactly where she was. But he knew if he revisited the streets of Chelsea and questioned the cab drivers that he would find someone who remembered driving an increasing woman home, or perhaps bringing the local midwife to her house. He bade his friends good night with a sleepy smile and made his way to his own lodgings.

The next morning he was up early and out before the baker's rolls had been brought out, their delicious fragrance stealing from beneath the green baize wrapping. He went immediately to Sidney Street and began reexamining the neighbors, who were once again sorry, but couldn't remember. Some few obviously couldn't. The rest, of course, didn't want to get involved. That was true in every case, and it didn't discourage him. Finally, just before noon, he came upon a hansom cab driver who not only had one of the few functioning memories on the street, but who was willing to talk.

"For a price, gov'nor. For a price. For 'ow do I know what the lady's gentleman will do to me hif 'e finds out I knew all along she 'ad become a mother? I could a told 'im, of course. But I likes Marie, I really do, and so I sacreeficed my own gain, I did."

"I admire your loyalty," said Naylor, quite seriously, for he knew how tempting it would have been for an ill-paid cabby. "But you need not worry that you will bring harm to Marie by this. Her lover need never know. I am not here to end a liaison, but save a marriage."

The cabby gave him Marie's address, which was two streets over. It was next to a haberdasher whom Naylor had already questioned, and who had already twice denied knowing the woman. Naylor gave a smile of exasperation and knocked on Marie's door.

"Is your mistress at home?" he inquired of the maid who answered his knock.

"Yes, sir," she said, eyes wide in fear at the sight of a runner.

"Please tell her that Gideon Naylor of Bow Street wishes to see her."

"Yes, sir." The young woman scurried off, leaving Naylor in the hall. It was a very nice house, as love nests went, he could see. Not luxurious enough for her patron to be an earl or duke, but whoever the officer was, he had done well by her.

The maid reappeared and led him into the parlor. "My mistress will be right down."

Naylor only had to wait a minute before a very pretty young woman appeared at the door. She was dressed less flamboyantly than he expected, but then, it was daytime. Her paint and powder was tastefully done, and the perfume she was wearing was pleasant, not cloying.

"Mr. Naylor?"

"Yes, madam."

"Has there been a crime in the neighborhood? Are you making inquiries?"

"No, not at all. I have come to see you."

She sat down and gestured him to a chair.

"I have been hired by Lord Holford, madam."

There was no change of expression on her face when he gave Jonathan's name.

"Lord Holford wishes to find the mother of his daughter. I believe her name is Rose," Naylor added gently.

Marie turned white. "Has anything happened to her? Does he not want her anymore?"

"She is in perfect health, from what I know. And he seems to consider her his own. No, it is that Lady Holford has been alienated from her husband by some gossip that only you can correct."

"Gossip? I can hardly do anything about society gossip, Mr. Naylor."

"It seems that the Holford's stable lad saw you on the steps with Lord Holford. He kept it quiet all this time and just dragged out the tale to impress a young kitchen maid. Lady Holford overheard and thinks that Rose is the child of a union between you and Lord Holford. She has taken their daughter to Somerset and is demanding a separation from her husband."

"I see. But surely she must have wondered who the child's mother was? Surely she should have guessed . . . she does *love* Rose?"

Naylor was surprised to find himself moved by the woman's concern. "You care about her then?"

"Of course. Why do you think I left her there. I wanted her to have a chance. Had I kept her, we would both be in the workhouse now," she answered passionately.

"Your officer never guessed?"

"No, and I am lucky to have good friends in the neighborhood who don't gossip. Those who aren't such good friends . . . well, I paid them off."

"Did he marry you?"

"What do you think, Mr. Naylor?"

"Likely not."

"He married someone his family picked out for him. But he is still my protector. I may have been wrong about the possibility of marriage, but he did and still does love me."

"So you have no regrets?"

"I have thought of Rose every day for a year," she said with tears in her eyes. "But no, as long as she is happy, I have no regrets."

"Will you come with me into Somerset?"

"Won't a letter do?"

"It seems that Lady Holford's conditions are seeing you and hearing the story from you."

"Will it make a difference to Rose?"

"I would think so, wouldn't you? She will have two parents again. And won't be reminding her mother of her father's supposed infidelity. Come on, luv, it will only be a day or two out of your life."

"All right, Mr. Naylor. I could be ready to go tomorrow."

"Tomorrow is the day before Christmas Eve."

Marie smiled a bitter little smile. "And Christmas is a time spent with wives and families, isn't it?"

"Of course. Can you meet me at eight tomorrow morning at Lord Holford's?"

"I will be there."

"Thank you, Miss de Wolfe." Naylor paused at the door as she led him out. "Miss de Wolfe . . ."

"Yes, Mr. Naylor?"

"I think you are to be greatly admired. It took courage to give Rose away."

Marie's eyes filled with tears. "Thank you, Mr. Naylor. No one has ever guessed how much it cost me."

Naylor placed his leather hat securely on his head and walked down the street. Marie watched him and

thought how odd it was that such a completely un-
prepossessing man was a runner. But then again, he
had found her!

The next day's journey to Meare was a quiet one.
Jonathan had greeted Marie kindly and had thanked
her for her help. She asked a few questions about
Rose, and he answered openly, with a father's love
and pride so clear on his face that Marie was again
reassured that she had done the right thing to leave
her child with him.

Instead of spending the night at an inn, they
pushed on. There was a full moon and the sky was
clear. The moon lit their way, and the stars looked
like diamonds spread out on a black velvet jeweler's
cloth. Jonathan could not sleep and found himself
wanting Maddy desperately.

They reached Meare in the early hours of the
morning, and Marie was sent up to a spare bedroom.
Jonathan lay in his bed, moonlight pouring into the
room, wishing Maddy were beside him, hoping that
she soon would be.

The next morning after breakfast he bundled Marie into the coach, and they set off.

"Will she see us, Lord Holford?"

"I think so. Her parents will make sure of that."

"But whatever will they think of me?"

"Don't worry about anything but telling Maddy
who you are," Jonathan said reassuringly, acting
calmer than he felt.

They were admitted by the butler and sent into the
drawing room. Lady Mansfield came in immediately.

"Jonathan, my dear. I am so glad you are here."

"You do not think me the villain of the piece then,
ma'am?"

''No. I suppose I should, but knowing you, whatever you did was from good intentions.'' Lady Mansfield suddenly noticed their other visitor and looked questioningly at her son-in-law.

''This is Rose's mother. Lady Mansfield, Marie de Wolfe.''

Marie stood up and gave a clumsy curtsy.

''She is here to tell Maddy the truth. Which is what I already told her. That I met Marie for the first time the night we found Rose and that my only deception was to pretend to know nothing of her origins.''

Lady Mansfield's face lit up. ''Thank you for coming, Marie. I knew there had to be some explanation. Let me get Maddy. She is up in the nursery with Rose.''

A look of longing passed quickly over Marie's face, but it went unnoticed.

A few more minutes, and then Maddy slowly entered.

''Maddy!''

Maddy put her hands up as though to ward her husband off.

''Please, Jonathan, nothing you can say will change things.''

''Maddy, this is Marie, Rose's mother.''

Madeline looked skeptical. Marie got up and walked over to her. ''I am indeed Rose's mother, Lady Holford,'' she said quietly. ''But I can assure you that Lord Holford is not her father. I never met him until that night last year, and indeed, I never knew who he was until two days ago.''

Maddy would not allow the wild hope that sprang up in her heart to overcome her suspicions.

''If you are indeed Rose's mother, then please tell

me your story. And begin by telling me what she was wearing that night.''

"She was wearing a flannel gown and a white wool cap which I crocheted for her. I embroidered it with pink roses.''

Maddy felt such a surge of joy that she almost fainted. The woman was Rose's mother. That much was true, so why should she not believe the rest.

"Please go on.''

Marie told her story briefly. "So you see, I would have left her in front of a vacant house, and God knows what might have happened to her, even if she survived the cold. Lord Holford saved her and me . . . and your marriage, I would guess?'' she added tartly. "Surely you should not condemn him for such a small deception. And if you still have any doubts, you may ask Gideon Naylor yourself, and he will convince you that my story is true.''

"I do not need to do that, whoever this Mr. Naylor is, Miss de Wolfe. I can tell that you are telling the truth. Jonathan, would you leave us for a moment?''

Jonathan nodded and left, wondering what else Maddy wanted to know. She seemed to believe Marie, but hadn't looked at him the whole time.

After he closed the door, Maddy took Marie by the hands and led her over to the sofa, where she sat them both down.

"Marie, I owe you so much that I can never repay you. I owe you Rose, who has brought the greatest joy to my life. And now I am indebted to you again for rescuing me from destroying my marriage. How might I repay you?''

Marie was looking down at their clasped hands. "I wonder if I might see Rose, my lady. I didn't come here meaning to ask that, you must believe,'' she added. "And I don't want to hold her or anything. I don't think I could bear that." Marie's voice broke, and Maddy gently stroked her hand.

"Are you sure you can leave her again?"

"Oh yes, my lady. Her father is still my protector. He never knew about her and never shall. I must leave her with you for the same reasons as before."

"Then let us go up to the nursery. She is playing with her nurse, and we can peek in from the doorway. If she is occupied, she will never know we are there."

When they got upstairs, the nursery door was open. Nancy was sitting in the rocking chair, knitting, while Rose was playing with her blocks, babbling softly to herself. Her back was to them, so all they could see was her chubby neck bent over her toys, and they watched her for a few minutes. Then Rose turned, as though sensing someone there, and her whole face lit up at the sight of Maddy.

Marie turned and quickly walked down the stairs.

"I will be right back, sweetheart," said Maddy, and she quickly followed Marie. She found her by the door, trembling and crying.

"Oh, Marie, I am so sorry."

"No, my lady. It was me that wished to see her. It was just the way she looked at you. You are truly her mother now, I realized, but it is still hard."

"You are a most courageous woman, Marie."

"You are the second person to tell me that," said Marie with a watery smile. "I wish to go back to London immediately, before I lose that courage."

"I will arrange it right away with Jonathan. We will send one of the maids with you in the coach."

"Thank you, my lady. And I wish to tell you something."

"Yes."

"I will never forget Rose, but I have one bit of happiness amidst the sorrow. That is knowing that you are her mother."

"Thank you, Marie. May I communicate with you from time to time? If it would not be too painful for you. I could let you know how Rose is doing."

"Oh yes, I would like that."

Maddy looked long and hard into Marie's eyes. "I can never, never thank you enough, Marie. The only way I can show my appreciation is to try to be as good a mother as you are."

Marie left within the half hour, after saying good-bye to Jonathan. He was exhausted by the last twenty-four hours and informed Maddy that he was going home to rest and then change for the Christmas Eve service. "I will meet you at church, Maddy. I have no energy to talk now."

Jonathan overslept, and he arrived late, just as the service had begun. The church had been transformed, cold stone warmed by candlelight, greens everywhere, and the altar piled high with hothouse flowers. Jonathan paused in the doorway. His family pew was in front and on the right. It was there that he must sit, of course, and he was sorry that he and Maddy had not talked, for it would look strange for him to be there all alone while she sat with her family on the left. But as he moved down the aisle he saw her, hymnal in her hands, standing alone in the Holford pew, and he knew that everything would be all right between them.

He clasped her hand and squeezed it as he slid in next to her, and they sang "Adeste Fideles." And when the service was over and all the neighbors gathered outside to give each other Christmas greetings, he had his arm tight around her waist.

He sent his coach ahead a little way and asked her to walk with him. "I know it is cold, but it is a beautiful night."

"I would love a few minutes under the moon and the stars, Jonathan." And so they walked, holding hands, neither wanting to break the peaceful silence between them.

Then Maddy began to sing, softly, an old carol:

"We know by the moon
That we are not too soon
And we know by the ground
That we are within sound . . ."

Jonathan looked down at her and smiled. "And is it too soon for a Christmas kiss, Maddy?"

"No, Jonathan."

He bent down and touched her lightly on the lips. "You do believe me now," he asked.

"I do. And I should have before, my dearest love. I should have trusted you."

"But I understand why you could not. Let us just be grateful to Marie and Gideon Naylor."

"Just who is this Mr. Naylor?"

"Later, Maddy," said Jonathan with a grin. The coach was before them. They climbed in, and Jonathan directed them to Meare.

"But Rose," protested his wife.

"Will have her parents first thing in the morning. For tonight, I want you all to myself."

They needed no candlelight, for the moon shone in on them, softly illuminating Maddy's curves and Jonathan's hardness. They made love slowly and tenderly the first time, for they felt under a spell. But when they awoke in darkness, for the moon had moved on, they came to one another hungrily. And in the morning Jonathan reached for Maddy again, only to find her gone. He lay still for a moment, and then he heard her retching in the dressing room.

"Maddy, are you all right?" he called to her anxiously.

She came in, looking pale and tired.

"You look dreadful, Maddy. Are you becoming ill?"

"Well, thank you, my lord. I looked different in the moonlight last night, I surmise?" She crawled back under the comforter. "I think, Jonathan, that my mother may be right."

"About what?"

"She suspects I may be increasing."

"How could that be possible after all these years?"

"I don't know, my love, but all the signs are there. I am beginning to believe it myself."

Jonathan looked at his wife with wonder in his eyes. "I can't believe that after all this time . . ." A broad smile lit up his face. "Oh, Maddy, what a Christmas!" He held her close to him and buried his face in her hair. "I thought I was as happy as a man could be, but this has almost sent me over the top."

They dressed quickly and drove to Mansfield where Rose had been up for an hour, asking for Mama and Papa. She ran into their arms as soon as she saw them and dragged them into the parlor where presents were waiting.

They watched her delight in ripping open the packages and laughed aloud at her startled face when she first played with her jack-in-the-box. Her grandfather had bought her a new doll, a French one, exquisitely dressed and coifed. "So we can get rid of that dreadful Miss Jones, Maddy," he whispered. But as much as she seemed to like her new toy, Rose never let go of Miss Jones. Miss Jones was with her when the jack-in-the-box popped open for the hundredth time that day, and Miss Jones went to bed with her, as always, that night.

Maddy and Jonathan held hands and looked down at their daughter.

"Do you think you will feel different about Rose, Jonathan, when we have a child of our own?"

"I am afraid of the opposite. I cannot imagine that I could love a child more than our little Christmas Rose."

THE BEST GIFT
OF ALL

by Emma Lange

"A RETICULE, Philip?" Lord Townshend regarded his companion in droll surprise. "You are making Barbara the gift of a reticule for Christmas?"

"Don't distress yourself, Charles," Philip Lindsay, Earl of Westphal, murmured without interrupting his study of the black beaded reticule he had accepted from an obsequious salesclerk. "The reticule is for my wife."

Though no longer amazed, Lord Townshend did not appear satisfied. "Well, surely a fancy comb would be more festive." He gestured to a nearby case. "They are all the rage this year."

Philip did look up then, only to shake his head. "No, no. Too gaudy by half."

And I prefer my wife's hair down.

The unbidden thought was not welcome. Philip turned abruptly to signal a lackey standing a respectful distance away, several packages in his arms.

"What of a necklace then?" Lord Townshend suggested. "All women like baubles. You could give her a sapphire. I believe I recall correctly, despite the quantity of port we drank before your wedding, that your countess has blue eyes."

Midnight blue. And her finest feature, but, one might successfully argue, for the thick, dark hair that flowed to her waist. Philip had seen it unbound that first morning at Chively. Unaware of his presence in their room, she had sat up with nothing to cover her but the fall of ebony hair.

Philip tightened his jaw, displeased to have his thoughts in so little control. "The reticule will do splendidly for her," he said curtly. "It has a distinct advantage over sapphires, besides the fact that she doubtless has dozens of costly baubles from her father. She's actually some need of a reticule. Freddy Livermore spilled port on hers at our wedding banquet and ruined it."

Charles did not mistake the note of finality in Philip's voice and said nothing more as the earl turned to the lackey waiting at his elbow and dropped the reticule onto the pile of presents the man juggled. "That's the last of the gifts, Carson. Pay the shot and take them round to Curzon Street for Fredericks to pack."

"You have decided to go to Wiltshire for Christmas, then?" Lord Townshend asked as he and Philip stepped out into the cold of the gray winter's day.

The earl nodded. "Mother's formed the notion that she must celebrate Christmas at Chively once more, now that the house has been restored to some degree of comfort."

Philip did not need to add as he settled his beaver hat upon his tawny head that Lady Camilla Westphal might not be up to another winter's journey into Wiltshire. Her health, never robust, had been seriously weakened by the strains of the last several years.

"All the Lindsays are convening, then?"

"I sincerely hope not every Lindsay in the country will join us," the earl remarked with a dry chuckle. "Ned has agreed to tear himself from his books; Uncle John and Aunt Katherine are to escort Mother; and Cousin Celicia is dragging Reginald down that she may inspect the progress of the restorations. Of the immediate family, only Margaret and her new, dearly bought husband will be absent."

Charles let that mocking "dearly bought" slip by without remark. He knew the sacrifice his friend had made that Margaret might have her heart's desire, a young viscount whose family could not afford to ally themselves with paupers, however illustrious and ancient the bride's family name might be.

But, reminded of the restoration work upon Chively, Lord Townshend did inquire about it, for like Lady Celicia Berkeley, he had long considered Chively one of the finest of England's country houses.

"You are confident then that your wife is restoring Chively as you would wish? I do not mean to question her taste, but . . ."

"You've every reason to question my wife's taste, Charles," Philip cut in coolly. "Darius Tarrant's daughter may have learned about percentages at her father's shrewd knee, but I doubt she had her tastes cultivated there. No, my friend, sharing your concern I hired an architect to guide her. He has been at Chively since I left."

"All this time?"

"Hmm. There are funds to keep him on for life, if . . . ah! But you were not concerned with Mr. Mackenzie's salary, I surmise." Philip's gray eyes lit suddenly. "You are concerned that the two of them . . ."

"Well, dash it all, Philip! You needn't grin in that odious way. You left her after only a week or so and have been absent three entire months. I don't know this fellow, Mackenzie, he may be hoary with age, but I do remember your wife. She may not be the stuff of legend, but she's pleasing enough looks . . ."

Pleasing enough . . . the phrase caught Philip. Perhaps his wife was pleasing enough, but she'd not the looks of the wife he'd have picked for himself, had he had the luxury of choice.

His father and brother, taken by the same carriage accident, had denied him that. The exact dimensions of the debacle they'd left him had been stunning. Of course, Philip had known they flew too high. 'Twas why he had bought his colors and left for the Peninsula. He could not stomach watching them drain the estates dry, but he had not known precisely how profligate they were. Unless he married, and not mere wealth, but dazzling wealth, even Chively would have to be sold.

It was Stodgkins, the Lindsays' solicitor, who suggested with a great many "ahems" that Philip consider the daughter of Darius Tarrant, or "Midas" Tarrant as the man with his fingers in dozens of lucrative pies was known in the city. . . .

"The old man's family is undistinguished yeoman stock, no more, but old Midas insists her mother's family can trace its lineage back to Welsh royalty. No doubt a bit of a hum, my lord, but I've met the girl, and I do not believe you would find her a disgrace. The most salient point, however, is that the old man longs like the devil to marry her into the nobility and is willing to settle a truly magnificent amount on her, if you are agreeable."

"Did he come to you?" Philip asked, disgusted to think Stodgkins had presented him to prospective fathers like so much horseflesh at Tattersall's.

The solicitor had done nothing so unacceptable, however. "Tarrant came to me, yes. I don't know how he got wind of your, er, situation, my lord, but Midas has ears in many places.''

''Would her dowry pay off all the debts?'' Philip asked, a hard look in his eye.

Stodgkins nodded. ''And more. You would have an income of fifty thousand pounds, my lord.''

For a long moment Philip could only stare. An income of fifty thousand pounds. It would require a man with the touch of Midas to provide sufficient capital to produce such an income.

''The girl is agreeable?''

Again the solicitor nodded. ''She is.''

She was agreeable, she who had never seen him. His title for her wealth. Tit for tat and bile to a proud man, who must put himself up for sale to pay for the sins of others.

Philip met her before the wedding, to determine if he could stomach her. Luckily, for, with so many dependent upon him—from his frail mother to Margaret, languishing without her viscount, to every last tenant—Philip could not have easily whistled fifty thousand pounds down the wind, the girl was, as Charles had said, ''pleasing enough.'' No more, though. Except for her purse, Philip would never have looked at her twice.

In truth, he did not wish to marry at all. He enjoyed very well his bachelor status, and his resentment at being forced into the parson's mousetrap showed after he was left alone in a comfortable parlor with Midas Tarrant's daughter.

''You are agreeable to this match then, Miss Tarrant?'' Philip said shortly and without softening preamble.

When his prospective bride did not answer immediately, Philip supposed he had miffed her. He'd no remorse. The prospect of allying himself forever with anyone, but particularly a slender chit who was neither in his style nor of his class did not bring out the best in him.

"Our marriage promises rewards for us both," he continued, without gentling his tone. "You will gain a title, and I funds I've dire need of."

Still she said nothing, only regarded him with eyes that were very blue and very wide. Philip resented her steady gaze. It seemed to demand more of him than he'd any intention of giving. Nor was he pleased that she remained mute. She was intelligent enough. He sensed it, and he resented that she maintained a dignified silence while he, as he saw it, was obliged to caper like a fool, proposing to a girl he did not even know.

Out of sheer perversity Philip added, "There is the question of issue. As I desire an heir, I shall oblige you to receive me in your bed until a boy is born."

He achieved a reaction. Megan Tarrant had a Welsh woman's coloring: dark hair, eyes of midnight blue, and a fair, milky complexion. Even a faint blush became obvious on her cheeks.

"I, I did not think to bargain over which wifely duties I would fulfill, my lord." She may have stumbled momentarily, to Philip's unreasonable satisfaction, but she kept her chin up, which he noted as well. "When I agreed to this marriage, I agreed to accept all a wife's obligations."

Philip had more to say, for he did not mean to be burdened with a young miss's romantic dreams, if indeed she was a young romantic and not a hardened title hunter. He meant to be certain she knew beforehand the kind of marriage they would have. "And did you agree to accept a wife's duties, as well, Miss Tarrant? I shall want you to oversee the restoration of my seat in Wiltshire when I return to town.''

She did not reply immediately. In the silence Philip could hear the distant shouts of children. Would she refuse him now that he had made it clear he did not mean to catapult her into society? Would she try to bargain with him?

Philip was to know only that Miss Tarrant did not mean to address the subject then, for when she spoke, Megan referred to the children playing somewhere in the house. ''I should like to take my brothers and sisters with me to Wiltshire, my lord. There are five of them, and . . .'' she paused before gathering herself to finish almost brusquely, ''and I do not expect my father to live much longer.''

It was Philip's turn to stare. Old Tarrant had not seemed ill when they met . . . though it was true he had appeared aged. Miss Tarrant apparently followed the train of his thought, for she added softly, ''He is only a little over fifty, my lord.''

Tarrant had looked at least twenty years older. Philip nodded slowly. ''I see. I am sorry for you, Miss Tarrant. As to your brothers and sisters, of course they may keep you company at Chively.''

Certainly, I shall not, he had added beneath his breath.

''Damn, Philip! Watch where you go!''

Philip blinked, then realized Charles had brought him up short before he could step into the path of a passing dray.

''Thanks, old man.'' He smiled at Charles, the charming smile that invariably inspired the person upon whom it was bestowed to smile in return. ''I'd have been flat as a pancake had you not brought me to my senses.''

''The least I could do! I ought not to have cast

doubt upon your countess. Really, she seemed too great an innocent to carry on behind a fellow's back, Philip. Ah, but look! Here comes a more pleasant topic to discuss. Do you see Cartwright's phaeton across the way there? Bought it yesterday . . .''

Philip tried to listen. He did not wish to think on his wife, her innocence, the night she'd lost it, or the subsequent week at Chively.

He'd not been in his cups when he stalked into their room after dinner that first night. He had helped himself to liberal amounts of claret at their silent dinner, but he'd felt too grimly aware of what was to come to be drunk. Reluctant virgins had never been to Philip's taste, and, too, he was so angry. Likely he had glowered at her when he saw her, the nearest person on whom he could vent his frustrations. He did not want a wife!

He might have taken her like that, almost vengefully, had he not, before she ducked her head, chanced to see her bite her lip to keep it from trembling.

His anger had not withstood the sight. Whatever the chit's faults, she did not deserve being taken in fear and trembling her first time. Philip had considerable experience. By the end of the night she had opened to him and sweetly. By the end of the week he had taught her abandon, though she had, even then, retained a certain indefinable, but appealing innocence.

Damn! It did not suit him to recall that week or her. She was too young, too innocent, and only "pleasing enough" to look upon. He had no intention of becoming enthralled by any woman, but least of all by a chit who did not have even good breeding to recommend her.

It had been difficult to leave her. Philip smiled

grimly. There. He had admitted it. He might not have left, in fact, had he not had the curricle race with Stafford—for exceedingly high stakes—to draw him back to town. He had even considered delaying the race. He'd only been married a week, after all. The very suspicion, though, that the chit who had bought him for his title could affect him, when he had determined she would not, had prompted him to keep to his original plans.

"I'll wager I know what subject has you so absorbed, I cannot get your attention even a half moment!"

Philip started, then smiled ruefully. "I am sorry, Charles."

"It is this Christmas business." Charles nodded sagely. "Selecting presents is a confounded nuisance. As you've chosen your wife's, I deduce it is Barbara's gift distracts you."

"There you are wrong. As I desired the pleasure of seeing Barbara in the flimsy nothing that caught my eye, I have already presented her her gift."

"You do not mean to say you gave Barbara no more than a flimsy nothing for Christmas?" Charles gaped. "Good Lord, Philip! She wheedled Hardwig into presenting her a string of pearls last Christmas."

"Then Hardwig is a fool," Philip murmured with a negligent shrug of his thoroughly masculine shoulders. "When a woman demands pearls to come to a man's bed, it is time he find a new mistress."

Charles could not but smile at his friend's unconscious arrogance. Philip possessed the best looks of any man in Charles's considerable acquaintance. He'd even, well-formed features, a hard, tall, broadshouldered body, and a pair of sometimes smoky, sometimes luminous gray eyes. Women besieged him, not the other way about, particularly when Philip's eyes glinted with a certain interested gleam.

"No, I suppose you don't have to pacify your mistresses with pearls," Charles agreed with something like a sigh. "I daresay Babs did not even cut up sharp over your plan to go to Wiltshire for Christmas."

"I didn't ask her opinion," Philip replied offhandedly. "But even had I, she'd have said nothing. She is to go to Somerset with George."

"The three of you could ride together for much of the way." Charles grinned at the thought.

Philip grimaced. "What a pleasure that would be, fighting off Barbara every time George fell asleep. I would not, you may be astonished to learn, care to cuckold George in his own carriage."

"Standards, standards," Charles chuckled. "Well, I wish you luck with your solitary journey. It looks like snow to me," he added, glancing up at the leaden sky. "And I also wish you luck with your wife. Surely even you, Philip, will need luck with a woman you've left unattended for three months."

Philip shrugged off the warning before he could recall exactly how still his wife had gone that morning when he had announced he was leaving her. "Megan knew before we married I did not intend to sit in her pocket at Chively. Now let us put our minds to what we wish White's to present us for luncheon. . . ."

"Will the snow keep the earl from coming, Meggie? Mr. Mackenzie said it snowed nearly two feet in all."

"You said we could go sledding when the snow stopped, Meggie!"

"Meggie, do you really believe stirring the plum pudding will bring us luck?"

"Wait for Lord Ned, Pris! Meggie, tell Pris she must wait for Lord Ned!"

"Please." The Countess of Westphal regarded the five children gathered around one of Chively's kitchen tables with a half smile. "My dears, I do believe you have caught Christmas fever! But to answer you, in reverse order: Pris, it would be impolite to begin stirring before Lord Ned arrives. Kit, I cannot say whether stirring the plum pudding will bring us luck, as Cook believes." The eldest Tarrant boy listened with his head cocked, for at twelve he was skeptical of superstitions. "However, I cannot see that stirring the pudding will do us harm."

"Will," she addressed a boy of ten, whose twin, Amanda, had scolded Pris, when the five-year-old had thought to stir the plum pudding prematurely. "I did promise to take you sledding if the snow stopped and the wind died. As of an hour ago, when I looked out, the first condition had been met, but not the second. As to your question, Becky," Megan addressed a gentle-looking girl of about fifteen, "I cannot say how bad the roads are beyond the drive. However, I am certain the earl will arrive at Chively as soon as he is able."

As soon, that is, as he is able to stomach again the wife he could endure no more than a week.

Megan's expression betrayed nothing of the thought. Pride aside, she'd not have worried the children. They knew her marriage was unusual, but they had been so awed by her husband when they met the earl at her wedding, that they accepted as a matter of course that such a man's marriage was unusual.

"Look, it's Coates!" Will waved at a young footman hurrying in from the hall. ''Has the earl arrived? Are you come to tell us?''

Megan tensed as she awaited the servant's response. Only when he shook his head did she breathe freely again, and then she felt a fierce anger at herself. She had vowed he would not unnerve her ever again! Did she mean to stare wide-eyed and tongue-tied as she had done that afternoon he had come to meet her?

To inspect her, rather. She remembered keenly those gray eyes of his assessing her, determining if she were worthy of giving him her purse and services as a brood mare.

That was not fair! Philip had not treated her so callously that week as she had feared he would. He had not merely used the girl who was as little up to his standards as Megan knew she was. Far from it, he had been all that was gentle and languorous and seductive.

Oh, so seductive. Megan could remember little of what she had done during the day that week, when Philip was attending to estate matters with his steward. She only recalled the evening and how her steps had quickened until she fairly flew to the summer parlor where he invariably awaited her, a light in his gray eyes that . . .

''Ah, here's Master Ned then, my lady!''

Megan started at Cook's exclamation and following the plump woman's gaze, saw the earl's brother was bending down to greet the children. A line of pink colored her cheeks, though no one, least of all scholarly Lord Ned, could possibly have guessed at her thoughts. But she knew their trend too well. Her body had even grown taut, prepared from habit for the images to come. Damn. Megan gritted her teeth. She had vowed she would not allow her husband to weave that sweet, fiery, magical spell around her again. If she did, she would only end by being miserably hurt, as she had been when he had coolly announced, after a night of heady lovemaking, that he was leaving within the hour.

He had warned her he would, Megan reminded herself. It had been her error to hope he had not meant what he said. Or that she could change his mind. She would not make that error again.

"Megan, I am sorry I am late." Ned Lindsay gave her an apologetic smile. "I promised Mother I would read to her until she fell asleep."

"I'm afraid Lady Camilla's journey taxed her heavily," Megan said, as she reflected almost wistfully that Ned Lindsay was the kind of man she ought to have married. He was not dangerously beautiful, or magnetic, or dripping charm when he chose. He'd have stayed with her. They'd have enjoyed companionable walks through the fall woods.

If the vision did not rivet her, Megan did not admit it. She truly liked Ned.

"Whatever the price of the journey, Mother pays it willingly," Ned replied. "You must realize, she feared she would never see Chively again."

He gave Megan a smile that she returned in kind, for if Ned was grateful for the wealth she'd brought into the family, she was grateful to him for treating her and her tribe of half brothers and half sisters with the same warmth he accorded the true members of his family.

"I hope your mother will feel free to stay as long as she likes. Lord John and Lady Kate too," Megan added, thinking of Philip's aunt and uncle, who had arrived with Lady Camilla the day before Ned came. Though she had not had much opportunity to speak with her mother-in-law, for Lady Camilla had needed rest more than conversation, Megan had found Lord John and Lady Kate to be surprisingly convivial. Actually, she suspected they had warmed to her so quickly because they adored whist, and Megan was very good at whist.

"Will Lord John and Lady Kate come sledding with us?" inquired Will, who was nothing if not tenacious in pursuit of a promised treat.

Ned's smile held a little surprise. "Well, I doubt they are up to sledding, Will. Are you venturing out today?"

"After we stir the plum pudding!" was Will's prompt reply, until, sensing Megan's glance upon him, he added, scrupulously, "If the wind dies down that is."

"Well we certainly cannot go sledding if we do not stir the pudding," Megan remarked. "We might break our legs, we'd be so out of luck. Here Ned, you take the first stir." She extended Cook's large spoon to the young man. "As the Lindsay representative the honor should go to you."

Ned made no move to accept the spoon. "You are a Lindsay now, Megan," he reminded her with gentle gravity. "And as lady of the house, you are the one must take precedence."

Megan flushed, embarrassed to have revealed how uncertain she was of her new position and how very little she thought of herself as part of her husband's family. But Ned seemed to understand, for there was no disapproval in his expression, only kindliness, and Megan relaxed. She smiled even, a warm smile that lit her face. "You are a very gracious gentleman, Ned Lindsay, and in honor of your eloquence I shall make the first great, enormous stir."

Hopefully the larger the stir, the greater the luck, Megan thought, as she passed the spoon to Ned.

And with a great deal of luck the last of Philip's guests, Lord and Lady Berkeley, would accept her as easily as Ned and his aunt and uncle had done. With even more luck, it was just possible Philip would get stuck in a snowbank and not come at all to cut up her peace.

"I shall hold you as tightly as Ned did, Pris. I promise."

"You are going down, Meggie?" Will beamed. "What a sport you are! You'll not regret it! Sledding is the most fun imaginable."

"It looks wonderful fun," Megan chuckled, seating herself upon one of the sleds the children and a footman had brought up the hill that curved gently down to the drive. From just below she could hear shrieks and laughter. Ned had taken Becky down with him and Kit had, quite purposely Megan suspected, bumped into them.

Will jumped upon his sled. "I will race you, Meggie!"

"Hurry, Pris! We've been challenged!"

Giggling wildy, Pris leapt on behind Megan and clung like a burr as they went careening down the hill, gathering speed as they went. When Kit suddenly loomed into view, seated in the snow, his overturned sled by him, Megan, a novice at sledding, for it was not a town sport, pulled more vigorously than necessary on her steering bar, causing her sled to veer sharply.

Unprepared, she and Pris did not make the turn, but flew off the sled, tumbling and sliding down the hill, Megan laughing helplessly while Pris shrieked, half in delight and half in terror.

"Look, Meggie! Hoesies!"

Weak with laughter, Megan did not quite comprehend what Pris said until she turned her head and saw there were, indeed, horses nearby. A carriage she had not heard approach had stopped in the drive only a few feet from them.

Megan could not see who had ordered the coachman to stop, but she did not need to see him to know his identity. The Earl of Westphal's crest was emblazoned upon the side of the handsome, highly polished carriage.

As she lifted Pris off her chest, for somehow her sister had ended there, Megan saw a lackey dart around to open the door and lift down the steps of the carriage. If she scrambled, she might be standing when her husband descended, but she refused to scramble, or to regret, for more time than it took to banish the thought, that he should have come upon her when she was dressed in her oldest pelisse and her heaviest boots, not to mention, wet, messy skirts and no hat at all. Her hair! Megan had not realized that her ribbon had come out. No. She bit her lip as she sat up. She would not refine for even a half second on the dishevelled state of her hair.

"May I be of assistance?"

Though she knew Philip had come, to hear his low, well-pitched voice and know, when she looked up, that she would see him caused Megan an alarming faintness of breath. Time seemed suspended as a large, gloved hand came into view. She'd no choice but to slip her own into it. And to look up.

Her heart performed a somersault, when Megan met her husband's gaze. She had thought herself armored against the effect of Philip Lindsay's glinting gray eyes.

"I did not expect I would be greeted by a snow maiden."

A corner of his so very appealingly shaped mouth lifted, and Megan found herself staring, no matter what she had intended. Philip Lindsay was so impossibly handsome, so carelessly assured, she could not quite take in that he was, in fact, her husband.

Ah, but she was his wife and standing before him more bedraggled than any scullery maid. She would not think on it! Nor would she stand witless and mute another moment.

A bracing sense of frustration stiffened Megan's spine.

"I hope your journey was not vastly unpleasant, my lord," she said. "As you can see, we at Chively are enjoying the snow."

"I am glad someone is enjoying this miserable stuff."

The speaker was not Philip, who had reacted to Megan's faintly challenging welcome by lazily arching a dark golden eyebrow. An overdressed dandy had descended from the carriage, Megan saw, glancing beyond her husband. Finding the fop's quizzing glass upon her, she became excrutiatingly aware all over again how little like a countess she looked.

"May I present Tony Havershawe, Megan," Philip said. "I found him and his party stranded at the Golden Bull. The roads to Somerset have been closed for two days, and those back to London are impassable by now. Jack and I"—Philip saluted the coachman on his box—"had to lead our horses some of the way. I hope we've enough beds for everyone?"

"I'll be delighted to double up, if need be."

Megan stiffened, not caring either for Mr. Havershawe's suggestive tone or for the fact that he continued to study her through his quizzing glass.

"We've quite enough beds, my lord." If she sounded cool, Megan did not care. The man could only be making sport of her, looking as she did. And drat this development! They did not have a surfeit of beds. Chively was enormous, but the restoration had proceeded slowly. Straining to see into the carriage, Megan hoped Mr. Havershawe's party was not large.

"Philip!"

It was Ned making his way through the snow, Megan's brothers and sisters behind him, their eyes as wide as his smile.

"Well, Ned, I see you have been showing Megan and, ah"—Philip seemed to take in the sight of the several children with a little surprise—"her brothers and sisters how to enjoy Chively in winter."

Ned grinned. "You've got it backward, actually. It is they who reminded me of winter's pleasures." Then Ned spied Tony Havershawe. "Havershawe?"

"Quite, dear boy," Mr. Havershawe drawled, a thin smile curving his mouth. "Philip rescued me from the least commodious inn in Wiltshire. Along with Babs and George."

"Babs and George?" Ned echoed.

The young man's tone rang oddly sharp in Megan's ears, but she was distracted counting rooms and beds now that she knew the party Philip had rescued numbered three. There were enough beds, but only enough rooms for everyone to have his or her own, if Lady Celicia Berkeley and her husband did not arrive.

Instantly Megan prayed that the roads to the south might be as bad as those to the west and east, for if Lord and Lady Berkeley did arrive, two people would be obliged to share a chamber.

Just the thought made Megan's heart race. She had taken courage from the assurance that she would have a separate room from Philip. A door between them had seemed a reliable measure of protection against him. But if she had to share his bed, her only protection against him would be . . . her own resolve.

"Now then, my lady, you look very well, if I may say so."

Megan's eyes met those of the brisk, elderly woman who had been her maid since she was sixteen. "You may indeed, Gibson, and thank you. You encourage me to hope I shan't suffer too greatly in comparison with the fashionable company awaiting me."

"You will not suffer in comparison to anyone, my lady," Gibson replied with the calm assurance of a woman who had attended one duchess and two viscountesses in her career. "You are fresh and genuine, qualities that cannot be found in a paint pot."

Touched, Megan smiled. "Beneath that efficient exterior, Gibson, you've the dearest heart in all the world. And now you've given me the confidence to force my feet from this room, I must get on with it. Because the children had the greatest difficulty settling down for their supper, I am late."

"Your guests will expect you to be taken up with your hostess's duties, my lady," Gibson advised steadily as she handed Megan a fine Norwich shawl. "Now you will have the opportunity to make a grand entrance."

Megan made no rejoinder as she departed. There was no point saying she could not hope to make a grand entrance when a woman of Lady Barbara Choumley's beauty, style, and elegance had entered before her.

Megan had heard the term "Diamond of the First Water," but until now she had never met a woman to whom it might apply. Lady Barbara Choumley could have few rivals even in London, with her

green, slanted eyes and that wealth of blond hair.
She'd a curvaceous figure too, Megan recalled, spar-
ing a grimace for her own merely acceptable decol-
letage.

A sigh escaped her as she straightened her shoulders.
Envy would not change her looks any more than it
could change her background and make her more
acceptable to . . .

"Ah, there you are, Megan. I was just coming to
look for you."

To have the very person she had just been thinking
of materialize behind her caused Megan to spin about
and give a little cry.

"You startled me, my lord."

To Megan's dismay her voice sounded tellingly
faint. Philip had taken her by surprise in more ways
than one. In evening dress he looked just as he had
when she had rushed into the summer parlor to begin
their evenings together. But she'd more than the tug
of bittersweet memory with which to contend. There
was present reality as well: Philip's tall figure su-
perbly turned out in elegant black, and his golden
hair set off by the snowy white of his cravat.

Determined that Philip should not completely
overwhelm her, Megan launched into speech immediately, even as she met his eyes and registered
how luminous a gray they were in candlelight. "You
came from your mother's rooms, my lord? I hope
she is not unwell? Is that why you wished to find
me?"

"No," Philip replied far more unhurriedly.
"Mother is much the same. She plans to rest tonight
to conserve her energies for tomorrow evening. That
is why I wished to speak with you. You do have a
fitting celebration planned?"

For over a month Megan had been doing little but

plan the Christmas Eve festivities, all alone. She'd enough of her father's temper to shoot back sharply, "It is a little late, is it not, my lord, to ask? If you'd your heart set upon a celebration of some particular sort, you might have sent word."

With that she turned on her heel, though she had not meant to behave so intemperately toward Philip. She had intended to be all that was serene, pleasant and entirely aloof in regards to him, but she would not regret her display.

He could have made her some kind of greeting, after all. It was the first moment they had had alone after three months apart. And he might have made a polite remark on her looks, no matter that Lady Barbara quite put her in the shade. And what of his house? His precious Chively. Had he even noted the work accomplished upon it, she continued to fume, quite unaware of the strong hand that reached for her.

Catching Megan by the elbow, Philip spun her about with ease. She was not short. The top of her head came to his chin, but she was fine-boned and slender.

"I asked a perfectly legitimate question, Megan, and I have no intention of being treated to a child's tantrum in response," he said levelly.

Instantly Megan regretted her pique. Philip made her feel a child, and not just because he had caught her up as if she were one. He did have a right to know her plans. It was his house, after all, and the people she must entertain were his friends and family.

Megan forced her gaze to hold his, though she felt a fool. "I tried to plan a celebration as much as possible like the ones you used to have here at

Chively. To do so, I consulted with your mother by letter and then with Dabworth. . . .''

"You consulted with Mother?" Philip interrupted.

"I was not aware how weak Lady Camilla is, my lord, but I don't believe I overtaxed her," Megan defended herself against his sharpened tone.

"No, no." Philip seemed to shake off some preoccupation. "I am certain she was up to replying. You surprised me. That's all."

Megan had surprised Philip, because his mother had made no mention of the letter. She had, in fact, given the distinct impression that celebrating Christmas at Chively had been entirely her idea. Philip knew why. His mother had feared he would not come for his wife alone, and soft-hearted as she was, she had not wished to think of anyone, even Darius Tarrant's daughter, planning Christmas festivities no one would bother to attend.

Philip remained silent so long Megan grew uneasy. "You do not approve, my lord?"

"Approve?" Philip repeated, no longer thinking of his mother's stratagem. His gray gaze had focused upon his wife. Irrelevantly, he noted an inescapable fact about her was that she did not look a cit. Dressed in quiet, good taste, she held her slender figure gracefully. The more-refined-than-not bones of her face, reminded him of old Darius's claim that his daughter was descended from Welsh kings. And then, of course, there were her eyes. They seemed a deeper blue than he recalled.

Perhaps it was that new spark animating their depths that accounted for the difference. He had noticed it outside in the snow, the moment their eyes had met, even before she'd given him that cool, even slightly combative greeting.

Charles had not been so wrong, it seemed. She
was not well pleased to have been left and then ignored for months.

"Approve?" Philip repeated. "Had you wished
to know what I would approve, you could have written to me, Megan."

The result of his experiment did not surprise him.
Her eyes flared brightly. "I did not wish to harry
you with trivialities, my lord. I'd the confidence that
you would advise me if there was some custom or
other you particularly wished to celebrate. Was I
wrong?"

Philip bit back a smile. The wide-eyed girl of their
first meeting had found her tongue. "No, you were
not wrong, Megan. I shall always advise you of any
particular wish I may have."

Philip had played unfairly. He had so much more
experience than Megan and knew to a nicety how
suggestive not only was the look he gave her, but
the tone he used. She blushed as prettily as ever.

"Now as to the matter of beds," he continued,
assuring that her cheeks remained attractively rosy.
"Dabworth has assured me we really do have a sufficient number of restored rooms and aired beds."

That Philip had asked Dabworth to verify what she
had already told him annoyed Megan enough that
her equilibrium was restored. "There will be enough
beds," she replied briskly, "but if Lady Celicia and
her husband arrive, there will not be sufficient rooms
unless Lady Barbara shares with her husband."

"Impossible," Philip said out of hand. "George
snores so dreadfully, we may actually be obliged to
sequester him in a wing of his own."

"But . . ."

Philip's grin came so unexpectedly that Megan's
heart turned over. "I was teasing you, Megan. You

needn't look so worried. There will be no need to put another wing in order by tonight. But I wasn't joking as to the other. Barbara will not share a room with George. Someone else will be obliged to give up her solitary splendor, if Celicia does come.''

Still unsettled by Philip's unexpected teasing, and unable to read his expression, Megan fumbled for an appropriate response. ''Yes, well, ah, Lady Kate and Lord John have already said, firmly, that they cannot sleep in the same room. In their case it is she who snores.'' Megan took a breath as she felt the heat rise in her cheeks. If only he would leave off looking at her so . . . so steadily. ''That would seem to leave only the two of us.'' There! She had said it.

''So it would,'' Philip replied. Megan thought she detected amusement threading his tone, but she was not to know for certain, nor to discover whether she or the thought of sharing a bed with her had amused him. Their guests waited, as Philip reminded her, holding out his arm. ''I believe it is time we go down. Your dress is very nice, by the by. A marked improvement over your sledding costume.''

''Ah, the earl and his countess at last. We had begun to despair of you, my dears.''

Mr. Havershawe's mocking drawl did not improve with repeated hearing, Megan decided as she entered the winter parlor on Philip's arm, and she was distinctly relieved when Lord John decided the question of whether she would sit on the side of the fire where the three members of the Choumley party were ensconced, or on the side where the far friendlier Lindsays had chosen to take their seats.

''My dear Megan,'' Lord John stretched out his hands to her. ''I intend to snatch you from my unworthy nephew, as I have not seen you all this day,

and my old eyes have been crying out to be revived
by your fresh beauty.''

Megan smiled her gratitude. She had not quite
trusted Philip's offhanded, rather equivocal compliment, but Lord John's gallantry made her feel welcomed among people who were not, she was
supremely conscious, her peers.

When Megan was seated, her impression that her
guests had divided themselves into two not entirely
convivial groups did not lessen. Lord George
Choumley displayed no interest in anyone as he
dozed before the fire. Near by him his wife reclined
upon a Grecian couch, looking the picture of indo-
lent beauty as she listened with a faint smile to whatever witticisms her brother was whispering into her
ear. Their private conversation was mirrored by the
one Ned was having with his aunt. Near Megan, they
spoke in low, indistinguishable voices too.

Only one guest remained apart from either group.
Megan had persuaded Mr. Mackenzie, Philip's architect, to join them for dinner, as he was to leave
the following day to spend Christmas week with
friends nearby, and she imagined Philip might wish
to have conversation with him.

The Scotsman had donned his best coat of superfine for the occasion, along with a severely starched
cravat, but despite his efforts his stocky, vigorous
figure looked out of place in the elegant company.
The self—conscious smile he gave Megan in greeting indicated he knew it, and she bestowed upon him
her warmest smile. Mr. Mackenzie might not be the
ornament Mr. Havershawe was, but in Megan's
opinion the architect was worth a dozen bored, frivolous dandies.

''I am glad to see you did not freeze in the west
wing today, Mr. Mackenzie,'' she said.

"I made certain the chimneys were the first things repaired, my lady. We'd fires to warm us, as well as the sight of you and the children frolicking in the snow. Did you enjoy your first sledding expedition?"

"I did very much," Megan assured him. If her guests had, as she'd the notion, maintained distinctly separate groupings before she entered the room, they united now to follow Megan's conversation with Mr. Mackenzie. Determined not to be self-conscious, she continued as companionably as she'd have done had she not been observed. "Speeding down the hill was most exciting. My only regret is that I went so much of the way without benefit of a sled. If you were watching us, I fear you witnessed the sad end to which I came, Pris perched upon my chest."

"I did not think you minded much," Mr. Mackenzie replied, a light, of which Megan was blissfully unaware, softening his gaze. "I could hear your laughter all the way to the second floor of the west wing."

"More likely you heard my shrieks." Megan laughed. "And Pris's. She left me half deafened, she screamed so."

"You've a, ah, good many brothers and sisters, Lady Megan." With very little pleasure, Megan turned to meet Mr. Havershawe's knowing eyes. "I declare they seemed a small tribe unto themselves, there were so many. And yet, I did not notice even one that favored you."

"How perceptive you are, Mr. Havershawe," Megan said. "They are my half brothers and half sisters, actually. In all, my father had three wives."

"Indeed." Mr. Havershawe's arched brow seemed to cry out, three wives? What lack of breeding!

Idly Megan wondered what the dandy would say

if she tossed the glass of sherry Ned had fetched her
in his thin, fox's face. But she did not require such
an extravagant gesture to defend herself against the
man's supercilious attitude. She had allies, as it
turned out.

To Megan's surprise Lady Katherine took up her
cause. "Only three wives!" The older woman gave
a typically blustery laugh. "My dear, your father
was too slow for words. My uncle—he was the Duke
of Redbourne and a dear, dear man—had five wives
and fifteen children in all. What a grand time I used
to have visiting Redbourne Hall in the summer! Ah,
my. One never lacked for playmates there."

Megan was not so surprised that Ned would speak
up. He looked inquiringly at his brother, who had
taken a place near Mr. Mackenzie and the fire. "I
believe our grandfather had several wives, did he
not, Philip?"

In contrast to Mr. Mackenzie, whose stalwart
stance resembled that of a captain upon the high
seas, Philip looked entirely at his negligent ease with
his shoulder propped against the chimneypiece and
a glass of claret dangling from his hand.

He nodded to his brother. "Four or so, I believe."

"Four?" Mr. Havershawe exclaimed.

Philip did not take the cue to make a story of his
ancestor. "Childbearing can take a toll," he said
quietly and flicked his glance to Megan. Before she
could determine whether there was any sympathy in
his eyes for the fate, as he seemed to have guessed,
of her mother, he looked to Mr. Mackenzie and
changed the subject.

Megan marked it in Philip's favor that he could
lift his glass to the Scotsman without appearing the
least patronizing. "You've done a great deal of work,

Mackenzie, and all of it excellent. I am particularly pleased with the hall. It is handsomer than ever. And I commend your thought to put French windows across the length of the library. There was never enough light in the room before.''

''I am gratified you approve my work, Lord Westphal,'' Mr. Mackenzie replied, his voice tinged with a burr. ''I fear, though, that I cannot accept your praise for the French windows. They were installed at Lady Megan's suggestion, you see.''

Philip glanced to Megan. She was flushing and shaking her head, as she looked, not at him, her husband, but at the architect, whose *tendre* for her was so obvious.

''You give me far too much credit, Mr. Mackenzie! I must protest. I only observed as, ah,'' Megan hesitated, uncertain suddenly how to refer to her husband. She had never called him by his given name in company, and though she suspected most of those present did, she could not seem to bring herself to it. He was no help either, she found when she glanced at him, hoping for inspiration. His gray eyes looked as remote as a stranger's. ''. . . as my lord did, that the room was dark for a reading room.''

''You remarked as well, my lady,'' Mr. Mackenzie reminded Megan, ''that you thought it would be pleasant to be able to walk out from the library to the gardens.''

Megan blessed Mr. Mackenzie. He replied so readily that, if any noted her formal manner toward her husband they were not given time to dwell upon it.

''It will not fadge, Mr. Mackenzie. I only presented the problem. You arrived at the solution,'' she said.

Mr. Mackenzie, not surprisingly, smiled broadly.

"Let us say the French windows were the result of a collaboration, then, my lady."

The thought pleased Megan, and she returned the Scotsman's smile unreservedly. "I think you do me too much honor, sir, but I am too delighted to quibble."

"Well, I wish to congratulate whoever it was had the inspiration to work upon the chimney in my room." Ned smiled. "It has been years since that fireplace drew properly."

All the chimneys had needed work, Mr. Mackenzie reported, but Ned's most of all, as a colony of bats had taken up residence in it.

Lady Barbara sniffed in eloquent disgust, but Lady Kate demanded the story of the bats, and Mr. Mackenzie obliged, recounting at great length and exaggerated detail one maid's reaction when a bat flew into her hair. Megan, though she had found little humor in the hysterics of the maid at the time, laughed helplessly along with Lady Kate at the story Mackenzie made of the incident.

Her humor died suddenly when she happened to glance to Philip and found he was watching her with an expression that led her to assume he considered her display of amusement ill-bred. Megan maintained her smile, however, for she would not have Philip believe that he could, in effect, decree whether she could laugh or not.

And what did he want of her anyway, she muttered to herself. As if they would give her the answer, Megan's eyes slid, of their own accord, to Lady Barbara. The beauty was regarding the interplay between Mackenzie and Lady Kate with a bored, disengaged expression that put her squarely in Philip's camp.

Megan's heart sank. There was no hope she could

ever lounge about as aloof and ornamental as Lady Barbara. She'd not the beauty to carry off such a pose.

Philip, it seemed, was doomed to be frustrated with his wife, and she . . . she was doomed to be like the fisherman's wife in the old story, who had wished for more than fate could fairly give her and ended with nothing.

Megan ought to have been satisfied when her first wish regarding Philip Lindsay had been granted.

She had known of him long before he came to her father's house that afternoon. She had seen him in the park, though Megan never went to the park at the fashionable hour, for she was not a fashionable person nor interested in becoming one.

She did like to walk out early, however, as the city was coming alive. Becky and Amanda had been with her the first time Philip had gone pounding by on a blooded chestnut, his golden hair gleaming in the sun. Tall and well built, he sat his horse with such ease Becky had breathed on a sigh that he seemed a centaur. Megan had not replied when Amanda demanded to know what a centaur was. Becky had had to explain, for Megan had been lost to all but the man riding by and wishing that she might be allowed to see him at least once again.

She had, and not just once. The Earl of Westphal was regular in at least some of his habits. He rode most mornings at eight.

Gibson had known his name, and in the way of a servant a great deal of his circumstances, but nonetheless the earl had never seemed a real person to Megan. He had been a figure of fancy to her, a god-made mortal, perhaps. He certainly was that handsome.

And then one day, her father, whose dearest wish,

as she well knew, was to wed her to a title, had come
into her room and offered her the man of her secret
dreams. He had offered her other impecunious no-
bles previously, but Megan had found it, if not easy,
then possible, to disappoint her father's hopes in their
cases.

But she'd her own hopes and fancies to battle when
it was Philip Lindsay her father dangled before her.
She could be his wife. Dazzled, and aware too that
her father wished desperately to settle her before he
succumbed to the illness plaguing him, she had challenged fate.

A fool, that was what she was. And a fool twice
over to continue to repeat her mistake. She must
cease to wish for more than she had. She was his
wife. She had the satisfaction of knowing her father
had died well-pleased.

In time her fascination for Philip would fade, particularly if she could avoid the silky seduction of his
lovemaking. There was the matter of his heir, true,
but Philip's interest in a son seemed to have faded.

She'd only this Christmas to get through, Megan
persuaded herself, and she had already composed
excuses to keep him in his own room. If only the
weather would prevent Lady Celicia . . .

Megan started from her thoughts upon hearing her
name spoken. To her surprise it was Lord George
Choumley who addressed her in a voice she found
oddly high and girlish, given his heaviness and middle age.

"Ah, there, do you not hear?" he was asking.
Dutifully Megan listened, and did, in fact, hear, with
an abrupt sinking of her heart, the sound of voices.
"Yes, I hear them more clearly now," Lord George
said. "I do believe, Lady Megan, that your last
guests have arrived."

Megan did not drift between waking and sleeping, drowsily wondering where she was. She knew instantly. And was acutely aware of the strong arm lying heavily upon her waist, of the hard, masculine body curved around hers, and of that body's heat.

Her body heated, but with shame. She had thought herself strong. She'd buried two stepmothers, both of whom, contrary to the fairy tales, she'd loved dearly. She had suffered the greater loss of her father stoically, and she had even held up when Philip left her, the week that had seemed so golden to her evidently meaning nothing to him.

But where had her fortitude been last night? Philip had not given her a word of explanation and certainly, heaven forbid, no apology for his three-month absence. She'd no notion if he meant to leave again the day after Christmas! Yet he had had only to touch her for all her resolve to hold herself apart from him to melt like a very thin patch of snow in the heat of the sun.

He had not played fairly! Asleep when he came to bed, she had been easy game. He had made her ache for him before she had been alert enough to marshal her defenses. By the time she had come fully awake, her body had been trembling for him. She had arched back into him, in fact, and had gotten what she desired. Philip's passion had run as hotly and urgently as hers. Within moments they came together in a fiery explosion of pleasure.

Megan stifled a groan. That had been the first time. There had been a second. Before she'd even caught her breath. Philip had begun to caress her again. More slowly this time and languidly, he'd set her skin aflame and made her want him all over again.

Perhaps she was a wanton. Surely it was not natural that a man who had treated her as indifferently as Philip had should be able to arouse her so. Even now feeling his smooth, hard body, she heated with something other than shame.

She must go and quickly 'else it would be her awakening him, an insupportable thought, especially as Megan had no notion how Philip would respond to her in the light of day. It seemed possible that he might be disgusted by her abandon.

Far later Philip awakened slowly. For a half second he could not think where he was or how he had gotten there. Bleary-eyed, he looked up, saw the blue canopy overhead, and remembered.

He had stumbled to bed very late, having stayed below to play cards with Tony and Reginald. Megan had been asleep, curled into a tight ball on the far side of his bed, and clad, he had seen by the light of the candle he held, in a flannel nightdress that was fastened all the way to the last button at her throat. Her soft, silky hair had been confined in a braid as tight as the ball she had made of her body.

Not exactly signs of welcome, which suited him, he had decided. He was as weary as the devil. The journey to Wiltshire had been long and trying. Yet he had not allowed the swirling snow or even the miserable sleet to deter him, as he told himself he persevered for his mother's sake.

And what had he earned for doing his duty? An annoying tweak of his conscience.

He had not known Barbara would be stranded at the Golden Bull. He'd thought her and her party safe in Somerset and had been stunned to come on them when he stopped for fresh horses.

It was not an unpleasant inn, despite what Tony

had said, but still, it was no more than a public hostelry, scarcely an inviting place in which to celebrate Christmas. He had known Barbara, Tony, and even old George for years. He could not abandon them merely to spare a wife he scarcely knew, should someone let slip the exact nature of his association with Barbara.

Philip's unexpected company had not, unfortunately, lightened his journey. Glad though they were to escape the Golden Bull, Tony and Barbara had thought nothing of complaining ceaselessly. If it was not the cold that displeased them, the leaden skies did, or the tedious pace Philip's coachman kept over the frozen roads, or the provisions the host of the Golden Bull had provided.

Even as they turned into Chively's drive, Tony had been carping over something, Barbara agreeing with him in a pettish way that had made Philip's eyes narrow. He had thought the day too dismal to save until unexpectedly, carrying on the cold, crisp air, a girl's gay laugh had penetrated the gloom of the coach.

He had not recognized the laugh and had been as astonished as anyone to look out and see Megan lying in the snow, still laughing, her dark hair spread like a silky fan about her.

As he had helped his wife up from the snow, Philip had seen that he must revise his opinion of her looks. Perhaps three months had changed her. Perhaps he'd remembered her wrongly. She'd not Barbara's classic beauty, it was true, but she was more than "pleasing enough" with her skin that was as smooth and pure as alabaster, her thick, black hair, and those blue eyes. Not as voluptuous as Barbara, she was, nonetheless, very attractive. After three months, Mackenzie was completely smitten by her. And after an acquaintance of only three days or so, Ned and John were enchanted.

Even starchy old Dabworth had been affected by the new Countess of Westphal. Though Philip had never been the favorite of the staff at Chively, the old butler had welcomed him home with a bow so stiff, he might as well have said outright he disapproved how long the master of Chively had left its mistress to languish alone.

Ned and John had used words, and had a great deal more to disapprove than Dabworth. Predictably, John had put the matter the most succinctly. "Damn, boy! However little you may care for the girl, I find it outrageous that you intend to make her entertain your mistress. It isn't done!"

Philip had reacted in character even to Ned's far gentler admonition. He'd given both men a cool look and let them think what they pleased. Certainly he had not stooped to protesting that he had more honor than to dally with a mistress in his wife's house.

Lying in his bed, one arm flung back behind his head, Philip admitted he had been unfair. What else was everyone to think? He had left Megan after only a week and resumed his interrupted relations with Barbara soon after. Celicia's titillated laugh when she spied Barbara ought not to have irritated him so. Likewise the disbelieving snort Reginald gave when, for what seemed like the hundredth time, the story of his chance meeting with the Choumleys and Tony was related. And he ought not to have been so exasperated with Barbara herself when she rose from her place beside him at the card table and gave him a significant look as she announced in a suggestive purr that she was off to her lonely bed.

Tony had looked at him sharply when he had not followed Barbara out of the room, and then after a moment, had made some silky remark about the power new challenges had to fascinate.

Philip had recognized the remark as a ploy designed to discover where Barbara stood. The two were close. Tony would wish to know, and Philip ought not to have shot back that what surprised him the more was how quickly old challenges lost their power to interest. He wasn't even certain he meant it.

But he'd not gone to Barbara's bed, not even when he discovered Megan in her off-putting flannel. No, he had fallen into his own bed. And though he'd been bone weary, his eyes had not closed.

Instead he had lain there listening to Megan's gentle, even breathing. And feeling her warmth. Her body seemed to radiate heat on that cold night, and he became aware too, as he lay there, of her soft, sweet scent.

Desire stirred. Or he became aware of a desire that had first stirred when he spied her in the snow.

Despite the evidence of Megan's flannel, Philip did not fear she would spurn him. He had taught her passion, then left her to pass three months without a man. And he was confident she had slept alone, even though for just a moment in the winter parlor, he had wondered. She had been very much at ease with Mackenzie. Too at ease, he had decided during dinner. She was a different kettle of fish from Barbara. She'd not have carried on unaffected had she betrayed her wedding vows. She would have avoided the Scotsman's eyes and blushed when she could not.

Adjusted to the morning light now, Philip smiled. Had his caresses been a test, she'd have passed with flying colors. She had responded to him that readily, arching back into him when he did no more than nuzzle the silky spot just behind her ear.

No, he had not kept away so long that she had dallied with the architect. His smile deepened. Nor so long that she had forgotten what she had learned about the art of making love, either.

"I must say you are a pleasure to encounter on this bleak day, Countess." Lord John smiled warmly upon his niece by marriage. "The sparkle in your fine eyes routs the gloom."

"It is Christmas Eve, sir," Megan replied in the same fond spirit. "Good spirits must be the order of the day."

Lord John shifted his attention downward to Pris, who held her sister's hand. The two had visited the kitchen, Megan to consult with Cook as to the preparations for dinner, and Pris to wheedle a cookie from the maids.

"It is indeed Christmas Eve!" Lord John exclaimed, his hushed voice calculated to make Pris's eyes go wide. "A day when only good spirits reign. Did you know, Miss Pris, that harmful spirits are entirely routed upon this day? Why, we may tell every ghost story we ever heard, speak of goblins even, and witches too without the least fear of rousing those dire creatures."

"Will wou tell us one, Lowd John?" Pris begged in an avid whisper.

"I shall, indeed! Where are your brothers and sisters? In the nursery?"

Pris nodded. "They awe making pwesents."

"Well then, shall we entertain them while they work?" Pris giggled when Lord John offered her his arm, but she laid her hand upon it, as if she had been born knowing the proper way for a gentleman to lead a lady. "Very nice," Lord John approved, then turned his smile upon Megan. "We shall leave you, my dear, though it means denying ourselves the sight of your lovely glow. You will be too busy to bother with us anyway, for the servants are bringing, I do swear, every bit of greenery they could find into the hall.''

"We shall have splendid decorations then," Megan chuckled. "And thank you, Lord John, for your attention to the children. They will be delighted to hear ghost stories."

"You needn't thank me, my dear! It brings back my childhood to tell ghost stories on Christmas Eve. I'd an uncle who told them every year."

Christmas Eve: a day for decorating the house, for telling ghost stories, drinking from the wassail bowl, and burning bright fires. It was indeed a day for good spirits.

Even Lady Camilla had been affected, for feeling stronger she had invited Megan to her rooms that she might assure her daughter-in-law how pleased she was by the work being done on Chively.

"You cannot imagine what a pleasure it is to know the house is being cared for again," Lady Camilla said between sips of tea. "Poor Harry, my husband, was a gay man, my dear, but alas, he was dreadfully shortsighted. He drained the estate for naught, really, and little by little repairs were let go along with most of the servants. Finally we were obliged to stop coming altogether, the house became so uncomfortable. Poor Harry. To the end he believed he could reverse his slipping fortunes with one more turn of the dice, but I hope I do not shock you with my plain speaking, Megan?''

In truth, Megan was a little amazed that her mother-in-law should be so forthcoming upon their first extended conversation. But she was not shocked exactly and said so.

Lady Camilla smiled. "I am glad. I've too little time left to waste words. And I did wish to assure you that Philip is quite unlike either his father or his elder brother." The older woman paused, and when she spoke, she seemed to pick her words carefully. "Stronger than they, he always chose his own course. That is what afflicts him now, of course, but he is no fool, Megan. He will come around. Only be patient, and give him time to see how exceedingly lucky he is."

Proceeding toward the hall where she could hear the servants bustling about, Megan recalled her mother-in-law's approval of her with pardonable pleasure. As to Lady Camilla's prediction that Philip would come about, however, Megan tried very hard to resist the temptation to take it to heart.

She could not quite forget it, however, and during the morning, as she went about making certain all was ready for the evening, her spirits lifted. The night before began to seem less and less a disaster. Philip's lovemaking had not been a merely perfunctory mating of bodies to beget an heir. He had desired her as much as she had desired him.

It was Christmas Eve, a magical day, as Lord John had said. No wicked or even gloomy spirits could darken the day, and Megan decided she would not think how Philip had taken pleasure in their bed before but still left her. She would only think how he had pleased her, though thinking on that would, she admitted, make her more than a little shy next time she encountered her husband.

"Megan! I hope you will not resent that I have begun to arrange some of this lovely greenery. I adore making the garlands and wreaths for Christmas!"

Megan returned Lady Kate's broad smile as she crossed the great hall to the table at which the older woman worked with a mound of fragrant greenery.

"I am delighted you have begun, ma'am. Now at least we've some hope of finishing before next Christmas comes."

Lady Kate chuckled. "It does look as if the servants brought in half the forest, does it not? I think their efforts indicate how pleased they are to have Christmas celebrated at Chively again. Also," she added, cocking her white head at Megan, "I do believe their enthusiasm is a mark of the esteem in which they hold their mistress. Ah, I have put you to the blush, my dear!" Philip's aunt gave a crow of delight. "And how lovely you look blushing, but I'll not have you deny what both John and I have observed. You've won over the servants, Megan, and that is a very revealing fact."

Both a little flustered and very pleased by Lady Kate's praise, Megan smiled the radiant, unaffected smile that set her face aglow. "You are very kind, Lady Kate. But tell me"—she went on in a brisker tone that indicated she would change the subject from herself—"are there any traditions at Chively concerning the greenery?"

"Dozens!" Lady Kate proclaimed. As she and Megan sorted through the greenery together, she told where they had used to hang the wreaths and how garlands had been fashioned to grace the stairs. "As to the mistletoe, the tradition at Chively is that the kissing boughs are hung by the men, but we shall have precious few hanging, if all our men continue to play slug-a-beds."

"Not all are, Lady Kate."

To Megan's chagrin the male who joined them was Mr. Havershawe. She guessed he had been in the dining room where breakfast was being served informally, for he came from that direction. With him came his sister, who made a general, negligent greeting as she regarded the greenery upon the table before Megan and Lady Kate with all the interest she might have accorded a butter churn.

"I am present," Mr. Havershawe continued, "and I would be rivetted to hang a kissing bough or two. Good morning, Countess." He bowed as he swept Megan with a flagrantly assessing gaze. "You are in enticing looks today, if I may say so. Not that you were not in fine looks yesterday, of course, but you must have had a most, ah, restorative night last night, to look so delightful this early in the day."

Although she could feel her cheeks heat at the man's very nearly impertinent and certainly suggestive reference to her night, Megan held his gaze steadily. "It is kind of you to flatter me, sir, but if I am in looks, I believe the cause is the day. I have it from Lord John that Christmas Eve is the only day of the year during which not a single malign spirit may roam."

To Megan's infinite pleasure, for a moment Mr. Havershawe did not look quite so superior. "I really do wonder, my dear Lady Megan," he said, his gaze distinctly sharper than it had been, "if you are not to be taken seriously."

Before Megan could wonder why he should bother to ponder such a thing, a high-pitched, rather breathy voice came from the stairs. "Seriously, Tony?" Lady Celicia had caught the one word. "But you never take anything seriously, dear man!" Tripping down the stairs, she greeted her aunt first. "It is just like the old days, Aunt Kate, seeing you among your greens. Babs! You are up early. How did you sleep?"

It was not an odd question, and Megan would have

thought nothing of it but for the moment's stillness that followed. Glancing up from the wreath she had fashioned, Megan saw Lady Barbara's green eyes had narrowed slightly as she regarded Lady Celicia, and her answer to the simple question seemed strangely obscure. "I slept quite as I expected," she replied finally, her voice striking Megan as not quite so world-weary as usual.

"Ah," Lady Celicia said and turned a speculative look on Megan. Mystified, Megan was half surprised when Lady Celicia's tone was entirely amiable as she said, "Good morning, Megan. I may address you so informally, may I not? I am your cousin now, after all. I trust you slept . . ."

"No, no, no! You may not bring ivy into the hall, boy." Interrupting her niece without apology, Lady Kate waved her hands furiously at a hapless servant. "You will bring us bad luck!"

Diverted from her interest in how people had slept, Lady Celicia laughed. "Do you believe that superstition, Aunt Kate? I shall be surprised if you truly do."

" 'Course I do," Lady Kate replied with a snort. "It is tradition to use ivy without and holly within. To flaunt tradition is to tempt Lady Luck. Ned!" she cried, spying her nephew ambling in from the direction of the dining room. "You've the authority of the scholar. Tell your cousin we would tempt fate to use ivy in the house."

Ned took a moment to make his greetings before he turned with a smile to his aunt. "I cannot say Celicia would be tempting fate, Aunt Kate, but perhaps she would be tempting Bacchus."

"Whatever do you mean, Ned?" Celicia demanded.

"Ivy is an emblem of the god Bacchus," Ned

explained. "That is why the early church leaders forbade its use inside houses of worship. The fathers did not wish their believers to sit beneath, and perhaps be tempted by, the symbol of the god of wine and licentiousness."

"Well, well, Ned," Mr. Havershawe drawled, "I think you have made a case for using armloads of the stuff."

"We most certainly shall not." Megan was as surprised by Lady Kate's sharp tone as by the look Philip's aunt gave Mr. Havershawe. "It is Christmas, Tony. A time for good will and honorable dealings."

"Here comes, Philip! He is master of the manor. Let us put the matter to him!"

At Lady Celicia's exclamation, Megan froze. She did not go absolutely still for long. She gained control of herself before anyone could notice, but for that one moment, she was aware of nothing but the failure of her head to lift that her mouth might curve in the welcoming smile a wife would be expected to give her husband.

"Put what to me?"

Megan forced her gaze up, afraid she would never do so if she did not then, when his attention was upon his cousin. He had been home almost a day, but still she was not accustomed to his looks, and as usual, she could not quite credit that a man possessing such masculine beauty was her husband. Then she blushed, recalling how very married they were, and all the things they had done together in their marriage bed, things that seemed in the light of day almost sinful.

Suddenly Philip shifted his gaze and caught her staring. Caught her blushing too. Megan knew he saw her hot cheeks, because he flicked his gaze to them, and a gleam flared to life in the depths of his eyes. To Megan's astonishment, not to mention embarrassment, her blood leapt in her veins when she caught sight of that gleam, and worse, Philip seemed to guess his effect upon her, because quite suddenly he half grinned, a corner of his mouth quirking, as their gazes held.

To Megan it seemed they stayed so, with the air between them vibrating, for ages. But it was a very little time in reality. Almost in the next moment Philip looked back to Lady Celicia who, apparently unaware of her cousin's momentary distraction, was rattling on about whether they should risk having a drunken, licentious Christmas by including ivy with the indoor greenery.

"I've no desire at all to celebrate a bacchanalia on the Roman order, if that is what you're asking, Celicia," Philip responded when he had heard her out. "However, I am not the final authority. Your question would be better addressed to the lady of the house. Megan?"

Megan did not allow herself to meet Philip's gaze then. Although his deferral to her caught her off guard and pleased her enormously as well, she was too keenly aware that the others were watching her to risk blushing like a schoolgirl again. She looked to Philip's aunt. "I shall defer to Lady Kate's wisdom. We shall use ivy on the door."

"Now that's decided," Philip declared, "I wish to announce that an expedition whose purpose is to find and fetch the largest Yule log possible is about to be launched. Any man willing and able is invited to join it."

"Tell Reginald, Philip!" Lady Celicia cried fondly. "He would adore . . ."

"You are quite behind the times, Celicia," Philip remonstrated with teasing sternness. "Reginald is even now donning his boots as are your brothers, Megan. I hope you do not object to them going outside on so cold a day?''

She could not avoid looking at Philip then and did with a smile that was, in all, shy. "Far from it. I am pleased that you will take them.''

"I am relieved you are pleased.'' Philip laughed wryly, and Megan's heart seemed to stop, for she had never seen her husband look quite so approachable. "I would not relish telling them I had spoken too soon. They are that excited. But what of you, Tony and Ned? Do either of you wish to venture out on this cold and blustery day?''

"I do!'' Ned stepped forward.

Mr. Havershawe, however, remained ensconced in the chair he'd taken. "I quite prefer ladies to cold, my dears. But do enjoy yourselves.''

As she watched her husband stride from the room, his arm about his brother's shoulders, Megan let out a long breath. How foolish her worry that he might despise her seemed. He had smiled at her! Even though she had blushed so . . . so foolishly. Truly, Megan thought, Christmas Eve did seem a charmed day.

Megan's mood improved still further when only a very little later Lady Barbara and Mr. Havershawe grew bored watching the greenery being fashioned and departed the hall. Megan had not liked Mr. Havershawe from their first meeting, and she could not say she cared much more for the man's sister. She had formed the opinion that Lady Barbara held her in disdain, and not merely because the woman continued to be so very cool. Once or twice Megan had glanced up to find the beauty studying her with a distinctly unpleasant expression. Megan could only assume the expression to be a sneer because she could not fathom why Lady Barbara should actively dislike her. Megan certainly had never done anything to her.

With the departure of the pair, Lady Celicia became markedly friendlier. Happy to chatter about the past at Chively, she delighted in telling Megan what Philip had been like as a child, how he, though the second son, had been the leader of the children, and how he had been adept at getting up to pranks. Laughing at a trick Lady Celicia described, Megan hoped rather wistfully that she might witness something of that lighthearted side of her husband's nature someday.

When, at last, the ladies hung the wreaths they had made, looped the garlands along the stair rail, and set out the clumps of mistletoe tied with pretty ribbon for the men to place as they saw fit, Lady Kate declared the effect of their efforts "truly lovely." Megan agreed as she surveyed the great hall, for festooned with the magic of greenery, it seemed aglow with Christmas good will and cheer.

Her fears that her Christmas would be at best a joyless occasion and at worst a disaster seeming completely groundless, Megan half floated to the nursery to look in upon Becky, Amanda, and Priscilla. She had no need to ask if they had been hard at work making gifts. The mound of debris upon the floor was testament enough.

There were many gifts yet to complete, however, and fearful they might fall short, the girls begged Megan to help. As she had been with her guests for some time, she agreed, and so, as it was Christmas Eve, having consented to the girls' further request that they be sustained by hot chocolate and cookies, she settled down to stitch tiny pink flowers upon the handkerchief they had designed for Lady Celicia.

The boys came bursting in some time later, momentarily disrupting the nursery's cozy atmosphere. But neither the hint of cold that clung to them nor their excitement for their expedition into the woods, could quite prevail, in the end, over the girls' sense of purpose, and even Megan, though she was deeply pleased they had enjoyed themselves, only listened to them with an abstracted smile as she concentrated upon finishing the third, or perhaps it was the fourth project she'd been given.

Eventually the boys were persuaded into taking up paper and pencil, or scissors, depending upon their separate talents, and once again the atmosphere in the room became purposeful, if still excited. All went well until it was discovered that no one knew precisely how a kestrel looked. The information was necessary because Will had learned that Lord Reginald's dearest possession was a large ketch he kept at dock in Southampton. The name of it being *The Kestrel,* the children had decided to draw a picture of the hawk for the gentleman's gift.

Having been sequestered in the pleasant atmosphere of the nursery longer than she had intended, Megan volunteered to go along to the library to find a book on birds to send back with a maid.

As the library was large and Megan was distracted trying to recall in which section she had seen the books with drawings of birds, she had taken a step into the room before she realized she was not alone.

A sigh alerted her. Later she would realize she had immediately recognized the sound as one a woman in the arms of a man might make, but at the time she looked about more quickly than her thoughts registered.

Megan recognized the pair instantly, despite the gloom of the day. No man in the party was so tall or well formed as Philip, nor had anyone hair his shade of tawny gold. His face was hidden from her, however, for though he faced her, he had bent down to kiss the only blond woman in the group.

It was no idle kiss, no swift Christmas greeting. Lady Barbara's arms were entwined about Philip's neck, and the pair seemed lost to all but their embrace.

Megan simply stood staring, seeming frozen in place, nothing coherent in her mind, only a single, endless oh, reverberating over and over. Oh . . . oh . . . And then, the first thought: Lady Barbara, of course, of course.

Such feeling flooded her then she might have given a little cry. Megan did not know. But without warning, Philip glanced up, his gray eyes locking with hers as she stood rooted to the ground.

In the next instant the spell was broken. Lady Barbara stirred in Philip's arms, and Megan whirled about, fleeing out the door.

Not for anything in the world would she have allowed Lady Barbara to discover her there, her mouth formed into an agonized O, as she gazed upon the scene like some impoverished child might gaze into a Bond Street toy shop.

Megan fled to the the west wing. Unheated, it would be empty, and she'd no room of her own in which to shut herself away.

When a shaky sob escaped her, she squeezed a fist tight against her lips. She must not cry! Not yet. Not here, where anyone might see her and guess at how all her stupid, silly, pathetic hopes had been shattered.

Dear God! He had brought his mistress to Chively! To her, to his wife, to entertain! And they all knew!

So much came clear now from Mr. Havershawe's sly, knowing expression, to Lady Celicia's specific interest in Lady Barbara's sleep. Little wonder Ned had exclaimed more with shock than surprise when he saw whom Philip had brought home with him. And . . . Dear God! Megan pressed her fist so hard against her lips, the pressure hurt her. Now she knew why her husband had abandoned her after only a week.

The west wing of the house was cold and silent as a tomb. There was no one to hear the sob that escaped Megan as she fell back against the door, her arms wrapped around her waist as if she must hold herself together physically.

Had they laughed together, Philip and his so beautiful mistress, at how easily they had fooled the naive chit whose only merit was her money?

Megan had known Philip did not love her, but she had had no inkling that he despised her so! Dear God! Why had he made love to her as he had last night? Why? Did he want an heir so much? A far worse possibility occurred. He had come to bed late. Had he gone to his mistress first and come to his wife only because he was unsated?

"Megan!"

Megan went rigid. He had followed her! She could not bear to see him. She simply could not.

"Megan, I know you are there, and I am coming through this door."

Megan did not heed Philip's warning and went reeling when he pushed open the door.

"Megan."

Philip reached out to steady her, but Megan scuttled back, uncaring if she fell. The last thing in the world she wanted was to touch him, who had played such a cruel game with her, making her a thing of sport, or alternately, and no better, a thing of pity, before his friends.

Philip let his hand fall, before the look Megan turned upon him. Her eyes were dark and wild. She would bolt, he knew, if he reached for her.

"Megan." He spoke slowly and quietly. "No, please do not run off again. I shall only have to chase you further, if you do. I must tell you. . . ."

"Stop!" Megan clapped her hands over her ears. "I do not wish to hear your lies, Lord Westphal! I will not hear them!"

"You've every right to be distraught, Megan, but I swear that I will tell you no lies. I wish to explain."

Megan skittered back out of Philip's reach when he extended his hand again. "Go away! I despise you! Do whatever you please with the money you married me for, my lord earl. Only do not come near me again!"

"Damn it, Megan!" Philip exclaimed, his temper strained by her refusal to even listen to him and by her reference to the money that was, indeed, the only reason he had married her. "That scene in the library was not what you thought."

Megan laughed at that, a sharp, derisive laugh. "Do you take me for a fool, sir? Can you possibly believe I do not now understand why the members of your family exclaimed so oddly upon finding Lady Barbara included among your guests? Do you imagine, my lord, that I am so stupid I cannot now comprehend what lay behind Mr. Havershawe's sly grins? That scene in the library was precisely what I thought. She is your mistress. And you brought her here for Christmas."

"No!" Philip's denial came sharply, even harshly.

She'd been all wild defiance until she said that last. Then her voice betrayed her, wobbling painfully, and she ended by biting her lip.

But Philip's negative was ill-advised. Before he could say another word, Megan shrieked, "You wish me to listen to you when you deny something so obvious I ought to have seen it from the first? Be damned to you and all your lies!"

She whirled to dart away, a set of darkened steps just down the corridor her objective, but Philip guessed her intent and caught her by the shoulders before she could escape. "I'll have my say, Megan."

An implacable light gleaming in his gray eyes, Philip opened his mouth to say that whatever may have passed between him and Barbara in London, nothing of the sort was taking place at Chively. He intended to add that he'd more honor than to shame a wife of his so, no matter her origins or the unsettled nature of their relations, but Megan would not listen.

She cried out furiously before he could speak. "You do not own me! And I owe you naught, given the mockery you've made of your vows! I wish to have done with this travesty! Go away!"

"Damn it, Megan!" Philip shook her as she twisted frantically from side to side. "I've no intention of going away. You will listen to me. Stop it, now. I mean you no harm. I swear it. You must listen."

"I will not!" She hit out at his chest with her fists. "Actions speak louder than words, my lord! You have demonstrated more than once the esteem in which you hold me. I . . ."

But before Megan could cry out that she hated Philip, a small, stricken voice sounded from the other side of the door Philip had banged shut behind him when he strode through it. "Meggie!" It was Pris calling out as she struggled to reach the door handle. "Meggie! Meggie!" she continued, growing more anxious, when no one answered.

For half a second Megan considered hiding herself from Pris. But then the child cried out again, and Megan knew she could not.

Philip let her go before she made a move to jerk free of him, and when she brushed ineffectually at her wet cheeks with the palms of her hands, he held out his handkerchief. "I think this will prove more effective."

For a moment Megan stared at the square of monogrammed linen, but when Pris called her name again, she overcame her revulsion at touching anything of Philip's, and snatching it, put the handkerchief to use as she hurried to the door, calling out with feigned calm, "I'm coming, Pris!"

She only stopped a moment to stab a pin into the tendrils of hair that had come loose as she ran, then she opened the door. "Pris?" Kneeling, she held out her arms to the child. "What is it, pet?"

"I . . . I was afwaid. I saw you wunning, Meggie!" The little girl looked on the verge of tears. "And the eawl . . ." She glanced fearfully over Megan's shoulder. "I thought he chased you, and . . . and was angwy and wished us to leave Chively." Her fears voiced, she gave a little sob and buried her face in Megan's shoulder. "Where would St. Nicholas find us then, Meggie? We don't have a house anymore."

Megan held her tightly, grateful, at least, that Pris seemed to have heard nothing of her shouting match with Philip. "You mustn't worry, Pris. We shan't leave Chively before St. Nicholas brings your gift. I promise you that. I was running, but it was only a game.''

"Were wou cwying?'' Pris asked, pulling back to inspect Megan's face for herself.

A few swipes with a handkerchief could not erase red-rimmed eyes, and so Megan nodded. "Yes, I did cry a little when I was caught, but it was nothing, truly. How could anything be very wrong? It is Christmas Eve. Speaking of which, I do believe it is time to go and ready ourselves, or we will be late to our own festivities.''

"And the earl?'' Pris whispered, peeping over Megan's shoulder at the tall, imposing man who appeared almost godlike to her. "Is he coming?''

"Yes.'' Philip took the opening before Megan could get out a negative. He had heard everything, including Megan's equivocal answer about whether they would leave Chively. She had not said they would stay, only that they would not leave that very night. Later he would clear that matter up with her. Just then he'd a very innocent party's fears to assuage.

"I wouldn't allow two such lovely ladies to find their way back all alone.'' He smiled, exerting all his considerable charm upon the child who regarded him so shyly. "If you take my hand, we may be off at once to the warm side of the house.''

He held out his hand, and to Megan's vexation Pris promptly deserted her in favor of the earl. Philip's display of charm proved nothing to her. He simply did not wish to upset the Christmas festivities that his family—not to mention his mistress—had traveled so far to enjoy.

Nothing would have pleased Megan more than to turn her back on the evening and let even those members of Philip's family who had been kind to her fend for themselves. But however little she cared about the adults in the house, she could not destroy the children's Christmas. And so, avoiding Philip's eye, she rose stiffly, and taking Pris's hand, retraced her steps that she might endure the remainder of a Christmas Eve that had made a mockery of Lord John's assurance that it was a blessed, protected, magical day.

"This is famous, my dear!" His face flushed with the seasonal spirits he had imbibed all the gay evening long, Lord John raised his glass to Megan where she sat at her end of Chively's long, festively decorated table. "A boar's head! You are magnificent!" he cheered, and the others joined in. At least Megan knew the people at her end of the table cheered. Her glance did not stray beyond midtable. "I can't think how you contrived to present us a boar's head, my dear," Lord John continued in a delighted roar, "but I am confident it is in my honor. We had one every Christmas at Queen's College to commemorate the student who was attacked by a boar on Christmas Day."

As it was Christmas Eve, the children had joined the adults for dinner, and their eyes were fixed upon Lord John when Kit voiced the question in all their minds. "But what happened to the student, Lord John?"

"What happened to him?" Lord John bellowed. "Why, I'll tell you what happened. He stuffed a copy of Aristotle into the boar's mouth and escaped unscathed! Best use Aristotle was ever put to in my opinion!"

Everyone laughed, including Megan. All evening she had laughed when laughter was expected and clapped when the others did, as when the Yule log

had been ceremoniously dragged into the great hall
by the men and lit by a faggot that Dabworth stoutly
maintained had been kept smoldering since Candlemas
last as tradition decreed. Megan's head had throbbed
from the effort it took her to appear gay, and the
effort it took her to avoid her husband's eyes.

As Dabworth proudly carried in the boar's head,
fashioned by Cooks's magic from roast pork and
sausage, Megan could feel Philip's gaze upon her,
but as she had all evening, she found reason to attend to someone near her.

She might yet burst into tears if she looked at him,
or worse, fling her wine glass the length of the table.
She could not trust herself. She had never behaved
as she had done in the west wing. He must know
why. He was no fool. A woman who had married
him only for his title would not have shrieked and
cried and lashed out like a madwoman.

If only he had not followed her! Not the least result of his effort to placate her was that she had not
gotten to cry out all her tears, and now her head felt
so heavy she could scarcely keep it from dropping.

Megan's mouth tightened a fraction. Philip had
not needed privacy in which to cry out what meager
heart he had. He'd been able to smile at the sight of
the little present factory in the nursery. When she
had caught the flash of his smile from the corner of
her eye, Megan had had to look away, afraid the
anger and pain that seized her would be writ large
upon her face for the children to see.

Nor had that one smile taxed the limit of Philip's
good humor. Megan may have longed to be as far as
possible from every human in the house, but Philip
had complied readily, when Will begged him to tell
the girls about the tradition of the Lord of Misrule,

saying, ''They will not believe Kit and me when we tell them all you told us in the woods.''

Grinning, Philip actually seemed happy to tell how, when he was very young, the Lindsays had maintained the old custom of crowning a Lord of Misrule to preside over Chively for Christmas Day. A merry fellow, the Lord of Misrule, as his name implied, turned all the staid, normal rules of life topsy-turvy. The children laughed, delighted by the antics Philip described, and eager to know more, barraged him with more questions than he could answer, for he had been quite young when his mother thought it wise to discontinue that particular tradition.

Megan had excused herself to go and dress when Becky asked Philip if he thought Lady Barbara would prefer a box decorated with feathers or tiny bits of tissue papers. She took Pris with her, in case the earl thought to insist that she hear out his soothing equivocations while she dressed herself for the evening she had once anticipated with as much excitement as the children.

Why had he gone to the nursery with her and then stayed even when she had left? Megan could only think Philip wanted to keep a close eye upon her until the evening began to assure himself she did not mean to make a scene before his family and friends. As to staying, perhaps he had found it soothing to surround himself with the children's innocence and admiration after he had played the lead role in the tawdry drama of the previous hour.

As the plum pudding was carried in with great fanfare an hour or so after the boar's head had been carried out, Philip glanced down the table at his

wife. She was looking, of course, anywhere but at
him.

He considered rising to toast her. She would be
obliged to look at him then. But he would not force
her to attend to him yet. Her composure might crack,
if she had to acknowledge him.

And she was composed. Not by so much as one
strained look did Megan betray how wretchedly her
evening had been spoiled.

She had looked forward to this evening greatly.
He did not know that from Megan, of course, but
from the boys. In the woods they had artlessly con-
fided how she had said since Christmas was a family
affair, they might enjoy themselves as much as they
liked, despite the fact that they were in mourning.
"It will be our antidote to sadness," she had told
them.

At least she had had the inspiration to entertain
everyone with a mummer's play after dinner rather
than the traditional dancing. Watching a play, she
would not have to be quite so careful to keep up the
gay charming facade with which she had fooled the
company thus far. Nor would she have to suffer physical contact with her husband.

Philip's jaw tightened grimly. He'd have found it
difficult indeed to feel her stiffen in his arms, or
worse, find some excuse to escape him altogether.

Megan finally had her excuse to escape the festivities after the mummer's play. The hour was late, and
the children nodding on their feet. The servants she
had cajoled into taking the mummers' parts had just
made their second bows when she rose to say she
would go up with the children.

When Philip bid his guests good night soon afterward, only Barbara failed to register surprise at his
early departure. Their kiss in the library had been,

at least on his part, a tepid token of farewell he had felt obliged by the rules of dalliance to accord his now former mistress.

Even before he'd left London, Philip had half suspected he would not resume his affair with Barbara when he returned. When he had caught sight of his wife in the snow, laughing, he had known with certainty.

Megan could not have known that when she stood in the library door, however. Damn and damn again. Philip took the steps two at a time. He had fought on the Peninsula and had seen men's eyes go wide with shock when they were hit in battle. She had looked like them, her blue eyes unnaturally wide and so dark as to be black.

Anticipating what he would say now that he finally had her to himself and anticipating as well making up to her in their bed for what he had inflicted upon her not only this afternoon but ever since their marriage, Philip fairly burst into the room.

She was not there. Abruptly he spun on his heel and stalked to the nursery. He found her after carefully opening three doors. She was in bed with Pris, sleeping on the far side by the wall where he could not get at her unless he awakened the child.

Irresolute as he had never been before in his life, Philip stood in that doorway a long time. He'd a fierce desire to grab Megan up, to shake her, to make her listen to him, but he would alarm Pris if he did.

Devil it, he swore. He would make Megan listen before she could leave Chively, as he suspected she planned to do after the children had opened their gifts from St. Nicholas. Or was she expecting him to leave first, to go off with Barbara and Choumley and Tony? George had announced they would leave on the morrow, though it was Christmas Day. The roads were passable, he said. He had had word from his coachman.

Megan let out her breath as Pris's door closed. She had been certain Philip meant to drag her back to his bed to get an heir on her as soon as he could, and she had been prepared to fight him. Never again would he touch her, no matter that the laws supported him. Were Megan to protest that Philip had broken his vows by taking a mistress beneath her nose, she would be laughed out of any court in the land, not to mention Philip's jaded circles.

No matter, Megan meant to leave Chively the next day. Whether Philip intended to remain or leave with the Choumley party, she did not know or care. She was going to her old governess. Miss Millicent would harbor her. She'd no money of her own: that had gone to save the Lindsays and fuel her own pitiful dreams, but her father had not handed over his entire fortune to Philip. By far the larger part had been put in trust for the other children. Megan knew the administrator of the trust well. Her father's solicitor since she was a child, Mr. Threatt would provide for her and the children.

The sight of Philip striding through the nursery door late the next morning took Megan so by surprise she felt almost as intense a pain as she had when she discovered him in Lady Barbara's sleek arms.

He was a beautiful man, really, with his height, his flawless features, and his warm, tawny hair. And it was one of the last times she would see ever him.

Megan bit down hard on her lip to keep it from quivering and thanked heaven for the children as they rushed to give Philip a noisy greeting.

"We were just coming down, Philip!" Amanda

said. "We've all our presents finished and wrapped. See!"

Becky blushed as she held out a small box. "I have yours, Philip."

It was the first Philip had thought of the presents he was giving. He had been too absorbed with . . . himself, he acknowledged grimly, to inspect what his secretary had purchased for the children. But Megan's present. How could he have thought a reticule would do? He looked down at the dark, sleek head she had kept averted since he entered and knew a ragged regret. There was not time to find something more.

"We are ready to come down, my lord," Megan said, rising. "I hope we have not kept you and your guests waiting over long."

She might have been the governess of his children, she spoke so impersonally.

"Merry Christmas, Megan," Philip said, feeling absurdly self-conscious with the children looking on.

"My lord," was all Megan said in return. Nor did she look at Philip as she deliberately neglected to wish him well on Christmas Day. She turned away to motion the children to the door.

Philip could not force her to acknowledge him with the children watching, and so he led the way from the room, Pris holding one hand and Amanda the other.

In the winter parlor they found the others already gathered around the fire and a mound of presents upon the hearth. When Philip heard Kit exclaim, "But some are for us!" he realized he had had no reason to worry over Hemmings's choices. Megan had prepared them to expect nothing from him.

Perhaps it was that lack of anticipation that made them appreciate so greatly what they did receive. Or that Hemmings, bless him, had a better understanding of children than Philip had realized. The supple riding boots and sumptuous dresses they received made them almost babble their thanks.

To their credit the children were quite as eager to give as to receive. Of course the gifts they had made were not much, but it pleased Philip that his family exclaimed over their feather pins and amateur pictures with the greatest delight.

The Choumley party reacted far more coolly, of course. Barbara, in particular, said "Ah, how nice," so tonelessly when she saw the box that had been decorated for her, that she mocked her own words. Philip caught sight of the ruby earrings dangling from her ears. He had not seen them before and guessed they were, along with the rose silk dress she wore, her Christmas present from George. Damn again. Rubies would compare rather well to a black beaded reticule.

After a pause during which warm punch and poppy seed buns were served, the adults exchanged their gifts. Feeling grimmer by the moment, Philip watched while Celicia unwrapped an emerald ring from Reginald, and his Aunt Kate made a great deal of a pearl-encrusted comb Lord John gave her. To Philip's relief, Megan opened nothing then. She alone had a token for everyone, even the members of the Choumley party.

She had chosen well, he was not astonished to see, from a pretty bed jacket for his mother to a finely illustrated copy of Milton's *Paradise Lost* that made Ned gape with surprised pleasure.

It was Pris who presented Philip the box with his name upon it. Inside, he found a heavy, silver pin handsomely wrought in the shape of a stirrup. "It is for you to wear in your cravat when you go out riding in the mornings, Lord Philip!'' Becky divulged, while he stood staring down at the elegant gift that put the one he had bought for Megan to shame.

He looked up slowly. "How do you know I go riding in the mornings, Becky?"

"Why, because we saw you almost every morning last spring," Becky replied. "Did not Meggie tell you? We often walked at the hour you rode, and we thought you resembled a centaur."

"That is a creature that is half man and half horse," Amanda piped up to explain proudly.

Philip scarcely heard her. He was looking to Megan. Her eyes were fixed upon the pin he held, but he could see a faint line of color on her cheeks. She had known of him before their solicitors met. She had not, as he had thought, accepted him sight unseen with only his title to recommend him. She had seen him many times, he repeated to himself, as the ground seemed to shift beneath him.

Feeling much worse for the new information, Philip only realized belatedly that the children were urging Megan to open the last present remaining upon the hearth, hers from her husband.

He almost stepped forward to stop her as she tugged at the wrapping. Everyone was watching, though, for they had all finished with their gifts, and all too soon Megan held in her hands the black beaded reticule it had taken Philip all of two minutes to choose.

The reticule received the response it deserved. For a half second there was an awkward, disbelieving silence. Philip opened his mouth to say something, anything to save himself, but before he could, Megan laughed aloud. "What a good choice, my lord," she said. "I do like useful gifts, and I had not realized you saw the gentleman spill his claret on mine.

Thank you. I haven't a fancy reticule, and I shall always think of you when I use this one.''

It was the most superb job of acting Philip had ever witnessed, and something tightened in his chest. No doubt she would think of him when she used it, though not with fondness. When she glanced toward him, smiling, her eyes never met his.

"I think you will have to take your husband in hand, my dear." Philip glanced sharply to Barbara. A thin smile curving her lips, she looked like a sleek, spoiled cat intent on harm. "A man must be trained to understand what constitutes a proper gift. I would not have these," she waved a white hand in the direction of her earrings, "had I not slyly pointed out what I wished to have."

"But I did not present you with those earrings, Babs!" Lord George, a stickler for the truth, pointed out. "You got those yourself."

"Hmmm," Lady Barbara purred, lifting her delicate eyebrows at Megan. "I did, indeed. Do you not like them?"

His temper evident in the lines about his mouth, Philip stepped in front of Megan. He'd have liked to slap Barbara for the lie at which she hinted, but his attention was all for his wife. She had gone unnaturally pale.

"Unfortunately I was not on hand for you to drop me a hint, Megan, and so I got you something I knew you needed." She was not looking at him, though to the others it might have seemed she did, for she had, in the interest of appearance, lifted her gaze to his chin.

Philip did not allow Megan's set expression to deter him, however. He reached for her hand and summarily lifted her to her feet. The gesture brought her eyes to his, and the astonishment in them made him smile just a little.

"Your fancy reticule is a token only, Megan. It is my way of saying you will have need of such when we take the wedding trip we missed. As soon after Christmas as possible, we, you and I and the reticule, are off to Italy."

"Italy?" Megan stared. "I . . . I cannot. I have too much . . ."

Philip cut her off firmly. "We employ Mr. Mackenzie to renovate, my dear. You may approve what he has done, when you return. Ah my," he sighed, "I do not think you are entirely persuaded even yet, my lady."

Philip's smile deepened though he shook his head sadly. Megan tried very hard not to be moved by the warmth and charm of his smile. Had he smiled as warmly when he gave Lady Barbara her earrings? Did he wish to acquire a harem of adoring ladies? Was that the explanation for this display of his charm?

Philip turned Megan to face the others when he saw her eyes darken. Keeping an arm about her waist, he pulled from his pocket a velvet cap that sported a sprig of mistletoe.

"With this cap," he intoned with mock solemnity. "I, the Earl of Westphal, crown myself Lord of Misrule for the entirety of this Christmas Day." The children, primed by his stories of the day before, cheered in delighted surprise. Philip bowed to them. "Should any of you lords or ladies be uncertain what a Lord of Misrule is, you've only to ask one of my minions there. They will tell you. I shall not be able to satisfy your curiosity, for I mean to abduct this lady. Perhaps I am tardy in realizing the prize she is, but I intend to correct my error without delay.''

Then, before she could credit he really meant to do it, Philip swept Megan up in his arms and strode from the room.

"But, my lord!" Megan protested in a furious undertone as most of their audience cheered. "I do not want to go! Dabworth is to bring in the frumenty and . . .''

A smile playing about his mouth, Philip shook his head. "Dabworth has been bringing in the frumenty since before you were born, Megan, my love. He will not require either of us to assist him. And I do wish that you would grant me the boon of my name for Christmas—it is Philip.''

He said it so softly, while his gray eyes gleamed in a way that even then made Megan's pulses leap. But if Philip had forgotten Lady Barbara Choumley, Megan had not. She returned Philip a stony, unflinching stare.

"I did not give Barbara those earrings, Megan,'' Philip addressed that look levelly. "She wanted you to think so, because she wished to hurt you. The kiss you interrupted in the library was a farewell kiss, on my part at least. She and I were lovers before I ever met you, Megan, and I only fell back into the affair because . . .'' he paused to boot open the door to their bedroom. "Because I was, temporarily, a fool,'' Philip resumed as he crossed to their bed. When he sat down upon it, he tightened his hold upon her, for Megan tried to swing free. "It is in no part easy to admit to being a fool, Megan. You will stay in my lap until I have delivered myself of a full confession.'' When she remained stiff as a board, he added, "Please?''

Philip's scent and warmth surrounded her. Her

bottom rested on his hard thigh, and she could feel the smooth, supple skin of his arm beneath hers. Then he said "please" in that gruff way. Megan nodded once, curtly, far too aware of the sudden warmth spreading through her to relax.

"Look at me, Megan." Philip gently nudged her chin up until her blue eyes met his. "I've behaved like the worst fool. I've no excuse, only the explanation that I've the devil's own pride. 'Tis why I resented you before I ever saw you. I felt like some nag being trotted out for your inspection. And when I suspected myself to be weakening toward the wife I was determined I would ignore, I ran like a hare. To prove I wasn't in any danger from you, I left after that one week, and for the same reason I took up with Barbara again. But the more I tried not to think of you, the more you crept into my thoughts. You plagued me, blast you, and now here I am, begging you to accept my apologies. Will you forgive me?"

"I . . ." Megan paused to clear her throat. "I want to, my lord."

"But you fear it might not be possible, given how shabbily I've behaved? I can't blame you, Megan. But if you won't forgive me just yet, will you at least allow me a little time to prove myself? You were planning to leave today, were you not?"

Megan started in surprise. "How did you guess?"

"I'd more than enough time to think last night. Not only did I divine your intention, but I realized how very empty life would seem without you."

Philip looked so grave, Megan swallowed past a lump in her throat. "And you, my lord? Will you stay?"

"By you, sweet Megan. I intend to be your shadow whether we are in Italy or in England. And if you learn to address me as Philip, I may even kiss you upon your neck just here, where your pulse is beating.''

A delicious thrill made Megan shiver when Philip kissed her where he said he would. ''Oh, that is unfair! I cannot think. Philip!''

His golden head came up, and he fixed her with gray eyes that had gone a smoky, sensual gray. ''I have longed for more time than I knew to hear you say my name like that. What can I give you, my love?''

''Do you truly mean all this, Philip?''

Philip understood her uncertainty. ''I did not bring Barbara to this house to bed her beneath your nose, Megan. I brought her here for precisely the reason I stated from the first, because she and the others were stranded at an inn. She's a beautiful woman, it is true, but she . . .'' He shrugged his shoulders abruptly. ''The measure of Barbara is that she lashed out at you for naught but the pleasure of causing you pain. By contrast, you are warmth itself, and luckily for me, quite the most delicious lover that any lady could be. I would say I have fallen head over heels in love with you, Megan, but I fear you won't believe me. Instead, I ask you to give me the opportunity to prove I have. Starting now.''

''Philip! It is daylight. We have guests and the children . . .''

''Our guests will be occupied by the children.'' Philip smiled a slow, persuasive smile as he continued the caress that had turned Megan's cheeks pink. ''And as to it being daylight, my dear, why all the better to see the most appealing Christmas gift any man ever received.''